WAGES
OF SIN

By Stephen Coonts

WAGES
OF SIN

STEPHEN
COONTS

ORION

Copyright © Stephen Coonts 2004

All rights reserved

The right of Stephen Coonts to be identified as the
author of this work has been asserted by him in accordance
with the Copyright, Designs and Patents Act, 1988.

First published in Great Britain in 2004 by Orion Books
an imprint of The Orion Publishing Group
Orion House, 5 Upper St Martin's Lane, London WC2H 9EA

A CIP catalogue record for this book is
available from the British Library

ISBN (hardback) 0 75284 629 9
ISBN (trade paperback) 0 75284 630 2

Printed and bound in Great Britain by
Clays Ltd, St Ives plc

To the archivist Vasili Mitrokhin

Whatcha gonna do when they come for you, bad boy?

—Ian Lewis *"Bad Boys* Theme"

WAGES
OF SIN

CHAPTER **ONE**

When Dorsey O'Shea walked into the lock shop that morning in October, I was in the back room trying to figure out how to pick the new high-security Cooper locks. I saw her through the one-way glass that separated the workshop from the retail space.

My partner, Willie the Wire, was waiting on a customer. I don't think Willie recognized her at first—it had been two years since Dorsey and I were a number, she had changed her hair, and as I recall he had only met her on one or two occasions—but he remembered her as soon as she said his name and asked for me.

Willie was noncommittal—he knew I was in the back room. "How long has it been, Dorsey?"

"I really need to see Carmellini," she said forcefully.

"You're the third hot woman this week who has told me that."

"I want his telephone number, Willie."

"Does he still have your phone number?"

That was when I stepped through the shop door and she saw me. She was tall, with great bones, and skin like cream. "Hey, Dorsey."

"Tommy, I need to talk to you."

"Come on back."

She came around the counter and preceded me through the doorway to the shop. I confess, I watched. Even when she wasn't trying, her hips and bottom moved in very interesting ways. But all that was past, I told myself with a sigh. She had ditched me, and truth be told, I didn't want her back. Too much maintenance.

In the shop she looked around curiously at the tools, locks, and junk strewn everywhere. Willie wasn't a neat workman, and I confess, I'm also kinda messy. She fingered some of the locks, then focused her attention on me. "I remembered that you were a part owner in this place, so I thought Willie might know where to find you."

"Inducing him to tell you would have been the trick."

Obviously Dorsey had not considered the possibility that Willie might refuse to tell her whatever she asked. Few men ever had. She was young, beautiful, and rich, the modern trifecta for females. She came by her dough the old-fashioned way—she inherited it. Her parents died in a car wreck shortly after she was born. Her grandparents who raised her passed away while she was partying at college, trying to decide if growing up would be worth the effort. Now she lived in a monstrous old brick mansion on five hundred acres, all that remained of a colonial plantation, on the northern bank of the Potomac thirty miles upriver from Washington. It was a nice little getaway if you were worth a couple hundred million, and she was.

When I met her she was whiling away her time doing the backstroke through Washington's social circles. She once thought I was pretty good arm candy on the party circuit and a pleasant bed warmer on long winter nights, but after a while she changed her mind. Women are like that . . . fickle.

I had the Cooper lock mounted on a board, which was held in a vise. I adjusted the torsion wrench and went back to work with the pick. The Cooper was brand-new to the market, a top-of-the-line exterior door lock that contractors were ordering installed in new custom homes. They were telling the owners that it was burglarproof, unpickable. I didn't think there was a lock on the planet that couldn't be opened without a key, but then, I had never before tried the Cooper. I would see one sooner or later on a door I wanted to go through, so why not learn now? I had already cut a Cooper in half—ruining several saw blades—so I knew what made it tick. I had had two pins aligned when Dorsey came in, and of course lost them when I released the tension on the wrench and walked around front to speak to her.

She eyed me now as I manipulated the tools. "What are you doing?"

"Learning how to open this lock."

"Why don't you use a key?"

"That would be cheating. Our public would be disappointed. What can I do for you today, anyway?"

She looked around again in a distracted manner, then sat on the only uncluttered stool. "I need help, and the only person I could think of asking was you."

I got one of the pins up and felt around, trying to find which of the others was the tightest. The problem here, I decided, was the shape of my pick. I could barely reach the pins. I got a strip of flat stock from our cabinet and began working with the grinder.

"That sounds very deep," I said to keep her talking. "Have you discussed that insight with your analyst?"

"I feel like such a fool, coming here like this. Don't make it worse by talking down to me."

"Okay."

"It's not that I didn't like you, Tommy, but I never understood you. Who are you? Why do you own part of a lock shop? What kind of work do you do for the government? You never told me anything about yourself. I always felt that there was this wall be-tween us, that there was a whole side of you I didn't know."

"You don't owe me an explanation," I said. "It was two years ago. We hadn't made each other any promises."

She twisted her hands—I couldn't help glancing at her from time to time.

"Why don't you tell me what's on your mind?" I said as I in-spected my new pick. I slipped it into the Cooper, put some ten-sion on the torsion wrench, and went to work as she talked.

"Every man I know wears a suit and tie and spends his days making money—the more the better—except you. It's just that—oh, hell!" She watched me work the pick for a minute before she added, "I want you to get into an ex-boyfriend's house and get something for me."

"There are dozens of lock shops listed in the yellow pages."

"Oh, Tommy, don't be like that." She slipped off the stool and walked around so that she could look into my eyes. She didn't reach and she didn't touch—just looked. "I feel like such a jerk, asking you for a favor after I broke up with you, but I don't have a choice. Believe me, I am in trouble."

Truthfully, when she dumped me I was sort of subtly cam-paigning to get dumped. I wasn't about to tell her that. And you don't have to believe it if you don't want to.

I glanced at her. The tension showed on her face. "You're going to have to tell me all of it," I said, gently as I could. At heart Dorsey was a nice kid . . . for a multimillionaire, which wasn't her fault.

"His name is Kincaid, Carroll Kincaid. He has a couple of videotapes. He made them without my knowledge when we were first dating. He's threatening to show them to my fiancé if I don't pay him a lot of money."

"I didn't know you were engaged."

"We haven't announced it yet."

"Who's the lucky guy?"

She said a name, pronounced it as if I was supposed to recognize it.

"So why don't you ask him for help?" I said.

"I can't. Tommy, even if I pay blackmail, there's no guarantee Kincaid would give me the only copies of the tapes."

"So you want me to break into his house and get the tapes?"

"It wouldn't really be burglary. He made the tapes without my permission. They are really mine."

Amazingly enough, when we were dating the thought never crossed my little mind that she might have a stupid stunt like this in her. I made eye contact again, scrutinized every feature. I decided she might be telling the truth.

I was trying to think of something appropriate to say when I felt the pick twitch and the lock rotated. It was open.

I put the tools on the table and was reaching for a stool when she moved closer and laid a hand on my arm. "Oh, Tommy, please! Blackmail is ugly. I am really in love, and it could be something wonderful. Kincaid is trying to ruin my life."

I reflected that sometimes having money is really hard on a girl, or so I've heard. And the prospect of burglary always gets my juices flowing. She gave me Kincaid's address. I made sure Dorsey understood that I wasn't promising anything. "I'll see what I can do." She gave me her cell phone number, started to kiss me, thought better of it, and left.

I sat wondering how that kiss would have tasted as I listened to her walk through the store. When the front door closed Willie came into the workshop.

"I don't know what you got, Carmellini, that drives all the chicks wild, but I'd sure like to have some of it. They're troopin' in here all the time wantin' to know where you are, what you're doin'—makes a man feel inadequate, y'know? Maybe you oughta open a school or somethin'. Sorta a public service deal. Whaddaya think?"

"I got the Cooper opened."

"How long it take you?"

"I wasn't timing it. I was—"

"Three minutes for me," Willie said with a touch of pride in his voice. " 'Course I wasn't looking at a dish like that when I did it. What does she want you to do—steal the silver at the White House?"

"I can beat three minutes blindfolded," I told Willie, and by God, I did. And I had to listen to a lot of his b.s. while I did it.

I went into Kincaid's place the following night. There was no one home and he forgot to lock the back door. When I found that the door was unlocked, I sat down at his backyard picnic table while I thought things over. For the life of me, I couldn't see what Dorsey would gain by setting me up. She was waiting in my car halfway down the block with a cell phone to call me if Kincaid returned while I was in the house.

If she was playing a game, it was too deep for me, I concluded. Even smart people forget to lock their doors.

I opened Kincaid's back door and went inside.

After thirty minutes I was certain there were no homemade videotapes in the house, although I did find three high-end video-cams and a dozen photographer's floodlights in the bedroom, which had a huge round bed in the center of the room and electrical outlets every three feet around the walls. This guy was more than kinky—he was set up to make porno flicks.

So where were they? There were boxes of videotape—all unopened, still wrapped in cellophane. Nothing that looked like it had been in a camera.

I was going through his files at his desk in his den—he was reasonably well organized, I must say—when I found a receipt for a safe deposit box at a local bank. From the amount he paid, he must have rented a large box. The receipt was dated a month ago. The box key wasn't in the desk, and I didn't expect it to be.

I couldn't find a receipt or record that hinted that he owned a storage unit. He might have stashed a suitcase full of stuff at a friend's house, but I doubted it. These days everyone had curious friends. His car was a possibility, though an unlikely one. If some kid took it for a joyride he could be ruined. Of course, he could have delivered the tapes to whatever lab processed them into movies. But if he did that with a tape of Dorsey and some porno kings, why try to blackmail her?

Dorsey was chewing her lip when I got into the car. "No videotapes," I said. "Has a nice little home movie setup, but no tapes."

"I could help you look. They must be there."

"They aren't. He didn't even lock the back door." I started the car and got it rolling down the street. "He's set up to film some hot porno action. The raw tapes would have to be digitized and edited, and the equipment for that isn't in the house."

Her color wasn't good. She didn't meet my eyes.

"When did he first approach you demanding money?"

She thought about it. "Three weeks ago, I think. Labor Day weekend. I had some friends over for a small party, and he showed up unannounced."

The time frame seemed to fit. I decided the safe deposit box was a definite possibility.

I didn't make a habit of burgling houses for ex-girlfriends, even if they were beautiful and rich and being blackmailed. During the day I worked for the CIA. It wasn't something agency employees talk about, and I had never mentioned it to Dorsey. I think I did once mention that I worked for the General Services Administration. She probably thought I was some kind of maintenance supervisor. Maybe that was the story I told her—I don't quite remember.

Usually I worked overseas, breaking and entering for Uncle Sam, planting bugs, stealing documents, that kind of thing. Every now and then I did a few black-bag jobs stateside for the FBI, strictly as a favor, you understand, one federal agency helping another. I sometimes heard rumors that the CIA asked the FBI to ask for my help on domestic matters, but being a loyal employee, I immediately discounted and forgot those ugly whispers. In those days I was just another civil servant beating in time, working toward that happy retirement on the old fifty-fifth birthday, followed by a life of golf and restaurant meals courtesy of future taxpayers.

After my abortive inspection of Dorsey's ex-flame's house, I took her back to her car and dropped her. She was in a foul mood, chewing her lip.

I waited until she got inside her vehicle, then drove away to find a bar. As I swilled beer I compared how I felt two years ago when she dumped me and how I felt walking through the porno guy's digs.

Oh, well.

A few days later I had to leave work after lunch for my annual physical, so after the doc finished with the rubber glove I took the rest of the day off. I went by the neighborhood bank where Kincaid had his box, parked, went in and rented one for myself.

It was a typical suburban branch bank, with a drive-through window and an interior lobby. A security door that had to be opened from the inside prevented people from entering the loan officers' half of the building, and that was where the small safe deposit vault was. I filled out the form and was admitted to the vault. A bank of boxes formed each wall. The largest boxes were on the bottom row. Beside the door was a cabinet that contained envelopes holding keys for the empty boxes, and on top of the cabinet were two steel boxes containing the cards that each patron had to sign every time he wanted into his box. A single surveillance camera was mounted high on the wall opposite the door to the vault.

My escort in the vault was a young woman named Harriet who was wearing a wedding ring and maternity clothes, although the baby wasn't showing much. I commented on that, and she told me she had five more months to go. It was her first child. She and her husband were so excited.

"You're lucky we have a large box available. This is the only one. It became available last week when the lady who had it was transferred to Europe. She's with the State Department."

She gave me my key, and we checked that it opened my new box. The locks for the individual boxes were lever tumbler locks, which is the universal standard in American safe deposit vaults. Each box had two keyways. As usual, she had to insert the master key, which she carried, into one keyway and my key into the other and turn them both simultaneously for the box to open. Fortunately Willie had a bank of four safe deposit boxes complete with their lever tumbler locks back at the shop.

I confess, I was a little disappointed, although I tried not to show it. Some banks were getting in the habit of breaking off one of their master keys in the lock of each box in the vault, then admitting box holders to the vault without an escort. Needless to say, these boxes were a breeze for guys like me to pop. I had my hopes up, but it wasn't to be. This bank was still doing it the safe, old-fashioned way.

I told Harriet I might be back in a few days to put some stuff in my new box, thanked her for her time, and departed.

Back in the shop Willie and I discussed lever tumbler locks and disassembled one from his safe deposit boxes. Lever tumbler locks require an L-shaped pick, the prong of which must be precisely the right length. I used my key to measure the length I needed and made myself three picks, each a slightly different length, just in case.

I spent the weekend practicing on Willie's locks. My best time was twenty-six seconds, but two minutes was the average, and if I hurried or wasn't paying strict attention, I couldn't get the lock to open. Willie spent some time watching me, and even opened one a few times himself.

Willie the Wire was twenty years older than me, a slim, dapper black man who worked Washington hotels in his younger days as a bellboy. Finally he quit carrying bags into the hotel for guests and specialized in picking locks and carrying luggage out—sans tip. The last time he got out of prison he promised himself an honest job, but with his reputation, no one would hire him. A friend of mine knew him and mentioned his plight to me. We had dinner a few times, and he showed me a couple of things I didn't know about locks, so I bankrolled this establishment and we became partners. He knew I worked for the CIA, but we never talked about it.

That weekend as we played with the locks on his sample safe deposit boxes, he wanted to talk about Dorsey O'Shea. "This might be a setup, man. You ever think about that?"

"Why would Dorsey want to set me up?"

"Maybe somebody who don't like you wanta burn you—how the hell would I know, man! You're the fuckin' spy, you tell me."

"I can't think of any reason under the sun."

"She look like real money. That right?"

"She's got it, yeah."

"You don't know what the hell you gettin' into, and that's a fact. This man got somethin' on her besides movies of her gettin' cock. Whoever looks at faces in those flicks, anyway? You in over your simple head, Carmellini."

Perhaps he was right, but Dorsey O'Shea didn't hang with Willie the Wire's crowd. Although being a porno star wouldn't hurt your rep in some circles, a lot of minds weren't quite that open. If Kincaid was a real son of a bitch he could squeeze her for serious cash.

That's the way I had it figured, anyhow. On the other hand, maybe I just wanted to see if I could pop Kincaid's box at the bank. I had never done a safe deposit box before, so what the hell.

I called Dorsey on Monday morning, right after I called the agency and said I was sick. "Today's the day. Pick me up at my house at ten o'clock."

She showed up ten minutes late, which was amazingly punctual for her. I got in with her and directed her to a costume place that a friend of mine owned in a strip mall in Silver Spring. When we came out, she was wearing a maternity dress. We had a hard plastic shape strapped to her stomach to fill out the dress. I thought she looked about seven months along. I pushed on her new stomach and it felt real to me—the proper resistance and give. On the way to the bank I drove and briefed her.

"I don't know if I can do this, Tommy," she said when I finished.

"Do you want those tapes or not?"

"I want them."

"You have two choices—pay up or do a deal. Killing Kincaid will leave the tapes for the cops to find. Odds are he has the tapes in his box at the bank. He thinks they're safe there. He may have duped them—I don't know. If we clean out that box we may get something he wants bad enough to trade for. Everything in life's a risk."

"My God!" she whispered.

"We're about a mile from the bank. Think it over."

When we pulled into the bank parking lot she looked pasty and haggard, which was fine. Anyone who looked at her could see she was not her usual self.

"All right," she said.

I went through it again, covering everything I could think of, including contingencies.

"Make it good," I said, and handed her the small bottle I had brought with me. She made a face and drank half of it.

"All of it."

"Jesus, this tastes bad."

"All of it."

She tossed off the rest of the goop and threw the bottle on the back seat.

We went into the bank and sat outside the security door until Harriet finished a telephone call and came to open it for us. I had a leather attaché case with me, but it was empty.

A female loan officer was seated behind her desk talking on the telephone in one of the small offices off the main office area. The walls of all these spaces had large windows in them so everyone could see what was going on everywhere in the bank. The only privacy was in the vault, a series of cubicles for customers to load and unload their boxes, and the employee restrooms, which were right beside the vault. I didn't see any other employees in this area of the bank.

Dorsey and Harriet compared due dates after I introduced them, then Dorsey sat at a chair by Harriet's desk. While Harriet retrieved the master safe deposit box key from her desk, I checked that none of the surveillance cameras were pointed into the vault. They weren't.

Inside the vault, Harriet asked, "Do you remember your box number, Mr. Carmellini?"

"Number six, I think. It was one of the large ones." I pointed at it.

Harriet opened the card catalog and looked me up while I watched over her shoulder.

She removed my card from the box. "If you'll just sign and date this . . ."

I did so and handed her my key. She inserted her master key into my box lock, then mine, and opened it.

"Do you want to take your box to our privacy area?" she asked.

Before I could answer, I heard Dorsey moan, then I heard a thud as she hit the floor.

"My God!" I said, and darted out of the vault. Harriet was right behind me.

Dorsey lay facedown on the floor, moaning softly and holding herself. The woman from the loan office rushed out and bent over her. Dorsey began retching.

"The bathroom," Harriet said, and grabbed one arm. The other woman took her other arm, and they assisted her to her feet. Dorsey gagged.

As they went through the door of the ladies', I faded into the vault. Bless Harriet, she had left the master key sticking in the keyway of my box!

I turned sideways to the camera and removed a halogen flash-light from my trouser pocket. I snapped it on as I aimed it at the camera. The light was so bright I had to squint for several seconds. I placed the light on the cabinet beside the card file and arranged it on a flexible wire base so it was pointed at the camera. The beam would wipe out the picture.

I knew that Carroll Kincaid also had a large box, based on the amount he had paid in rent. It took just seconds to find his name in the card catalog. He had box number twelve and hadn't visited it since he rented it.

Leaving the lock on my box open, I used the master key on Kincaid's, inserted one of my picks and a torsion wrench in the second keyway, and went to work. After ten seconds, I decided I had the wrong size pick and tried another.

I closed my eyes so that I could concentrate on the feel.

Perspiration beaded on my forehead. That never happens to James Bond in the movies; it's a character defect that I just have to live with.

Time crawled.

I concentrated on the feel of the pick.

Bang, I got it, and felt the lock give the tiniest amount. Keeping the tension on the torsion wrench, I turned the master key . . . and the lock opened.

Kincaid's box had something in it. I didn't open it. I merely transferred his box to my vault and put my empty box in his, then closed the lock flap. I replaced the master key in the lock on my box, closed it, retrieved my key and the halogen flashlight, and was waiting in the lobby with my attaché case when the women came out of the restroom.

Dorsey looked as if she had been run over by something. Her face was pasty and her hair a mess.

Harriet and the other woman helped her toward the door.

"I'll get her home," I said, and slipped an arm around her. "Thank you *so* much."

Dorsey murmured something to the women, then put her hand over her mouth as if she were going to heave again. Harriet opened the door and I half carried Dorsey through it.

I put her in the passenger seat of the car and got behind the wheel.

"You son of a bitch," she snarled. "I nearly vomited up my toenails."

"Remember this happy day," I remarked, "the next time somebody wants you to star in a fuck movie."

"Did you get the tapes?"

"I got something. I'll go back in a couple of days and get whatever it is."

"I'll go with you. I want those tapes."

"Those women have seen you for the last time. When I get the tapes, I'll call you."

She didn't like it, but she was in no condition to argue.

When I went back Wednesday afternoon, Harriet gave me a strange look. "How's your wife?"

"Better, thank you. You gotta be tough to have a baby."

She obviously had something on her mind. "After you and your wife left Monday, I had the strangest call from our security officer."

"Oh?"

"Apparently the surveillance camera in the vault stopped working while we had your wife in the restroom."

I shrugged. "Did it break?"

"Oh, no! Merely stopped working for a few minutes. They monitor them from our main office in Silver Spring."

"That is odd," I admitted. "While you were in the bathroom I used the time to put the items I brought into my box."

"The master safe deposit key was still in the lock of your box after you left."

"You have it now, I hope."

"Oh, yes."

"I really appreciate the way you and the other lady helped my wife," I said warmly. "I apologize for the inconvenience, but you know how these things are. I've written a letter to the president of the bank. I feel so fortunate that the bank has such wonderful employees."

Harriet beamed.

We opened the locks, and I pulled my box from its shelf. I carried it to a privacy cubicle. There were a dozen videotapes, four whopping big stacks of cash with rubber bands around them, and a Smith & Wesson .38 revolver, which was loaded. I put a handkerchief around my fingers as I checked the pistol. The box was the best place for it, I decided; I left it there. The money and tapes I put in the attaché case.

Harriet and I chatted some more while I put the box away, then I left.

I played the tapes on a VCR I had at home. Dorsey was on three of them. The same men were on all twelve. I didn't recognize any of the other women. When I finished with the nine tapes Dorsey wasn't on, I smashed them with a hammer and put them in the garbage, where they belonged.

The cash amounted to twenty-seven grand in old bills. I held random bills up to the light, fingered them, and compared them to some bills I had in my wallet. It was real money, I concluded. Tough luck for Carroll Kincaid—easy come, easy go.

I met Dorsey that Friday evening in downtown Washington at a bar jam-packed with people celebrating the start of the weekend. As the hubbub washed over us, I gave her the three remaining tapes. I put my mouth close to her ear and asked, "Is any of these men Carroll Kincaid?"

"No." She refused to meet my eyes. "I don't want to talk about it."

"For whatever it's worth, you weren't the only one."

She grunted and slugged her Scotch down as if it were Diet Coke.

"A thank-you would be in order," I said.

She laid a hand on my arm, tried to smile, got up, and walked out.

I drank a second beer while I contemplated the state of the universe. On my way home I stopped by the first church I saw—it was Catholic—and went in to see the priest.

"Father, I have unexpectedly come into some serious money. I won't burden you with an explanation, but I wish to donate it to the church to use in its ministry to the poor."

The priest didn't look surprised. People must give him wads of cash every day. "As you probably know quite well, the need is great," he told me. "On behalf of the church, I would be delighted to accept any amount you wish to donate."

I handed him the money, which I had put in a shoebox and wrapped in some Christmas gift wrap I had left over from the holidays.

He hefted the box and inspected my wrapping job. "Do you want a receipt?" he said, eyeing me.

"That won't be necessary." I shook his hand and hit the road.

A few weeks later the agency sent me to Europe, where I spent most of the winter and spring. I didn't hear from Dorsey O'Shea during my occasional trips back to the States, and probably would never have run into her again had I not gotten into a jam the following summer.

CHAPTER TWO

On the first Tuesday in July I found myself driving west from Washington on I-66 under a huge warm front that was stalled over the mid-Atlantic region. It was a gray, rainy day. The wipers squished monotonously on the windshield of my old red Mercedes coupe. A leak between the windshield and the hardtop that I had fought for years dribbled on the passenger's seat. Apparently the weeks the car had spent this winter alternately baking and freezing outside my apartment building had been too much for the goo and do-it-yourself rubber seals that I used to plug the leak last summer.

I had only been back in the States a week, which I had spent writing reports, cleaning up routine paperwork at the office, replacing the leaking water heater in my apartment, and putting a new battery in my car. The mindless routine and endless rain had me in a gloomy mood on Monday when my boss, Pulzelli, called me into his office.

Pulzelli was a bureaucrat to his fingertips, a man who loved the thrust and parry of interoffice politics. He was famous in the agency for his habit of picking his teeth with a pen, which left his enamel splotched with whatever ink color happened to be his current favorite. He was also a bit prissy about saying "damn" and "hell" at the office; I could clean up my act when around quality folk, so that didn't bother me much. The thing I liked best about Pulzelli was his willingness to do battle to protect the people who worked for him. All in all, he was a good guy to have on your side when the fan was splattering the smelly stuff all over, as happened at the agency a couple times a day. It seemed that we lurched from crisis to crisis, but perhaps that was only my perception.

"The chief wants me to provide someone for a week at the Greenbrier River facility," he said. "How about driving up tomorrow morning?"

The "facility" was really a safe house deep in the heart of the Allegheny Mountains surrounded on three sides by national forest. The cover was that the estate belonged to a wealthy novelist who was rarely there and was paranoid about his privacy when he was. A grass airstrip and a hangar were visible from the highway; the rest of the structures were completely out of sight of the motoring public and could only be reached by a mile-long gravel road. Although the property was fenced and continuously patrolled, the agency beefed up the security detail when the use of the facility warranted it. Apparently this was one of those times.

On two prior occasions I had spent a week there assigned to the security detail while Russian defectors were being interrogated. If the facility was used for anything other than defector interrogations, I didn't know about it.

"From the French Riviera to the Allegheny Mountains," I said to Pulzelli. "Talk about culture shock—I don't know if my heart can stand the strain."

He grinned, and I saw several stains on his teeth that could have only been blue ink.

"Another defector?"

"No one said anything to me."

We batted the breeze for a few minutes. He didn't mention what the security detail was guarding at the safe house, nor did I ask again. He couldn't tell me what he didn't know, which was precisely the rationale for classifying information and restricting access to those with a need to know.

Four people worked for me. Just now one was in the Mideast, one in Japan, and one in China. The only one currently in town was Joe Billy Dunn, the new guy who had just arrived from Delta Force. He strolled in after lunch that Monday, fresh from a training session for new recruits.

"You're in charge for the rest of the week," I told him. "I'm going to be out of the office on assignment. I'll call you from time to time, see how things are going."

Dunn was thirty-two, a few inches short of six feet, wedge shaped, and hard as a brick. He threw himself into his chair, plopped his feet on his desk, laced his fingers behind his head, and sighed contentedly. "Three weeks in headquarters and already I'm in charge. Cream always rises to the top, my mama used to say."

"Right."

" 'Course my ol' daddy said that shit floats."

"Philosophers, both of them."

"The rate I'm going up, about Christmas they're gonna put me in charge of this-here outfit."

Dunn wasn't a yokel, although he liked to play the role. He had a trace of southern accent in his voice, which he exaggerated from time to time. He struck me as one of those people who are best taken in small doses.

"Don't start World War III while I'm gone," I told him.

Why the powers that be assigned Dunn to my section was a bureaucratic mystery. The people in my section traveled the world breaking and entering, planting bugs, tapping lines, and running wireless surveillance equipment. We didn't do it all by ourselves, of course; we were merely the experts called in when the local station chief needed more expertise than he had available.

Dunn's field was counterterrorism operations. He could jump out of planes in the dead of night, handle and repair any weapon in the army arsenal, speak Arabic and French, and survive indefinitely on mice and snakes in places I wouldn't even want to fly over. He was quite adept at unarmed combat. Armed combat, too, for that matter. He knew very little about clandestine surveillance. Maybe they expected me to train him. Oh, well.

So here I was on Tuesday morning, watching rain fall from a slate sky and stream across the windshield, thinking about the problems at the office. I wasn't in the mood for the radio. The monotonous sounds, endless traffic, and subdued light all had their way with me, so I stopped at a McDonald's near Front Royal in the Shenandoah for coffee. The hot java and the pit stop helped and I soon felt better.

I took I-81 southeast down the valley. Sandwiched between trucks, trying to avoid the spray from their tires at seventy-five miles per hour, I rolled by the towns of Strasburg, New Market, and Harrisonburg. I was relieved when I saw the exit I was looking for near Staunton and got off the interstate.

Another stop, this time for gas as well as coffee, and a handful of paper towels to wipe off the water from the passenger seat of the car. On through the rain I went, westward along a twisty two-lane highway into the mountains. The road attacked the grain of the mountains at right angles, so soon I was downshifting and working my way through switchbacks and blind curves. Over the top and through switchbacks and blind curves down the other side. Across a small stream and up the next one.

The clouds came down, shrouding the mountaintops in dense fog as the rain grew even heavier. The road ran through a great hardwood forest; in the rain all that could usually be seen was vivid wet, dripping green. The road was so slick I didn't have time to do much looking. After creeping over three mountains I went through the village of McDowell. A mountain later, Monterey. Three more mountains and I found myself driving through a widening valley toward Bartow. At the bridge across the Greenbrier River I turned south.

Five miles later I entered another wide, open valley, the largest I'd seen since leaving the Shenandoah. When I saw the barn and hangar in the huge meadow on the right side of the road, I turned in at the gate and drove slowly along. I knew that the security gang was watching me on cameras mounted on the barn, so I took my time, even stopped alongside the hangar, got out and stretched my legs in the rain so that they got a good look at my face and had time to do a computer check of my license plate. I didn't want anyone jumping from behind a bush, sticking a submachine gun in my face—shocks like that were hard on my adrenal system.

I was dressed for the hinterlands today: hiking boots, jeans, and a dark green Gore-Tex windbreaker that shed the rain nicely. I pulled the collar tight to keep water from trickling down my neck.

A half dozen deer grazing in the meadow a hundred yards or so away lifted their heads and watched me, more curious than afraid. I stared right back. One of them was a buck growing a decent rack of antlers. They ignored the cold rain. Finally they tired of watching me and went back to munching grass, which reminded me that I, too, was hungry. And cold.

It was cooler here than in Washington . . . at least fifteen degrees cooler. If the air cooled off much more, I thought, this rain could turn to snow. Wouldn't that be the icing on the cake? From the tanned bikini babes of the French Riviera to an early summer snowstorm in these old mountains! I shivered at the thought, turned up my collar, and got back into the car.

Speaking of babes, I had a date for this coming Friday night. I had forgotten to cancel it. I removed my cell phone from my coat pocket and looked at it. No service.

Of course not. Now I remembered! We were only a few miles north of the National Radio Astronomy Observatory, smack in the middle of a huge radio quiet zone.

I put the cell phone back in my pocket and made a mental note to call the lady on a landline.

I drove on, crossed over a narrow bridge with no guardrails, then followed the road into the wet, dark, dripping forest.

The road came to a four-way intersection, and I took the road to the left, which was hard-packed gravel. The road paralleled the valley for several hundred yards, then turned to follow a creek into the hills. Two hundred yards after the turn there was a wide place, a pullout barely large enough for one car. I parked, got out, and stretched, sucking in a deep lungful of cool air smelling of wet earth and fragrant blossoms.

The woods were quiet, the treetops enshrouded in clouds, the leaves glistening.

There was a dim pathway up the slope to the right. It was difficult to see, but I knew it was there and didn't have to search for it. The forest floor squished under my feet.

Fifty yards up the hill was a small one-story security cabin made of logs. It was surrounded by laurel and difficult to see from more than ten yards away. This was the security post that monitored the surveillance cameras trained on the barn and hangar and mounted high in trees at various places. The people here could use a radio to summon armed guards in four-wheel-drive vehicles to intercept intruders.

The door to the cabin was ajar. I climbed the steps, crossed the small covered porch, and went in.

"Hey, guys, don't you—"

There were two men in the single room, both dead. One sat slumped in a chair facing the bank of monitors; the other lay on the floor in the middle of the room. Both had been shot numerous times. There was little blood. Several dozen spent 9 mm cartridges lay scattered on the floor.

I froze. There was a small restroom in one corner of the building; the door was closed. It was unlikely the shooter was in there answering nature's call, but . . .

I turned the man on the floor just enough to pull the pistol from his shoulder holster. It was a 9 mm auto. I thumbed off the safety, tiptoed to the restroom door and opened it with my foot. Empty.

I knew the man in the chair from my prior tours here. His name was Fred. I touched his cheek. Still warm. Very warm. His hand was limp and supple. He had at least eight bullet holes in him that I could see, and none of them had bled much. I fingered one of the wounds. The blood was still fresh and oozing.

These men hadn't been dead long. Just a few minutes.

I had seen no traffic on the road. Now that I thought about it, the pathway up here showed no footprints. I glanced at the radio—it had a half dozen bullet holes in it. The telephone . . . I picked it up, didn't get a dial tone. I put it back on its cradle.

Something was going down, but what?

I stepped to the door and looked at the porch. I could see other wet footprints. I slipped out onto the porch, walked along it to the end. Depressions in the leafy forest detritus were visible, at least two trails. One coming, one leaving? Perhaps the shooter had come this way, along the side of the hill through the forest, parallel to the road below. Then he retraced his path leaving. I knew what lay in that direction—the main complex.

I went back in the cabin and looked at the surveillance camera monitors. They were still working. The killers must have shot these men immediately before I pulled up at the hangar or after I left it. Or perhaps they were so busy drilling these guys they didn't notice me on the monitors. If they had seen me, they would have met me down on the road or here at the cabin and killed me, too.

Later on I realized that this would have been an excellent time to jog down the hill to my car and beat a tactical retreat to the safety of the nearest village, where I could have called Washington with the news. There was nothing I could do for the men in the cabin. Unfortunately that thought didn't occur to me then.

I checked the pistol. There was a round in the chamber and the magazine was full. I put the safety on and, with the pistol in my hand, started off through the forest following the tracks.

He knew his wife was probably dead. He had heard the ripping of the silenced submachine guns—still loud—and knew precisely what it was. She had been in the kitchen eating when he came into the bathroom, just moments ago.

He held his hands to his ears, trying to stop the sounds. Oh, God, all his nightmares were becoming reality!

He was completely unarmed, knew nothing of unarmed combat, knew it would be suicide to leave the bathroom. As the staccato bursts sounded closer, he surveyed the small room. There was a chute for towels . . . he opened it, wormed his way into it. And fell.

He landed in a pile of towels and sheets on a hard concrete floor. The basement.

He looked around, desperate for a place to hide. Oversized laundry machines were mounted against the wall—two washers, two dryers.

He had always had the ability to think quickly and function flawlessly under pressure; he had been doing it for twenty-five years under the noses of the paranoid professionals of the KGB. He used that ability now. Without wasting a second, he opened a dryer and crawled in amid the sheets and pillowcases, then pulled the door shut after him.

The thought occurred to me that if I wasn't real careful, I could end up like Fred and his colleague. Whoever shot them used an automatic weapon, and I was carrying a peashooter.

I'm no hero—far from it. I've been around long enough to know I'm not bulletproof. I also know that revenge is something people only get in movies—not in America in this day and age. I kept going anyway. I wanted this guy. Wanted to shoot him my very own self . . . as long as I could do it safely, without doing any serious bleeding. I liked Fred, but friendship has its limits.

I took my time walking through the woods, pausing frequently to look and listen. The sound of rain hitting the leaves and big drops falling off the trees masked all other sounds. With the leaves on the trees and brushy plants and the reduced visibility from fog, I couldn't see far. Still, the depressions in the wet leaves were easy to follow—even for a city boy like me.

It took about twenty minutes at my slow pace to get to the edge of the main complex clearing. Using the trees as cover, I sneaked to a spot where I could see, right behind a large tree. Flat on my face, I inched my head around the trunk. The main complex consisted of a two-story log structure that functioned as a dormitory, a garage for vehicles, and the main building itself, a huge, two-story log house with a covered porch that wrapped all the way around it. There were no vehicles in the gravel driveway.

A body lay on the front porch. From the way he was sprawled I knew he was dead.

A muffled ripping reached me, a second or so of sound, then another burst. The sounds seemed to be coming from the main house. I knew what those sounds were—bursts from a silenced submachine gun. The killers were still hard at it, slaughtering people.

Killers. There had to be more than one. The pistol felt useless in my hand.

Only a suicidal fool would charge in there with a pistol to face an unknown number of men armed with submachine guns. I'd certainly played the fool on numerous occasions in my life, but I sure as hell wasn't suicidal. Lying behind that tree on wet, soaking leaves, I knew there was simply nothing I could do. I checked my watch. It was seventeen minutes after twelve.

Several minutes passed. The shooting seemed to be over. After those two bursts I heard, there had been nothing else. Now black smoke began to waft from the chimney.

I had been in the main room of the house on several occasions and remembered the huge, cut-stone fireplace.

The smoke became a column.

Maybe the bastards were setting the place on fire.

At twenty-nine past the hour a man wearing a camo outfit came out onto the porch. He had a submachine gun cradled in his arms. He walked to the end of the porch and, facing in my direction, made a come-here motion with his arm.

I froze, holding my breath. Certainly he couldn't be motioning to me!

That was when I had a bad shock. A bush near a solitary tree twenty yards in front of me suddenly stood up and began walking toward the porch! It was a man in a ghillie suit, a web of cord and leaves and strips of rag that covered him completely and allowed him to sink to the ground and mold himself into the landscape. I could see the round sausage-shaped silencer on his weapon protruding from the suit.

If I had moved in any direction from this tree, he would have spotted me and killed me.

Every Tom, Dick, and Harry wore camouflage clothes these days, but silenced submachine guns and a ghillie suit? These men had the look of professionals. Military snipers, perhaps. Uh-oh! Right then I thanked my stars that I was wearing a dark green jacket, not my yellow one. The air went out of me, and I seemed to sink into the earth in my attempt to disappear from view.

I was also doing some hard thinking. When I saw the man in the camo clothes glance at his watch and take a two-way radio from a holster on his belt, I knew I was in deep and serious shit. They might have hiked across the hills through the national forest to get here, but I was willing to bet my pension these dudes were now waiting for a ride. Someone was going to drive a vehicle up the only road, and that someone was going to see my car—and call these guys on their handheld radios, which would cause them to come looking hard for little old me.

Even as that thought shot across my synapses, I heard the radio in his hand come to life. In that still air the sound carried, although I could not distinguish the words. Yep, both of them took a quick glance around.

Uh-oh!

That was when I realized I should have taken the car to the village to telephone the cavalry.

The inadequacy of my hiding place also hit me hard. Stretched out behind a tree, I was invisible to these two as they stood in the yard, but if they began circling the perimeter of the clearing, they would see me easily.

I backed straight up, keeping the tree between them and me. When the ground permitted, I rose to a crouch and began waddling back the way I had come as fast as I could. They would see my tracks, of course, but I had a few minutes before they found them. I intended to see if I could get back to my car before they did.

Fifty yards into the woods I began jogging toward the guard cabin. I didn't jog far—the tree trunks, dead limbs, fallen trees, rocks, and uneven ground made it impossible. The best I could manage was a fast walk, going over, under, and around obstacles, just as I had coming from the cabin. The heel marks and boot prints in the sodden forest carpet were nearly a path by now, plainly visible. And here I was trucking along this little highway, begging for someone to shoot me.

After about four minutes of this, I stopped and shucked my hiking boots, tied them together with the strings, and put them around my neck. The wetness went through my socks instantly, nearly freezing my feet.

Trying to disturb the leaves and dirt as little as possible, I climbed up the hill away from the path at right angles. When I had gone forty feet or so, I sat down to put my boots back on. My feet were already cold—there was no way I could walk very far without the boots.

I was tying the lace on the second one when I caught a glimpse of movement out of the corner of my eye. A rotten log partially concealed me on that side—the side toward the guard cabin. I ducked down, huddled against it, and waited.

Perhaps a minute went by. Then he came, following the tracks. He was wearing camo clothes and carried a silenced submachine gun in his hands, the butt braced against his right hip. I could see a slender boom mike across his face; the headset was under his camo hat. He moved slowly and steadily, scanning alternately the trail, then the woods right and left.

He must have had a lot of experience in the woods, because when he came to the place where I left the trail, he recognized the footprints going away and turned toward me, still scanning. I held the pistol sights dead center on his chest as I squeezed the trigger.

CHAPTER THREE

In the silence and gloom of the forest, the shot was the loudest noise I'd ever heard.

The man I fired at dropped instantly.

I didn't wait to see how bad he was hit. I leaped up and ran at him, the pistol at the ready.

The guy never moved. Looked to me like the bullet went right though his heart and stopped it. Stopped it dead.

The man was a stranger. He was wearing a headset that contained an earpiece and a mike. A cord led from it to a radio in a holster on his belt. I helped myself—he didn't need it anymore.

The submachine gun was an MP-5 with a red dot sight and a silencer. It had a doubled banana clip, each side holding forty rounds.

I slapped his pockets, found another double clip, and took it, found he had a pistol and pocketed that, too. No car keys. My hair was soaked, leaking water down my forehead into my eyes, so I wiped my face on my wet sleeve, then jammed his camo hat on my head.

The radio was on, but no one was saying anything.

The heft of the MP-5 gave me a fool's confidence. I was cold, wet, scared, and mad. I started back toward the main complex with the submachine gun braced against my hip, my thumb on the safety. The gentle mist of rain was now a drizzle.

The dude who worried me the most was the one in the ghillie suit. When you are playing with guns in the woods, the man who sees the other fellow first has a huge advantage. The ghillie suit was the ultimate in camouflage, but only if the person wearing it stayed immobile, settled in to become one with the surrounding land-scape. Movement negated the value of the suit.

Nearing the clearing, I stopped behind a tree to look and listen. Took a few steps to the dubious safety of another tree and scanned everything. I crawled the last twenty yards to a large tree that gave me a view of the house and yard.

I was thanking my stars the bushes and weeds were well leafed out, providing me some cover, when a large SUV drove up the road and stopped in front of the main house. The driver didn't turn off the engine.

"I'm here, Joe."

This had to be the ride they were waiting for, the one that dropped the man I killed.

Flat on my belly, I eased the muzzle of the MP-5 through the bushes and settled the red dot of the sighting reticle on the driver of the vehicle. The range was perhaps a hundred yards, maybe a few yards less.

The thought of the guy in the ghillie suit stopped me from pulling the trigger. Without moving my head, I scanned every-thing I could see in that gloomy wet universe.

They had undoubtedly heard the pistol shot and knew their

man hadn't reported on the radio. My only edge was that they didn't know where I was. I hoped.

The guy in the ghillie could be anywhere in the brush surrounding the clearing waiting for me to reveal my position. I had no illusions—with an MP-5, he didn't even have to be a good shot. Any one of that clipful of 9 mm slugs he could hose at me would be quite sufficient to terminate my miserable existence.

A man in a camo suit with a weapon in his hand came out onto the porch. He looked around, then keyed the radio on his belt. "Joe?"

The silence that followed that word was pregnant.

The seconds ticked by one by one, then another male voice spoke into my ear. "This intruder must have boogied, Frank. Maybe we'd better get the hell outta here, too."

"I never saw so much goddamn paper." That was the man on the porch, I thought. "Take at least an hour to burn all of it in the fireplace."

"We don't have an hour, man."

"Come help. We'll set the house on fire and get the hell out of here."

That was when a bush off to my right began to move down the hill toward the house.

The man on the porch went back inside. The driver of the SUV turned off the ignition and climbed out. He took the steps to the porch two at a time and disappeared inside.

I waited until the walking bush was nearing the porch, then eased the red dot onto him. Bracing the gun against my shoulder, I thumbed the fire selector to full automatic, then squeezed the trigger. The noise was about as loud as a .22 rifle. The weapon walked off target and I muscled it back on, then released the trigger.

The bush collapsed on the ground; his weapon fell several feet away.

I had fired about a dozen rounds, I thought. A one-second burst or a little over. I pointed the MP-5 at the porch and waited, examining windows. Perhaps I should have moved, but I was betting they didn't know where I was. Movement might give me away.

A flicker of light showed in one of the ground-floor windows. The bastards had indeed fired the place. The fire grew quickly in intensity.

They must have used thermal grenades!

I snuggled the weapon in against my shoulder and waited. Anyone desiring to leave by SUV was going to get perforated.

They went out the back.

I didn't see them go, but after a minute or so several of the lower windows shattered and smoke began puffing out of the upstairs windows. I didn't think they were going to immolate themselves, so concluded they must have gone out the back and over the hill, precisely the way they had come in.

I took a deep breath and sprinted for the cover of the SUV.

That sprint would have gotten me a roster spot in the NFL. I have never run so fast in my life.

No shots. As I huddled behind the SUV and listened to the fire in the house snap, crackle, and pop, the thought occurred to me that one of those dudes might have stayed behind just for the fun of icing me point-blank as I went up the porch stairs.

If so, he was behind the door.

I emptied the magazine into the door, put in a fresh magazine, then put a burst into each window.

Feeling a tad bit better, I ran up the stairs and into the house, ready to shoot the first thing that moved.

They had used thermal grenades. The heat and smoke were intense. Yet the fire looked worse than it was. Crouching, I could see that the main room was covered with paper, heaping piles of it. And three bodies.

Two more bodies in the kitchen.

The back door was standing open.

I threw caution to the winds and hurried through the building, looking for anyone still alive. And sorta hoping I'd meet a bad guy, so I could have the fun of shooting him with the MP-5.

I did find someone, hiding in an upstairs closet.

She screamed as I jerked her out of there, screamed and went for my eyes with her fingernails.

I pushed her roughly, and she fell to the floor. "Goddamn, lady, get a grip. I'm one of the good guys." I must have shouted it, because I was pretty pumped.

She stared at the submachine gun with eyes as big as saucers as the smoke roiled through the room. Her eyes rose to my face. I must have looked like something from the Black Lagoon standing there with that weapon in my hand, soaked to the skin, and covered with dirt and leaves.

"Who are you?" she whispered, staring at the weapon, her eyes wide.

"Let's get the hell outta here, lady, and do the introductions some other time." I jerked her off the floor and pushed her toward the door.

"The suitcase," she shrieked, pointing back toward the closet.

"We ain't got time for your fuckin' clothes. The goddamn house is burning—"

"That's what they came for! That's what they wanted!"

I jerked the suitcase from the closet—it must have weighed fifty pounds—and pushed it at her.

"Get down the stairs and out of the house, right now, while I check to see if anyone else is alive up here."

She disappeared into the smoke dragging the suitcase—it was just a bit too heavy to carry.

I ran from room to room, looking in closets and under beds, coughing and shouting. I didn't find anyone; not that I searched everywhere, but I just ran out of time. The smoke was bad and getting worse. I could feel the heat in the floor and walls. I charged for the stairs hoping that I hadn't waited too long. The staircase was like a chimney, funneling smoke and heat to the second and third floors. I held my breath and went down blind.

At the bottom of the stairs I tripped on something and went sprawling. She had collapsed coming down the stairs and lay in a heap beside the suitcase.

The fire was raging by then and the heat was unbelievable, but there was a little clear area near the floor, maybe two feet high. I crawled over to her, grabbed her by the arm, and began pulling. I couldn't manage both girl and gun, so I abandoned the weapon.

When we reached the porch I half carried, half dragged her down the steps into the yard.

Then I lost my footing and dropped her. I went to my knees, gagging and retching and trying desperately to get some air. I stayed down until my head cleared somewhat. She was breathing shallowly. I put her on the grass, turned her over on her chest, and began pushing and pulling on her arms. After about thirty seconds of that she gagged, then gasped, "The suitcase! For Christ's sake, get the suitcase!"

Okay, she was going to make it.

Figuring she knew more than I did, I went spider-walking back into the house for the damned suitcase and the MP-5. I wanted the gun more than the suitcase. The guys who iced these people and set the house afire might come back; if they did, I wanted that shooter. In our uncertain age, you must do unto others before they do it unto you.

Going back into that burning building was one of the dumber things I have done since I got out of diapers and stopped eating mud. The heat and smoke were damn near intolerable.

Miracle of miracles, I found the gun and suitcase and reversed course for the door. Got lost and started getting dizzy again from the smoke, then found the door just in time. I tossed the case into the yard and fell beside it on the grass.

While I gagged and coughed, she loaded the suitcase into the SUV.

Finally I got my breathing under control. I struggled to my feet and almost fell on my face. After thirty more seconds of hands on knees, I stood. She was bent over the dead man in the ghillie suit. She had pulled off his headpiece and had it in her hand.

"You know him?" I managed.

"No," she said, and tossed his head rag on the ground. She turned back toward me.

"Name's Carmellini, lady. Who the hell are you?"

"Kelly." She said her last name, but I didn't catch it. She was about medium height, had short dark hair and large brown eyes, and was in her late twenties, maybe a few years older. She might even have been pretty; it was hard to tell. Her face and clothes were covered with soot and grime. Behind us the fire was roaring. The heat was getting worse, and I found myself moving away from it. She did, too. Although she glanced at the fire from time to time, most of the time she kept her eyes on me.

"Well, Kel, this is how it is. Those assholes shot everyone they could find and set the goddamn house on fire. The worst of it is that they may come back. I suggest that we borrow this fine vehicle and get the hell outta here."

I managed to stagger over to the SUV and look in. The key was still in the ignition. I picked up the MP-5 and put it in the rear seat, then got behind the wheel. Kelly got into the passenger seat.

We were sitting ducks if the killers elected to stay around to ambush us, but I was praying they hadn't. Still, Fred's pistol felt good in my lap. As the wipers smeared the water on the windshield, I got the SUV going and turned it around.

The guy in the ghillie suit looked like a small brush pile in the lawn.

I put the transmission in park, leaped out, and ran over to him. I turned his head and took a good look. Nope. Never saw him before. And he had an MP-5 lying beside him. I had forgotten about it. Hell, I could have left the other one in the house and just taken his.

His weapon sported a double banana clip in it that might come in handy later, so I jerked it out. I left the weapon.

"Where did you get your submachine gun?" she asked, her eyes on my face.

"The guy carrying it left it to me in his will."

She glanced back at the house, then at the suitcase on the rear seat.

As we were going down the drive, I asked Kelly, "What happened back there?"

"They came this morning. I was upstairs, heard the shooting, went to the top of the stairs. There's a place where you can look over the balcony into the main room downstairs, and I saw they had shot Mikhail. That's when I grabbed the suitcase in his room and hid."

"Who is Mikhail? What's in the suitcase?"

She took a deep breath before she answered. "Mikhail Goncharov was the chief archivist for SVR, the successor to the KGB. He was like . . . their librarian, in charge of the central records depository. He defected last week. We had just started to debrief him. He spent the last twenty years making notes from the case files of the Soviet foreign intelligence service, and then Russia's after the breakup. He had seven suitcases full of notes that he brought with him when we extracted him."

She jerked her thumb over her shoulder. "That's the last one."

With the house on fire, the man hiding in the washing machine in the basement decided he could wait no longer. He could smell the smoke, hear the roar of the fire, and knew if he waited much longer, he would never get out of the building.

Perhaps he had already waited too long . . .

The basement had not yet filled with smoke. There had to be an exit door . . . somewhere! He ran from room to room, fighting back the panic. There was a furnace in one room, several storerooms full of canned food and large freezers . . . and at the end of the hallway, a door.

It was locked with a massive dead bolt, one that could be opened from the inside. The man opened it, and found himself in a stairwell. He went up it slowly, trying to see, as the fire raged in the house above him.

No one in sight. Scraggly grass covered with autumn leaves for forty yards, then the forest.

The man ran toward the forest.

Safely behind a large tree, he paused and looked back at the house, which was engulfed in flames.

The blood pounded in his temples.

Biting his lip, trying to contain his emotions, he turned his back on the burning house and walked into the dark dripping forest.

CHAPTER FOUR

When we reached my car, I ran the SUV off the road and parked it. There was just room enough to turn my car around.

"Why did you park here?" Kelly asked as I put the suitcase full of paper into the trunk.

"There's a guard shack up the hill. The agency sent me to do a week of guard detail, so I wanted to check in with the guys before I went up to the house. They were both dead. Shot with an automatic weapon, it looked like." I didn't think I'd need it, but I put the MP-5 on the ledge behind the coupe's seats.

After I got the car turned around and we were headed for the hard road, she said, "Say your name again."

"Tommy Carmellini. Why were you here?"

"I'm a Russian translator. All the notes are in Russian. That was the only language Goncharov spoke."

"The suitcase contains his notes?"

"Yes."

"So you saved them," I mused, and glanced at her. She didn't look like the toughest broad on the block, but she had backbone. Of course, one wondered how much. Those dudes with the camouflage and automatic weapons were supposed to kill everyone at the safe house and destroy all the notes. They were the A-team, but whose A-team?

Someone was going to be very peeved when he heard that there were two survivors. I glanced at her, wondered if that thought had occurred to her yet.

We crossed the bridge and took the graveled road across the meadow and airstrip and past the hangar. I felt naked. We had just turned onto the paved road when the first fire truck rounded the curve from Bartow. Fortunately no one in the truck could have seen our car come across the meadow ... I hoped. As the truck went by, I slowed and looked back into the low hills. Although the rain was still coming down steadily, the ceiling had lifted enough so that I could see a column of smoke rising above the trees and merging with the clouds.

I eased the clutch out and got the car in motion again. Three cars with small flashing lights on the roofs, driven by volunteer firemen probably, went racing by us and turned into the gravel road, following the fire truck. They roared across the meadow, over the bridge, and disappeared up the road into the forest.

"I missed your last name, Kelly. What did you say it was?"

"Erlanger."

"So what's in the notes?"

"Everything. Goncharov summarized or copied verbatim every KGB file he thought significant during the twenty-some years that he was the head archivist, then smuggled the notes out of the building every evening when he went home. The collection filled seven suitcases—a mountain of material. We were just starting to dig into it. I'm guessing, but I would say roughly half the material deals with Soviet internal politics. The foreign intel files I saw were about recruiting and running agents—mercenary and ideo-logical—illegal residents, assassinations, disinformation, payoffs, subversion of foreign regimes, support for indigenous Commu-nists around the globe, running arms . . . you name it. Think of every dirty thing the KGB did before the collapse of Communism and every dirty thing it did since then, and you got it."

"How far back do the files go?"

"Lenin, Dzerzhinsky, Stalin, the purges . . . Goncharov had ac-cess to every file in the archives until he retired four years ago. He was fascinated by the way the party used the NKVD and KGB to eliminate opposition and maintain its hold on power, then lied about it. His superiors or high-placed members of the government periodically ordered files destroyed—getting rid of the evi-dence—so he copied them before they went to the shredder and furnace."

We came to the bridge at Bartow and turned right, toward Staunton and the Shenandoah, which was seventy-five miles and seven mountains away. As we accelerated away from the intersec-tion, I glanced in the rearview mirror. A large SUV coming from the north made the turn and fell into trail behind us. It wasn't the one I had parked when we transferred to this car—it had come from the wrong direction, and besides, I had the keys to that one in my pocket.

"Those bastards," Kelly Erlanger said hoarsely. "Goncharov and the others didn't have a chance. They were slaughtered like steers. Murdered. Gunned down."

I glanced at her. Tears were leaking from her eyes. She was staring straight ahead at nothing at all, remembering . . .

The SUV was still in trail, back there eight or ten car lengths. I was making fifty-five along the narrow, straight, wet highway, charging up the valley. A plume of road spray rose behind me. I slowed to fifty. The SUV stayed the same distance behind.

Shit!

"His wife defected with him. I don't know what happened to her."

"There were two dead women in the kitchen," I said. "One of them was in her late fifties maybe. Perhaps early sixties, gray hair, sorta plump. The other was maybe thirty, tall."

"Bronislava Goncharova was the older one. She didn't speak any English. The tall woman was Natasha Romerstein. She was a translator, too—she and I worked together at the agency. Her parents were Ukranian; she was born in America. She had a two-year-old son."

We were approaching a Y intersection. The road to the right was the one I had always driven to and from this valley—it was the only one I knew—so I took it. The SUV followed me.

We were still in a narrow valley. The stream meandered back and forth, but the road ran straight for almost a mile, crossing the stream several times on small bridges. Then it went into a long sweeping left turn and continued for another mile. Only at the head of the valley did the road began to wind and twist as it climbed Allegheny Mountain. I checked to see that Kelly had her seat belt on. She didn't.

"Put the belt on," I said over the growl of the engine.

She snapped herself in, then looked behind us. The SUV was not falling back. I kept the car at fifty.

"They've been behind us since Bartow, keeping their distance," I told her. "If we can't outrun them going up the mountain, this is going to get messy. Can you shoot an MP-5?"

"No."

She pulled a cell phone from her pocket, looked at it, then announced, "No service."

"Who you gonna call?" I asked.

"Why . . . the agency! My supervisor."

"Those guys weren't Russians. They were Americans. I listened to them talk."

"What are you saying?"

"Don't jump to conclusions. Yeah, the Russians may have hired some Americans to assault that house to kill Goncharov and burn the notes, but how did they know he was there?"

While she was mulling that over, we reached the head of the valley and started climbing the mountain. I downshifted and put the hammer down. Although the road was wet, the Mercedes had good rubber.

The SUV wasn't as agile in the curves as the coupe. They must have had a hell of a mill under the hood, because even with my maneuvering advantage the big SUV hung in there. I felt my back end start to break loose on one of the horseshoe turns halfway up . . . I managed to save it and kept the throttle on the floor as the SUV slid into the berm and gravel flew. The driver swiftly recovered without losing much momentum and stayed on my tail.

Right, left, higher and higher on the mountain, working the clutch and stick, I kept the Mercedes as near the adhesion limit as I could. Kelly used both hands to brace herself.

We didn't pass a single car climbing the mountain. We topped the ridge—blew by the sign that read radar detectors were illegal in Virginia—and went into a long, descending sweeper down the eastern slope. I let the Mercedes accelerate . . . past sixty, seventy . . . the distance was opening . . . then braked hard for a blind right-hand turn.

Too fast . . . the rear end broke loose and we slid across the road, headed for the berm and the edge. Of course, on that curve the state had not gotten around to putting up a guardrail. The edge was right there, like the Grand Canyon. The added friction of the rocks saved us.

With gravel flying, I threw the car back on the road and missed a shift, almost stalled the engine, then was accelerating hard again.

In the rearview mirror I got a glimpse of the SUV sliding across the berm and going over the edge.

I slammed on the brakes.

"Why are we stopping?" Kelly shouted as the deceleration forces threw her against her shoulder belt.

"They went off the road, over the edge," I told her as the Benz slid to a halt and I slammed it into reverse. "This is our chance to find out who those dudes are and who the hell they're working for."

I backed up at full throttle, the engine howling, then braked to a stop on the berm where they went over. I popped the shifter into neutral and jammed the parking brake on, then bailed out with Fred's automatic in my right hand.

No one was moving in the SUV, which was impaled on a large tree trunk thirty feet down the slope. It had slammed into the trunk of the tree just behind the driver's door, and the tree had arrested it. The glass was gone; the vehicle was badly twisted from impact. I could see two heads—the driver's and passenger's—and they weren't moving.

I slid down the mud and gravel of the slope, struggling to keep my feet under me, until I reached the wreck.

Three men were in the vehicle. The passenger and the man on the back seat were dressed in camo pants and shirts, while the man behind the wheel was wearing jeans and a pullover. At first glance, it looked as if the air bags had saved their asses. Not the guy in back, however. His neck was obviously broken. His corpse was partially on the floor, partially on the seat.

I felt the passenger's carotid artery. He was still alive. And out cold. He had a snub-nose .38 in a holster on his ankle and an MP-5 between his legs. A two-way radio lay at his feet. One of his legs was broken—apparently he fractured it on the weapon during the crash.

I reached across and felt the driver's artery. No pulse.

I was struggling to get the passenger door open when I heard the Mercedes engine wind up. I started up the muddy slope, took two steps, and quit. Standing there in the rain, ankle deep in mud, leaves, and roadside trash, I listened to my Mercedes going down the mountain until the sound completely faded.

What a hell of a day this turned out to be.

I hadn't been smart enough to pull the keys from the ignition, so ol' Kelly what's-her-name made like a jackrabbit, leaving me with two corpses and a comatose killer ready for intensive care. It was enough to piss off the pope.

A common, coarse word seemed to fit the situation, so I said it aloud, then repeated it because I liked the sound of it.

CHAPTER FIVE

The injured man's seat-belt buckle was jammed; I had to cut the belt with my pocket knife. I dragged him from the passenger seat and laid him out in the mud. I wasn't too careful about how I handled him. If he croaked, so be it.

He didn't even twitch. No wallet, naturally. Not even a car key. I unstrapped his ankle holster and put it on.

There was a Virginia car registration certificate and proof of insurance card in the glove box of the vehicle, which I pocketed.

The driver had a wallet. I had a devil of a time getting it out of his pocket due to the way his corpse was jammed into the twisted seat. When I succeeded, I looked through it, found the driver's license, and extracted it. Didn't recognize the name. Address was Burke, Virginia. I put it in my pocket. Looked to see what else he had in there. Some credit cards and an AAA card, all in the name that appeared on the driver's license. Maybe that was his real name. Then again . . .

I heard a car or pickup coming, paused, and listened. It was climbing the mountain and didn't slacken its pace. Went around the curve above me and continued upward.

The corpse in the back with the broken neck was jammed down between the seats, and I wasn't in the mood to try to get him out of there. I doubted if he had any more ID on him than the man lying in the mud.

I was about to give up when I saw a bulge in the driver's shirt pocket. Jackpot! A cell phone. I pocketed it and the two-way radio.

The rest of it I left—corpses, weapons, ammo, and the comatose dude lying in the mud in the rain.

Kelly hadn't been gone three minutes when I finished and climbed the bank back up to the road. I was a royal mess, mud from the knees down, soot and fire filth from the knees up. And I was wet, tired, and pissed off.

As I inspected the skid marks in the gravel, I put Fred's pistol behind my belt in the small of my back and made sure my jacket covered it. Someone would see those skid marks and investigate, sooner or later.

I set off down the mountain, plodding along. Two more vehicles passed, both descending the grade. The rain continued to fall.

Twenty minutes after I left the wreck, when I was almost at the bottom of the grade, a farmer in an old pickup stopped and waited for me to catch up. He was white-haired, wearing well-worn overalls and a John Deere cap. And he was dry.

"You look like you could use a ride," he said when I opened the door.

"Car slid off the road back up the mountain," I told him. "I'm a real mess. If you don't mind, I'll ride in back."

"Hell, son, you won't hurt this truck. It's about as old as you are. Hop in and I'll give you a ride to Staunton."

"Thanks," I said gratefully. I climbed in and pulled the door shut.

He walked through the dripping forest, around rotting logs and broken limbs, over boulders and piles of dirt where trees had been uprooted by some ancient wind. The going was hard in the wet, slippery leaves on the forest floor, last autumn's rotting collection. And he wasn't wearing enough clothes.

His thoughts were all jumbled up, memories that flashed through his mind in no particular order. His wife's face haunted him.

She was dead—he was sure of it.

Murdered.

Like his mother and father. His very first memories as a toddler were of the night the NKVD came for them, took them away. He remembered the cold . . . and his mother sobbing, hysterically denying something. He had been but a tot. Lord, that was a long time ago . . . over sixty years. Stalin had purged the military and the party of his enemies, who were executed or sent to slave labor camps.

He didn't know what happened to his parents. They had disappeared into the great vastness of Soviet Russia and were never seen or heard from again . . . leaving only ghosts to haunt the thoughts of those who remembered them.

Tears ran down his face as he worked his way aimlessly through the forest, scrambling over slick, rotting logs, avoiding thickets and steep places, going more or less in one direction . . . perhaps.

In truth, he no longer cared.

All his life he had known they would come for him eventually. Just as they came for his parents.

He remembered sitting on the floor of the apartment crying after they took his parents. How long he had waited there for his parents to return he couldn't recall—he had been too small and it happened too long ago. Years later the woman who took him in said that he had been without food or water for three days when she found him, huddled on the floor, nearly dead of dehydration and hypothermia. She had picked him up, wrapped him in a blanket, and taken him home with her . . . at the risk of her own life.

Evil maims or kills, and good saves us. Sometimes. When he became a man he often contemplated the contrast between good and evil. The world was full of people who didn't believe in moral absolutes, people who could rationalize whatever course of action they wished to pursue, usually one that benefited them. They cheated, stole, lied, temporized, apologized, explained, and assured themselves and each other that everyone did it. He wasn't one of those people.

It wasn't that he was better than everyone else. He was no stronger or weaker than most. He, too, suffered the ravages of regret, the torture of remorse. Yet he refused to surrender to evil, even for a moment, even to preserve his life. He had lived in intimate proximity to it all his life and thought he knew all its faces. He had never surrendered, had fought it, tried never to give in to the constant fear, the terror of being discovered, the panic as he contemplated their revenge.

His wife understood. She had stood beside him, shared the risks, and . . . paid with her life.

He walked on through the forest, wet, shivering, remembering . . .

The old man talked all the way to Staunton, and I tried to hold up my end of the conversation, with dismal results. I had too much on my mind to pay much attention to the details of his life story and that of his children, of whom he had five or six . . . I got a little confused there in the middle.

He dropped me at the Wal-Mart in Staunton, and I shook his hand gratefully. An offer of money might have insulted him, so I didn't risk it.

After he drove off I went into the store and bought a new outfit from the skin out, then went to the men's room and changed into it. I dumped my wet, muddy clothes in the trash. At the snack bar I downed two hot dogs and two cups of hot, foul, black coffee while I sat thinking about things.

Mikhail Goncharov . . . the archivist for the KGB, a man who copied top secret files, lots of them, seven suitcases worth. Secrets from the cold war, buried where no one would ever see them, were now about to be exposed to the light of day. I was sure that many people all over the world would find the prospect horrifying, if they only knew. Obviously someone did know and was extremely unhappy.

I wondered who that someone was. Some people in the CIA knew of the Goncharov collection, probably some folks in British intelligence. And, perhaps, in Russia.

It seemed improbable to me that the Russians figured out where the agency was going to debrief their note-taking ex-archivist and managed to arrange a hit squad in less than a week. More likely, I thought, someone at the agency told someone . . . somewhere . . . something. The location perhaps, and obviously the need for haste.

Whoever wanted Goncharov silenced and the files destroyed had almost succeeded, at a terrible cost. That person wouldn't quit now, not when he learned that some of the files had escaped destruction—and that one of the people who had read the files was still very much alive.

I left a tip for the waitress and strolled out of Wal-Mart. A bank of pay phones stood near the front entrance. I went back in the store and got ten dollars' worth of quarters, then returned to the phones. Pulzelli was still at the office.

"Tommy Carmellini, Sal. I have some bad—"

His voice dropped to a hiss. "Where are you, Carmellini? The FBI has been here with a search warrant and gone through your desk."

"My desk?"

"They want you for questioning. Someone took out the Greenbrier safe house this morning, killed everyone there. They think you may have been involved."

"Jesus H. Christ!" I exclaimed, even though this was Pulzelli and he hated coarse language. "You just told me to go up there yesterday. Do they think I went off my nut or what?"

"They want to ask you some questions. Tell them everything and they'll go away. Where are you?"

"You answer a question for me. When you were told to send someone to Greenbrier for guard duty, did they ask for me specifically, or did you just choose me?"

"I chose you. The FBI knows that. Now tell me where you are."

"Sal, you've always played straight with me, so I'm going to level with you. The killers were there when I got there, and one of the translators escaped them. From what she told me, it appears that there has been a leak at the agency. These killers may even have been agency employees—I don't know yet."

"Talk to the FBI."

"That's probably good advice, but now I know too much. If there are some rotten apples at the agency, they could set me up to take this fall and there wouldn't be much I could do about it. Watch your back, Sal, and stay out of the line of fire."

I severed the connection before he could reply.

The rain outside had slackened to a gentle drizzle, almost a mist. Standing in the middle of the Wal-Mart parking lot with the cell phone in my hand, I got a little damp, but not wet. I stood there soaking up the liquid sunshine while I wondered how the FBI got onto me so quickly.

I had been the unexpected glitch, the witness who sees too much and doesn't drop dead on command.

It seemed logical to assume that one of the killers must have given the license plate number from my car to that someone in the agency or the FBI, and that person had decided to frame me. Or permanently shut me up.

Or, more than likely, do both. If you've murdered eight or ten people to hide guilty secrets, what's one or two more?

Sitting in an FBI office in Staunton jabbering into a tape recorder didn't appeal to me much, not while there were still bad guys running around with silenced MP-5s.

I put the cell phone back in my pocket and went back to the pay phones. My next call was to my lock shop partner, Willie the Wire. I dialed his cell number and got him on the third ring.

"Hey, man, I need some help."

"I've been telling you that for years and you still haven't been to see a shrink."

"A woman ripped off my wheels. I don't want to call the cops, but I want the Mercedes back. Don't you have a friend who works for LoJack?" LoJack was an antitheft system that allowed the police to locate stolen cars. I had had a LoJack beacon installed in my car when I acquired it.

"Yeah. Been a while since I talked to him, so I don't know if he's still working there."

"Give him a call, will ya? Tell him I need to find the car and don't want the police notified. A lover's spat. See if he can turn on the beacon and get a location."

"Ain't nobody love you, Carmellini."

"A lot you know. I've got hot women stashed in cities and towns, villages and farms, all across the length and breath of this great land."

"Right! Washington, you think?"

"Somewhere in the suburbs, I'll bet. Her name is Kelly Erlanger." I spelled it for him. "The spelling is just a guess. See if she's in the telephone book."

"Okay."

"One more thing. Today sorta went sour. The FBI is looking for me. If they show up at the shop we haven't had this conversation and you have no idea where I am."

A low, dry chuckle. "What the hell you been into now, Tommy?"

"You wouldn't believe it if I told you. As you know, I live a quiet, holy life, studying the scriptures and praying. My cell phone is off. I'll call you this evening from a pay phone."

"Luck, fella."

My cell phone felt heavy in my pocket. I had it off so the feds couldn't use the cellular network to locate it, once they figured out who I was and learned my cell phone number. Once the phone was turned on, it only took a few seconds for the phone to log on to the network, and then they would have me. With the power switch off, the telephone should be unable to talk to a network if queried. Theoretically. But with the techno-wizards marching bravely on to God knows where, who the hell knew? I ditched the phone in the trash can by the main entrance of Wal-Mart.

Now to get to Washington. There was a car dealership a few hundred yards from where I stood, so I walked over and inquired about renting a car.

An hour later I was on the way to Washington in a four-year-old sedan with seventy grand on the odometer that a local entrepreneur brought to the front door of the dealership. The only cool thing about the car was the bumper sticker: FREE THE FRENCH—WHACK CHIRAC!

Thank heavens the wipers worked—the misty drizzle had turned to rain again.

What a crummy day!

CHAPTER SIX

The miles flew by as I zipped north on I-81. Before I knew it, I was at the turnoff for I-66, which would take me into Washington's western suburbs. A few miles later I got off the interstate at the Front Royal exit and went south about a hundred yards to the McDonald's. There was a pay phone on a low mount beside the parking lot. Although the telephone book attached to it with a woven wire was ripped to shreds, I got a dial tone when I lifted the receiver. I went into the McDonald's and traded a five-dollar bill for more quarters.

Willie answered on the second ring.

"Hey, pal. It's me."

"They were here. Three of them came in about a half hour ago. Said you were wanted on a material witness warrant."

"FBI?"

"Yeah. They wanted to search, but I wouldn't let 'em. They'll probably be back with a warrant in a little while."

There was nothing in the shop that I didn't want the law to see, so that news didn't worry me.

"What about the woman, Kelly Erlanger?"

"She's got an unlisted number." He read me the number and address. "Better hope the car is there. My friend at LoJack is out sick. I called his house, and his old lady says the son of a bitch is shacked up someplace or on a roaring drunk—she hasn't seen him in two days."

"How'd you come up with Kelly's address?"

"Got a friend's wife who works at the telephone company."

Willie's circle of friends and acquaintances never ceased to amaze me. "Where in hell did you meet all these people?"

"I met this woman's old man in the joint, which is where you're gonna wind up if you ain't real careful."

"I've heard that song before. Can even hum it."

"I don't know what the hell you're into today, Tommy, but these were heavy federal dudes on a mission, not desk jockeys doin' some damn background investigation. I figure they'll have a tap on this line within an hour."

"Thanks, Willie. I'll be talking to you."

Oh, boy. If the FBI was a bit quicker than Willie estimated, they now had Kelly's number and home address.

I needed money. I figured that the FBI would take a few hours to freeze my bank accounts, so I had better get some walking-around money fast. The convenience store next to McDonald's had an ATM sign on its pole, so I went in and tagged it for three hundred from my checking account. I also bought a Coke and a bag of jerky.

Rolling toward Washington, I tried to put everything in per-spective.

The FBI! How did they get into this mess so quick?

Why did Kelly Erlanger steal my car and jackrabbit?

Who wanted all those people at the safe house dead? Russians, probably. If Erlanger was telling the truth, of course the Russians wanted their ex-archivist dead and the file copies destroyed. But those shooters this morning weren't Russians—I would bet my life on that.

Mikhail Goncharov found the cabin by the river well after sunset, just before the onset of total darkness. He was staggering along beside a creek when he came to the culvert and the road. Beyond the road was a river.

He was desperately cold, his clothes sodden from the rain, so cold he was near the point of collapse.

He wasn't thinking anymore, just walking, trying to stay upright.

Standing on the road as the last of the twilight faded, he couldn't even see which way the river was flowing. Didn't matter, really. Upriver or down, there was really no difference. Without conscious thought he turned right because he was right-handed and walked along the road.

Goncharov hadn't gone far when he found a road leading off to his right, away from the river. He followed it. A hundred yards along he found a cabin. There were no lights, no car in the parking area.

Summoning the last of his strength, he climbed the three steps to the porch, tried the door. Locked. With a padlock.

The mind of the archivist began to work again. If he didn't get shelter and warmth, he would die of exposure tonight.

There was a woodpile beside the cabin. He used a billet of wood as a hammer on the padlock. He ran splinters into his hand, but after an eternity of pounding the hasp tore loose from the wooden door.

Feeling his way around inside the cabin, he found a bed with blankets, one of which he wrapped around him. Further exploration revealed an iron stove in the middle of the single room. Fumbling in the dark, he found matches, newspapers, and wood.

Somehow he managed to get a fire going in the stove, then fed in wood until the stove would hold no more. As the stove crackled and popped and warmth spread in the darkness, Mikhail Goncharov pulled the blanket tightly around him and sank into the nearest chair.

He couldn't sleep. The scenes ran back and forth through his mind—

fire, shots, blood, his wife's face frozen in death, faces from his past, the files, the fear . . . the terror!

Under the overcast the night became very dark. The rain stopped, finally. Occasionally cars and trucks drenched my windshield with road spray, so I kept busy fiddling with the wipers while I tried to figure out what in hell I should do next.

I didn't like being in this predicament. Sure, before I got black-mailed into joining the CIA I spent a few years outwitting the law, but I was always meticulously prepared before I made my first move. I had never been a fugitive.

Funny how a man's life goes. If my partner in that big dia-mond heist hadn't got busted and finked on me, I might still be in the business. I will never forget the day that a CIA recruiter buttonholed me after class and suggested we have lunch in the student cafeteria. I was only a month away from graduating from Stanford Law School. She asked about my postgraduation plans, sounded so innocent. After I finished blowing air she re-marked that a prosecution for stealing the Peabody diamond from the Museum of Natural History in Washington might give any law firm interested in me food for thought. Naturally, as the conversation progressed, the CIA became my number-one job choice.

Now I was legit as a postal clerk, right smack-dab in the mid-dle of the great American middle class, accoutered with credit cards, debts, a savings account, and a green paycheck every month. Yet on this miserable wet July night, this loyal, paper-pushing government employee was dodging the law as if he had never been persuaded to add his name to the civil service payroll. Ah, me . . .

I didn't have a map of northern Virginia in the car, so I stopped at a convenience store in Manassas and purchased one. Thirty minutes later I was cruising a subdivision in Burke, Virginia, looking for my car.

There it sat, red and dirty, in the driveway of Erlanger's house.

I drove past and looked the neighborhood over. It was a newer suburb, with twisty streets with cutesy names that were all dead-ends and small two-story houses painted earth tones. Judging from the size of the decorator trees, the subdivision was perhaps three years old. Every house had a garage and driveway—no cars parked on the street. Lots of streetlights, fenced backyards for dogs and tots.

If the FBI was also onto Erlanger, they were here, somewhere, watching and waiting for me. Even if they hadn't yet learned that she had survived the massacre that morning, if they had the telephone line to the lock shop tapped, they were here or on their way.

I didn't see anyone in any of the cars.

They might be waiting in Erlanger's house.

Only one way to find out. I parked in her driveway beside my car. The MP-5 was just visible behind the seat of the old Mercedes. The driver's door was locked.

But not the passenger door!

The electric door lock was broken, had been for months—the passenger door had to be locked manually. Obviously Erlanger hadn't checked the passenger door after she pushed the button.

I kept a spare key in a magnetic box under the driver's seat. I was sorely tempted to jump in the Benz and boogie. With the key in hand, I stood beside the car for a few seconds thinking about it.

Kelly Erlanger was a ditz—stealing my car proved that. The last thing I wanted to do was play white knight to some dingdong airhead who thought I might be a hit man.

I could always call the guy in Staunton and tell him where his heap was, mail him the key.

Of course, the guys who smacked all those people this morning were still running around loose, and the people who sent them were going to get aggravated at me before too long.

The light was on in Erlanger's living room. I saw no heads looking out. The daffy broad was probably calling the damned cops.

I muttered a four-letter word that I thought summarized the situation and transferred the submachine gun to the rental heap. My clothes and some burglary tools were in the trunk of the Benz, so I transferred them, too. God knew when I'd see this heap again—and the Benz was completely paid for. I spotted my emergency roll of duct tape, pocketed that. I closed the Benz's trunk, made sure it latched, then selected a pick as I walked up to her front door.

I could hear something going on in there—music or a voice.

Five dollars against a doughnut she was talking to the 911 operator.

I twisted the knob on her door, made sure it was locked, then inserted the pick.

The thought occurred to me that I was going to be in big, big trouble if she had a gun. She had struck me as a politically correct academic, which meant feminist, pro-life, anti-gun, and all the rest of the chorus, but what the hell, these days you never knew. Maybe she carried a shooter in her purse just in case. Please God, don't let her shoot me!

I raked the pick while maintaining pressure on the knob. I felt one of the tumblers go up. I raked the pick savagely, releasing and reapplying subtle pressure to the knob, trying to make all the tumblers pop up at once and catch them there.

After six or eight rakes, the door opened. Yes!

She *was* on the phone, staring at me wild-eyed, screaming, "He's coming through the door now!" I must have been a fearsome sight—it had been a long day and I had seen too many dead people, some of whom I killed myself.

I bounded across the room and popped her once on the jaw before she had time to rabbit. She went down like a sack of potatoes.

The suitcase full of paper was right there on the floor by the coffee table. She had been going through the contents when I showed up.

I shoved everything into the suitcase and tried to close it. Had to put it on the floor and use a knee on it to get the latches snapped. Then I threw her over my shoulder. Out on the porch I put the suitcase down and closed the door until it latched. I must not have been thinking too clearly, because I took the time to wipe off the doorknob. As if they didn't know who I was.

The suitcase went in the trunk of the heap. She went in the passenger seat.

Out on the street I glanced at my watch. How much time did I have?

I drove toward the subdivision exit as far from her house as I could get and still see her driveway, which was only about seventy yards due to the way the street curved. There was a house sitting there with black windows and a FOR SALE sign in the yard, so I backed into the driveway and killed the engine. Then I used the duct tape on her wrists and mouth, then taped the seat belt to her arms so she couldn't pull them out of the belt. She was moaning and starting to come around as I snapped the seat belt in place to hold her. I checked her jaw—didn't seem to be broken, although the bruise was turning yellow and purple and swelling up right before my eyes.

She came to slowly, began thrashing as she realized she was restrained, eyed me wildly.

"Did you call 911?"

A look of defiance crossed her face.

"We'll just sit here and see who shows up," I said, and rolled down my window to let some air in—and so I could hear a chopper overhead, if one showed up.

After two or three minutes, she calmed down. At least she stopped squirming, trying to get loose. I ignored her facial expressions, just watched the street. I had about decided that everyone in the neighborhood had burrowed in for the night when a hardy soul wearing a raincoat came along walking his dog. Apparently the dog needed a potty break rain or shine. The man paid no attention to us in the car, didn't even look our way.

Ten minutes passed, then fifteen. I checked my watch occasionally. After twenty minutes had gone by, I remarked, "These Virginia cops are certainly Johnny-on-the-spot. Good thing you weren't getting murdered or raped, huh?"

After twenty-two minutes a ten-year-old rattletrap rolled down the street—woofers thudding—and parked in a driveway two doors away from Erlanger's house. The driver went inside.

The bad guys arrived in two unmarked cars twenty-seven minutes after I parked in the driveway. I pushed her down and ducked my head as they went by. The cars went slowly down the street, one behind the other. At least two men in each car. They stopped in front of Erlanger's house, doused the lights.

"Doesn't look like cops to me," I remarked. "Plainclothes, no cruisers."

She was watching intently. Although the distance was about seventy yards, the streetlight beyond her house limned the men. One of the four men stayed by the cars while the others went toward the house, out of our line of sight.

"Seen enough?" I asked her.

For the first time she looked my way. There was fear in her eyes.

I started the car, snapped on the lights, and got under way toward the subdivision entrance. No one followed me.

When we were rolling out on the freeway, I ripped the tape from her mouth. She screamed.

"Hurts like hell, doesn't it?"

"Who are you?"

"I told you, lady. Tommy Carmellini, CIA."

"Who were those men back there?"

"They sure as hell weren't street cops speeding to assist an honest taxpayer in distress."

"They came to kill me, didn't they?"

"Probably." I shrugged. "A friend of mine got your address from the telephone company. The only reason I reached you first is because I knew your name."

"Why me, for God's sake?"

"Someone doesn't want Goncharov's notes read by anyone. You've seen them. You might know too much."

"I don't know anything!" she shrieked, then began sobbing.

I was fresh out of sympathy. The ditsy broad stole my car, which was now sitting abandoned in her driveway. Whatever slim chance I once had of talking my way out of trouble had evaporated. No doubt the hit men were looking for me, too.

The rain started again. I turned on the wipers and tried to concentrate on driving but found that impossible. What should I do now? How was I going to stay one jump ahead of hit men who showed up when someone called the police? If the police were tipping them off, intentionally or inadvertently, no doubt the FBI was also cooperating. Hell, maybe the hit men *were* FBI.

I felt like a man driving to his own execution.

"Get this tape off me," she said.

"You gonna bail at the first stoplight?"

"No."

I thought a little clarification wouldn't hurt. "Those people back there came to kill us, lady. I thought they'd show up before long looking for you, which is why I went to get you out of there."

"A knight in shining armor," she said acidly.

"You've been told. You want out of this car, that's fine with me. I'll drop you anywhere you say. Call the cops, the FBI, your boss, your boyfriend, your mama, whoever. Someone kills you, that'll be your tough luck."

I pulled over to the side of the road and ripped the tape off her arms. It must have hurt like hell, but she stifled the scream.

"You got a cell phone on you?" I asked when we were rolling again.

She swabbed her face with the tail of her blouse. When she finished she said, "Yes."

"May I use it?"

She removed it from a pocket and passed it over. I threw it out the window.

CHAPTER SEVEN

The neighborhood where my lock shop partner, Willie the Wire, lived was quiet that soggy evening. I drove through once, looking for cars parked with people in them. Didn't see anyone, so I decided to try the dead man's cell phone.

I turned it on, waited for it to find the network, then dialed Willie's number.

"Yeah," Willie growled when he picked up his phone. He answered the telephone at the lock shop the same way—a nasty habit I had tried to argue him out of.

"It's me." He had told me a dozen times that relying on other people to recognize your voice was impolite, an ego trip, but I wasn't going to drop it until he said hello in the conventional manner. Okay, so we were both a bit childish.

"Where are ya?"

"Driving by on your street."

"Give me two minutes, then drive by again. I'll jump in."

"It's a four-door sedan, white. Not the Benz."

"Okay."

He was on his stoop as I braked to a stop. He intended to get in the passenger seat. When he saw Kelly he got in the back. I had the car rolling before he could get the door closed.

"Kelly Erlanger, Willie Varner."

She wasn't talking to me at that point—still fuming about me tossing her telephone, I suppose—but she tossed off a "Hi" to Willie.

He grunted at her, then addressed me. "Carmellini, you idiot, what have you got your silly ass into this time?"

Keeping my eye on the rearview mirror, I told it straight, leaving nothing out. The stuff about the archivist was classified, of course, as was the existence of the CIA's Greenbrier River safe house. Being a convicted felon, Willie Varner couldn't have gotten a security clearance if his life depended on it. As I saw it that night, one more little felonious security breach wouldn't blacken my character more than it already was. What the heck, the killers that morning probably didn't have security clearances either.

When I finished my tale of woe, Willie gave a low whistle. "Jesus, Carmellini. Send you out of town for a day and all hell breaks loose. I never saw you so deep in shit before, man. Gonna need a backhoe to dig yourself out."

"I should have let them shoot me?"

"Sounds like somebody's gonna do you sooner or later."

"You going to help or not?"

"Oh, sure. I'll pop over to Langley tomorrow and ask to see the director. Get this all cleaned up."

"Terrific."

"Like, whaddaya want me to do?"

I held the cell phone up, offered it to him. "I took this off the guy who was driving the crashed car. There must be a bunch of telephone numbers on it. I want to know who they belong to. All of them."

He didn't reach for the phone. "I don't want to go back to the joint," he said. "I been there and I didn't like it."

I took my foot off the accelerator and half turned to look at him.

"Oh, all right!" He grabbed the phone. "Goddamn you, Carmellini."

As we headed back for his house he muttered—loud enough for me to hear, naturally—"As if I didn't have enough misery in my goddamn life . . . goddamn Russian assassins now."

I could never do anything with Willie when he got pouty, so I didn't try. Kelly Erlanger knew this mess wasn't my fault, and she was in high dudgeon, too.

When I was braking to a stop in front of Willie's house, he said, "They bust down my door and shoot my innocent black ass, Carmellini, I'll torture you in hell until the end of time."

He got out and slammed the door. As we drove away, Erlanger said, "What if he calls the police?"

"He won't," I assured her. "Willie Varner's my best friend."

She made a rude noise, which I ignored.

Erlanger was sulking, doubtlessly angry the killers didn't wax her, when I remembered Dorsey O'Shea.

Well, why not, I asked myself.

Dorsey lived on that estate overlooking the Potomac, five hundred wooded acres complete with tennis court and swimming pool and a little three-story brick shack with fifteen or twenty rooms, five fireplaces, and a dozen commodes. Ol' Dorsey owed me big for getting her cute little heinie out of the clutches of her porno boyfriend last spring. Surely she wouldn't mind if Kelly Erlanger and I dropped in unannounced and hid from the law and the outlaws for a few days.

I pointed the car in Dorsey's direction. We had been driving for fifteen or twenty minutes when Kelly asked, "Where are we going?"

"To visit a friend of mine."

"She a plastic surgeon? You and I are going to need one if we hope to live out the year."

"Naw. She's a rich socialite. Never worked a day in her life, inherited a huge heaping pile when her parents had the grace to die young."

"So how do *you* know *her?*"

"I was her boy toy for a while," I said flippantly.

"Good Lord! She must be ancient if you were the best she could do."

"She's a real old prune," I snarled. "And she's got servants. A maid and a cook. Better keep your lip zipped and let me do the talking or we're liable to wind up in drawers at the morgue."

"This is your gig, hero. I'll cling to you and look deeply into your eyes while you talk us into the house. But I want my own bedroom."

I wasn't about to tell Erlanger about robbing a safe deposit box for O'Shea. "You don't know Dorsey," I explained. "She's a friend. She'll be delighted to help. You'll see."

Dorsey O'Shea had a long winding drive, which was cool; you couldn't see the house from the road.

A Porsche was parked in front of the place. I didn't think it was Dorsey's, because she always parked in the garage around back. I parked the heap beside the Porsche and hoisted the suitcase from the trunk. Kelly climbed the stairs and crossed the formal stoop and pushed the doorbell.

I joined her on the stoop with the suitcase.

After a bit the porch light came on.

I heard someone unlocking the door, then it opened.

Dorsey was wearing a slinky black silk thing and a set of high-heeled slippers, and apparently not much else. She had a glass of wine in her hand. It was brutally obvious we had interrupted something.

"What in the name of God are you doing here, Carmellini?" she snarled.

Kelly Erlanger tittered. She leaned against the doorjamb and held her hand over her mouth, and her shoulders began to shake as the laughter went off the scale and she fought for air.

I pulled her hands down. "Hey, get a grip."

Her whole face contorted and she lost it. Just went to pieces.

I picked her up in my arms and marched through the door, pushing Dorsey aside. "Get the suitcase," I growled at O'Shea. "This woman's been through hell and needs a place to sleep."

As I strode through the living room to the grand staircase, I got a gander at Dorsey's romantic interest, a balding twit twenty pounds overweight standing by the fireplace with his mouth open.

The guest room that I picked had a nice double bed all made up. "A glass of whiskey on the rocks would be appreciated," I told Dorsey, who followed me up the stairs and stood twisting her hands in the doorway. She scurried away. I stripped off Erlanger's shoes and put her between the sheets, then sat down on the edge of the bed as she tried to control her sobbing.

"You keep doing that, you're going to get the hiccups something terrible."

Dorsey was back with the whiskey within a minute. I took a sip, just a taste test, then offered it to Kelly. She shook her head no.

"Hey, this is medicine. Settle you down."

She grasped the glass with both hands and took a long pull as if it were milk.

The sobs stopped. She hiccupped once, then belted back another big slurp.

"How can you be so calm?" she asked.

Dorsey was still in the room. I heard her moving behind me. "What should I be doing?"

"I don't know." She worked some more on the whiskey.

"The best thing we can do for those people who got murdered is to make sure their killers don't get away with it."

She thought about that, then nodded.

"To do that, we have to stay alive."

"Okay."

"These people whacked Goncharov at a top secret safe house. Before we go walking into a police station or FBI office, we had better figure out how they did it. We make one mistake, we're dead."

She tossed off the last of the whiskey, then snagged a piece of ice and sucked noisily on it. She looked at Dorsey, then met my eyes. "I want to see the bastards dead."

"That's the spirit." I stood and took the empty glass. "Get a good night's sleep. We'll talk in the morning. I warn you. Don't make any telephone calls. The killers know we got away. They're going to be moving heaven and earth to find us. Let's not make it easy for them."

"I've got a boyfriend," she objected. "And parents and a couple of girlfriends who really care about me. They are going to be worried sick."

"We'll worry about that when and if your name gets in the press."

"You don't think that—?"

"Bet the press never hears a whisper. Now get some sleep. We'll talk in the morning."

"Okay."

I shooed Dorsey out of the room and turned off the light, then pulled the door shut.

"Who's the guy?" I asked Dorsey, referring to the pork chop by the fireplace.

"Just a friend."

"Sorry about dropping in on you like this. If you'll give him a raincheck, I'll tell you how we spent our day."

To her credit, Dorsey didn't hesitate. She led the way down the stairs. I went to the kitchen while she said good-bye to her guest. I knew where the liquor and ice were, so I made myself a drink while she attended to that. When she came into the kitchen I was sitting in the breakfast nook working on bourbon and a chunk of cheese from the fridge.

She poured herself some wine, then sat down across from me.

"How you been?" I asked conversationally.

She brushed that aside. "You used the word 'killers' to that woman upstairs. This had better be good."

"Your cook and maid? They here tonight?"

"No."

I shrugged. We needed her cooperation, so I told her about the bodies in the rain, the assassins, and the fire.

The archivist awoke when the woodstove began cooling. It took several seconds for him to remember where he was, why he was there. The stove still had glowing coals in it, so he added more wood. He left the iron door to the stove open and, when the wood burst into flames, used the dim light to explore his surroundings.

The cabin had no electricity. He found a candle and lit it. With that in hand, he examined the contents of the cupboard. A box of crackers caught his eye. He stripped off his damp clothes, arranged them on a chair to dry, then wrapped himself in the blanket and attacked the crackers.

Bunks lined the wall opposite the door. Fishing rods stood in one corner. An old coat hung from a peg near the door. The little cabin was snug and warm, much like the vacation dacha he used to visit in Russia. With Bronislava.

All that was past, finished. She was dead, murdered.

The killers would probably find him soon. If they thought him dead in the rubble of the CIA outpost, he would have a little time before they came. But they would come. Of that Mikhail Goncharov was certain. He knew the Russian secret police—for more than twenty years he had spent his working life reading their case files. They never gave up. They would hunt an enemy of the state to the ends of the earth no matter what the cost, no matter how long it took. They would get him. One day, as inevitably as the turning of the earth, they would find and kill him.

He had traded his life and her life for . . .

For what?

He fed more wood into the stove and sat staring at the flames.

He had spent his life surrounded by evil. In the end it had consumed all that he loved. Consumed everything and left him with nothing.

CHAPTER EIGHT

When I finished my summarization of the day's events, Dorsey O'Shea asked, "Who *are* you, Tommy? Really?" She was sitting across from me in her breakfast nook in her silk hostess dress that looked as if she had nothing on underneath, her chin on one hand, staring at me with narrowed eyes.

"Just a guy in over his head."

"You don't expect me to believe all that hooey, do you?" She got up from her chair. "Killers, car wrecks, Russian spies . . . sounds like something from a movie. Things like that don't happen in real life. Give me a break!"

The irony of the moment was not lost on me. Why do women refuse to believe me when I tell the truth, yet buy every word when I lie to them? I finished my drink and stood. "Help me unload the car."

She didn't want to—that was plain. While she was trying to figure out a way to toss me out of the house on my keester, she reluctantly trailed along behind me. The first thing I pulled from the trunk of the car was the MP-5. I handed it to her. "Carry this. And be careful—it's loaded."

I got my soft bag, closed the trunk, then led the way back into the house. She followed along carrying the gun in both hands.

I sat down on one of the sofas near the fireplace, took the gun from her, and laid it on the floor.

"That's a submachine gun?"

"Yep."

"Never saw one before."

"Help me with this suitcase." It was sitting by the end of the couch. I pulled it around and opened it, then brought out several handfuls of paper, which at this stage of the game were smashed in there like so much trash. I passed her a couple handfuls.

Goncharov had tiny, cramped handwriting, nearly illegible. The fact that he used the Cyrillic alphabet and wrote in Russian didn't help. It could have been Sanskrit for all I knew. I pondered that verity for a moment—the bodies I had seen that morning had been real enough, and the man I killed hadn't faked it, yet I had no verification for Kelly's statement that these notes were purloined copies of KGB files. Were they? Really?

After a minute or two Dorsey put the pages I had given her back in the suitcase. She placed two more slabs of wood on the fire, poked it up some, then sat down beside me on the sofa and stared moodily at the flames.

The silence grew and grew. "Was the guy the fiancé?" I asked finally.

"Oh, no. We broke up months ago." She shrugged dismissively. "Geoff is an outside artist. I am thinking about sponsoring him."

"Outside? He does statues in the park?"

"No, silly. He's outside the establishment. He has no formal artistic training."

"Oh." The fire popped a few times, then settled down. "Guess I'm an outside artist, too."

She gave me a withering look.

"How come you never suggested sponsoring me?"

"For Christ's sake, Tommy! You killed several men today, and now you're sitting here in front of my fire trying to be funny."

"I'm just happy to be alive."

"I never met anyone so callous."

I made a rude noise. Then I kicked off my shoes, stretched, wiggled my toes, and indulged in a huge yawn. Frankly, I felt pretty good . . . tired and mellow. You gotta admit, being alive has its attractions.

"I want a drink," she said, and stood. "Do you?"

"Sure. Whiskey, please."

While she was gone I surveyed the room. It didn't look as if she had changed anything since I last saw it, back when I thought that she and I . . .

Dorsey's great-grandfather was a bootlegger, had been mobbed up, bribed cops and judges and county officials, shot it out with the competition, all of that . . . got modestly rich and retired when they repealed Prohibition. He bought this estate in the thirties and built the mansion. He had only owned it a few years when his ticker stopped dead one night while he slept.

The bootlegger's only daughter married a fast-talking salesman who thought cars were the coming thing. He used the bootlegger's money to build a string of car dealerships around Washington in the late thirties. During and after World War II he got rich when Washington's population exploded and the mass exodus to the suburbs began.

The car dealer's daughter, Dorsey's mother, was a hippie. She flitted off to San Francisco, smoked pot, sang peace songs, and stretched the concept of free love nearly to the breaking point, according to Dorsey. She and Dorsey's father—another hippie who didn't need to dirty his hands with work after he married Dorsey's mom—filled their days with manifestos, politically significant demonstrations, general hanging out, and recreational drugs. They joined communes several times. They were in California protesting the Vietnam War and searching for the meaning of life when they drove their car over a cliff near the ocean one morning during the wee hours. Dorsey thought they were probably strung out at the time.

When her grandparents died Dorsey inherited it all, the mansion, the estate, the money, and the dealerships. She dabbled in starving artists and porno filmmakers and hard cases like me.

She came back from the kitchen with the whiskey and nestled beside me on the couch. Amazingly, after the day I'd had, the heat and pressure of her body against mine felt very good.

"Aren't you chilly in that outfit?" I asked.

"A little."

I pulled an afghan from the back of the sofa and put it over her.

"So what are you going to do about this mess?"

"Haven't decided." I couldn't help myself. I draped an arm over her shoulder and pulled her close.

"Could call the police, you know."

"And have a hit team show up instead of the cops? No thanks."

She rested her head on my shoulder.

The fire burned down as we sipped our drinks. I was acutely conscious of how she felt snuggled up against me. And smelled.

My eyelids grew heavy. Getting up the stairs was going to take some doing. "Sorry to barge in on you like this," I said.

"I'm glad you came. The artist was a bit of a snob."

"A big house like this, moldy old money, a beautiful woman? What the hell does he want?"

"It was pretty obvious that I didn't know much about art."

"So it *was* a rescue! Glad I got here in the nick."

"Oh, Tommy, what's wrong with *us*? You and me? Why didn't it work for *us*?"

"If I could answer questions like that, woman, I'd be getting rich with my own call-in radio show." Actually I had a theory, but that didn't seem to be the time or place. The fire felt good and she felt better, snugglely, with promising bulges and curves.

As I sat there basking in her aura, my mind wandered. Who were those guys?

That was a problem I couldn't solve just then.

I dropped it and slid my hand inside the afghan. Yep, she was wearing nothing under that slinky thing. A scene from one of those porno flicks shot through my little mind. Feeling guilty, I retracted my stray appendage and used it to put the whiskey where it belonged.

When I finished my drink, the moment could be avoided no longer. "What bed do you want me in?"

"Mine."

That response made me smile. "I was hoping you would say that," I told her warmly. I hoisted the submachine gun and carried it up the stairs while she locked up and turned off the lights.

I awoke about three in the morning. I had been sound asleep and a moment later was fully awake. Dorsey O'Shea was curled up with her back against mine, breathing deeply, totally relaxed.

I checked my watch, then lay in the darkness listening to the sounds, wondering why I had come so fully awake.

I sneaked out of bed, and pulled on trousers and a shirt. The submachine gun was where I had left it, propped on its butt in one corner. I put the pistol in my trouser pocket and picked up the MP-5. Dorsey didn't awaken as I eased the door open and crept out. I pulled the door shut behind me and stood in the darkness listening.

The old house was deathly quiet. The bootlegger built it solid.

I eased open the door to Kelly Erlanger's room, stood and listened to her breathe as she slept. Finally I closed the door as softly as I could, making sure it latched.

I worked my way slowly down the stairs, stopping frequently to listen.

Okay, maybe I was being paranoid. I didn't think yesterday's killers could possibly find us this quickly, but what the hey, I had a lot to be paranoid about. The truth of it was that I was damned worried. I assumed the Russians wanted Goncharov dead. Yet those guys yesterday weren't Russians. And they knew precisely where to find Goncharov, ensconced in a top secret government safe house and surrounded by armed guards. They arrived armed with serious weapons—you can't buy MP-5s at your local sporting goods store. These popguns came from an arsenal somewhere . . . probably a government arsenal.

And who were the killers? What did they do during the day when they weren't sneaking around in ghillie suits gunning people down? Where did they live? Were they on some kind of retainer, or were they an ad hoc group hired for one job?

Regardless of how those questions shook out, if the assassins wanted to make the job a clean sweep they were still after Kelly Erlanger and me.

I was going to have to find out who was hiring these dudes if I wanted to get very much older. Somehow, some way, I had to put that someone out of action.

I padded around the old house from window to window, cradling the submachine gun in my arms and looking out into the dark, wet night, thinking about the problem.

The guy I needed on my side was my boss, Sal Pulzelli.

Dorsey kept her telephone books in the kitchen in a large drawer under the phone. I rooted through the one she had for northern Virginia. There he was, in Dunn Loring. An apartment building, apparently. I made a note on a piece of scratch paper and put the telephone books away.

Most householders in metro Washington have books of maps; Dorsey was no exception. After locating Pulzelli's street, I figured out how to get there. I took the map with me, just in case.

At this hour White's Ferry at Leesburg probably wasn't running, so I drove southeast to the beltway and crossed the Potomac on the Legion Bridge. Traffic on the beltway was fairly light at that hour of the morning. The eternal rebuilding efforts were apparently occurring someplace else that summer.

As I drove I thought about Salvatore Pulzelli, a career soldier in Washington's army of paper-pushers. He didn't smoke, drink, or cuss—a real party animal, I'm telling you—watched his weight, wore conservative department-store suits and drab, uninspired ties, kept his desk neat and shipshape, and, truly, was a decent sort of guy. If he had any hobbies he didn't talk about them.

I knew very little about his personal life. He never wore a wedding ring, nor had I ever heard him mention a wife. I didn't know if he had a girlfriend or boyfriend or whatever. When I first got to know him I had wondered if perhaps his demeanor was an act—perhaps he lived a secret life in the Washington kinky sex scene—but finally I realized that was pure fantasy. He wasn't the type.

I sure hoped he lived alone, though. Without a dog.

It was ten minutes after four in the morning when I found Pulzelli's building. There were four apartment buildings in a row along the street, each about about ten stories high. The street was a wide one decorated with speed bumps to keep the local auto mechanics fully employed. Pulzelli lived in the first building. I drove on by and parked in the parking lot of the second one.

I got out and locked the car—I left the MP-5 in the trunk—and stood looking and listening. There wasn't a soul in sight, just a sea of cars under lights mounted on poles. The stark scene was relieved somewhat by scraggly young trees in the ribbon-thin borders.

No security patrol, no early risers or late partygoers that I could see. I walked toward the nearest apartment building, then around it, keeping in the shadows. Once around the building, I angled across the parking lot toward Pulzelli's tower.

I was hoping the FBI wasn't watching everyone I knew, waiting for me to break cover. Of course, if a watcher was sitting in one of these cars, I was dead meat. It was a serious risk, but a necessary one. I needed Pulzelli's help.

The lobby of Pulzelli's hive was empty. Security cameras were mounted high in every corner. A computer sat on a small podium where perhaps a security guard had once stood vigil. It looked as if the owners had bought a computer and fired the guard. I typed Pulzelli's name into the computer . . . voilà! Apartment 310.

I called him on the telephone, which rang and rang. After ten rings I gave up.

Seventeen minutes after 4:00 A.M. Don't tell me he's out partying! Pulzelli?

The elevator required a card to activate it. I walked around the elevator shaft to the door to the fire stairs. This door would be fitted with a push bar on the inside so that anyone coming down the stairs could exit through the door, yet there would be a conventional lock securing the door from this side. That lock I could pick.

When I saw the door a cold chill ran up my spine. The door had been forced with a crowbar, which bent the metal so that the lock no longer latched. It had taken a strong man to do that.

The door came open with a groan—the hinges hadn't seen oil since the building went up. Once inside the stairwell, I removed the pistol from my belt and checked the safety. I went up the stairs making as little noise as possible, which meant anyone but a deaf man could have heard me. Sound reverberated around inside that concrete staircase as if it were a kettledrum.

At the door to the third floor, I paused, checked the pistol again, then eased the door open with my left hand. No one in the hallway.

Pulzelli's apartment was four doors away from the elevator. The lock appeared intact.

I knocked. Waited . . . no sound.

Finally put my ear to the door.

The lock wasn't any big deal. I hoped he didn't have the chain on, though.

Took me about two minutes to pick the lock and open the door. No chain.

I went in with the gun in my hand.

Salvatore Pulzelli was lying naked on the living room floor. Apparently he had been strangled with a wire garrote. His arms, chest, and crotch were smeared with blood, which hadn't completely dried. His pajamas were on the floor near him, so I used the top to swab at one arm. Lots of little cuts.

He must have opened the door for them. They tortured him, then killed him.

The apartment wasn't large. In addition to the living room, which doubled as a home office, there was a kitchen, a bath, and two bedrooms, one of which was obviously for guests. I checked the rooms to see that they were empty—anything was better than looking at Pulzelli.

Standing in the living room with my back to the body, I managed to get my stomach under control and tried to get my brain in gear. Did the killers ask him about me? Was it me they were trying to find?

The killers hadn't been gone long. Pulzelli's blood hadn't dried to a crust.

I used a kitchen towel to keep from leaving fingerprints on the telephone in the kitchen. Willie Varner's telephone rang and rang. He didn't answer.

Oh, man!

I remembered to pull the apartment door shut behind me and checked to ensure that the lock engaged.

CHAPTER NINE

I couldn't get Pulzelli's face out of my mind. God, he looked bad, the muscles in his face contracted, baring every tooth, his eyes bulged out and staring at infinity. The poor guy . . . he didn't want much out of life, just a comfortable job, decent clothes, and a pension to look forward to. He had planned to travel when he retired in three years—I recall him mentioning that one time when I caught him perusing travel brochures at his desk. He envied me, he said, because I got to travel a lot. I told him that I would gladly trade: He could travel while I put in forty hours a week behind his desk and got seriously involved with three or four hot women.

Maybe Pulzelli liked women, too.

I couldn't help him now. That was a fact.

Willie Varner lived in a second-story flat on a dumpy street in northwest Washington. The assassins I saw at the Greenbrier safe house were white, and Willie's neighborhood wasn't. Maybe that mattered—I didn't know.

Washington was a seedy town. Outside of monumental Washington one found endless miles of row houses in various states of disrepair. Most would have collapsed long ago if they weren't all jammed together, holding each other up. Undereducated, unemployed black males lined the sidewalks selling drugs. The inner city was one giant drug bazaar. I had made that observation to Willie the Wire one day, and he got all huffy. He had lived here all his life, except when he was in prison, and was sorta proud of the town, although he would never admit it. He growled at me and gave me the outsider stare. I knew what it meant: "You ain't black."

I spotted an empty parking space two blocks from Willie's place, said a word of thanks to whoever was running the universe this week, and wheeled the car in. Believe me, I locked the doors and tugged on both the driver's and passenger's doors, just to make sure.

Even at that hour of the morning there were people out and about, all black. A couple of winos sat on a curb, one was sleeping in a doorway, and a young man in baggy trousers and a shirt three sizes too large was striding along toward me, arms going, eyes moving ceaselessly from side to side like a predatory animal. He looked me over as he approached and didn't slacken his pace. Yet when he was ten feet away he looked elsewhere, pretended I wasn't there as he walked on by.

There was a car double-parked in front of Willie's.

Staying on the sidewalk, I eyeballed everything as I walked up. Man behind the wheel. White man. No other white guys around.

I left the sidewalk in a bound, passed behind his car, and drew the pistol as I walked up on the driver's side. Stuck it right in his ear.

"Freeze, asshole. Hands on the wheel."

He froze all right, wide-eyed and rigid as a frozen steak. He was maybe thirty-five, white, balding on top, with medium-length dark hair, wearing an earring.

"Turn off the ignition and hand me the keys."

As he started to move I jabbed him with the piece. "I'll blow your brains out if you twitch." He did as ordered, slowly extracted the keys, and held them out with his right hand. I took them with my left and pocketed them.

"Hands where I can see them, out of the car."

He came, slowly and steadily.

He had a pistol in a belt holster on the left side, an old five-shot .38 revolver with a two-inch barrel. I took it, shoved it in my pocket. Standing behind him, I patted him down. He had a wallet. I helped myself.

"If this is a stickup, better think twice," he said. "I'm a federal officer."

"Yeah, right. Got a badge?"

"Not on me. I . . ."

No knife . . . if he had had a knife, I would have drilled him then and there. Maybe. Well, I sure would have been tempted. He did have a cell phone, which I liberated since he didn't need it anymore.

"I'm going to count to five," I said, "then start shooting. You can run like hell or die right where you stand. One . . . two . . ." He glanced over his shoulder at me, then began running. I raised my pistol and aimed it. He ran faster.

After he rounded the corner and disappeared, I surveyed the street—this was a "mind your own damn business" neighborhood if ever there was one—and glanced up at Willie's apartment. I could see a glow from behind the curtains, so the lights were on there. I went into the building with both hands on the piece and the safety off.

The stairs were at the very back of the dark hallway. As I went tiptoeing along with the pistol at the ready, I regretted not shooting the guy out front. He wasn't on his way to the airport to take a six-month sabbatical. What if he came charging upstairs while I was in the middle of delicate negotiations? Or did a knife job on me next week? Of course, the law generally frowned on people who took it upon themselves to waste assholes; there were so many, and where would it stop?

The stairwell had an old-building mustiness to it, a delicate aromatic mixture of stale tobacco, marijuana, and beer vomit. Willie lived in the flat on the left at the head of the stairs. There was a window at the end of the upstairs hallway that faced the street; the only light in the hall came through that glass. I seemed to recall a fixture up here, so I looked. Right at the top of the stairs, a naked bulb on the ceiling. I could just reach it.

The bulb was loose in the fixture. Some thoughtful soul had screwed it out far enough to extinguish it. I left it that way.

I put my ear to the door. I could hear muffled voices but couldn't distinguish words.

The shortest and quickest way into that apartment was through that door. If it was locked, I wasn't going in. The door was a security door—wooden panels over steel—and wore four locks, including a new Cooper. It would take me a half hour to pick them all, and everyone inside would hear me do it.

I got a firm grip on the gun, then grasped the doorknob and applied pressure. It refused to turn.

The only other way in was the fire escape.

There was no help for it—I eased down the stairs and headed for the door. Just in time I remembered the jackrabbit that had been behind the wheel. He was nowhere in sight.

The alley was a home for garbage cans. There must have been a dozen in there.

The bottom of the fire escape consisted of a ladder with a weight on the bottom, but it appeared to be chained up, no doubt to discourage overweight burglars. I hoped it would hold me . . .

and the noise wouldn't inspire someone in Willie's to lean out the window and shoot my sorry old self.

With a pistol in each hip pocket, I ran and jumped as high as I could reach. Got one hand on the rusty metal, then the other. The whole contraption creaked, but it held.

I did a chin-up, then hooked a leg and squirmed my way up. On the next flight I came to Willie's living room window. Gun in hand again, I inched my head around . . . and I saw Willie. They had him naked with a plastic tie on his wrist, sitting in a chair from the kitchen. They were working on him with a knife.

How many of them were there?

I could see two.

White guys.

Two deep breaths, then I squared myself in front of the window and drilled the nearer guy in the back, which drove him to the floor. My second shot spun the knife holder halfway around, so I shot him again. He was a big fucker: He stayed up, spun toward the window, released the knife, and tried to get a pistol out of a belt holster. I gave him two more bullets, the second one in the face. That one snapped his head back, and he toppled.

I kicked out the rest of the glass and stepped through the window. A man rushing from the kitchen snapped off a shot that stung my arm. He had started running when he heard the shots and entered the room before he knew my location, which proved to be a fatal mistake. I nailed him dead center before he could shoot again. He lost his weapon and his legs folded and he somersaulted forward onto his face.

Willie was still conscious. The sadist with the knife hadn't gotten to his crotch yet. His girlfriend was gonna thank me someday.

I got the little .38 out, and with a pistol in each hand I checked the rest of the apartment. No one else there.

I cut Willie loose with a kitchen knife and used a towel to clean him up some. There was blood everywhere. Then I half carried, half dragged him to the bedroom and put him on the bed. He had some Scotch tape on his dresser, so I used that. Slapped tape on the worst of the cuts to hold the edges together and slow the bleeding.

"Come on, man, we gotta get you to the emergency room."

"That you, Tommy?"

"Yeah."

"You get the motherfucker with the knife?"

"Yeah."

"He dead?"

"Seems to be."

"Shoot the fucker again. Drive a stake through his goddamn heart."

I began working pants and a shirt onto him.

"They wanted to know about you," Willie said. "Where you were, when I talked to you last, who your girlfriends were, everything. . . ."

"What did you tell them?"

"Everything I could think of when that prick got to cuttin' on me with that fuckin' knife."

The hell with his shoes.

"You're gonna have to help me, Willie. I can carry you, but we'll both be dead if we meet another of these bastards."

"Okay."

I draped one of his arms over my shoulder and lifted him. He could barely stagger. I half carried him into the hallway and made sure the door locked behind us.

"You've lost a lot of blood and you're still bleeding, man."

"Tell me something I don't know."

"You tell them about Dorsey?"

"Who?"

"Dorsey O'Shea."

"Probably. Fuck, I was jabberin' my fool head off there at the end."

"Who were they?"

"Cops."

"How do you know?"

"By the way they asked questions. The good guy, bad guy routine, all of it."

"You're guessing."

I almost put him down and went back to search the corpses, but he was still leaking blood at a good rate. It was the hospital quick or the morgue later.

Going down the stairs he said, "I been grilled by cops all my life. I could tell."

We took the hitters' car. Willie was not in any shape to do the two blocks to mine, that was certain. I drove back to my rental heap and took the time to collect the MP-5, then headed for the nearest hospital that I knew about. I asked Willie if indeed the one I was thinking of was the one, but he had passed out by then.

I whipped into the ambulance entrance and carried him into the emergency room. There was a vacant gurney there, so I put him on it. An attendant rushed out to help me.

"He's lost a lot of blood. Some guys cut him on his arms and chest. No drugs. He's not allergic to anything that I know of."

As the attendant rushed the gurney through the swinging doors, I turned to the window where the admitting lady sat with a client.

"I'll be right with you, sir," she said. "Please take a seat."

"I'll park the car and be back," I said.

As I got behind the wheel and headed for Wisconsin Avenue, I wondered if Willie did tell them about Dorsey O'Shea. Well, they were dead, so even if he did, it didn't matter.

Unless they called someone, of course. Maybe that was what the guy in the kitchen was doing when I rudely interrupted. I didn't recall seeing a cell phone in the kitchen. Of course, he might have put it in his pocket as he drew his pistol, after I fired the first shot.

Perhaps I should go back to Willie's and search the bodies.

I decided to do it. I had the brains to come down a side street and look toward Willie's before I turned that way and committed myself, which saved my silly ass. Two cop cars with lights flashing were parked in the street.

I turned the other way and fed gas. As I drove I heard the moan of an ambulance.

My arm was leaking blood where the bullet had grazed me.

I hoped they were dead. All three of the sons of bitches.

Fifteen minutes later I pulled into a McDonald's and parked. The sky was turning light. The sun wasn't up yet, but it soon would be. The vehicle registration certificate was in the glove compartment. The car was registered to a Donald P. Westland in College Park. His insurance certificate verified the address. I used his cell phone to call information.

"I'm sorry," the operator said. "I don't have a listing for a Donald Westland in College Park."

"Could it be an unlisted number?"

"No. I have no listing at all for anyone by that name."

I read her the address. "It might be under his wife's name," I said.

After a moment of silence, she said, "I'm sorry, sir. I have no Westland listed."

I thanked her and broke the connection.

I was getting quite a collection of cell phones. I punched my way through the stored numbers on this one, looking for one I recognized. They were all new to me.

I turned the telephone off and sat there trying to think. My heart was still beating a mile a minute. I was leaving bodies all over, and I didn't know who these guys were.

What if this was a government car, and the name and address on the registration and insurance were merely cover? I got out, opened the door, looked for an oil change sticker. And there it was: Jiffy Lube.

I opened the wallet. The driver's license was for one Johnson Dunlap, Bethesda. The mug staring at me from the license was the balding getaway driver outside of Willie's. That certainly wasn't conclusive—my employer routinely issued fake ID to back up false identities. The credit cards were also in the name of Johnson Dunlap. Couple hundred dollars in bills in the wallet, several credit card invoices, a dry cleaning stub, and an AAA membership card.

I turned on the telephone and called information. The operator gave me a number for Johnson Dunlap. That number was one of the ones stored on the telephone memory. I dialed it.

After ten rings I broke the connection.

Perhaps Johnson Dunlap was a real man. I tapped his driver's license on the steering wheel as I considered. If he was a cop or federal employee and lost his wallet containing his real driver's license while committing a serious felony with three colleagues— now dead—whoever was running this show was going to be very unhappy with Mr. Dunlap. He would undoubtedly realize that. Would he share the bad news with them?

I had another wallet in my pocket, the one I took off the driver who wrapped his SUV around a tree on Allegheny Mountain yesterday. I got it out and gave the driver's license a close look. Jerry Von Essen, Burke, Virginia. I called information. They gave me a telephone number, so I dialed it.

After four rings, I got a sleepy female. "Hullo."

"Is Jerry there?"

Talk about a hot woman—she went thermonuclear in two seconds. "The son of a bitch hasn't come home yet," she snarled.

"Think he'd take the time to call? You see the bastard, tell him I'm not taking any more of his shit! I'm moving out."

Before I could reply she slammed the telephone down.

Johnson Dunlap. Should I go check on him, or should I hotfoot it back to Dorsey's? Willie probably blabbed Dorsey's name, so they would show up before too long.

I glanced at my watch. My sense was that I had a little time, and God knew I needed information.

I thought about calling Dorsey, warning her. Hell, she didn't even own a weapon. The only thing she could do would be to load Kelly in a vehicle and run for it. Or call the police. Neither option seemed very attractive to me. I couldn't protect the women if they were running around the country, and I wasn't ready for the police.

Yesterday's clouds had dissipated. No rain today. Terrific.

CHAPTER TEN

J ohnson Dunlap lived in an older tract home in what had once been a fashionable neighborhood, perhaps sixty years ago, immediately after World War II. The maples, oaks, and tulip poplars that blocked out the sky looked about that old.

His house looked similar to every other house up and down the street—single story, brick facade, not much grass in the front lawn due to the deep shade cast by the huge trees. The driveway was empty.

I checked my watch, then drove down to the main arterial and along it until I came to a convenience store. I bought a newspaper from the box near the door and got back behind the wheel to look it over. The paper contained nothing on the massacre yesterday in West Virginia, not an inch. No story on a massive manhunt; nothing at all on fires and murder and corpses in the forest.

I started the engine and drove back to Dunlap's. I parked in his drive in front of his single-car garage.

As I walked around the house I checked for a security system, which would have been out of place in this neighborhood. Nope.

I let myself into the backyard through a gate. There was dog poop scattered about, so I wasn't surprised when the pooch began yapping inside the house as I picked the lock on the kitchen door. As I opened the door a small canine fluffball shot through. Apparently he, she, or it was more interested in relieving bladder pressure than taking a hunk out of my leg. Once in the kitchen, I firmly closed the door behind me.

There were several stacks of mail on a small stand near the kitchen table, but I bypassed them and headed for the bedroom. Sure enough, there was Baldy and a woman in framed photos on the dresser and nightstand. So Baldy was indeed Johnson Dunlap, a real person. Somehow establishing that fact seemed important.

I glanced around the bedroom and went back to the mail in the kitchen. If there was a pay stub or pay summary in one of those piles that gave the name of his employer, it would make my day. I was flipping through the envelopes when I heard another car pull into the driveway.

The dog in the back yard began yapping. I sat down at the kitchen table, got out the automatic, and laid it in my lap.

From where I sat I could see the front door. The key turning in the front door lock was plainly audible. The door opened and a woman in her early thirties dressed in a nurse's white uniform entered the house. She had a bag in her arms and was so intent on getting in and not dropping the bag or her keys that she didn't see me. She closed the door and turned to walk along the hallway to the kitchen. That's when she saw me.

She stopped, tried to recognize my face. The light wasn't great, so she took several more steps toward me.

"Johnson?" She raised her voice. "Johnson?" Then to me: "Where is he?"

"I don't know," I said. "I came alone."

"But the car?"

"I borrowed it from your husband."

She entered the kitchen. She set the bag containing groceries on the kitchen counter and extracted a half gallon of milk, which she placed in the refrigerator. She had short dark hair, was a tad plump, and had had an accident with some food during her shift—there was a stain on her blouse. It looked like mustard.

"Did you just get off work?" I asked.

"Yes." She named the hospital. She glanced around the room again, noted the dog in the back yard, made eye contact with me and asked in a worried voice, "Where is Johnson? Has he been hurt?"

"He'll be along shortly."

"How'd you get in here?"

"You left the back door unlocked."

She passed over that—she probably had forgotten to lock the door many times in the past—and said, "Would you like some coffee?"

"I could use a cup," I admitted.

She was getting a little steamed, I could tell. "You have a name?" she asked as she went about putting a filter and coffee and water in the machine on the counter.

"Tommy Carmellini. And you?"

"Michelle."

When the coffeemaker was going, she turned to face me, crossed her arms, and leaned back against the counter. "Want to tell me what this is all about?"

"Who does Johnson work for, Michelle?"

"Don't you know?"

"We met only once, earlier this morning."

She stood silently with her butt against the counter, staring at me as the coffeemaker gurgled.

"He's in trouble, isn't he?"

"Yes."

"How much?"

"A lot."

She visibly sagged. "What agency are you with?"

"CIA."

She covered her face with both hands. After a bit she lowered her hands and tried to get her breathing under control.

"I don't know who he's working with or for. He said he could make some serious money. For the last two weeks he's been working odd hours."

I didn't say a word. She waited for the question that didn't come, examined my face carefully, then continued: "He's been looking for a real job since he left the FBI. That was last August. He couldn't find anything. Since they forced him out, he couldn't use the bureau as a reference, couldn't get any law enforcement agency to talk to him. He's got a degree in law enforcement, worked for a police department for five years before he got accepted by the FBI. He's never done anything else. I thought, this time . . ." She ran out of steam and had to use a hand to brace herself against the counter.

"I'm sorry, Mrs. Dunlap."

She bobbed her head.

"What's he done?" she said, her voice a whisper.

"I—"

"Tell me the truth!"

"They killed some people."

She tried to keep a straight face. She looked around, saw the coffeepot, got cups from the cupboard, and poured. She brought one over, handed it to me, then sat across from me.

"I'm sorry," I said.

She bit her lower lip.

"So you don't know . . . ?"

She shook her head.

I tasted the coffee and realized I didn't want it. I got up, and put the pistol behind my belt in the small of my back. She watched me do it, didn't say anything. I went out the front door, closed it behind me, got in her husband's heap, and drove away.

I guess I was pretty paranoid as I drove back to Dorsey's shack in the forest. These guys had gotten to Sal Pulzelli and Willie Varner—it was only a matter of time before they got to Kelly Erlanger and Dorsey O'Shea. I had figured I had a few hours. Now I was hoping I hadn't figured wrong.

Amazing how the mind works. My pea brain, anyway. Johnson Dunlap had seemed important two hours ago—now he didn't. I'd forgotten how time was rushing on. Now, as I drove toward Dorsey's, I could think of nothing else. I must have looked at my watch fifty times. Of course, when you are in a hell of a hurry every old fart and white-haired lady in the state gets out on the street in his or her Lincoln or BMW or Cadillac and drives slowly and erratically. They had nowhere to go and all day to get there. Me, I knew my time was fast running out.

I passed cars and vans and trucks on the right and left, ran a couple red lights and pushed the speed all I dared. If I had been stopped by a traffic cop, I don't know what I would have done. Wrap him up and take him along would have been my only option. Actually, I could have used a cruiser with a siren and overhead lights right about then.

So these dudes weren't Russians, weren't suicidal ragheads. They were plain old American scum who killed for money and the sheer fun of it.

That fact relieved me somewhat. At least when I caught one of them and put the fear in him, he would know my language. If he died before he could get his conscience polished clean, at least we wouldn't have had one of those tragic failures to communicate.

I used Westland's cell phone to call Dorsey. I had difficulty remembering her phone number. I never used to forget the number of a beautiful woman—so either the lack of sleep was getting to me or I was losing it as I aged.

The telephone rang four times before she answered.

"It's me. Are you and Kelly still alone?"

"Where *are* you, Tommy? I have never in my life had a man sneak out of bed after sex. What's the matter—wasn't I good enough for you?"

"Hey, babe, I had a few problems I had to check on. I'm on my way back to your place. Are you two women alone?"

"Very much so."

"For Christ's sake, don't call anybody. I'll be there in a few minutes. Keep the doors locked and stay away from the windows!"

I tossed the phone onto the passenger seat.

"Get outta my way," I shouted at one old lady who slowed a half block before she turned left. I was tempted to give her the finger, but reserved it for a van driver who looked as if he learned to drive yesterday.

I whipped across traffic into Dorsey's drive and stopped. No one was parked nearby. The traffic kept flowing past. I zipped back to the trunk and unobtrusively rescued the MP-5. Put it on my lap and checked the safety and tried to think logically.

These guys might come through the woods like they did at the Greenbrier safe house, avoid the driveway altogether. I looked at my watch again. It was still there—right on my wrist.

Ahhh shit! How did I get into this mess, anyway?

I drove slowly up Dorsey's drive, looking around like a naked shoplifter. Saw a lot of trees. In addition to money, Dorsey had a zillion trees, by God. Didn't see a living soul.

After consideration, I parked the car at the place where the driveway exited the trees, just before it widened out. There was no easy way for a vehicle to get around it, so if the villains came up the drive, they were going to have to park behind the heap and get out. If I was in the right place waiting . . .

I charged for the house, knocked on the door.

Dorsey opened it. She was wearing a robe and no makeup. I went in past her, pushed the door shut behind me.

She was certainly angry, but when she saw my face the anger gave way to fear.

"My God, Tommy, what is going on?"

"These guys were cutting on Willie the Wire when I showed up at his place. I think I got him to the hospital in time, but I'll bet they're still sewing him up."

"They're coming here?"

"They might. That's a fact. Have you called anyone, anyone at all?"

"Yes. The maid and the cook. Told them not to come today."

"Anyone called here?"

"You did. And the artist who was here last night."

"No one else?"

"No."

"Where's Erlanger?" I strode for the stairs, carrying the submachine gun in my right hand.

"She's in the kitchen."

I changed course, went past the staircase and made a beeline for the kitchen. Kelly was sitting on a stool sipping coffee with a pile of Goncharov's notes in front of her.

"Sleep okay?" I asked as I went by. The view of the back yard out the kitchen windows was excellent. There was about thirty yards of grass between the house and the forest. There was no way one man could cover every approach to this house. We could run, of course. But where?

I turned to face Erlanger. Dorsey was standing beside her. "These people cut up my partner, Willie Varner, this morning. He told them about you, Dorsey. They might have telephoned someone before I showed up—Willie didn't know."

"What do you think we should do?" Kelly asked.

I took a deep breath. "We can't stay here long term, but I need some time to think about our next move."

I opened the refrigerator and looked inside. I was hungry enough to eat a road-killed possum. Fortunately Dorsey had some gourmet cheese. I grabbed the whole package and a quart of milk.

"I'll go outside and sit under a tree while the brain percolates. Kelly, it would help if you would read as much of Goncharov's notes as possible. Dorsey, you could throw something in a suitcase, get ready to go. You and Kelly are about the same size—maybe you have something that might fit her."

I took a swig of milk and a bite of cheese.

"Your arm is bleeding," Dorsey said.

"Yeah."

Dorsey's face was a study. "Tommy, we have to call the police."

"One of the guys who cut up Willie was ex-FBI. Willie thought the others were cops. If you call the cops, these are the dudes who will show up, just like they did last night at Kelly's house."

"My God, Tommy!"

"I need to do some thinking," I insisted.

Kelly lifted the notes and said, "Everything I've looked at concerns KGB shenanigans in Russia. All these papers seem to be about the dirty tricks the KGB pulled to control the party."

"Check everything in the suitcase," I said to her, and headed for the door. Dorsey tagged along behind. At the front door I gave her the snub-nose .38 revolver I had liberated earlier that morning.

"There're five shots in this thing. No safety. Hold the pistol in both hands at arm's length, aim right at the dude's belly button, and squeeze the trigger slowly."

She took the pistol and held it against her breasts. "This isn't supposed to happen in America."

"Don't I know it!"

I found a thick bush in the middle of a thicket at the corner of Dorsey's garage and crawled under it. From there I could see the heap and the driveway and the east side of the house. I was completely blind behind me, and the garage blanked out everything on the west side of the house. This spot would have to do.

I lay there munching on cheese and wondering what I should do next. Staying alive was looking more and more difficult. And there were the women. Should we split up or stay together?

I stripped a few cartridges from the backup banana clip on the submachine gun and used them to fill up the magazine of the automatic. It wasn't much, but it was all I could think to do.

Mikhail Goncharov spent the morning sitting beside the cabin in the sun, with his back against the chopping block. The day became hotter and the shadows shrank. Finally the sun slipped behind a large oak that shaded the area where he sat. He watched birds and chipmunks and listened to the gurgle of the distant river.

Sometime in late afternoon he was watching a chipmunk search the forest floor for nuts that had somehow escaped his attention this past winter when he heard a car. He sprang to his feet and hid behind the woodpile.

The car pulled into the parking area for the cabin, fifty feet or so down the hill.

A woman and a man got out of the car and began to load their arms with items to carry into the cabin.

The fear leaked out of him, leaving only lethargy. As they came up the path with their arms full of boxes, he stepped out from behind the woodpile and resumed his seat. Startled, the two people spoke to him in a language he didn't recognize.

The Russian shook his head. After several attempts at conversation, the man went inside the cabin and looked around, then came back outside and spoke to the woman, who was still standing there with a box of groceries in her arms.

Goncharov ignored the people and turned his attention to the chipmunk, who seemed oblivious to the company.

After a while both the visitors went into the cabin. They eventually began making trips to and from their car, carrying bags and luggage. The archivist remained seated against the chopping block in the sun. He didn't recognize these people, nor could he remember how he got to this place. Where was it? Why was he here?

It was all confusing, like something in a dream, fragments of reality that he couldn't put into a familiar pattern. Perhaps he should try harder to remember . . .

He was getting tired.

Finally he arose, relieved himself behind the nearest tree, and lay down in a sunny spot near the woodpile. In minutes he was asleep.

CHAPTER ELEVEN

This isn't supposed to happen in America."

Isn't that what Dorsey said? The words kept running through my mind as I lay under that bush waiting to find out if those dudes at Willie's made their telephone call before I killed them.

At least it wasn't raining.

Ah, me! What day is this, anyway?

Let's see. Yesterday was Tuesday, so this must be Wednesday. Believe it or not, a mere twenty-four hours had passed since the shit hit the fan. I checked my watch. Twenty and a half hours, to be precise.

I lay there listening to the insects, watching a snail, thinking about the problem. I needed a place where these two women and I could drop out of sight for a few days while Kelly read the Goncharov files. Of course, we only had one of the seven suitcases containing his notes, but still, there might be something in that mess that pointed the way.

An hour ticked away. I was proud of myself. I only looked at my watch twenty-three times in that hour. I stopped glancing at it finally, and let the warmth of the air of that June day and the cool, moist earth on which I was lying sort of settle me down, put things in perspective. I must have dropped off. How long I slept I don't know, but a movement to my far right brought me instantly awake.

I lay there under that bush like a dead man, with only my eyes moving. Something had alerted me, but what?

I was completely awake, totally alert . . . and couldn't see anything out of the ordinary. I listened. Birds, very distant traffic noises from the road beside the river . . . the droning of an airliner. The buzzing of a small plane, fading . . . and . . .

And . . .

I began moving my head to the right. Glacially, as slowly as I could make my muscles move. Of course, that would be the direction the threat would come from since I had thought it the least likely and the bush obscured my vision—and hid me—and I would have the devil of a time getting the MP-5 turned that way. I already had my eyes two-blocked that way, so as I moved my head I could see . . .

Limbs, leaves . . . more leaves . . . and *a man.*

No ghillie suit this time, just a head-to-toe camouflage outfit. He even wore a camo hat and had grease on his face. I spotted him initially only because he was moving. He hadn't yet seen me because I wasn't, and because I was embedded in vegetation.

I lay there motionless as a week-old corpse.

He had appeared from behind the house and was moving to my right, toward my rear. Every step he took put me at a larger disadvantage.

He was carrying some kind of assault rifle.

Oh, Jesus, I was up against the first team! This guy knew what he was doing and he was hard at it, sneaking along with every sense alert, looking for something to kill.

The stupidity of my choice of an ambush position became brutally obvious. I was hidden, all right, but I had no ability to change positions or engage the man. If I twitched a muscle, I was dead. I knew it and lay frozen with sweat popping from every pore. A few minutes of this and he would smell me.

He was sneaking out of my range of vision to my right. Since I couldn't move, I looked around in the other direction.

If there were two of these camo guys out here I might as well shoot myself now and be done with it.

I didn't see anyone else. That didn't fill me with confidence—this guy was so good he didn't need any help. I had a nearly overpowering urge to pee and restrained it with difficulty.

I was going to have to do something soon. He was moving behind me, and when he saw me he would finish me instantly, without remorse. Exactly the same way I'd shoot him.

My mind was going a hundred miles an hour and I couldn't think of a goddamn thing!

He was going to finish me in just a few seconds. My whole life . . . and it was ending. Here! Now!

Whump. I heard the noise and for a second it didn't register. Then I heard it again. Shots! Two of them. From inside the house.

I took a chance, turned my head another inch to my right.

He had turned and was surveying the windows of the house. Now he looked around, scanned everything quickly, then advanced toward the back of the house, back along the direction he had come. One of his buddies must have gone in the back door.

I lay there frozen until he passed behind the house, out of view. Then I came out of that bush, as quickly and silently as I could, and got pointed in the right direction, the MP-5 in my hands.

I ran for the corner of the house, came up short, and eased an eye around.

He was standing outside the basement door, looking in the other direction, about to enter.

I snicked the safety off, shouldered the weapon as I rounded the corner and gave him a hell of a burst, at least half a clip. The bullets spun him, knocked him off his feet, hammered at him until I released the trigger. I ran toward him while looking around to see if there was anyone else.

Didn't see another soul. The camo man lay sprawled out like he'd been hit by a Freightliner. I don't think one of those 9 mm bullets missed. There wasn't much blood. He looked unnaturally plump. I bent down, tugged at his shirt. He was wearing a bullet-proof vest, which hadn't saved him from the slugs that hit him in the head and neck, at least three of them.

I eased the door open with my left hand—the glass had been cut out and the lock opened from the inside—and passed through, the submachine gun at the ready.

Taking my time, I slipped through the basement, a room I had never been in, until I found the stairs up. I could hear a woman sobbing.

I climbed as silently as possible, then pushed the door at the head of the stairs open inch by inch and looked out. I was in the passageway just off the kitchen. The sobbing was louder now.

I moved toward it, the submachine gun at the ready.

Dorsey was sitting on the bottom stair, her face in her hands. She was sobbing. Kelly Erlanger was sitting beside her, her arms around Dorsey's shoulders.

In front of them lay a man. He wasn't moving. Blood was everywhere, a widening lake.

Keeping the gun on him, I walked over, stood in the blood, and turned him onto his back with one foot.

It was Baldy from this morning, Johnson Dunlap. He looked at me, tried to focus his eyes, and went limp, staring at nothing at all.

She had fired twice. The first bullet hit him in the body apparently—I could see the bullet hole in his shirt—doubling him up but not injuring him; he, too, was wearing a bulletproof vest. The second slug, however, whacked him on the inside of his right thigh. Severed the femoral artery. Johnson Dunlap had bled to death in Dorsey O'Shea's hallway while she sat sobbing on the stairs.

I wouldn't have tried to save the bastard either.

After running my fingers through Dorsey's hair, I unlocked the front door and went out that way. I thought maybe I ought to make a circuit of the house, just to make sure there were only two men sneaking about. Undoubtedly there was a getaway car somewhere, but I had zero chance of tracking these guys back through the forest to find it.

On the bright side, maybe now Michelle would get herself a better fella.

Basil Jarrett and Linda Fiocchi stood on the porch of their vacation cabin on the bank of the Greenbrier River staring at the sleeping form of Mikhail Goncharov, stretched out in the sun by the woodpile. They knew nothing about him, not his name, nationality, age, or condition . . . nor, of course, were they aware of the previous day's events at the CIA's Greenbrier facility six miles from their cabin. Not only had the CIA not informed the press or local law enforcement agencies of the murders at the facility, the fact that the spy agency owned anything at all in this state was classified. Jarrett and Fiocchi had never even heard a CIA rumor.

Basil Jarrett owned two sawmills that manufactured decorator fencing. His fences lined suburban lawns in thirty-seven states. Fiocchi, his cabin co-owner and live-in girlfriend of ten years, was an accountant. "He's not a drunk or doper," Jarrett said.

"How can you tell?"

"Look at him! He's a healthy man in his mid-sixties, I'd say, properly nourished yet not fat, reasonably fit, seems to have most of his teeth, bathes regularly . . ."

Fiocchi didn't argue. She, too, had seen her share of derelicts, and obviously the sleeping man wasn't one of them. "So who is he?"

"I haven't the foggiest." Jarrett held up the clothes Goncharov had come in, which were now dry. The new trousers and shirt were brands that were sold in many large clothing chains nationwide.

Fiocchi shrugged. "He knows we are here and went to sleep anyway. On the other hand, he did break into the cabin. Should we wake him and demand an explanation, or should we go to Durbin to call the law?" There was no telephone in the cabin—no electricity at all—and no cellular service this close to the Radio Astronomy Observatory.

"Take hours for a deputy or trooper to get here," Jarrett replied gloomily. "They have to come all the way from Marlinton. Maybe we should find out who he is before we toss him overboard. Maybe he's sick or crazy and wandered away from a cabin or farm around here."

Linda Fiocchi didn't think much of the police option either. "He's probably sick. He looks harmless enough." She went into the cabin for a blanket, which she arranged over the sleeping man.

I loaded the women, the submachine gun, and Mikhail Goncharov's suitcase in Johnson Dunlap's car and set sail on the highways of America. At my insistence, we left the two thugs right where they had fallen. I also left their weapons beside them; I could use the ammo, but I decided to buy what I needed at a sporting goods store. When the police found those dudes—which would probably happen sooner rather than later—I wanted the record to accurately show the weapons they brought with them.

I figured that the police were already involved in this somehow and might be looking for cars—mine, Kelly's, and possibly Dorsey's. I just hoped they weren't looking for Dunlap's. Yet.

Every time we passed a police cruiser I twisted for a look, and ogled the mirrors, waiting for the driver to turn around and snap on the lights and siren and give chase. What I would do if a cop did give chase I didn't know, but I was absolutely certain that I didn't want to kill or wound a cop. If cops were involved, they were merely following orders from their sergeant or captain or whoever. Johnson Dunlap, the camo man, and the dudes who were slicing up Willie Varner were a different breed of cat. They weren't trying to arrest anyone—they went to kill. I had no regrets icing them and I certainly wouldn't lose sleep over them.

Dorsey would, however. When I wasn't rubbernecking for cops, I watched her in the rearview mirror. She was in the back seat staring out at traffic and the scenery. I didn't think she actually saw much of it. Her eyes were dry, but she had a look on her face that hadn't been there before.

I debated telling her about my visit with Michelle Dunlap earlier that morning, then decided against it. Maybe it was best for Johnson to remain an anonymous thug who broke into her house to kill her. She didn't need to hear a sob story or a description of the widow.

See, that's the way guys think. As far as I was concerned Dunlap and his pals were assholes who sold out to another asshole and went sallying forth to kill people they didn't know for money. Dunlap got wasted—his tough luck. Dorsey didn't appear to see it that way or she wouldn't have been leaking tears earlier or staring out the window now.

For Christ's sake, I wasn't crying about the camo man. I was actually sort of pleased that I used the submachine gun and hosed him good before he did it to me. I hadn't suspected he might be wearing a bulletproof vest; if I had only squeezed off a round or two with the pistol, my dick might have been on the chopping block. We played for keeps and he lost. What's for dinner?

Kelly Erlanger was busy reading files in the passenger seat. She had arranged the pages into some sort of order and was skimming through them. Reading in a car always made me sick, but it didn't seem to bother her.

"So who's hungry?" I asked brightly.

Erlanger didn't look up from her reading. Dorsey kept her face pointed out the window.

I stopped in Annapolis at a hamburger joint. "Anyone need to use the facilities?"

No response.

They never pee in James Bond movies either.

I went inside, visited the men's, then ordered burgers, fries, and three soft drinks—Diet Cokes, of course. A county mountie sneaked in while I was paying, and I didn't see him. I nearly dropped the load when I turned around and found him behind me in his Foster Grants watching me juggle the bag and the drinks. Gave him a noncommittal "Hi" and walked on by. Not a friendly, neighborly "Hi" or a go-to-hell, kiss-my-ass-fool kind of "Hi," but more of an I-don't-give-a-shit "Hi." You know, just a "Hi." I guess he didn't see the automatic under my shirt, because he didn't pull his piece or shoot me or even say "Hi" back.

I used my butt to open the door of McDonald's and stuffed the food in the car and fed it gas. Neither of the women was hungry or thirsty.

We crossed the Bay Bridge and headed east.

I turned on the radio and got an easy listening station in Baltimore; rolled down my window and stuck my elbow out.

"Where are we going?" Dorsey asked, the first words she had spoken since she gunned down Johnson Dunlap.

"To visit a friend."

"Let's see . . . You've roped me and Willie Varner into this mess already. I had to kill a man and Willie is in the hospital—you did say you took him to the hospital?"

"Uh-huh."

"Anyone else?"

I hadn't yet mentioned Sal Pulzelli to her and now didn't seem to be the right time.

"Now you have another friend in mind. What do the Catholics call it when the devil comes calling?"

"I don't know."

"If your friends hold up a crucifix, will you still cross their threshold? Or will it take a silver bullet through your heart to slow you down?"

I bit my lip. You can never win these kinds of arguments with women, and only a fool would try.

"Being your friend is a dubious honor, Tommy. What do I have to do to get my name erased from the list?"

I almost said to stay away from porno movie producers, but managed to stifle myself. The miles rolled by while Kelly Erlanger read and Dorsey glowered at the back of my head. I kept the car five over the speed limit, slurped on a diet Coke, and listened to the radio.

CHAPTER TWELVE

They were in their apartment in Moscow when they came to arrest him. They came in the middle of the night, as they always did. They smashed at the door with a sledgehammer. The furious pounding woke him, the sound of wood splintering, someone somewhere screaming. Bronislava was beside him, startled awake.

He could see everything in the small apartment in the light from the street that came through the window, see the door panel bulging and splintering under each impact, hear the grunting of the man swinging the hammer. And there was no other way out. No exit. They were trapped! When they found his notes he and Bronislava would be taken to the Lubyanka, thrown into the cells, and interrogated and tortured until they told everything or died. He had seen them there so many times, people praying to die . . . and now it was his turn. The hammering . . . they were almost through the door . . .

He awoke in a lather, fighting the blanket that was over him. He sat up, stared at his surroundings.

Oh, God, where was he? Nothing looked familiar . . . nothing. Only the dream had been real, the same dream that had tortured him for twenty years . . .

There was a woman sitting on the cabin steps—a young woman, perhaps thirty years of age, with medium-length dark hair, wearing a blouse, slacks, and a sweater. She spoke to him in a language he didn't understand. He shook his head slowly, completely lost, confused.

He urgently needed to go to the bathroom. He stood, folded the blanket that had covered him, and, with it draped over one arm, stepped behind some bushes and relieved himself. He zipped up his pants and stood looking around.

The woman found him there. She had a cup of something hot. He accepted it gratefully, sipped, then she took his arm and led him back to the steps of the cabin. By gestures she motioned him to sit beside her on the top step. He did so, sipped at the drink, glanced around at everything, trying to remember.

She spoke again. He understood not a word. While she was talking a man joined them on the porch. He was slim, apparently in his mid-thirties, with a lean, tan face and short hair. He spoke to Goncharov also, and to the woman, back and forth. Mikhail Goncharov had no idea what they were discussing.

After a while she led him inside. He looked around again. Everything was strange. He sank into the nearest seat, scanned the entire room, then arranged the blanket over his legs. He was chilly.

The woman made him a sandwich. He ate it slowly, savoring every bite. She gave him more of the hot liquid to drink.

When he finished the food, the man brought a notebook and a ballpoint pen. He handed them to Goncharov, pointed to Goncharov's chest, then widened his hands before him in the universal gesture of a question.

A name, Goncharov thought. He wants my name.

But what is it?

Startled, his eyes widened as he realized he didn't even know who he was.

He picked up the pen, made the point go in and out, examined the white paper, but for the life of him he could think of nothing to write.

"He doesn't know his own name," Linda Fiocchi said heavily.

"Apparently not," Basil Jarrett agreed.

"So what should we do?"

"Damn, woman, I don't know." Jarrett went to the woodstove and opened it. He wadded up a sheet of newspaper from a nearby pile, added kindling, and struck a match. When the paper caught, he closed the door and adjusted the draft.

What should we do with a man who is obviously suffering from some kind of severe mental confusion? Not that Linda or I know a solitary thing about mental illness. Boy, you come to the cabin for a quiet, restful weekend, some fishing, reading, wine, and lovemaking . . . and you've got a mental patient on your hands.

When Jarrett turned around, Linda was sitting beside the older man holding his hand. The man seemed to be paying no attention. He stared fixedly at something far, far away.

Civilization had reached Rehoboth Beach, Delaware, I decided as I cruised slowly through, checking out the scene. The Wal-Mart was huge, spanking new, and had a couple of acres of parking lot. Inside would be 9 mm and .38 Special ammo, not to mention underwear and jeans, socks and shirts. All the necessities for classy, with-it guys like me.

The house I was looking for was about a mile south of downtown on the beach side of the highway, on a dead-end street. It looked about as I remembered it, a medium-sized two-story bungalow with a large screened-in porch and a crushed-seashell parking area big enough for four cars. I wheeled in, killed the engine, sat looking it over. Only two of the other bungalows on this street that dead-ended at the dune had cars parked beside them.

"Whose house is this?" Dorsey O'Shea asked from the back seat.

"Guy I know."

"One of your friends you are about to curse with your presence. Do you have permission to stay here?"

"Uh, he won't mind."

"So the answer is no." She harrumped. "I thought not."

I turned in my seat to face her. "I've had about enough of your lip. I'm sorry you had to shoot that bastard this morning, but I'm not real damn sorry. He came to kill all three of us. It was him or us. He was a rotten cop and he fell in with rotten people."

"You knew him?"

"I know his name, yes."

"Jesus, Tommy, I don't want to have to kill people, for any reason at all. Ever again." Her voice had a hard, brittle edge to it. "Do you understand?"

"I understand."

"What kind of man are you, anyway? You kill a man at my house, watch another die before your eyes, and you drive all afternoon with your arm out the window and the radio playing, like you don't give a good goddamn." The pitch and volume of her voice were rising. "What kind of animal are you, anyway?"

"I can answer that," Kelly Erlanger said calmly. "Yesterday morning Tommy Carmellini ran into a burning building and dragged me out, saving my life. Men like the ones this morning went through that building shooting everyone they could find, then set the place on fire to burn the bodies. Last night he went to my house and got me out of it just before more men arrived to kill me."

She turned in her seat so that she, too, could see Dorsey. She held up a handful of paper. "These are copies the KGB archivist made of the files in his custody. He spent twenty years copying these files and smuggled them out of Russia after he retired. Never in my life have I read such a chronicle of evil. Tommy Carmellini? He's one of the good guys."

She got out of the car and closed the door behind her, leaving me alone with Dorsey.

Dorsey wouldn't look at me. After a bit she said, "I know there is evil in the world, but I don't want to live with it. I don't want to fight it. I don't want it bleeding to death in my foyer. What's so wrong with that? Do you understand?"

"I think so," I told her. "But you'd better keep that pistol handy. You may need it again if you want to keep breathing."

It only took me a couple of minutes to pick the lock on the front door of the bungalow. I opened the door, went through turning on lights, then went back to the car to carry in the weapons and baggage. The women came inside. After they used the facilities, they walked through the house examining everything.

"You really do know the owners?" Dorsey asked sharply.

"Yes."

"They won't mind you using this place?"

"I don't think so."

"Why don't you call them and ask? There's the phone."

"I would rather not. The fewer people who know we're here the better. If there's a problem, I'll make it right with the owners later on."

Kelly took a deep breath and announced, "I'll take the bedroom on the left, upstairs. I saw a swimsuit up there that looks like it might fit me. Dorsey, would you like to go for a walk on the beach?"

Dorsey's shoulders sagged. "Yes," she said. "I guess I would."

While they were changing clothes I rooted through the kitchen drawers until I found a spare house key. I gave it to Kelly as they trooped past on their way out, with borrowed towels over their shoulders.

I stood beside the car watching them walk down the street. After they disappeared across the dune, I got in the car and headed for Wal-Mart, which even had groceries.

That Kelly . . . she had her share of guts. I liked that.

The sheriff was a man in his fifties, balding, with a modest pot gut and a quiet voice. He stood in front of the cabin listening to Basil Jarrett explain about the man they had found when they arrived midday, the man who had spent most of the afternoon asleep near the woodpile.

When he had told him everything he could think of, Jarrett led the sheriff inside. He sat down beside Mikhail Goncharov, asked him his name, where he was from, all the usual questions. For his troubles he received a blank stare.

The sheriff took the pad, wrote his name upon it, and held it up so the man could see the similarity between the name on the pad and the sheriff's name tag above his left pocket, just below his badge. Then he offered the man the pad and pen.

Goncharov took them, examined the pen, stared at the white paper, and finally laid them in his lap. The sheriff rescued the pad and pen and wrote out two questions. *What is your name? Where do you live?* Goncharov didn't appear to even read them when they were held in front of him.

The sheriff sat for a bit more, chatting with Goncharov and receiving no response, then finally arose from his chair and motioned to Jarrett and Fiocchi to follow. Standing in front of his cruiser, he said, "He's not from around here. Never saw him before."

"Do you want to take him with you?"

"Well, about all I could do would be take him to the county lockup for transport to the regional jail. We could get some prints, send them to the FBI, see if they can figure out who he is. Gonna take a while, I suspect."

"You'd leave him in jail while the bureaucrats are piddling along?"

The sheriff settled his hat onto his head and looked searchingly at each of their faces. "Seeing as how he's apparently incompetent, the mental health commissioner will have him examined by a psychologist or psychiatrist, hold a hearing. If the commissioner finds he's incompetent, regardless of who he is, he'll send him to the state mental institution for treatment."

"I see," Basil Jarrett said, glancing at Fiocchi. "So you're saying he'll probably wind up in the nut house?"

"I sorta suspect so," the sheriff admitted. "This fella doesn't have a wallet or money on him—you told me that. It's been my experience that there are very few people without some kind of identification on their person unless they are running from something." He shrugged, then continued, "He doesn't appear to be under the influence of alcohol or drugs. He won't talk to me in any language, won't write down his name or tell us where he lives—he seems unresponsive. Abnormally so."

The sheriff got out a pack of cigarettes and lit one, taking his time. When he had it going he said, "He appears to me to be unable to take care of himself. I call that incompetent. What do you think?"

While the sheriff smoked, Jarrett and Fiocchi walked out of earshot and talked the situation over. In a moment they came back. "Is there any way you could fingerprint him and send the prints to the FBI? And leave him here until you hear something?"

"You don't know who this man is," the sheriff pointed out. "He could be a fugitive, a killer, or an escapee from a prison or asylum.

He could be bedbug crazy. He could be any damn body. Do you really want the responsibility of caring for this man for a while? Might be as long as a week?"

They went away and discussed it animatedly. Finally they returned. "Yes," Jarrett said. "He's sick, having severe nightmares, and we think he has amnesia. We don't think jail is the place for him. I have to go to work on Monday, but Linda could stay here with him if necessary."

"I've got some office supplies in the trunk," the sheriff said. "Seem to remember an ink pad in that bag." He made no move to open the trunk but stood smoking. When he finished the weed, he dropped it and ground it out beneath his shoe. "This guy seems pretty harmless. Let's hope he is."

When I got back from Wal-Mart that afternoon, I did some sit-ups and push-ups to get the kinks out, then went for a run. I stood on the dune looking until I saw the women—they seemed deep in conversation—then I ran the other way along the beach.

That night I fixed steaks and potatoes for dinner on the charcoal grill that sat beside the house in the small yard. While the food was cooking I made a salad. I had even remembered to buy a six-pack on my shopping expedition, so we washed our meal down with beer.

The women didn't have much to say that night. Kelly dove back into the Goncharov treasure and Dorsey selected a book from the shelves. She read on it a while, then put it back on the shelf and went upstairs. I heard the shower running, then nothing. I figured she went to bed.

I sat on the screened-in porch and thought about the last two days. Bullets, blood, fire, murder . . . it was like we were in the middle of a war.

Me, I was just a thief who liked breaking into places I wasn't supposed to be. The agency kept me busy cracking safes, planting bugs, photographing documents in private offices, and the like. All in all, it wasn't a bad job—I got paid adequately and regularly, although I wasn't getting rich, and presumably someday I would retire on a comfortable pension if someone didn't shoot me or I didn't open a booby-trapped filing cabinet. Or a rope didn't break while I climbed the side of a building. Or I didn't get thrown into some third-world dungeon to rot. Or I didn't pick up a fatal intestinal parasite somewhere or other. Or these hired killers who were chasing me and Kelly—and now Dorsey— didn't catch me.

What was there to worry about?

Truth be told, I thought about quitting the government off and on for years. Tell the CIA to shove it and go out on my own, burglary for fun and profit. Then I would think about guys I had known, guys like Sal Pulzelli, who didn't live to retire, and I would think, what the heck, I'll hang in there. Keep on keeping on. So I'd been hanging in, keeping on. Now Sal was dead and Willie carved up and . . .

I knew exactly how Dorsey felt.

Why me?

There were some blankets neatly folded on a chair in the living room, so I carried them out to the covered porch and bedded down on a couch. Kelly was still curled up reading.

It must have been about midnight when I awoke to find a woman crawling under the blankets with me. At first I thought it was Dorsey, but it wasn't. It was Kelly. She was wearing cotton pajamas and she wasn't interested in anything but sleeping. She snuggled up against me and promptly dropped off.

I wrapped an arm around her and went back to sleep myself.

CHAPTER THIRTEEN

When I awoke Thursday morning I found myself alone on the couch with the breeze whipping through the screens. I opened an eye, looked out. The day was here, but the sun had not yet risen. Or maybe it had. There were a lot of clouds up there.

I heaved myself out, put on shorts and my tennis shoes, and went outside. No one sitting in cars, no one peering out a window. Only a few folks out and about at this hour, joggers and dog walkers. I trotted down the street and thundered over the boardwalk across the dune. Birds probed the surf runout, and a garbage truck with balloon tires drove along emptying trash barrels. Here and there people combed the beach for treasures that might have washed up during the night. There was more trash than treasures. Amazing how many plastic milk jugs find their way into the ocean, to drift for months until they wash up somewhere.

I puffed along watching the gulls and the solid gray clouds racing overhead. On the way back I stopped running and walked to cool down.

So what was next? Where should I go from here?

The only leads I had were the contents of the wallets and cell phones I had taken from the dead and injured thugs. Of necessity, the trail must start with those since there was nowhere else.

Should I leave the women here and hunt these people alone?

The women seemed to be sleeping when I got back, so I got a pot of coffee going and went out for doughnuts and a copy of every newspaper sold in this town. When I returned to the house thirty minutes later, I took a quick shower, then settled at the kitchen table drinking coffee, munching doughnuts, and scanning the papers. I could not find a single word about the massacre in West Virginia or the shootings yesterday in Washington. *Nada.*

I was on my second cup of coffee when Kelly came downstairs. She was dressed in shorts and one of my T-shirts. She poured herself coffee, snagged a doughnut, and sat down beside me to look at the paper.

"Good morning," I ventured.

She grunted. Well, some women are like that B.C. Before Coffee.

I decided I wasn't going to mention sharing the couch until she did.

"There's nothing in here on the shootings yesterday," she said when she finished with the *Washington Post.* She put that paper down and picked up the next one.

"I didn't see anything," I agreed.

"So it didn't happen?"

"Apparently."

When she had scanned the lot, she helped herself to more coffee. She took her time examining the doughnut possibilities before selecting her second victim.

"I've read about two-thirds of the files," she said, "scanned them, anyway. Every one is on political double-crosses and murders and hounding dissidents and faking evidence for show trials of state enemies. The names are coded, but as near as I can tell, every person mentioned is a Soviet citizen or a prominent American or British traitor. I just can't see anything there that would make anyone in Europe or America feel threatened."

"Were all the files Goncharov copied about Soviet internal matters?"

"My understanding was that only some of them were. Apparently the only surviving files are on KGB dirty tricks."

I finished my coffee and frowned into the cup. Put it on top of the newspapers and stretched.

"Can you finish the rest of the files today?"

"I think so."

I took the magazine from the automatic and checked that the column of shells was full, then pushed it back in place.

"Where do we go from here?" Kelly asked. She was leaning against the counter, watching my face.

"I've got a couple wallets and cell phones."

"What does it mean that none of this mess made the newspapers?"

I eyed her. She wasn't innocent, naive, or ignorant. Or scared. She was smart and tough. And pretty decent looking. She had been a nice armful last night, but I suppose I shouldn't be thinking things like that.

"It means that some really big weenie is keeping it out," I said sourly. "That's why the cops were cooperating with the killers. We are up to our eyes in a very large pile of shit."

"I figured that out Tuesday."

"We're going to have to be very careful if we hope to keep breathing. No telephone calls, no e-mails, no nothing. We make the slightest noise, they'll be after us like hounds after a rabbit. What we have to do is figure out who the hounds are."

I broke the antennas off the two cell phones, then turned them on—neither had voice messages queued up, which was a shame—then got into the stored numbers. I wrote them down on a sheet of scratch paper and sat staring at the phones. Technology scares me. If the cops were cooperating with the killers, perhaps the cell phone people and the folks at the National Security Agency were, too. I turned the phones off, took out the batteries, and stored them in my overnight bag. The wizards were going to have to rewrite the laws of physics to find those cell phones without batteries in them.

I sat studying the numbers. Three numbers appeared on both phones. I made a tick beside them.

The contents of the wallets didn't even cover the kitchen table when I spread them out. One guy had a hundred fifty-three dollars in currency, the other had forty-two. I examined each bill for notes or numbers and put them back in their respective wallets.

Driver's licenses and credit cards made up the bulk of the remainder. Both guys had credit cards that looked as if they doubled as ATM cards. One of the guys had a bunch of dry-cleaning receipts. One of the guys belonged to AAA; one was a card-carrying member of the Harley Owners Group. In one wallet there were a few scraps of paper with telephone numbers on them—this was the dude who habitually didn't let his main squeeze know his whereabouts. Women's telephone numbers, I figured, but maybe I was being uncharitable. I added these numbers to my list.

That was the crop. I made sure I got the proper stuff back into the proper wallet.

The rain started about the time Dorsey O'Shea came downstairs. She looked disdainfully at the doughnuts and rooted through the pantry. She found a box of healthy cereal and ate a couple of dry handfuls between sips of coffee.

"That stuff has a lot of sugar in it," I said, just to be nasty. She ignored my comment.

Kelly was out on the screened-in porch reading. Dorsey joined me at the kitchen table. "How long is this going to go on?" she asked.

I didn't like that tone of voice, and we weren't even living together. "What's going to go on?"

"Hiding out like criminals?"

"That's what I'm trying to figure out. I've been waiting for Kelley to finish reading the files, hoping something promising would turn up."

"We must go back to Washington, talk to the authorities."

"What if they arrest us, accuse us of espionage and murder? Won't be any bail for that. My main concern is that we'll be killed before we can tell what we know. The people that tried to murder everyone in a CIA safe house can certainly reach into a city or county lockup."

She helped herself to another handful of dry cereal, which she ate as she thought about the problem. I could tell from the expression on her face that she was remembering the fear as Johnson Dunlap came at her with a gun in his hand. Memories like that remain with you all your life. She was still scared. Hell, I was still scared. Which in a way was good. If you're scared enough, maybe you'll be careful enough to stay alive.

"How do you live like this?" she muttered.

"Well, I only hole up in hideouts a couple times a year, then only for a week or two."

"Asshole."

"Hey, kid. I know you're scared. I am, too. So is Kelly."

She broke into tears. She pulled away when I reached for her.

"I never had to deal with anything like this," she sobbed, then headed for the stairs. After a while I heard water gurgling through the drain from the upstairs bathroom.

Outside the rain came down hard and smeared the windows.

When it began blowing across the porch, Kelly brought her papers into the living room and settled on the couch.

The rain set in for the day, a nice steady early summer soaker. I read all of the newspapers I could stand and went from window to window, looking out.

I was fast running out of patience. Knowing *they* were out there looking for us made the forced inaction very difficult. I turned on the television, flipped through the channels, snapped it off. Ten minutes later I did it again.

At one point I found myself standing at the living room window with the pistol in my hand, out of sight below the sill, watching the occasional passerby. I would hate prison. They would probably carry me out in a straitjacket before the first month was over.

Augh!

I was cleaning the MP-5 on the kitchen table when I thought I heard a female voice upstairs. I glanced at the couch—Kelly Erlanger was asleep with papers heaped in piles on the floor and around her.

I picked up the telephone. Dorsey's voice. I slammed it down, shot up the stairs two at a time. She was sitting cross-legged on one of the beds, a towel around her head, talking on the telephone. I grabbed it out of her hand and slammed it down.

"Are you crazy?" I snarled.

She was full of righteous indignation, which meant that she knew she had crossed the line. I knew her too well. "That was a friend of mine, I'll have you know. What gives you the right to be my jailer?"

"Who was it? Gimme a name."

"Zara Raja."

"Gimme a break, goddamnit!"

"That isn't her real name, of course—it's her professional name. Her real name is Suzy Rollins."

"Uh-huh."

"She's my spiritual adviser."

I was shocked. "I didn't know you were into religion," I said. Dorsey O'Shea, of all people!

"She's not a minister, not in the conventional sense—she's in tune with the universe. Tommy, I need to touch base with someone who really cares." She clouded up. "I feel so . . . icky. Helpless, defenseless." Tears rolled down her cheeks.

Now I remembered why Dorsey and I broke up two years ago. Beneath that gorgeous, sophisticated exterior was the soul of a twit.

I gritted my teeth. "Hey, babe, those people found your house. To find you they can check your telephone records on the phone company computer, find out who you call, tap some of the most frequently called numbers, and simply wait. When you call a tapped number they trace it."

"That's illegal!" she said indignantly.

I couldn't believe she was giving me this crap. "So is murder, Dorsey. Get a grip. These people aren't playing by the rules. Stay off the damn phone."

She dissolved in tears. I put an arm around her shoulder and tried to calm her down. She got clingy, but I wasn't in the mood. I finally went downstairs and poured a stiff vodka tonic and made her drink it.

When Basil Jarrett went fishing he took Mikhail Goncharov along. The day was overcast, with low ceilings, not much wind. Goncharov was sitting outside on his chopping block when Jarrett came out of the cabin in his waders carrying two poles and the tackle box. He tugged at Goncharov's sleeve to get his attention, showed him the rods, then made motions that he was to follow.

They walked to the road, then walked along it parallel to the river for a hundred yards or so until they came to a gravel bar that Jarrett was fond of. He rigged a fly on a line and handed it to the silent man beside him. Then he turned his back and selected a fly for his rod.

When he turned around, Goncharov was standing at the water's edge whipping the fly into the eddies with an expert flip of his wrist. In and out, in and out, he made the line dance, then stopped and let the fly drift for a moment with the current.

Although Goncharov wasn't wearing waders, he was soon in to his knees.

Basil Jarrett laid down his rod and stood watching. After a while he found a seat.

The Greenbrier was a fabulous trout stream, flowing swiftly over a wide, shallow bed as it snaked its way through the steep hills covered with forest, which came literally to the water's edge.

A half hour after he began fishing, Goncharov caught a small trout. He held it up so that Jarrett could see it, then deftly took it off the hook and tossed it back. When Jarrett took the fly box to Goncharov to allow him to make his own selection, the man grinned.

Basil Jarrett slapped him on the shoulder and returned the grin. Then he picked up his own rod and waded into the stream.

That evening I flipped on the television to catch the news. I'm not a TV guy—an occasional ball game or movie and now and then the news takes all the time I am willing to devote to television, which is not much. That Thursday evening the network's big stories were an earthquake in southern Russia, a flood in Bangladesh, another accounting scandal—this time at a big HMO—and lots of political news. This was an election year. The first convention was in ten days; the other one the week after that. According to the pundits the president had his party's nomination locked up, so most of the coverage was of the opposition's front-runner and his two closest rivals. When the broadcast was over I flipped off the idiot box.

It was merely a matter of time before the bad guys learned we were here and came for us—the only question was, how much time did we have? I wanted to boogie right now and get on with the business of tracking these guys down. What was I going to do with the women? Where would they be safe?

I was mulling over that question when I heard a car roll into the parking area near the front door. Ten seconds later I heard a door slam. I grabbed the pistol, went to the window, and took a fast look.

Thank God! It was the owner of the house. And his wife. And ... an elderly, white-haired lady. I ran for the door and threw it wide.

"Admiral Grafton, am I glad to see you!"

Jake Grafton looked at me in amazement. "Carmellini! What on earth are you doing here?"

"It's a long story. I needed a hideout and picked the lock. Hope you don't mind."

It took a lot to shake Jake Grafton; this was nowhere near enough. He grinned at me. "Good to see you."

"Tommy, we were just talking about you the other day," Callie Grafton said as she got out of the car on the passenger side. She smiled at me. "Come over here, meet my mother-in-law, Mother Grafton."

The old lady couldn't walk without help. "Goddamn hell to get old, young man," she told me as I helped her up the stairs into the house, carrying her walker. "Jake said the house was empty. What are you doing here, anyway?"

"I brought a couple of girlfriends over for a long weekend. I knew the admiral wouldn't mind."

She gave me the eye to see if I was serious. "Only two?" she said. "In my day single men went around with as many as they could afford."

"Two is about my limit," I told her glumly. "These days everything costs more." I introduced Kelly, then got Mrs. Grafton started off in her walker toward the downstairs bathroom.

Perhaps I should tell you about Jake Grafton before I go any further. I met him a few years back in Cuba when he was in charge of a carrier battle group. He had been mixed up in a few things since, and I had worked with him on several occasions. He was now retired from the Navy. About six feet tall, he had thinning hair, gray at the temples, which he combed straight back, and a nose that was a tad too large for his face. Without a doubt, he was the toughest, most capable man I had ever met. Having him here was a huge relief.

His wife, Callie, was one of the nicest people on the planet. She was tough as shoe leather, too, although you wouldn't know it looking at her. She taught languages at Georgetown. She and Kelly Erlanger were soon engaged in an animated conversation—in Russian! Dorsey O'Shea came downstairs and I introduced everyone, then I took Admiral Grafton out onto the porch, closed the French doors, and told him how my week had gone.

I chattered away, trying to hit all the important facts, telling everything as fast as I could. As I was talking Dorsey came out, closed the door, and found a chair. She listened in silence.

CHAPTER FOURTEEN

I t's someone high in the government," Jake Grafton said after listening to my tale. "They've kept it out of the newspapers and have police cooperation—those factors alone point to someone very high up."

Dorsey O'Shea thought he was ignoring the most important point. "There is a body lying in my foyer in a pool of blood," she said coldly. "I want someone to remove it and the corpse lying beside the house."

"Indeed," Jake Grafton murmured after an appraising glance at Dorsey.

"Just who are you, anyway? Tommy evaded the question when I asked who owned this house."

"I'm a retired naval officer, Ms. O'Shea."

"I have a great-uncle who was an officer in the Navy. As I recall, he commanded some kind of ship. That was years ago, of course."

Grafton glanced at me, then murmured, "Umm." I managed to maintain a straight face.

Dorsey decided the long-retired nautical relative was a conver-sational dead end. She pressed on. "What can *you* do about this mess?" she asked the admiral.

His reply came immediately. "I don't know. Tommy and I will have to discuss that."

"I'm going to have my entire foyer torn out and redesigned," she said. "Unless that room is drastically changed, I will see that dead man and all that blood every time I pass through it." She pressed her fingertips against her forehead. "I haven't talked to the police, and I think I should. They may arrest me. I feel so out of control . . . so . . ."

We were going to have to hold Dorsey's hand for most of the evening if I didn't do something fast, so I said to her, "Didn't you tell me the other night that you had an invitation to go to Europe?"

"Yes."

"Who invited you, anyway?"

"Dino LaGassa. He wanted me to join him on his yacht in July. You met him several years ago at the Spencers' party. He's tall, with long hair and—"

"Oh, yeah," I said, as if I remembered the guy and gave a rat's ass. "Ol' Dino. Truthfully, this might be an excellent time for you to go to Europe. I recall you mentioning that you know three or four people who are spending most of their time there. Call them when you get to Europe. If you don't know or like Dino well enough to drop in for a visit, you might look up some of these other folks. When the police get around to investigating, you can make a statement for the authorities in Europe to pass along or come back and make a statement. In the interim you can hire a lawyer."

"I have a firm I use from time to time."

"Right."

She brightened. "Perhaps I should go." She paused before she added, "It was self-defense, that man I shot. He broke into my house. Two women, there alone—my God, surely there will be no question! When the police investigate, I'll be delighted to cooperate."

"I'm sure the authorities will see it as self-defense," Jake Grafton said.

"On the other hand, perhaps I should go to the police now, make a statement, tell them how it was. They can get the bodies, I can arrange for a contractor, then go to Europe with this behind me."

"What if they arrest you?" I asked.

She sat staring at me, her mouth slightly agape.

"Tommy can call you from time to time, keep you advised how things are going here," the admiral said sympathetically. He could read her like a book. It had taken me six months, way back when, to figure her out. Slow on the uptake—that's always been one of my failings. So Grafton was an admiral and I was just a grunt in the spy wars.

"I don't have any clothes," she pointed out with a frown.

"Do like the common people do," I said curtly. "Buy some."

She ignored the tenor of my remark. We discussed the location of her passport—a dresser drawer in her bedroom—and I promised to get it for her tomorrow.

On that note we went inside to see about dinner. I confess, I was feeling better already. I had someone to share the load with, and I was getting rid of Dorsey.

Once inside, Dorsey sailed off to the restroom. That's when I whispered to the admiral, "Corpses get so gross if you leave them lying around the house."

"I've heard that," he said, nodding solemnly.

Mrs. Grafton—Callie—opened cans and defrosted and warmed a precooked ham. Kelly chattered with her in a language I assumed was Russian while Callie worked. Every now and then Callie glanced at Dorsey or me as the tale progressed. I had had about all of Dorsey I needed for a few years, so I sat beside the admiral's mom and chatted her up.

After we had gone through the usual questions—where do you live, did you grow up there, etc.—and the conversation slowed to a trickle, the admiral said, "Tomorrow is Mother's birthday."

"What do you want for your birthday, Mrs. Grafton?" Dorsey asked brightly.

"I don't want any more fucking robes, I can tell you that," the old lady declared. "Got more of them than I'll ever use."

Jake winked at me, I bit my lip to keep from laughing, and Dorsey looked flustered.

I decided this would be a good time to show Admiral Grafton the submachine gun, so I did that while the beautiful Dorsey O'Shea, an heiress and socialite who had never worked a day in her life, attempted conversation with an old farm woman from western Virginia who had known nothing but hard labor all of hers.

"Nice shooter," Jake Grafton said to me as he hefted the MP-5. "Right out of a government arsenal."

After he looked it over I returned it to the corner near the porch where I could get to it quickly.

"Do you really think letting Dorsey go to the airport is a good idea?" I asked. Yeah, it had been my idea, but now I was having second thoughts. "If there's a warrant out for her, they'll red-flag her passport. She'll be arrested at the airport."

"I'll lay money there's no warrant for her," Jake said. "For you, sure. Erlanger, perhaps. But why Dorsey?"

"Someone has to take the fall for the bodies at her house."

"You, more than likely." He looked me square in the eyes. "The real question is what degree of cooperation the person organizing this chase is getting from the various law enforcement agencies. The more he wants, the more he has to reveal. Do you really think he wants Dorsey hauled in on a material witness warrant to tell the authorities everything you told her?"

"I guess not."

"I doubt it, too."

Dinner went reasonably well, considering. While things were looking up, I couldn't get those killers out of my mind. They were out there, they had the resources of the police agencies at their disposal, and I knew it was just a matter of time before they found Kelly and me. When they did, it was going to be really bad. Our lives were on the line, and perhaps the lives of Dorsey and now the Graftons. As Dorsey so elegantly pointed out, the circle kept expanding with everyone I talked to. How much time we had left I didn't know, but I could feel it slipping away.

I wondered how Willie Varner was getting along. Poor Pulzelli, sliced up by assholes who knew damn well he didn't know diddly-squat.

I guess I had a sour look on my face, because Callie Grafton said, "Is the food okay, Tommy?"

"Sorry. I was thinking about something a thousand miles away."

She smiled gently.

"What I want to know, young man," the admiral's mom asked loudly, "is how you got into this house without a key."

"He's a cat burglar," Dorsey said with her mouth full, defying all the social conventions. "He picks locks."

"Well, hell," said old Mrs. Grafton. "A man's gotta do something in this world, don't he?"

I gave her a big grin. Some of these old ladies were real dears.

We were drinking coffee afterward when Jake Grafton excused himself and went upstairs.

Twenty minutes later he came downstairs and motioned for me to follow him.

As we stood beside his car, he said, "I'm going to make some telephone calls from a pay phone, just in case." He pulled a small address book from his pocket just far enough that I could see what it was.

"Who will you call?" I asked. He knew half the people in government, yet one or more of them were hunting me with a vengeance.

"Relax," he said. "I know a few people who can be trusted." With that, he got in his car and drove away.

Jake Grafton pulled into a filling station with a pay telephone mounted on a pedestal where drivers could use it without leaving their cars. After getting five dollars in quarters from the station attendant, Jake stood beside the phone to use it. He dialed a number from his address book.

"Hello."

"Sarah, this is Jake Grafton."

There was a moment's hesitation before Sarah Houston said, "How are you this evening, Admiral?"

"Sneaking right along. Howgozit at NSA?"

"So-so."

"By chance, are you alone?"

"Yes." She didn't sound full of enthusiasm, but then her history with Jake Grafton had its serious ups and downs. The name her parents gave her was Zelda Hudson. She was a certified genius who became a master computer hacker, programmer, and network guru. She got her start in business hacking into government and defense contractor computers to steal secrets to sell. Although she was getting rich on that gig, she masterminded the theft of a U.S. Navy submarine in order to get richer; Grafton had hunted her down, and she wound up pleading guilty to thirty-seven felonies. Later he had been instrumental in springing her from the pen to help set up a computer network to hunt down terrorists importing nuclear weapons into the United States. Of course she had had to change her name: The FBI provided a new identity, and she became Sarah Houston. After that adventure Grafton even managed to get her a research job at the National Security Agency.

Tonight Jake told her, "A friend of mine tells me someone took out a CIA safe house on the Greenbrier River in West Virginia this past Tuesday, killed most of the folks there. Have you heard anything about it?"

"Not a peep. Nor would I."

"There have been no public announcements, no requests for lo-cal police assistance, none of that. I want to know what the agency is doing to find the killers."

"I can't get into the CIA computers," she said flatly. "Once upon a time, but not in this day and age."

"There was a fire and a bunch of bodies—at least six, perhaps a dozen. The local fire department responded. The bodies must have gone somewhere, and someone must have queried the FBI fingerprint files in an effort to identify them. More than likely the FBI is involved."

"I could check that," she said tentatively.

"There was a shooting in downtown Washington early Wednesday morning," Jake continued. He read her the address that Tommy had given him. "And two people were shot on an es-tate in Montgomery County, Maryland, Wednesday morning." He gave her that address, too. "I need to know who these people were, who they worked for, what is being done to investigate these crimes."

"You still in the Navy, Admiral?"

"Nope."

She gave an audible sigh. "I suppose you don't want anyone to know that you and I are inquiring?"

"You're a mind reader."

"And you have a good reason for asking these questions?"

"You bet."

"Want to share it with me?"

"No."

"When I got up this morning, I thought life was going too well. If I didn't owe you big-time, Admiral, I'd tell you where to stick that telephone."

"Ain't it great having friends?"

"I want you to know that I like my job and don't want to go back to the joint. You're asking me to hang it all out, risk everything."

"Yes."

She said a cuss word, then said, "Call me back tomorrow night at this number, about this time or later."

They said a curt good-bye.

I bunked on the porch of the Graftons' beach house that evening, the MP-5 within easy reach. When he got back that evening, the admiral told me he had called Sarah Houston . That's all he said. I had been working for him when he sprung Sarah because she was the best hacker on the planet. If anyone could figure out what was going down, Sarah would be the one.

I handed him the automatic when he went upstairs to bed and kept the MP-5.

After the house quieted down and the lights were out, Kelly Erlanger came downstairs and crawled under the blanket with me. She was wearing pajamas—didn't say anything, just curled up with her back to me and drifted off to sleep.

I was beginning to wish that she was a little more romantic. After everything we had been through this past week, maybe this wasn't a good time. Still . . .

She was gone when I woke up, sometime before dawn. There was a nice breeze. I lay in the darkness listening. Occasionally a vehicle passed on the highway. The rumble of the surf was steady as clockwork. I was about to get up when I heard footsteps in the crushed-seashell street. The noise woke me completely.

I rolled off the couch as quietly as I could, picked up the MP-5, and crawled forward a few feet to a place I where could see up and down the street. I eased the silenced muzzle of the weapon forward, tried not to breathe.

Something was out there, something evil.

There—under the last streetlight, near the beach, someone with a big dog on a leash, walking toward the boardwalk over the dune.

Was I going to spend the rest of my life jumping at every footfall, every little noise?

A little disgusted with myself, I went inside and made a pot of coffee.

At ten after one on Friday afternoon I parked the car on a deserted country lane on the top of the bluff overlooking the Potomac and hiked through the woods toward Dorsey O'Shea's mansion. I carried the submachine gun in my arms and had the automatic in my pocket. That morning I offered to leave the MP-5 with Admiral Grafton, but he said he had an old pistol in a drawer upstairs, and that would do.

Needless to say, I had no desire to run into anyone on this hike—uniformed police looking for someone to drag off to the clink would be bad, but camouflaged killers packing submachine guns lying in wait for anyone happening by could be fatal. I had seen those shrub-heads in their ghillie suits, so I knew how hard they would be to see. I took my time, kept the eyeballs going as I slipped through the woods, watching every step, every twig and branch, alert for anything that shouldn't be there.

Believe me, I was sweating. One mistake and I was a goner. I knew it and was doing this anyway, which says more about my testosterone level than it does about my intelligence. Actually I didn't have a choice—I was already in this mess up to my eyes. Marching into a police station and making accusations looked as attractive as a weekend of Russian roulette. Anyone who could reach into a CIA safe house to whack someone could get to me in any hole I picked.

When I got my first glimpse of Dorsey's house, I got down on my belly and lay still for the longest time, looking and listening. Finally I crawled to where I could see better.

Lying there on the forest floor felt good. I didn't want to move. Thought of a dozen reasons why I shouldn't.

Finally I forced myself to do it. Stood and walked to the side of the house and pressed my back to it. Worked my way along the house to the corner and eased one eye around it.

The body of the man I had killed wasn't there.

After a careful look all about, I walked over to where he had fallen and examined the grass and earth. The rain had almost washed out the bloodstains. I eased on over to the spot where I did the shooting. Sure enough, someone had picked up the spent cartridges. I have good eyes, and I looked—and didn't see a single one.

Dorsey had given me a key to the kitchen door. Although she was a rich single woman living alone on the edge of one of the nation's worst sewers—Washington, D.C.—Dorsey didn't have a burglar alarm in her house. Go figure. I pushed the door open, then stood waiting for the hail of bullets that didn't come. Finally I sucked it up and eased through the doorway.

I kept my shooter at waist height, leveled and ready, my finger off the trigger, and moved as slowly and silently as I could.

I was dripping wet with perspiration. If they didn't hear me coming, they would smell me.

The body was gone from the foyer. Dorsey was going to be

pleased to hear that whoever had carted off the corpse had also cleaned up the blood. I couldn't see any stains.

I did the whole house room by room, floor by floor. Only when I was absolutely certain that I was the only person in the building did I go back to Dorsey's room and root through her drawer for a passport. She gave me a list of things she wanted, makeup, dresses, swimsuits, and such, but I didn't bother. She was wearing her Rolex and had her purse with credit cards, checkbook, and address book—she was ready to fly. Young women in her socioeconomic group didn't wear jewels, which meant hard times ahead for guys like me if that trend didn't change. Maybe I *should* stay with the government.

I locked the place up when I left, took a last look around, then set off back through the woods.

Who removed the bodies?

CHAPTER FIFTEEN

I headed for the Baltimore–Washington International Airport to meet Jake Grafton and Dorsey O'Shea. Traffic was heavy, as usual. Five million people in the metro area, and every one of them is out on the highway driving his own car when I want to get from here to there.

I was nervous—probably still tense from sneaking around the Rancho Dorsey trying to get shot. I didn't think the police had hauled away those two bodies. If they had, they would have put up a mile of yellow crime scene tape and still be there taking pictures, lifting prints, and doing all that stuff the CSI dudes do on television.

Musing on these weighty matters, I became aware of a white sedan three cars back that was keeping pace with me as I rolled east on the interstate. The other cars darted in and out of traffic and occasionally peeled off to dart down an exit, but this guy stayed back, matching my speed.

Tommy, don't be paranoid.

I allowed my speed to creep up another five mph, just for grins. The guy didn't fall back.

I changed lanes, slid over behind a semi, which meant I had to slow down about five. The sedan changed lanes, too, yet he fell back a little when two cars cut in between us. They took the next exit, which left about fifty yards between me and the white sedan.

Just when I was starting to get worried, the white sedan dropped down the next exit, leaving me to motor along with my random companions. No one else seemed to be following.

It was late in the afternoon when I parked on the top deck of the close-in parking at BWI and rode the elevator down to the pedestrian bridge that led to the terminal. I was sitting in the lobby across from the airline counter when I saw them approaching. I handed Dorsey her passport.

"That's all you brought?"

"I don't believe in overpacking. That other stuff would just weigh you down."

She bit her lip and tossed her hair. Grafton and I stood in line with her to present her passport and get her seat assignment. I told her that someone had removed the bodies from her house, and she nodded. I felt like the Roto-Rooter man telling her the drain was open.

After she did her business at the counter, Grafton and I escorted her to the security gate.

"You didn't bring that thirty-eight along, did you?" I asked, trying to be casual. It would be just my luck for her to be arrested for smuggling a shooter through security. She would spill her guts in a heartbeat. Grafton and I wouldn't make it out of the terminal.

"I left it at the admiral's house," she said distractedly.

She shook Grafton's hand, then held out a hand to me. "Goodbye, Tommy."

Well, what the hey! I wasn't the guy for her, and she certainly wasn't the gal for me. "So long, kid," I told her, shaking her hand.

She went through the metal detector okay, but the security personnel decided to search her handbag. Probably thought they saw a nail clipper in there.

"Think they'll send someone to Europe after her?" I said, referring to the hit men.

"Not a chance in a thousand," Grafton said. "Don't worry about it."

The security guard finished stirring through Dorsey's purse and returned it to her. She picked up her carry-on bag and joined the throng going down the concourse. She didn't look back.

"Let's get out of here," Jake Grafton said, turning away.

As we walked I told him, "On the way over here I thought someone followed me from Dorsey's, then they turned off."

He walked on, didn't say anything.

"Maybe I'm being an idiot."

That's when Grafton spoke. "If they're any good they have three or four cars on you. No one follows along as if he's on a leash."

"If they were watching Dorsey's place, they may be on me."

"The bodies were gone from Dorsey's?"

"Whoever took them away did a pretty good job cleaning up," I told the admiral. "No visible blood inside and just traces on the lawn, which will wash away in the next rain shower."

Grafton gave me his cell number and the telephone number at the beach house. I wrote them on my left hand. "We'll go separately," he added. "Don't go to the beach house unless you are absolutely sure you are not being followed."

As we rode up in the parking garage elevator, I asked, "What do you think, Admiral?" Perhaps I wanted some reassurance. If so, I didn't get it.

"I think you and Kelly are in a hell of a tight spot," Jake Grafton said, then got off the elevator on the fourth floor. The guy sugarcoats everything.

Up on the roof I stepped out of the elevator and hiked a foot up on the nearest trash can. While I worked on my shoelace I scanned the scene, looking for . . . I wasn't sure what. People were getting into and out of cars, walking toward the elevator carrying and pulling luggage; several cars were cruising around looking for spaces near the elevator, even though the entire back row of the area was empty.

I plopped my foot down and headed for my car, trying to hike along as if I hadn't a care in the world except crabgrass in the lawn.

It's just that I had this itch between my shoulders, one I couldn't reach to scratch. Maybe it was nothing, but it was there, this feeling that things were going badly wrong and there was nothing I could do to stop it. I wanted to shout, "I don't know *anything!* Erlanger doesn't know *anything!* Leave us alone."

Leave us alone—isn't that the prayer that defines our age? We ask it of the government, the people with causes, the addicted, the crazy, and the starving and oppressed in all those third-world sewers. Leave us alone! Let us live our comfortable little lives without your burdens. Please.

That's the prayer, and no one ever listens.

I didn't see Grafton's car—I wasn't really looking. I was trying to figure out if anyone was following me. Crazy how your mind works—it seemed as if everyone was following, everyone was looking at me, everyone was going where I wanted to go. When I changed lanes, the car behind me did, too. The guy or gal in front drifted over into the right lane for the off-ramp to Annapolis and the Bay Bridge.

Paranoid. I was paranoid. Relax, I told myself. Drive safely and normally and relax, for Christ's sake.

So I was doing just that, motoring along at the speed limit like the good citizen I will never be, when a police cruiser changed lanes to get behind me. I glanced at him in the rearview mirror and saw that he was using his handheld mike.

Oh, great!

I checked the other mirrors, looked at the terrain, thought about flooring the accelerator to try to outrun the guy. In this heap?

After a minute and a half the dome light of the cruiser illuminated and began flashing. I drove for another twenty seconds or so, then put on the blinker and began slowing. I pulled off the road, stopped, put the car in park, and lowered the driver's window.

I watched the cop walk toward me in the driver's side window. Mid- to late twenties, cool wraparound shades, a buzz cut, wearing a bulletproof vest under his uniform shirt. I'd opened my mouth to ask him what the problem was when he drew his service pistol and said loudly, "Out of the car, slow and easy, hands where I can see them."

"Officer, what—"

"Out! Now!"

I took my left hand off the wheel, unlatched the door. He backed off just enough to let me open it. I did so, then got out.

He had the pistol leveled in a two-handed combat stance. "Take two steps toward the front of the car, turn toward the hood, and put your hands on it. Now!"

This guy was spring-loaded to shoot. Since I had no choice, I did as he said. "What's this all about, officer?"

"The computer says your car is stolen, sir. Please cooperate and we'll get this all straightened out."

He got too close and I could have knocked the pistol away and decked him, but I didn't. Ten seconds later, when he kicked my feet aft and deftly pulled the automatic from behind my belt, I wished I had. My opportunity was gone by then, of course.

"On the ground. Lie on your face."

If he got those cuffs on me, I was dead meat, with a life expectancy that could be measured in hours. The heck of it was I didn't want to hurt or kill him.

As he snapped one of the cuffs around my left wrist, I rolled hard into him. He fell, grunted as he hit the ground.

I was all over him, fighting him for the pistol, which I knocked out of his hand. It went skidding under the car. He was young, strong, and desperate, probably sure I was going to kill him. All those years of rock climbing and working out had given me tremendous strength in the upper body, and believe me, I needed it then. We rolled around on the ground, grunting and cursing, each of us trying to subdue the other as traffic roared by on the interstate.

There was no way around it—at the first opportunity I popped him in the jaw as hard as I could hit. Stunned, semiconscious, he relaxed, and I leaped up.

The radio was squawking, something about backup help being minutes away. My young fool hadn't waited; if I had been a killer he would more than likely be dead. He didn't know that, though, and probably never would.

I couldn't leave him lying beside the road to be run over, so I picked him up bodily and tossed him in the back seat of the cruiser. I threw his pistol in with him and retrieved mine from where he dropped it. Then I grabbed the key from the ignition and threw it as far as I could. I was sprinting for my car when two unmarked sedans skidded to a halt, one behind the cruiser and one in front of my heap. The drivers and passengers came boiling out of the cars. There were four of them in civilian clothes, and they came on a dead run with drawn weapons.

"Freeze!" the man in front roared, his weapon leveled at my belt buckle.

It wasn't as if I had a lot of options. I lifted my hands. One of the men dashed in and snapped the dangling cuff around my other wrist, then two of them hustled me into their car. Behind me I heard a shot.

One of them got behind the wheel, and the other jumped into the passenger seat. In seconds we were rolling.

"You fucking assholes!" I roared. "For the love of fucking Christ! You people didn't have to shoot that cop!"

The guy in the passenger seat turned and slapped me in the face with his pistol, which threw me sideways and stunned me.

When I managed to get back to a sitting position, he stuck his pistol in my face and snarled, "I want the address where Kelly Erlanger is hiding, and I want it now."

"Or what? You'll kill me like you did that cop? Stick it up your ass!"

He whacked me again with the pistol and I passed out.

"He spoke to me today in Russian," Basil Jarrett said to Linda Fiocchi as they ate dinner. They and Mikhail Goncharov were sitting at the small round dining table in the cabin by the Greenbrier eating trout fillets that Jarrett had cooked in a pan over an open fire. Goncharov held his knife and fork in the European manner and ate with gusto.

Goncharov's glass was empty, so Jarrett poured him another glass of wine, then refilled his and Fiocchi's glasses. That killed the bottle.

"He seems to have regained his appetite," Fiocchi said wryly. Goncharov was working on his third fillet.

A few minutes later she said, "He never sleeps for more than an hour, then he wakes up talking and thrashing. Nightmares, I think. He wakes me up every time."

"So how did a man who speaks only an eastern European language get out here in the heart of the Allegheny Mountains?"

"I don't know."

Jarrett helped himself to another fillet. He was hungry, too. "I've been thinking about it all afternoon. Your guess is as good as mine."

Goncharov finished his fish and his wine, smiled at his hosts, then wrapped himself in his blanket and lay down near the stove. He went to sleep while Jarrett and Fiocchi sipped coffee. The first nightmare came fifteen minutes after he drifted off. The room he was in was afire, he was choking on smoke, men were shooting . . .

When I came to, the guy in the passenger seat was using a cell phone as we rolled along an interstate choked with traffic. I was leaning back against the seat, slumped toward the right door, with my hands cuffed in front of me. I took two deep breaths, waited a few seconds for my head to clear.

Nobody needed to tell me I was in real trouble. Obviously these guys had followed me from Dorsey's to the airport. They must not have had enough men to follow both me and Grafton, so they had stayed on me. They were going to get Jake Grafton's name and address from me one way or another, then they were going to kill me. I knew it and they knew it. They weren't going to ask nicely or appeal to my better nature. Even if I managed to say nothing before they beat me senseless or shot me to death, I had Grafton's telephone numbers written on my left hand in ink. They would find them eventually.

I thought about this, took one more deep breath, then reached forward, put my hands over the passenger's head, and jerked backward with the cuffs against his neck while I rammed my head into the back of his. I used every ounce of strength I had . . . and heard his neck snap.

The driver glanced sideways at me, his eyes as big as saucers, the car swerving dangerously. I didn't take the time to get my hands away from the dead man—I smashed the driver in the head with my left elbow as hard as I could.

The car caromed off a semi that was in the fast lane, then headed toward the right side of the highway. I managed to get my hands free of the corpse and got both hands around the driver's neck as we shot off the highway, went up an embankment, and smashed head-on into a huge aluminum light pole. My death grip on the driver's neck kept him from going through the windshield, because in the excitement he hadn't put on his seat belt.

The seat back broke loose, and I wound up jammed against the dashboard, the driver half under me. I still had a good grip on his neck, so I used it. Strangled him like a chicken.

Every window in the car was broken; glass pebbles covered everything. In the silence that followed the crash I could hear imperious noises coming from the cell phone. It was on the floor. I could hear it but couldn't see it. I jammed my hands down there, groped all over, and a miracle happened. I found it.

I said into it, "I'm coming to get you, motherfucker," then snapped the mouthpiece shut and put it in my pocket. The car doors were too twisted to open, so I went out through a window and headed for the woods at a hell-bent trot. The thought that there was another car full of these dudes roaming around someplace had finally occurred to me. Mom always said I had a one-track mind.

Deep in the trees, well away from the lights of the cars whizzing by on the highway, I stopped to empty my stomach. When the spasms stopped, I leaned against a tree for a while. I couldn't stop shaking. Too much adrenaline, I guess.

Personally, I think this James Bond gig is vastly overrated.

In the evening gloom under the trees I was temporarily safe. That calmed me down. When my stomach was under control and I had caught my breath, I managed to get a small pick set out of my pocket. It looked like a jackknife and contained three picks mounted as if they were blades and a torsion wrench that could be removed from the handle. I selected the pick I wanted by feel and inserted it like a shim under the teeth of the left cuff, jamming open the ratchet that held the cuff. Ten seconds later I had the right one off and tossed the cuffs away.

As the shock and adrenaline wore off, I realized I was oozing blood from the side of my face. Not from where the guy slugged me with the pistol, but from whacking my head on the dashboard when the car hit the pole.

I saw the flashing lights of a police car slow and stop by the wreck. Time to boogie. Ten minutes later I came out of the woods in a residential neighborhood. Walked between two houses and found myself on a paved street. Several cars passed me from time to time. An hour passed before I finally came to a convenience store with a pay telephone mounted on the outside wall of the building. I had been reading street signs, so I knew roughly where I was. I called Jake Grafton on his cell phone and told him what had happened in as few words as possible and gave him my location.

"Move down the street about fifty yards and wait for me," he said.

I went inside the store, cleaned myself up in the men's room, and bought a bottle of water. Fifty yards down the street was a hardware store with a van parked beside it. I sat down between the van and the building to wait. It was completely dark by then so I was difficult to see.

I was massaging my sore wrists six minutes later when a police cruiser drove by. The officer slowed to a crawl passing the convenience store, then turned right and went up the street into the subdivision I had walked out of a few minutes earlier.

CHAPTER SIXTEEN

When Jake Grafton rolled up, I walked briskly to his car. As we left the area we passed another cop on the way in. I motormouthed, told Grafton everything I could think of about the death of the traffic cop and the two men I killed. When I ran down, he asked for the cell phone I had taken from the car. I passed it over and he pocketed it.

"They must have had a beacon in the car you were driving," he mused. "When you went to the airport, they didn't have enough people to keep you under constant observation. They must have been pulling in people while we put Dorsey on the plane."

"If they had made you," I remarked, "they would have left me dead beside that cop and be on their way to the beach house."

"Or my apartment in Rosslyn," Grafton muttered darkly.

I could tell by the way he gripped the wheel that he was really pissed. Which made me feel better. Honestly. I knew Jake Grafton. He had been the military's go-to guy for a lot of years. I had seen him in action a couple of times myself, and let me tell you, he was the very first man I'd pick when we were choosing sides for anything, be it softball, hand grenades, or World War III.

I must have fallen asleep—in fact, I was exhausted—because I awoke with a start when the car stopped. We were sitting in front of his beach house.

"I want you to go inside and get something to eat, then get some sleep. I'll keep an eye on things tonight."

I opened the car door and lifted a leg out. It took effort. I was stiff and sore. "Aren't you coming in?"

"In a little while. I have some telephone calls to make."

He drove off while I climbed the steps.

Callie Grafton and Kelly Erlanger looked shocked when they saw me. They were alone in the house—the admiral had dropped his mother at the nursing home where she resided on his way to the airport with Dorsey. Tonight Callie made me a bowl of soup and a sandwich while I took a shower. When I undressed, glass pebbles cascaded onto the floor.

Looking in the mirror, I had to admit, I was a sight. I had two red, swollen, inflamed welts on my face where that guy had smacked me with his pistol. The one along my jaw had bled some. My hands, face, and neck were scratched in dozens of places from flying glass. I also raked some tiny glass fragments from my hair. No wonder I had itched.

Erlanger sat beside me while I ate. Callie hovered nearby. I summarized my adventures, omitting the parts I didn't even want to think about.

The admiral returned later and took the downstairs couch. He had an old 1911 Colt, which he put on the floor by the couch. The MP-5 was gone—it was in the trunk of the car I had abandoned on the freeway. I inherited the little .38 Dorsey had used to defend her castle. I made sure it was loaded and put it in my pocket. I was getting stiffer by the minute and had to work to climb the stairs to the guest room.

Erlanger was already in the bed with the lights out.

I undressed and crawled between the sheets. She snuggled right up to me. She was warm, smelled good, and settled right in with her head on my shoulder.

I thought the romantic side of our relationship could use some work, but I was too tired that evening. That must have been the last thought I had before I dropped off to sleep.

When I awoke the next morning the sky was gray. Kelly was still asleep, curled up against me, so I started to get out of bed. She wrapped her arms around me and gave me a big hug, then let me go.

I wasn't sure what it all meant. Maybe we were working up to something, or maybe I was a substitute for the teddy bear she had left at home.

Jake Grafton already had coffee made when I came downstairs. He was sitting at the kitchen table, his Colt lying beside his coffee cup, watching a cable news show.

"You're making quite a splash in law enforcement circles," he said, eyeing me to gauge my reaction. "Somehow you're the bad guy who killed all those folks at the safe house, murdered those guys at Willie Varner's, and, I have no doubt, killed that cop and those two other guys last night."

What a way to start a morning! "Well, I figured that," I admitted. "Death row, here I come. I'm going to have to get a hobby, something I can do in a small room." At least the coffee was hot. "Sarah Houston tell you all that?"

He nodded. "She was full of information. One of the tidbits I thought would interest you is the fact that Mikhail Goncharov may still be alive."

I decided the coffee needed milk and got some from the refrigerator. Then I sat down across the table from him.

"The safe house is in Pocahontas County, West Virginia. The county sheriff passed a set of prints to the FBI that they have been unable to identify," he continued. "The powers that be haven't made the connection between these prints and the people at the CIA safe house, but Sarah thought it curious. The prints of every person the CIA had there last Monday were on file. Goncharov's prints weren't, of course, because he has never been fingerprinted by any American agency."

"Where is this person?"

"You'll need to see the sheriff."

"Have they put me in the crime computer?"

"Yes. On a national security warrant, arrest and hold. No charges listed."

"Terrific." I thought about that for a moment, then said, "If it is Goncharov, he only speaks Russian."

"Take Erlanger with you."

We discussed it. He agreed to rent a car this morning for me so it wouldn't appear in my name if anyone ran a computer check at the car rental companies.

"What about the phone number on that cell phone I gave you last night?"

"Belongs to a Dell Royston."

I wasn't as stiff this morning as I was last night, but I still felt as if I had been run over by something big. I worked on the soreness in my shoulders as I tried to recall where I had heard Royston's name.

"Wasn't he some big weenie at the White House?"

Grafton nodded a fraction of a millimeter. "He was chief of staff," he said. "Left three months ago. He's running the president's reelection campaign, I think."

"He was the asshole I shouted at on the telephone last night?"

"Perhaps."

"Those numbers I gave you from those other two phones?"

"Don't think you'd recognize the names. Sarah is working them."

"So what's going down?"

Grafton got up and went to the window. He looked out, then turned to face me and leaned against the sink. "Something was in those files. Six of the seven suitcases may be ashes, yet Goncharov may remember something."

"Sorry," I said, shaking my head. "I'm not quite following you."

"Something that connects someone at the White House with the KGB or the foreign intelligence service."

I stared. "Naw."

"Someone really high up in government," Jake Grafton said, tugging at his nose. "Someone with the power to make things happen."

"Erlanger translated some of the stuff in the intact suitcase for me," I told him. "The files she saw have code names for every agent, every contact. The code names are rarely identified, and they are always in capital letters, BLUE, FOREST, MAX, something like that."

"Callie translated several files for me last night," he replied. "I doubt that any of these files on domestic dirty tricks by the KGB are what we are after. The file we want would have been a First Chief Directorate file, foreign intelligence. If we had the file, even with code names, if we knew the time and place well enough, we could make a shrewd guess who the agent might be."

He threw up his hands. "But we don't have the file. I want you to find Goncharov, talk to him, see what he knows. There may have been a foreign intelligence file that piqued his interest."

"Kelly said he hasn't had access to KGB files since he retired, like four years ago," I objected. "This administration wasn't in office when he made his notes."

Grafton shrugged.

"What should I do with him when I find him?"

"Talk to him, then call me. I may have an epiphany or two by then."

"Yes, sir."

I don't know why, but that word "sir" often slips out when I am talking to Grafton. My mind was elsewhere. *The president of the United States.* Holy . . . ! I hadn't fallen in a hole, I'd fallen in the Grand Canyon.

I poured a cup of coffee for Kelly and took it upstairs. I kissed her cheek, and she rolled over and kissed me back. When she smelled the coffee her eyes popped open.

"We're going to West Virginia this morning," I told her as she sipped. "Mikhail Goncharov may be alive."

Her eyes widened and she stared at me.

"I'll need you to translate."

"Alive? How could that be?"

"I don't know. The county sheriff sent an unidentified person's prints to the FBI. The prints may be from Goncharov. We're going to see if we can beat the crowd, interview him first."

"How did you learn about this?" she said, and had another sip of coffee.

"Jake Grafton knows people." I wasn't about to tell her about Zelda Hudson/Sarah Houston, who was supposed to be in prison. "They tell him things."

"Let's hope his friends are right," she said. She put the coffee cup on the bedside table and moved my hand under her pajama top.

When we got downstairs Callie was fixing breakfast while watching *Good Morning America,* which was doing a segment on the political convention that was starting a week from Monday in New York. The president had the nomination sewed up, of course, but had yet to name his vice-presidential running mate. The current VP had decided for health reasons not to run again.

The reporters had an inside tip, they said, that the VP nominee would be a woman.

By the time Callie and Kelly had had their breakfast, the admiral was back with the rental car. He tossed me the keys, and Kelly and I were soon on our way. Just to be on the safe side, he passed me the Colt .45.

Jake Grafton stood on the porch of the beach house and watched Tommy Carmellini and Kelly Erlanger disappear around the corner onto the highway. He went back into the house and climbed the stairs. Carmellini's and Erlanger's bags, such as they were, were still in the guest room. He searched everything in both bags, then spent an hour going through the room and adjoining bath.

When he finished he found Callie—she was on the screened-in porch reading files—and asked her to accompany him.

"Where are we going?" she asked.

"The library. I need something to read."

The first place I stopped was a bank in suburban Virginia. I left Erlanger in the car. Even though we made love that morning, I took the ignition key with me—maybe I'm not as good in bed as I hope I am. Inside, I visited a safe deposit box I kept at that bank under another name. I won't bore you with details, but back when I was in the burglary business, I opened a couple boxes in the metro area under fake names and kept IDs and cash in them, just in case. We live in interesting times. I also had boxes in Los Angeles and New York, but that's another story.

When I walked out of the bank, my new name was Zack Robert Winston Jr., and I had a driver's license and a couple credit cards to prove it. The credit cards were no good, but they looked nice. I also had three thousand in cash in my pocket.

I told Kelly about my new name. She looked at me sort of funny. "Who are you, anyway?"

"A civil servant, the same as you."

"Right."

She eyed me one more time, then got busy with the radio. By the time we hit I-66 westbound, she had a jazz station tuned in.

I rolled down my window and stuck my elbow out. After all that had happened, who would have believed I made this same drive this past Tuesday? Erlanger apparently felt the same way. She didn't say much, merely listened to the music, lost in her own thoughts.

To tell the truth, I was kinda hoping she was thinking about our romantic interlude earlier that morning. I sure was. I liked the way she kissed. Some girls sort of peck at you, but Kelly opened her mouth and glued herself to you. Just thinking about her kisses made me sigh. I glanced at her from time to time, but she was looking out her window. She had mentioned a boyfriend at one time; I drove along wondering about the state of that relationship. Was I merely a warm body who happened to be available?

By the time we reached Strasburg it was nearly one o'clock, and we both needed a pit stop. I parked in front of the Hotel Strasburg, a ramshackle white Victorian building that looked as if it predated the Civil War. We used the facilities, then ate lunch in a period dining room with real tablecloths. The food was delicious. Kelly wasn't very talkative, so I asked about her past to get her mind off the mess we were in.

She grew up in Illinois, she said, attended Vassar and majored in Russian. She was recruited by the CIA while she was still in college, decided that she could make more money working for the government than she could in a company trying to do business in Russia, and took the plunge. That was six years ago.

"Was it a good decision?" I asked.

"Well, if I was working in the private sector I would probably be doing a lot of traveling, translating, negotiating, and whatnot. With airline travel being what it is these days, I'd just as soon stay home. With the agency I don't travel at all except on vacations. I also work on more interesting material, I suspect, than I would in the private sector."

"Going to stay with the agency?"

"My sister has been after me to resign and move to Santa Barbara. She owns a bakery. Right now that looks pretty good. Maybe, if I get out of this fix alive . . ." She gave me a wry grin. "I'm just a paper-pusher. People killing each other—I hate it. It's against everything I believe."

"Yeah," I said.

The grin disappeared and she said with conviction, "The world shouldn't be like this."

Platitudes usually stop a conversation, and that one did. Some of the air leaked out of my romantic balloon.

We skipped dessert, slurped down coffee, and hit the road again.

Sarah Houston—her name was prominently displayed on the access pass that hung on a chain around her neck—was one of the upper-level wizards at the NSA. She spent most of her days with mathematicians creating codes for the U.S. government and military and breaking foreign government and military codes, and those of corporations, criminals, terrorists, and private citizens around the world who thought their communications should remain private. It was heady, cerebral stuff, and the people engaged in it were among the smartest in the world. Mental chess was a common office pastime, with moves being shouted across the room or exchanged in the corridors or break room. The former Zelda Hudson fit right in—she usually had three or four games going at any one time and won her share.

Yet her specialty was computers, so she regularly consulted with people who were designing state-of-the art software for data-mining other people's networks. She paid a call that Saturday morning on a man in one of those offices and flirted with him a little while they discussed the problem he was currently working on. He had designs on Sarah's body and was campaigning for a weeklong vacation together in August on Fire Island. When he mentioned the trip again this morning, she told him she was thinking about it.

As it happened, they were sitting in his secure space when the telephone rang and a colleague asked him to come to his office for a minute. He said sure, hung up the phone, and glanced at Sarah, who was looking at a printout of software code.

"I'll be right back," he said, and left her alone in the office with his computer logged onto the network. It was a violation of the security regs, but what the hey, they were friends, with a relationship that he wanted to go someplace special. And it was Saturday, with only a few people in the office.

The instant the door closed behind him, Sarah attacked the keyboard. Two minutes later she was back reading the printout, and she was still at it when her friend returned, five and a half minutes after he departed.

"Sorry about that," he said. "He needed the help now."

"No problem," Sarah Houston said, and smiled.

When she got back to her office after lunch she logged onto the network. She now had access to the deepest data-mining and surveillance capabilities of the NSA network, which she had granted herself. She began tapping in telephone numbers. The first three numbers she typed belonged to Dell Royston: his home, office, and cell.

CHAPTER SEVENTEEN

The sheriff's office was in a substantial, three-story cut-stone courthouse with oak floors. There wasn't a soul in sight that Saturday. Our footsteps echoed on the wide staircase and in the empty hallways. When we found the door labeled SHERIFF, I half expected the door to be locked and was relieved when the knob turned in my hand.

The sheriff was a pleasantly plump fellow pushing sixty. He had his feet under his desk and was working on a report when the receptionist showed us into his office. I stuck out my hand. "Zack Winston, Sheriff, like the cigarettes. Sorry to bother you, but we're looking for my girlfriend's uncle, who might be lost in this county."

The sheriff looked at me and raised his eyebrows. "You lost him?"

"He wandered away from our camper when we made a pit stop in the northern part of the county last week." I looked at Kelly. "It was last Tuesday, wasn't it?"

She nodded.

"And you waited until now to report a missing person."

I looked sheepish. "We've been looking, believe me, and just haven't found him. We didn't even know he was missing until we got to Staunton and stopped for gas. He must have got out of the back of the camper at one of our stops."

"He got a name?"

"Mikhail Goncharov." We had to give his real name. He might have given it to someone, although if the sheriff knew it when he sent in the prints for an ID, it seemed to me he would have said so.

"That sounds Russian."

I nodded. "He's a refugee. Russian is the only language he speaks. He's here visiting Kelly." I introduced her to the sheriff.

"You both look like Americans to me," the sheriff said dubiously. "Either of you speak Russian?"

Kelly reeled off a sentence or two. It sounded Russian as hell to me, and it must have to the sheriff, too, because he relaxed and smiled.

"We may have found him. Something wrong with him?"

"Alzheimer's," I said, nodding.

"Well, he's staying with a couple up in the northern end of the county at a fishing camp along the river, fellow named Jarrett. Go to Durbin and take the river road south about six miles. His name is on the mailbox."

"Thanks," I said enthusiastically. "We've been so damned worried, let me tell you." I pulled out a hankie and mopped my brow. "I feel like such a fool."

"Glad to be of service. But the person you should thank is Linda Fiocchi, Jarrett's girlfriend. She took him in, wanted him to remain as their guest while we tried to identify him. Aren't many people that kind in this world."

We talked about that for a bit. The sheriff really admired Jarrett's girlfriend. "Fiocchi's a class act. I think she thought he might be an illegal," the sheriff said, watching my face.

Kelly laid her hand on my arm. "Let's go get him now," she said to me, and smiled warmly at the sheriff. "I can't thank you enough."

"Wish you had put in a missing persons report," the sheriff said.

"He's scared to death of the police," I explained. "Living in Russia . . . perhaps you can understand. We were afraid that if he saw a policeman . . ."

"Seemed fine to me when I saw him," the sheriff said gruffly, giving me the eye. If he wanted to think Goncharov was an illegal, that was okay with me. In the abstract everyone wants the immigration laws enforced, but when the problem is reduced to real people, few people are ready to send them back to whatever they fled to get here. This county sheriff in the heart of the Alleghenies had not called the INS, and I doubted that he would.

We thanked him profusely and made a hasty departure.

I stopped at a filling station to call Jake Grafton. As I was using the pay phone, Kelly went to the ladies'.

"The sheriff says he's staying at a fishing camp on the river, near the facility," I told the admiral when he answered. "Sounds to me as if he's no more than five or six miles from it."

The admiral grunted. "Dell Royston has been busy today. He's made over a half dozen calls in the last two hours, a couple of them to numbers that you gave me. Something's up. Don't know what."

"Okay."

"Better find Goncharov and get him out of there."

"Yes, sir."

"Be careful, Tommy."

"I will," I said, and hung up. Kelly was still in the ladies' when I went into the men's.

It seemed to me that there was no time to lose. Whatever Royston might be up to, it couldn't be good. And the sheriff might just decide to drive up for a visit with Goncharov and his niece; I wanted to be gone before he arrived.

I waited in the car for Kelly. Why do women always take so long in the john?

At least now we had a name for Mr. Big. That was an accomplishment in itself. I remember reading about Royston these last few years. He had become a public personality while on the White House staff. I seemed to recall that he had spent most of his career as a political consultant, one of those professional cynics who creates an image for whatever politician signs up to foot the bill. The president was Royston's horse.

How in the world had Royston gotten into the KGB's files, if indeed he had? Did he analyze American politics for them or write op-ed pieces for *Pravda*? Perhaps the KGB paid him to write op-ed pieces for the *New York Times* and *Washington Post*. The second possibility seemed more likely, but I was just guessing. Or had the Russians paid him to kill Goncharov before he could talk?

Kelly came out of the restroom and plopped herself into the passenger seat of the rental car, and I fed gas.

"You did good in the sheriff's office," I said as we rolled out of town.

"Hope he bought it," she muttered, and half turned in her seat to look behind us. I glanced in the rearview mirror. No cruiser yet.

Durbin was almost forty miles from the county seat along curvy two-lane roads. The state highway department was busy, and that delayed us, and we got stuck behind several logging trucks that we had to follow for miles before we found places to pass. The drive took over an hour.

The river road out of Durbin was well marked. After I had gone a couple of miles along it, I began slowing at every mailbox, reading the names. It's been my experience that most folks aren't very good with distance estimations. Four-point-two miles south of Durbin, there it was. Basil Jarrett. I drove up the driveway, turned the car, and parked it pointing toward the exit.

"Same story?" Kelly asked.

"More or less. Let me do the talking."

A woman opened the door before I had a chance to knock. "I heard you drive up," she said.

"We're looking for my girlfriend's Russian uncle. The sheriff said he might be here."

"Oh, my God! I'm so glad you came! I'm Linda Fiocchi. Please come in, please! I think he's here." She held out a hand to Kelly, who took it. "You must have been so worried!"

"We've been frantic. He walked away from our camper on Tuesday, and we didn't know where he left us."

"We haven't been able to talk to him."

"He speaks only Russian."

"He's only spoken once, just a few words that we didn't understand. He seems . . . ill."

Kelly nodded knowingly, released Fiocchi's hand and used a finger to swab a tear.

I was surprised. Kelly Erlanger was an excellent actress. It was something to think about.

This sob scene would go on for quite a while if I didn't move things along, so I gestured toward the overhead loft and asked, "Is Unc taking a nap?"

"Oh, no. He and Basil are fishing."

"Ahh . . ."

"He loves to fish. He took a rod and went out at first light."

"He always loved it," Kelly said, nodding.

"We came downriver from Durbin and didn't see them," I said. "Are they farther down the river?"

"I don't know which way they went."

"I'll go look for them," I said. Kelly took a step toward the door, but Fiocchi wanted to talk about her houseguest. "He's such a nice man, but he's having severe nightmares. I thought he might have amnesia."

I left Kelly to keep Fiocchi occupied and took the car. The road ran right along the river, so the car should be quicker than walking. For some reason that I couldn't put my finger on, I had this nagging suspicion that time was running out.

I found the two men several miles down the river. They were wearing hip boots and working the shallows with fly rods. From Erlanger's description of Goncharov, I recognized him immediately. The other man, Basil Jarrett, was about forty, and he, too, knew how to fish. I watched them from the bank for several minutes before Jarrett looked in my direction. I waved for him to come over to the bank. He continued to cast while he worked his way toward me.

When he was twenty feet or so away, I said, loudly enough to be heard over the gurgle of the river, "Having any luck?"

"Did pretty well this morning. We released them all, of course. Slow right now. They'll start biting again when the sun goes behind the mountain."

"My name is Winston," I said. "I'm here to talk to your guest."

Jarrett began cranking in his line. "Do you know him?" he asked, glancing at me.

"Yes."

"He doesn't seem to speak English."

"He's Russian."

"How did you know where to find him?"

"The sheriff told us. I brought his niece. She speaks Russian."

Jarrett waded ashore. He shook my hand, sized me up. "You're not Russian."

"I'm as American as Freedom Fries. His niece is my girlfriend."

He handed me his rod, then waded out to where Goncharov was standing. He pointed at me, made gestures that Goncharov should come in. Goncharov reeled in his line, then waded over and climbed the bank. He was agile enough and surefooted. However, his face reflected little curiosity.

"Do you speak Russian?" Jarrett asked.

"Not a word. Jump in the car and we'll run up to your place."

After I turned the car around, I gave Jarrett the spiel I gave the sheriff, about losing the uncle from a camper last week. Jarrett listened in silence, asked no questions. "We were certainly worried," I said, summing up. "The sheriff said we owed you and Ms. Fiocchi a real debt for taking him in."

"Forget it. He's obviously a sick man. Least we could do."

As we drove he asked me where I lived, what I did, etc. I was chattering along, all lies, of course, when we rounded the curve just below the entrance to his cabin. There was a car turning into the driveway. I applied the brakes, stopped the car.

"Who is that?" Jarrett asked. "Someone with you?"

"No." Even as I said it, the car stopped, backed out onto the road, and started toward us. Then it stopped.

Oh, shit. I had been lucky as hell against these guys up to now, but there is a limit.

A man got out of the passenger's side, then reached back into the car. He pulled out a weapon, then began walking toward us. He was about fifty yards or so away, but even at that range I recognized the gun. MP-5. He kept walking, apparently trying to make up his mind.

The weapon held me mesmerized. If he lifted it, though, we were out of options.

"Get down," I shouted at Jarrett, and jammed the accelerator to the floor. As I did I reached over, grabbed his head, and pulled him down toward me.

The dude with the submachine gun leveled it, then hesitated as he faced the car rocketing toward him, faster and faster.

He squeezed off a burst that shattered the windshield—the glass just exploded—then he tried to jump out of the way. Too late.

I hit him a hell of a lick; he flew backward through the air and landed in the road.

I felt two thumps as I ran over him. I jammed on the brakes. The car slid toward the other car, coming to rest parallel to it, with the right front fenders almost touching. I slammed the transmission into park and bailed as I jerked Grafton's Colt from behind my back.

The other car shot backward, its tires screaming. The driver opened his door, stuck his head out, and spun the rear end into Jarrett's drive. I squeezed one off and missed him. The car ripped forward before I could get off another shot. It accelerated away toward Durbin, its engine howling.

I glanced behind me at the guy I had run over. He wasn't moving.

But was that the only car? Or had another vehicle preceded it up the driveway?

I ran to the driveway and looked. Couldn't see the cabin. Ran up the road fifty yards until I could. No other cars.

I lowered the hammer on the Colt and put it back behind my belt, then walked down the drive to my car. Jarrett was kneeling beside the man on the road.

He looked up at me as I approached, his face drained of color. "He's dead," he said.

"I hope so," I replied curtly. I didn't have any juice to waste on one of those sons of bitches. I looked in the car. Goncharov was sitting in the back seat, carefully picking pebbles of glass from his clothes.

I walked around to the dead man. He was a mess. The car had rolled across his abdomen, bursting it. I intended to search him, but when I saw the corpse I lost interest.

Jarrett turned his back to the corpse. He retched once but nothing came up. With his hands on his knees, he took some deep breaths. He looked at me. "Your face is bleeding," he said.

My cheek and forehead were burning. I explored them with my hand. Yep. I extracted several glass shards.

"Lucky that glass didn't hit your eyes," Jarrett said.

My eyes? The bastard was shooting at my head! I picked up the MP-5. It didn't appear damaged. I could see the gleam of spent brass lying in the road. "I'm fucking shot with luck," I muttered. "Just hope to Christ I haven't used it all up."

"Who the hell are you?" Jarrett asked.

That's when I violated every security reg the agency had. "Name's Tommy Carmellini, Mr. Jarrett. I'm with the CIA." I pulled my Langley building pass from my hip pocket and handed it to him. My honest phiz and real name were encased in plastic.

Jarrett examined the plastic and matched the picture to my face. As he returned the pass he tittered nervously. "A spy for the CIA!"

"I work for the agency, but I am not a spy. Get a grip, Mr. Jarrett."

He rubbed his face with both hands.

I nodded toward the car. "That is Mikhail Goncharov. He's a Russian defector, used to work for the KGB."

Jarrett gestured at the corpse. The Russian was squatting beside the body, examining the face. "Who's he?"

"Some son of a bitch who came here to kill Goncharov and the rest of us. Tough shit for him. Come on, let's go up to the house."

Goncharov had managed to get his hands covered with blood. He stared at the blood, rubbed his fingers together to feel it, smelled it.

"Jesus Christ," Jarrett said. "This man is coming apart."

Jarrett took off his shirt, and we cleaned up Goncharov as best we could, then put him in the back seat of the car.

"You want to wait here at the cabin while I go get the sheriff?" Jarrett asked me as he inspected his bloody shirt.

"No. I've got to collect the translator and get the hell out of here with Goncharov before more of these guys come back. I strongly suggest you and Fiocchi do the same."

"What about your car?"

I looked at the heap. No windshield and a pretty good dent in the grill and hood. Thank heaven Grafton was on the rental agreement—he was going to have to explain this one to the rental agency. I wondered if he had paid extra for the liability waiver.

"We're going to have to trade cars, Mr. Jarrett. My agency will reimburse you for any loss. You drive this heap into town and call the sheriff. Maybe he can get you a ride home."

That is what we did. Thirty minutes later Kelly Erlanger, Goncharov, and I were crossing Allegheny Mountain, heading east. I kept the MP-5.

We left the squashed guy lying in the road beside the river.

CHAPTER **EIGHTEEN**

As we motored over the mountains toward the Shenandoah Valley, Kelly Erlanger sat in back chattering in Russian with Mikhail Goncharov. She was getting a lot of monosyllable answers, so I knew it wasn't going well, though in truth I had other things on my mind and wasn't paying much attention.

Unless I missed my guess, the sheriff was going to be mighty unhappy after talking with Basil Jarrett. He had a violent death on his hands, a mutilated corpse spread all over a county road, and the guy who did the killing and mutilating was leaving the jurisdiction as fast as he could reasonably go. Jarrett would probably tell the sheriff it had been self-defense all the way—the shot-up rental car sort of spoke for itself—but the sheriff would undoubtedly want to question me. Especially when he heard my real name and ran it on the crime computer. When you're famous, everyone wants to talk with you.

My CIA pass had been enough for Jarrett, so he acquiesced in my "borrowing" his vehicle, but in truth he didn't have a lot of choice. I had just intentionally run over one man and whanged away at another with a pistol. I hadn't threatened him, though. Still if the sheriff started talking about Jarrett being an accessory after the fact, he might remember that he had been intimidated.

That was the way I reasoned it out, so I was on the back roads in case the sheriff called his Virginia colleagues. I planned to drive county roads only, no highways or interstates, all the way to Delaware. I planned to avoid Washington by crossing the mouth of the Chesapeake at Norfolk. I figured we would be lucky to get to Grafton's by daylight tomorrow.

Then there was the little matter of how the killers learned Goncharov was at Jarrett's. Perhaps the FBI fingerprint inquiry had come to their attention, but if so, why didn't the sheriff mention that someone had called, asking the whereabouts of Kelly's lost uncle?

No, something was out of kilter here. The killers weren't far behind us, and that fact would have to be explained.

I glanced over my shoulder at Kelly.

Naw. She wouldn't have called someone, would she?

She had been in that burning house, trying to save that suitcase full of files. The man Dorsey shot in her foyer had been after her.

So what was going on?

Grafton?

Or Sarah Houston? He had called her, asked for her help. She had been the source of the FBI fingerprint tip—I was certain of that. Who else had she told?

Houston. The more I thought about it, the more I was sure she was the leak.

She had never liked me, and she was too slippery by a bunch. When she was Zelda Hudson I had seduced and drugged her. We took fingerprints and eye prints and used them to get access to a place she claimed she worked in London. But she had conned us. She didn't work there; she wanted me to get into that computer and see the names of top American military officers, which I did.

Then she stole a submarine and tried to get rich in the chaos that followed. After she went to prison she never liked me much, even when I helped get her out. Women are so ungrateful.

And she was slippery. Too smart, untrustworthy, greedy, and a little light in the ethics department.

Of course, people said the same about me. Still, I concluded, Sarah was probably the one who dropped the dime on us.

Ten minutes later I changed my mind. Grafton kept her out of prison after the warhead hunt, and she owed him. Somewhere, I thought, in that hard little heart of hers was a smidgen of loyalty.

By the time we reached the Shenandoah, I decided I was over-thinking this. Sarah Houston was the logical suspect.

After a while I noticed that there was no more conversation going on in the back seat. Kelly was watching the road, so she saw me looking at her in the rearview mirror.

"He doesn't remember anything," she said flatly.

"You're kidding."

"He doesn't even know his name."

"Amnesia?"

"Seems so."

I adjusted the rearview mirror so I could observe Goncharov. He ignored my scrutiny, or perhaps he was unaware of it.

Amnesia? Or faking memory loss? After all, he had only seen Kelly for a few hours a week ago, and he didn't know me from Adam. Maybe faking memory loss was a last-ditch ploy when he had no other weapons left.

Yet I didn't believe he was faking. I'd seen the expression on his face a few hours ago as he rubbed blood on his hands.

I smeared a man all over the road, we're running from the

law—again!—and all we had to show for it was a Russian with amnesia who couldn't remember his own name!

It had been dark for several hours when we rolled into Richmond. We were hungry, and the SUV was low on gas. I found a gas station with a pay phone on the wall and fueled the vehicle. While Goncharov and Erlanger were making pit stops, I used the phone to call Jake Grafton.

The telephone rang and rang. That spooked me. What if they got to Jake and Callie? Killed them? I broke out into a sweat.

I hung up after fifteen rings and got my quarters back, then fed them into the box again and dialed his cell phone.

On the third ring, he answered. The relief hit me like a hammer, and I found myself leaning against the wall to remain upright.

I explained what had happened in West Virginia as quickly as I could, all the while looking around to ensure I wasn't overheard. Summing up, I said, "Kelly says this guy can't remember anything. He doesn't even know his own name. He might be faking, of course, though I doubt it. You should have seen him with his hands in blood—holy damn, that was scary."

Jake Grafton was silent for a long moment before he said, "He's been through a lot."

"Who hasn't?" I replied bitterly. I was thoroughly sick of the whole damned mess. Probably shouldn't have been thinking of myself, but I was. At that point I was ready to jump a banana boat to Central America and never come back.

"And Sarah Houston probably sold us out," I added savagely. "Somebody did, sure as hell."

"Somebody," he echoed.

"You and Callie had better clear out of your house. Those bastards may come for you, same as they did Sal Pulzelli and Willie

Varner. I saw Pulzelli after they finished butchering him. Believe me, that is one tough way to go."

"Seventy-five cents, please." The female operator cut in.

I fed in more quarters.

"Do you have enough money for a motel room?" Grafton asked.

"Yeah."

"Get one room with two beds. I'll meet you tomorrow at the house around noon."

"Okay."

"Watch yourself, Tommy. There're some real heavy people involved with this. And there are more guys out there with guns."

I knew that. No matter how many cockroaches you kill, you never get them all. Still, it was nice of him to express his concern. "Yes, sir," I said, and hung up.

We wound up with a room in a motel near the Norfolk airport, just a couple miles from the causeway that led across the Chesapeake to eastern Maryland and Delaware. It was nearly midnight by the time we got inside and locked the door.

While Kelly was in the bathroom, I got my first chance to observe Mikhail Goncharov closely. He was wearing old clothes a size too large; Linda Fiocchi said she had gotten the duds from a neighbor near Durbin. He was unshaven, balding, perhaps thirty pounds overweight, yet looked reasonably healthy. He looked tense, tired, wary. On those occasions when he met my eyes he didn't smile, didn't even acknowledge me.

The former KGB archivist must know as much as any man alive about the evil that men do to one another. Considering all he had been through—somehow evading the assassins who came to murder him, the assassins who did murder his wife—he must be aware that someone important wanted him completely, totally dead. After a career in the KGB, he well knew how ruthlessly efficient merciless men can be—he had been reading their reports for twenty-plus years. The thought that that someone also wanted my worthless hide tacked up on the wall certainly gave me goose bumps. If he really had amnesia he wouldn't be worried about that. Perhaps he just felt lost in a world where nothing was familiar.

After we had all done our evening ablutions and I turned the lights out, Kelly crawled into bed with me.

"What do you think?" I asked, referring to our roommate.

"I think he's a sick man," she said, and pushed her bottom into my side. "And I think I'm damned tired of chasing around the country with you playing hide-and-seek with every scumbag on the East Coast."

"Does get old after a while."

"I think we ought to hold a press conference and tell the world everything we know. Then we'll be off their list."

"Sure," I said. If only life were so simple.

Goncharov began snoring. Before long Kelly relaxed completely and also began breathing deeply. I lay there a while longer tossing and turning, thinking about how that guy looked lying in the road with his guts smeared all over. Before the sons of bitches got me, I would sure like to get even with whomever sold us out. Torture would be good, something that made them really suffer.

I was past torture and pondering some real iffy stuff to do to them when Goncharov stopped snoring. I heard his teeth grinding, then he said something. He was talking in Russian, I believe, but his words were just sounds to me. I could hear him tossing in the bed, flailing around. He awoke with a start.

Kelly also woke up.

"What's wrong?" she whispered.

"Goncharov was having a nightmare."

It was a long night. He woke up four more times that night with nightmares. Once he was awake for two hours before he drifted off again. I couldn't sleep either. The image of the car rushing toward the man shooting at us played itself over and over in my mind. The image of his face in that split second before the car hit him wouldn't go away. I tried to think of other things and couldn't.

At one point during the night I found myself in the bathroom staring at my face in the mirror. The overhead light threw the planes of my face and my eyes into deep shadow. The man in the mirror looked as if he had been dead for weeks.

I was more than a little worried the next morning, which was Sunday, as we motored north toward Delaware. We had breakfast at a truck stop, and I called Grafton again from the pay phone on the wall by the register.

"Your passenger still have amnesia?" he asked.

"So Kelly says. He isn't sleeping well. Nightmares kept him awake last night."

"We'll see you for lunch."

"Admiral, what if those dudes show up at your place?"

"I don't think they will."

"Sir, I don't mean to sound paranoid, but—"

"Come on up here, Tommy. Callie wants to talk to your passenger." He said it in a way that didn't leave much room for discussion. That's what happens when you spend too many years wearing a uniform.

"Yes, sir," I said cheerfully. As if I had a choice.

Sipping coffee and watching trucks come and go through the window, I wondered if maybe the bad guys were already at Grafton's. What if they were holding the admiral and his wife as hostages at gunpoint, waiting for me to bring Goncharov to them so they could make his loss of memory permanent?

Seated across from me in the booth, the archivist picked at an omelet. He had maybe four real bites before he quit. I wasn't hungry either. Kelly Erlanger was doing all right by a couple of eggs, though.

I sort of eyed her as she ate, wondered where she and I were going with this sleeping-together thing. You'd think if she had the hots for me she would show it a little more. Except for that one passionate moment—which had been terrific, by the way—our relationship was more like sister and brother than boy-girl. I confess, I felt as if I was eight years old, sleeping with a neighborhood kid in a tent in the back yard.

I wondered if indeed she did have a boyfriend. Would that explain it?

When we were fed and coffeed, I paid the bill and we rolled north. No one followed us that I could see.

As we drove along, I explored my options. Should I park somewhere and sneak over to Grafton's, just to see who was really there? Or should I drive in bold as brass and hope no one started shooting?

His voice sounded tired, yet . . . confident. In control.

I knew that voice. Jake Grafton was a fierce, determined warrior. If he had been held at gunpoint, I decided, he wouldn't have told me to come there, even if it cost him his life. After they shot Goncharov, they would kill him and Callie, and he knew that. Jake Grafton would spit in their faces.

Kelly's thoughts were running in the same vein mine were, but she didn't know Jake Grafton. "What if someone is waiting at Grafton's for us?" she asked.

"I know the admiral pretty well. They aren't. Trust me."

She didn't say anything else. Mikhail Goncharov sat in the rear seat looking out the window. His face was a study. I wished I could read his thoughts!

I drove into Grafton's parking area and parked beside his vehicle. His car was there; no one else's. We got out, walked up on the porch, and rang the bell. He opened the door, held it wide. "Come in." He didn't smile.

I let Kelly go first, then Goncharov. Callie was right there. She spoke to Goncharov in Russian, then led him into the kitchen.

I plopped down on the admiral's couch. "Hell of a trip," I said. Kelly sat down beside me.

Jake pulled a pistol from his pocket and sat in a chair opposite. He laid the pistol in his lap. "Ms. Erlanger, why do you think those men showed up at Jarrett's cabin a half hour after you did?"

Kelly shook her head. "I have no idea."

"Surely you've thought about it."

"Obviously they learned where he was. Perhaps they are monitoring telephone calls, perhaps the FBI called the sheriff and he told them where Goncharov could be found, perhaps the sheriff called the FBI and told them we were there inquiring for Goncharov. Those are the possibilities. I don't know how it went down."

"There's another possibility," Grafton said. "You called someone after you learned where Goncharov was."

She stared at him.

"She has a telephone, Tommy. Find it."

I held out my hand in front of her. She didn't take her eyes off Grafton.

"The easy way or the hard way," I said.

She turned to me. "You don't believe him, do you? You and I have been together for days. I didn't make any telephone calls."

"You went to the bathroom alone. Give me the phone."

She leaped from the couch and bounded for the front door. I tackled her. She tried to scratch my eyes out and managed to draw blood on a cheek.

After a bit of a scuffle, I had her under control. She had taken her purse with her as she charged the door, so I passed it to Grafton, then patted her down.

"I've got it," Grafton said, removing her cell phone from the purse.

Erlanger ceased to struggle.

"Get off me," she said through gritted teeth.

"Right." I picked her up, threw her onto the couch.

She ignored me. She was watching Grafton like a hawk as he pushed buttons on the telephone. "She called Royston," he said, then lowered the phone and leveled his gaze at Erlanger.

"Want to tell me about it?"

"What's there to tell?"

"You help us get Royston and whoever is behind him, the prosecutors may go easy on you. Multiple counts of murder could put you in prison for a long, long time. For all I know, they still have the death penalty in West Virginia."

"You can't prove anything."

"I'm beginning to see it," I said softly, not taking my eyes off her. "I've been wondering how they learned Goncharov was at the safe house."

"Erlanger was the leak," Grafton said. He sounded tired. "She told them as soon as she received the translation assignment."

The scene at the safe house replayed itself in my mind. "When I went into that burning house, she was busy burning the files, not trying to save them," I said, thinking aloud.

"Your presence was an unexpected complication," Grafton mused. "You were a witness they couldn't seem to kill. Worse, you shot back. They didn't expect that. Erlanger didn't want to die, so she went along until she could steal your car. When you showed up at her house that night, she was going through the only surviving files, trying to determine if the important one was there." He addressed her. "Were you thinking of blackmailing someone?"

She didn't turn a hair. "You can't prove anything."

Jake Grafton pulled a file from the bookcase behind him. "You didn't look hard enough."

Now an expression crossed her face, and it was ugly.

"You can't prove anything," she insisted.

Grafton tucked the file back in the bookcase between two books. "Tell Royston I have it," he said.

"You're letting me go?"

Grafton shrugged. "It's your choice. Cooperate for a reduced sentence or rabbit off to Royston and take the consequences."

She stood. I stepped aside. She walked to the door, opened it and went out without even glancing at me.

Okay, okay. So I don't know shit about women.

"She'll tell them you have that file."

He grunted.

"What's in it?"

He pulled it out of the bookcase again, passed it to me. I opened it. Inside was a section of the *Washington Post*.

"There's nothing here." That comment just slipped out.

Grafton shrugged. "Royston will suspect that's the case. But he won't know, will he?"

"Is that why you let her go, to tell them about the file?"

"They'll listen to what she has to say, then kill her."

That comment stunned me. He said it without sorrow or remorse. And he was right. Kelly Erlanger had to die.

"Why didn't you tell her that?"

He levered himself from his chair. When he was upright he looked straight into my eyes. "I made her an offer—cooperate or suffer the consequences. Death is the consequence. She won't believe it, though, until they point a pistol at her head and pull the trigger."

CHAPTER NINETEEN

W hat is your name?" Callie Grafton asked in Russian.
The archivist sat silently at the kitchen table, apparently thinking about the question. "I don't know," he said at last.

"What kind of work do you do?"

"I don't know," he repeated hoarsely. A sheen of perspiration appeared on his forehead.

"Are you married?" Callie sat beside him and held his hand.

"I don't know?" he said, obviously bewildered.

"You came to my house a few moments ago with two people. Do you remember their names?"

"Oh, yes. The woman is Kelly. The man is Carmellini—that's an Italian name, I think."

"Is he Italian?"

The Russian pondered it. "He might be," he said at last. "But perhaps not."

"If he is not an Italian, what nationality is he?"

Her questions didn't trouble Mikhail Goncharov, but they obviously confused him. She thought it interesting that he was not curious about the answers to her questions, merely surprised and troubled that he didn't know them.

"Are you thirsty or hungry?" she asked finally. And for the first time she got an affirmative answer.

After Kelly Erlanger took a powder, Jake Grafton wandered into the kitchen. I trailed along behind. Mikhail Goncharov was sitting at the small round table drinking soda pop and Callie was fixing sandwiches.

"Would you like a sandwich, Tommy?" she asked. "Ham and Swiss or tuna salad?" She didn't remark on the commotion in the living room, nor did she ask if Kelly Erlanger was going to join us. The thought occurred to me that Callie Grafton was as tough as her husband.

"Ham and Swiss, please." I dropped into a chair beside Goncharov. "Is it amnesia?"

"He doesn't seem to remember anything," she said without turning around.

"I've heard these hard-drive crashes are sometimes temporary," I said, just to make conversation. "Of course, what I know about it wouldn't fill a thimble." There was a napkin dispenser on the table. I helped myself to one; I used it to swab at the scratch on my cheek, which was still burning. There was a trace of blood.

Jake Grafton pulled three beers from the fridge and handed me one. It tasted great. He opened another and put it in front of Goncharov, who abandoned the soda pop and took a long swig.

After I had a couple of slurps, I said to him, "Kelly must be making a beeline for a pay phone. She might have already told them about this house. They could be here in the next five minutes."

Grafton savored a swig of beer, swallowed it, and nodded.

"Maybe I'm just a nervous Nellie, Admiral, but if they hit us here in this house, we're dead."

"I called some friends yesterday," Jake said. "They arrived this morning."

"Oh."

Callie put a sandwich in front of Goncharov and one in front of me. She had even put mustard on mine. I took a bite and worked on it a while. "Who are they?"

"Snake-eaters. There are a half dozen of them out there."

"I didn't see anyone . . . and I was looking."

"They're hard to see," he admitted. When Callie served his sandwich, he sat down beside me. "Tell me about yesterday, everything you can remember."

I was still talking when Callie took Goncharov upstairs to the guest room for a nap. He had only eaten a few bites of his sandwich.

Telling Jake Grafton everything I knew made me feel better. He asked a few questions to clarify points, but other than that, he had little to say. When I had run down and he was out of questions, I asked one. "Do you really think they'll kill her?"

"She called Dell Royston from every stop. Sarah Houston said it sounded like there was water running in the background every time. She said Goncharov had amnesia, told him where you were going, the name of the motel where you spent the night, my name, address, everything she could think of."

"Why didn't they hit us in the motel?"

"Too dangerous, too many witnesses, and Royston didn't want you killing any more of his people. Apparently they signed up for murder, not combat."

Dell Royston, a political operative at the White House. "Is Royston Mr. Big, you think?"

"That's the question," he muttered. "Let's go make some telephone calls. I'll drive. I want you to sit beside me with the MP-5 on your lap."

When we went outside to get in the car, I looked around casually. Didn't see a soul. And there were, Grafton said, six people out there right now armed to the teeth and burrowed in. Just goes to show . . .

We drove south along the beach to Ocean City. Grafton backed into a space in front of a convenience store so that I had a good view of the parking area and the street beyond. No one seemed to pay us any attention. I glanced at Grafton in the rearview mirror. He made four calls from the pay phone mounted on the exterior wall of the building, taking his time on all of them.

An older car eased to a stop near the gas pump and a couple of Mexicans got out. One went inside for a bit, then came back out and began pumping gas. The other checked the oil. On the end of the row where I sat, some kid was listening to rap on his car radio; he liked it loud, and he had every window in the car down. The Mexicans were finished with the gas and washing their windshield when two large boys on skateboards came flying down the sidewalk and across the parking area. They sat on the sidewalk sipping soft drinks from cans. Jake Grafton finished with his telephone calls and went into the store. He came out in a few minutes with a couple of fountain drinks.

When he got behind the wheel, he passed me one. As I sipped he said, "Your buddy, Willie Varner, was released from the hospital today. Going to be all right, the doctors said. Two of my friends are baby-sitting. He'll be okay, I think."

The images of Willie and Pulzelli slashed and bleeding flashed through my mind, made me feel like I was going to puke. I put the pop in the cup holder and took a very deep breath.

What causes amnesia, anyway? Do too many bad memories overload the system, cause circuit breakers to pop, drives to crash?

How close was I to a massive brain fart?

Between sips of Coke, Grafton briefed me. Sarah Houston was his spy, and she was a good one. She was monitoring the telephone numbers I had supplied, he said.

The people at the upper levels of the FBI and CIA believed that the Greenbrier safe house had been hit by Americans in the pay of the Russian foreign intelligence service. They were convinced the Russians had learned of Goncharov's defection, Grafton told me, and had moved swiftly and violently to plug the leak and minimize the damage. Someone had sold the boys in the corner office the theory that I was one of the American traitors. At the insistence of the White House, the incident was being treated as a national security matter, which was the reason nothing had leaked to the press. The relations between the Western world and Russia were too important to be jeopardized by the shenanigans of intelligence professionals—you could almost close your eyes and hear the White House advisers arguing that point in the Oval Office.

"The people at the top apparently don't know about Royston, about his involvement," Grafton said, thinking as he talked. "Sarah says he has five people still working for him that he talks to via cell phone on a regular basis. If Kelly confirms that Goncharov is at the beach house, he may send them to hit it."

I already knew that, and he knew I did, but this was Jake Grafton, thinking aloud. He had that habit. Then everyone knew precisely what was on his mind and could predict the directions in which he might go. I thought it a solid leadership technique. All the listener had to do was keep his mouth shut. That's what I was thinking when he asked conversationally, without a change of tone, "What do you want to do about Dell Royston?"

I glanced at him, wondered what was going through his mind.

"Cut his nuts off and feed 'em to him," I replied curtly.

Grafton drummed a few licks on the steering wheel with his fingers. "He's going to be in New York next week for the convention. Could you bug the hotel where he'll be staying?"

Apparently he was fishing to see if I still wanted to do the warrior thing. Well, I was good for a little while longer, I told myself, which was a real whopper. I never squander my best lies on other people—I tell them to myself.

"Sure," I said aloud. We discussed it, the equipment I'd need, when and where I could get it, and when the best time would be to do the jobs.

"Hang loose," he said, and got out of the vehicle to make some more telephone calls.

The dude who liked rap got his ride under way. In the relative silence that followed his departure I could hear a baseball game playing on the convenience store's sound system.

Right then I would have traded a couple months' pay to be sitting in a ballpark watching a game, smack in the middle of the American summer with nothing on my mind but the possibility of another beer. Oh well, a man can dream.

Mikhail Goncharov awoke from a nightmare bathed in sweat. He had been in one of the cells in the Lubyanka being interrogated by five experts. They wanted him to confess to something, though now, awake, he couldn't remember exactly what it was. He lay in bed thinking about the dream as it slowly faded.

Finally he began to take notice of his surroundings. Nothing seemed familiar.

Then he remembered the lady who fixed the sandwiches and brought him to this room.

The window was open—he could feel a warm breeze. Hear traffic noises. And . . . something rhythmical, a deep sound. He listened intently. The steady sound that repeated was . . . surf! He was near the ocean. He could hear surf pounding on a beach.

Galvanized, he rose from the bed, realized he was not wearing shoes, and automatically searched until he found them, then put them on.

In the room downstairs he found the woman. She was wearing shorts and a blouse. "I can hear surf. Where is the beach?"

"Come," she said. "We will go together."

Before he saw the ocean, he could smell it, salty and clean. Crossing the dune on the boardwalk, he saw the sun glinting on the swells. He stopped and stared as the warm sea wind played with his shirt and trousers. Before him was the beach. Beyond it the great blue ocean stretched away until it met the sky.

The woman waited patiently, watching him. He was so absorbed in the scene before him that he was unaware of her scrutiny.

There had once been an ocean and a beach . . . and another woman. He could see her face, remember how her hand felt, how the cold water felt as it swirled about his feet. Her name—it was right there on the edge of his memory, just out of reach, but her face was plain, her smile, her eyes staring at him, her hand on his cheek.

The memory was there, but the specifics wouldn't come. It was in the past, but not too long ago; he sensed that. And it was not here. Not this beach.

With a jolt he again became aware of the presence of the woman beside him. She was kind—he could see that. Very kind, with warm, intelligent eyes.

Despite the wind, the sun was warm on his skin. He took a deep breath, let the smell of the sea fill his lungs and head.

"Who—?"

He had to clear his throat, then he began again. "Who am I?"

At a kiosk in an Ocean City mall, I bought two cell phones and signed up for service while Jake Grafton watched from a bench fifty feet away. New phones on an account that couldn't be tied to me or Grafton would allow us to communicate with each other and Sarah with more confidence. Sarah thought she had a handle on the telephones the CIA and FBI were monitoring, but . . .

I used my Zack Winston driver's license as my ID and paid cash, gave the fake address on the driver's license as the address for the account. They would close the account eventually, but I had a couple months to use the phones before that happened. "So you live in Virginia?" the girl manning the kiosk asked. She was a trim brunette with a great smile.

"Uh-huh."

"Get down this way often?"

"Now and then."

I got the impression that I could get a date with her if I worked at it a while. She whacked away on her computer for a minute, then put the telephones in a bag and handed them to me.

"You're good to go," she said, flashing that smile again. "You should charge the phones overnight before you use them. The batteries will last longer."

I liked the way she grinned and brushed the hair back from her forehead. She didn't look a bit like Kelly Erlanger. Or Dorsey O'Shea, come to think of it. I gave her my absolute best smile and strolled away with my purchases in a bag.

Callie was out on the beach with Mikhail Goncharov when we returned to Grafton's beach house. I wandered upstairs and took a good look out each of the upstairs windows. Were the Russians pulling Royston's strings? I knew a little about him, Grafton knew a little, and we talked about what we knew on the way home.

Dell Royston was one of the president's political loyalists who had been with him all the way. He was a Washington lawyer who had only practiced for a few years when he hitched his wagon to the future president's—his new law partner's—rising star. He campaigned, directed door-to-door canvassing efforts, shook hands, raised money, did it all on the president's first run for statewide office, as the state's attorney general. He had been there on the unsuccessful first run for governor, and the successful second one. The Senate had followed, then the first run for the presidential nomination—which had failed—and the second run, which won the nomination and the presidency.

There were people who supposedly knew about these things who said Royston was the real political brains in the administration. Others said the president would never have won the White House without him. Who knew the truth of that? In any event, the president didn't seem inclined to change horses at this date, which was why Royston had resigned as chief of staff and was now heading the reelection committee.

Neither Grafton nor I had ever been in the same room with the man, much less met him. To me he was merely a figure on the evening news or a black-and-white photo in the newspaper. Looking out the windows of Grafton's house, I tried to recall his image. Balding, with chiseled features and no extra fat.

Personally I didn't think the Russians were pulling Royston's strings. His loyalties were on the public record for all to see.

So, was it the president? Did he order the trigger pulled on all those people at the safe house, on Willie Varner and Sal Pulzelli?

We were going to find out. One way or the other.

I remembered how casually Grafton asked the question, "What do you want to do about Royston?" Royston might know politics and politicians, but he had never met a warrior like Jake Grafton. I would bet my bottom dollar on that. I was equally willing to wager that he was going to meet the admiral before he got a whole lot older.

From the upstairs guest bedroom I saw Callie and Goncharov coming across the dune on the boardwalk. Callie had her sweater pulled around her, with strands of her hair adrift in the breeze.

She was a fine figure of a woman, every bit as tough as Grafton. I wondered if I would ever meet a woman like that.

Well, to tell the truth, I did once. A Russian named Anna. If I ever got the chance, that was the woman I wanted for a wife. If.

When Callie and Goncharov neared the house, I went downstairs to open the door for them.

CHAPTER TWENTY

I got a great night's sleep that Sunday night and awoke at dawn feeling much better. Didn't think about the mess I was in for almost ten minutes.

I thought about slipping out for a run along the beach, then thought how easy it would be for some asshole to shoot me as I jogged along, got mad at myself and went anyway.

Grafton went out for a paper, and Callie and I made it last, passing the sections back and forth. I even spent twenty minutes with the classified ads. Maybe this summer I ought to sell the Mercedes and get another ride. It was pleasant thinking about the prospect.

Goncharov wandered the house, sat for hours on the porch, occasionally flipped though magazines. He looked haggard, haunted. He wasn't sleeping much, that I knew. Callie took him for a walk along the beach. She spent most of Monday evening chatting with him in Russian, but she did most of the talking.

We still had Basil Jarrett's SUV parked in front of the Grafton bungalow, and that had to change. Driving it didn't seem like a red-hot idea either. Sarah had told Jake Grafton that the vehicle was listed on the national crime computer as stolen, with an armed and dangerous driver. Presumably that was me. At least I was appreciated.

About ten that night I borrowed Grafton's car, which was not yet on the crime computer, and sallied forth. Four hours later I was cruising by Kelly Erlanger's place in suburban Washington. My old Mercedes coupe was still in her driveway. There didn't seem to be anyone watching the house, although the car was also in the crime computer as stolen. I would have bet my last dollar that there was a radio beacon in the car so it could be tracked.

It would have to sit there until this mess was resolved or I signed it over to criminal defense lawyers as partial payment on a fee.

Thirty minutes later I stopped by a huge apartment building in Silver Spring. Sitting in the parking lot, I called Sarah Houston at her office in the NSA. She was there tonight and answered on the first ring.

"It's me," I said.

"You going to kill somebody, Carmellini?"

"Don't say things like that over the telephone."

"They are questioning everyone about you, trying to establish a link between you and the Russians, although they don't come right out and say it."

"Subtle guys."

"I had to admit I know you. Really took me down a notch professionally, I can tell you. I told them you like caviar."

"If I go down the slide, I'll know who to thank. I'm going to call him now."

WAGES OF SIN — 203

"Okay."

I closed the phone, which I had borrowed from Grafton, and dialed the number.

A sleepy baritone answered. "You had better not be a telephone solicitor," he growled.

"I'm selling male sexual enhancers. We're counting on you for a big order. Sorry about the pun."

There was a moment of silence, then he said, "That you, Tommy?"

"No names."

"You asshole, it's . . . it's damn near three o'fucking clock in the morning. Couldn't this have waited until daylight?"

"This is the only time I could sign out of the sewer where I'm hiding."

"No shit. What do you want, anyway?"

"Is that any way to talk to your boss?"

"What do you want, asshole?"

"I want to talk to you. I'm in front of your building. Buzz me in."

Silence. "And to think I could be getting a good night's sleep in a hole in Afghanistan right this very minute." He hung up. I'll admit, Joe Billy Dunn had a rough personality. The system sent me a holy warrior from Delta Force that I was supposed to transform into a cool, collected, accomplished burglar.

The door clicked, and I entered the lobby. I stood there with the cell phone in my hand, waiting. If Joe Billy Dunn called the cops or CIA security, Sarah would immediately call me. I checked my watch. A long minute passed, then another.

Maybe Dunn couldn't find the telephone number. Then again, how hard is it to dial 911?

After three minutes I called Sarah.

"Nothing," she said.

"Okay." I walked over to the elevator and pushed the up button.

Standing outside Dunn's door, I patted the Grafton's Colt for reassurance. I didn't want to shoot him for any reason under the sun. I needed his help. On the other hand, if he had a gun in his hand when he opened the door, this might get a little dicey.

Of course he did. A Beretta 9 mm. He stood back, waved me in.

"You packing?" he asked when I was in the center of the room with my hands up.

"Yeah." So much for the Mexican standoff.

"Drop it on the floor, real slow."

I did as he asked.

"Now sit on the couch."

Only when I was well away from him did he bend down to pick up my shooter. He squatted, never took his eyes off me. The Beretta looked like it was welded into his hand. Okay, maybe he was as good as the Army said he was.

"Explain to me why I shouldn't call the agency and tell them that I'm holding a traitor who sold out to the Russians at gunpoint in my apartment."

"Because you know I'm not a traitor."

"They're looking all over hell for you, Tommy. Claim you murdered a bunch of agency people in West Virginia."

"I was there. We were hit by some guys. I got a couple of the killers and got away in one piece."

He took a seat on a chair against the far wall, as far from me as possible. Although he was wearing only his underwear, there was not a sliver of doubt in my crooked mind that Joe Billy Dunn was a first-class pro who could handle anything in my limited repertoire.

I went through it, explained everything, holding nothing back. When I finished he put the pistol on the countertop and asked, "Want some coffee?"

"Sure."

"They wouldn't tell me anything at the office. Just that you were wanted and to call them immediately if I heard a peep out of you."

"Why didn't you?"

"I didn't believe a damn word of it. Not that I've known you that long, but I can't see you for cold-blooded murder. I've known a few killers. They like it; you can sense that." He went into the kitchen and began making coffee. I retrieved my shooter and took a seat in front of the counter. His pistol was lying beside my elbow.

I took my phone out and laid it beside the pistol. Sarah would call me when and if she learned someone was on the way to arrest me. If they had the place bugged and were merely listening, she wouldn't know that unless someone called a telephone she was monitoring. Every minute I was here was a risk.

If you think that I knew Joe Billy was on my side, think again. It had crossed my mind that he might be planning to pump me and dump it in person at the office tomorrow. If he did that I was screwed.

Joe Billy got his coffeemaker going, then turned and leaned on the counter. He crossed his arms. "So why haven't you called in?" he asked.

"Would you?"

He took his time before he answered. "No, I guess not."

"The president is going to be nominated for his second term next week in New York. His campaign is using the New York Hilton as their HQ. I don't know if the president will stay there, but Dell Royston, the campaign manager, surely will. We want to bug the Hilton."

Joe Billy whistled softly.

"Going to need your help to pull it off."

"We going to share a cell in the joint, or will we each get our own?"

"Hey, man, you can say no. I'm in this to my eyes, but you aren't. You don't want to dive in, I understand."

He busied himself with cups and milk from the fridge, then poured us coffee. Only when we were both sipping did he say, "What do you want me to do?"

"I need bugs and transmitters and a truck."

"Have to steal it."

I nodded, sipped some coffee. It was too acidic for my taste, but I drank it anyway.

"You know what I heard? When I got assigned to your division? Someone said you were a jewel thief before you were recruited for the CIA."

I let that one go by without comment.

"There was also a rumor that you were a suspect in the murder of a microbiology professor a couple of years ago."

"Jesus!" I roared. "What watercooler have you been hanging out at?"

"Never end a sentence with a preposition."

". . . Hanging out at, asshole?"

"Much better," Joe Billy said. "I deserve that, I suppose. Okay. I'll get you the stuff. Shouldn't be too hard—just gin up a fake work order and put it though the system, then pick everything up at the warehouse."

"How come?"

"You remind me of my older brother."

"Who is?"

"Dead. Killed by a suicider in Iraq."

"Okay." I didn't ask any more questions. I guess I didn't want to know. I gave him the specifics of what we needed and my cell phone number, shook hands, and left.

At some level you just have to trust people, yet when the stakes are large, it's damned hard.

I took the elevator down.

As the door opened at the bottom I started through it—and found myself staring at the muzzle of a silenced pistol. The silencer looked as big as a sausage, but the hole in the middle made it all business.

The man holding the pistol pushed it at me, and I stepped backward. He climbed on the elevator and glanced at the buttons, then pushed the top one.

He was about forty, of medium height, reasonably fit. He grinned broadly as the door closed. "The great Carmellini. You ran over a friend of mine, then shot at me." He raised the pistol and sighted over the silencer at my head. "You don't look so god-damn tough—"

His mistake was talking when he should have been shooting. And he was too close to his victim. I lashed out with my left hand, sweeping the pistol aside, and kicked with my right foot. Got him in the balls.

The pistol popped as he crumpled. I grabbed the weapon with both hands and ripped it out of his hands. Then I kicked him again, this time in the stomach. The third kick, in the neck, crushed his larynx.

He convulsed. With both hands around his throat, he writhed on the floor, trying to get air somehow.

I picked up the gun. Working fast, holding him down, I checked his pockets. He had a ring of keys, which I appropriated. He also had a cell phone, which I didn't think he'd need anymore.

He had pushed the button for the top floor in the building, so when the elevator stopped and the door opened, I pulled him out into the corridor, which at that hour was of course empty. He was turning blue by that time, still making little noises.

I got back into the elevator and reached for the button for the first floor.

Ah, hell.

I didn't have a pocketknife on me, nor did he. He did have a ballpoint pen, though. I rolled him over, sat on his chest, and pinned an arm with each leg. He was still bucking, with eyes bulging, so maybe there was time.

I jammed his head back and rammed the pen into his trachea below his crushed larynx. A little blood squirted around, but not much. Pulled the pen out, took it apart, then inserted the empty plastic barrel into the hole in his throat to hold it open. His eyes were riveted on me.

He sucked hard pulling in air—and getting nowhere near enough—but his color began to improve. I put his fingers on the thing so he could hold it in.

"You come here alone?" I asked.

He nodded affirmatively. His chest continued to heave up and down.

"Did you call Royston?"

A side-to-side head shake.

"If there's ever a next time, you're gonna be dead."

His eyes followed me as I went into the elevator and stayed on me until the door closed.

I inspected the pistol as the elevator hummed me down. It was an old Colt Woodsman in .22 rimfire. I popped out the magazine, checked it, then snapped it back into the weapon. The bullet that he fired in the elevator had left a tiny hole in the ceiling tile. The small spent cartridge gleamed on the floor. I picked it up and pocketed it.

So how did this guy know to wait for me to come down in the elevator? It didn't take a genius to figure out that Joe Billy Dunn's apartment was bugged and this guy had been listening. Obviously he decided to solve the Carmellini problem himself.

The lobby was empty this time. I held the pistol down beside my leg and walked out of the building. Ducking down, I scuttled over to the nearest vehicle and hunkered down beside it, then scanned the parking lot carefully.

Assuming the listeners weren't in an apartment in the building—which is where they would have been if this gig had been set up as a long-term surveillance—then they were in a vehicle parked near the building with the equipment to receive wireless transmissions from the bugs. All I had to do was find the vehicle, which was probably a van of some kind, with room for people to work a radio and computer and stay out of sight. And I didn't have much time. I was praying these guys hadn't called Royston with the news that Grafton and Carmellini were going to bug the New York Hilton. If they had, it seemed to me that Sarah Houston would have called me. If all the fancy techno-shit worked the way it was supposed to.

The parking lot was nearly full, of course, but there weren't that many vans. I began circling the building, mentally marking likely vans. There were only three that I could see.

Staying low, I went toward the closest. Nope.

I bingoed on the second one, a panel van. While it was marked with a construction company name and logo and sported Maryland plates, it had four antennas protruding from the top.

The driver's seat looked empty as I approached. It was parked nose-in to a row of cars with not much room for either door to open.

If there was someone in it, I needed to find out fast. Squatting, trying to stay below the view of the outside mirrors, I tapped on the sheet metal with the silencer and waited with my ear against it. No noise. If there was someone in there, he was being damned quiet about it.

I lifted the driver's door handle as quietly as I could, taking my time while sweat coursed off my face and soaked my shirt.

One deep breath, then another. Still no noise inside. If someone was in there, he was going to blow my silly head off when I jerked this door open.

If I hadn't pocketed a wad of keys from the guy in the elevator, I wouldn't have touched that van with anything less than a flamethrower.

No guts, no glory, they say. That isn't very inspiring, but the truth is, you can only die once. In a way, that is comforting.

I jerked the door open and waited. Nothing.

Stuck my fool head inside and looked.

Empty!

Then I upchucked on the asphalt.

I was so weak I had to bend down and grab my knees to keep blood in my head.

When I was feeling better, maybe a half minute later, I closed the door and checked the killer's keys. Found one labeled Dodge and tried it in the door. Yep.

I went back upstairs to have another little visit with Joe Billy Dunn.

A key on the killer's ring worked on the outside door of the building, which figured. That was how he got into the lobby so he could wait for me. I rode the elevator back to Dunn's floor, knocked on his door until he opened it.

I went through in a rush, sweeping him onto the floor. He was tough as nails—he went down under the rush and would have thrown me off and wound up on top if I had let him. I didn't. I jammed the silencer against his teeth and growled, "One more twitch and I'll start pulling this trigger."

That took the fight out of him, but his eyes were blazing.

"This apartment is bugged. You know about that?"

The look in his eyes was enough. He didn't know. I backed up, holding the Woodsman on him.

"Met the guy in the lobby who was listening. He was carrying this piece. His van is parked outside—it's the receiving post for your bugs."

He was eyeing the little spatters of blood on my shirt. "Who is he?"

"Didn't know him." I put the Woodsman behind my belt and looked around. "Let's find a few of the things. The van and these bugs should be everything I need."

"He dead?"

"Uh, no."

It took us six minutes to find ten bugs. They were the latest and greatest, ultrathin, transparent, and capable of being hidden darn near anywhere. Dunn gave me a plastic trash bag from under his sink, and I stowed them in it.

"We might not have gotten them all, but these will do," I said. "Thanks for your help."

"Where is the van dude?"

"On the top floor in the corridor. I gotta get going before someone finds him and calls the police."

"Okay."

"You still willing to help?"

He eyed me without enthusiasm. An affirmative answer would be proof he needed psychiatric help.

"Like when?"

"Now."

"Doing what?"

"Follow me around town while I dispose of the van, then bring me back here to get Grafton's car." I told him where and when to meet me, then left before he could say no.

I heard a siren as I drove out of the parking lot. Didn't see the patrol car or ambulance, whichever it was, and he didn't see me.

I am so lucky.

CHAPTER TWENTY-ONE

I stopped a block from Willie Varner's and looked the situation over. Two of Jake Grafton's friends were watching the place, so I knew I would be seen. The admiral had made a telephone call earlier that evening to tell them I would be coming, but you never knew.

I crawled into the back of the van and looked over the equipment. Yep, just as I thought, it was an FBI rig, complete with radio receivers, digital recording gear, signal monitors, police scanners, computer, all the goodies. I knew how to operate most of it. That came from watching experts work with the signals from bugs I planted.

Ah, me. The things you learn in a misspent life.

I locked up the government van and walked toward Varner's, thinking again what a crummy neighborhood it was. I passed a wino nipping from a bottle on a stoop and a kid on the corner waiting for a customer who needed a fix before I turned in at Varner's building. The light in the stairwell was still out. Terrific!

I clumped up the stairs, consciously making noise. The role of honest citizen doesn't come naturally to me.

As I was raising my hand to knock on the door, I heard a noise in the darkness behind me. Someone was on the stairs. "Freeze," the voice said conversationally. "I've got a gun. Don't turn around."

I stood there like the Statue of Liberty with one hand in the air.

"You got a name?"

"Carmellini."

"He's probably asleep. The door is unlocked."

"Thanks." I lowered my hand, turned the knob, and pushed the door open.

"That you, Tommy?"

"Yeah, Willie." He was propped up in his easy chair with a blanket over him.

"I couldn't sleep."

"You met those guys outside?"

"Great guys. Couple of brothers. Retired from Special Forces. One of them is always nearby."

I turned on the light by Willie's chair and looked him over. He was heavily bandaged.

"So how you doing?"

"Making it, thanks to you. That son of a bitch sliced me up pretty good. They take out some of the stitches on Thursday."

"You going to be okay?"

"Some nerve damage here and there, the doc said. Hell, I'm so sore you couldn't prove it by me."

"Sorry this happened, Willie."

"Those brothers outside—they told me you stumbled into something that should have got you killed."

"That's about it."

"You crawl though enough sewers, you're gonna meet rats," Willie said. "You gotta get outta the fuckin' sewers, Tommy."

"I'm working on it."

"I bet."

I pulled a stool over to his chair.

"Before you get comfortable," he said, "fix me a drink. You, too, if you want one."

I poured him a bourbon on the rocks and brought it over. He didn't have any trouble getting it down.

"I need a favor," I said. "Got a government van I need painted quick by someone who will do a first-class job and won't talk. Need some new plates for it, too, something not too hot. Know anyone who can help?"

Willie the Wire scowled and took another swig of whiskey. "You ain't quitting?"

"No."

He grunted, drank some more whiskey, and gave me a name and an address.

The sky was turning light when I left. I unlocked the van and drove off to find some breakfast.

Tuesday morning in Washington. July. Already it was steamy hot and the traffic was terrible, as usual, even though the worst of rush hour was over.

Joe Billy Dunn was waiting for me in a McDonald's parking lot. Cursing under my breath, I looked the area over carefully before I drove in. There was a police cruiser in the parking lot ... and through the windows I could see the two uniformed cops standing in line for Egg McMuffins or whatever. I drove through the parking lot and Joe Billy followed me.

I found the shop Willie Varner had recommended in the warehouse district of Washington, near the railroad tracks north of New York Avenue. Fortunately Willie had called ahead or they wouldn't have given me the time of day. The place had one entrance off the street, which opened into a large area filled with vehicles of all types in various stages of disassembly. I parked inside. A bald-headed fat black man in the filthy small office beside the entrance eyed me without enthusiasm through the fly-specked window.

"Hey, I'm Carmellini. Willie Varner sent me."

He removed a soggy stogie from his mouth, then said, "How is Willie these days?"

"Just got out of the hospital. Some dudes carved on him."

"Did he ever get over that stroke he had . . . what was it, five years ago?"

"He never had a stroke."

"Were you in the joint with him?"

"Nope. He and I are partners in a lock shop."

Apparently I passed the smell test, because he pried himself out of his chair and waddled out the door to look at the van. I got out of his way, stood back while he checked it over.

"What color you want it?"

"White, with commercial letters on both sides—Century Security. And a telephone number, 212 area code."

"Okay."

"Need a new VIN number on the dashboard and a set of commercial New York plates, not too warm."

He turned to face me, worked the cigar around in his mouth while he considered. His eyes narrowed. "Little blood on your shirt."

"I cut myself shaving."

He could see that was a lie, but he dropped it. "Plates will cost you another grand," he said.

"What's the total gonna be?"

"Three thousand."

"I think Willie and I got maybe twenty-five hundred in our account. I'll give you two grand. The rest we need to keep Willie eating until he can get back to work."

He took the butt out of his mouth and spit on the concrete. "The Wire says you're good people."

"He and I have been in business together since he got out of the joint. He's my best friend."

"That's what he said about you."

I shrugged.

"Okay, two grand. Cash. Pick your ride up two nights from now."

"Thanks." I held out my hand and we shook, then I handed him the key.

Joe Billy was waiting for me behind the wheel of Grafton's car. "What are they going to do to the van?" he asked as we drove away.

"Paint it. Put new plates on."

"Who do you have to know to get garage service like that?"

"The owner of a chop shop."

"Guess you have some real friends."

"A friend of mine does, anyway."

"I didn't like it when you stuck that pistol in my face. Don't do that again."

"I had to see if you knew that shooter was going to be downstairs and didn't have the time for a long discussion."

"And you decided I didn't know." That wasn't a question but a statement.

"That's about it."

"What if you thought I knew?"

I shrugged.

"You'd have killed me, wouldn't you?"

"I hadn't thought that far ahead." I hadn't told him about the incident in the elevator, but he had seen the blood.

He drove along, not saying anything, glancing at me a time or two. After a while he said, "Yeah, I guess you would." If he wanted to think that, it was fine by me.

He headed back toward his place. He had called in sick to the agency today, so he wasn't in a hurry. Me? I was tired and sleepy and had too much to think about, none of it pleasant. I began asking him questions about himself, just to make conversation.

"What did you do in the army, anyway?"

"Whatever it took to get the coon. I was in Delta Force."

"Uh-huh."

"Trooped around in Afghanistan a while with a couple guys, sitting on mountain passes, popping off al-Qaeda warriors sneaking in or out of Pakistan. Used .50-caliber sniper rifles mainly; people think they're only good to a thousand yards or so, but if you know what you're doing, you can score hits at twice that. Then did some time in northern Iraq when that went down. Worked with an agency covert team sniping, some sabotage, that sort of thing, making life uncomfortable for Saddam's boys. The agency guys sorta talked me into joining up with them, so I applied for a transfer. Decided I wasn't cut out to push paper in an office somewhere. Now look at me, stuck working for you at Langley. Can't seem to get on one of the teams."

"Something will open up. Always does."

"Yeah, and I'll be in a federal prison someplace."

"Well, you won't be dead."

"People are trying hard to stick you in one of those wooden planters. Might get splattered just being around you."

"No one lives forever."

"The good thing about Delta Force was you knew who the bad guys were. This seems a lot more iffy."

"Anybody shoots at you, shoot back."

"You didn't tell me shit, Carmellini. There's a bunch of killers chasing you and this Russian defector, and you don't know why."

"That's the truth of it."

"The agency always like this?"

"Hell, no. We normally do this crap only on weekends. This has been going on all week."

"So who is this admiral?"

I told him a little about Jake Grafton. Not a lot, but enough to explain that Grafton wasn't just another retired ship driver hanging out at the golf club in a logoed shirt sipping suds.

"So what does he think?"

"I dunno for certain. Looks to me like he's going to follow the trail anywhere it leads. Being around Grafton is always interesting."

"This little gig certainly is." Joe Billy glanced at me and grinned.

I was beyond tired. After I crossed the Bay Bridge, fatigue hit me like a hammer. Suddenly I was having trouble staying awake. I sang out loud, chewed on my lip when I couldn't think of anything to sing.

When I began to have trouble seeing, I knew I was in real trouble. At the eastern edge of one little village was an abandoned produce stand. I pulled off there, drove around back so the car would be out of sight, and killed the engine.

I must have gone to sleep instantly.

It was midafternoon when I finally awakened. I crawled out of the car and answered nature's call against a tree. Stood there swaying, still tired, looking around, trying to get all the synapses firing again.

The sun was out and there was a bit of a breeze.

Try as I might, I couldn't get the sight of that guy I left on the top floor of Dunn's building out of my mind.

Yeah, he came to kill me. Would have, too, in just a few more seconds if I had stood there flat-footed waiting for it. I knew that, but still . . . I felt dirty. Exhausted, burned out. I was living my life with the dregs of humanity, wasting the days.

If you must deal with sewer rats you must guard against becoming one. That's what Willie Varner was trying to say. He was telling me not to become a rat.

That said, I'll tell you here and now that there were a couple people I'd like to kill.

One was Dell Royston.

I doubted if Royston was the true villain of this piece. He had spent his life as somebody's dog. Probably still was.

Unfortunately I knew who owned him.

I got back in the car, fired it up, and headed for the beach.

CHAPTER TWENTY-TWO

I awoke on Jake Grafton's couch during the night, with the wind sighing around the eaves of the beach house. I could also hear the occasional car or truck passing on Route 1, which was only a block west. When the wind was from the east you heard surf; from the west, traffic. Looked at my watch. Almost 2:00 A.M. I tossed and turned a while, then gave up and went outside to sit on the stoop.

The evening news, which I had watched on television before crashing on the couch, spent half the show's airtime on the up-coming political convention at the Javits Convention Center in New York. The drama was over who would be the president's choice for VP. The president would run the convention, of course, through the head of his reelection campaign, Dell Royston, who would be dug in like a spider in a hole at the New York Hilton.

Sitting on the stoop, I tried to remember what I had seen in my two or three visits to the Hilton, certainly not New York's newest or flashiest, yet according to rumor one of the largest hotels east of Las Vegas. I had been in the lobby just last year—I think I went in to give the jewelry store a once-over—and could remember the high ceiling and plush carpets. The decor was modern, or rather, modern opulent. The architect must have been given his orders: Make it "with it" and "worth it." He had done his darndest.

I closed my eyes and enjoyed the wind playing with my hair.

I must have dropped off to sleep, because the next thing I saw was Jake Grafton passing under a streetlight, walking toward me from the beach. He came up to the stoop, stopped and looked me over, then said, "Got room for another bottom on that thing?"

"Sure, Admiral." I patted the boards beside me. "Park your fanny."

I glanced at my watch when he turned his back to sit. 2:36 A.M.

"You staying up late or getting an early start?" I asked.

"Goncharov went out for a walk. I followed along just to see that he didn't get lost. He's right behind me now."

Even as he spoke, I saw the Russian stroll into the light of the streetlamp. He walked toward us in no particular hurry, nodded when he saw us, and climbed the stairs. I gave him room. He went inside and we heard his tread on the stair.

"He's having it rough," the admiral said. "I heard him pacing the floor, then finally he went out."

"Think he'll ever be able to remember anything?" I asked.

"Maybe," he said. After a bit he added, "Then again, maybe not. His memories won't be good."

The image of Sal Pulzelli came to mind. "I know how he feels," I muttered.

Changing the subject, I asked, "How many guys are out there tonight?"

"Two. They are on twelve-hour shifts. Twelve on, twenty-four off."

"Aren't they getting tired of doing nothing?"

"Hell and high water couldn't pry them off this house. Sarah Houston said that Royston hired a guy. He uses a false name and she isn't certain, but she thinks he's Stu Vine. I passed that to them."

I whistled softly. Stu Vine! This was getting serious. I had never met the man and hoped I never would, but he was reputed to be the best killer on the planet. The CIA used him occasionally to go after agency defectors. Rumor had it that Vine was a sniper by trade, although he had been known to use a pistol, knife, and poison on occasion. Apparently he wasn't prejudiced.

"I thought he was dead," I said softly, so softly that Grafton almost missed the comment. I was slightly ashamed the words came out so muted. It was almost as if I were afraid that Stu Vine would hear me.

"Anybody could use that name," Grafton said dismissively. "Sarah could be wrong. That would be the first time in several years, but it's bound to happen someday."

"Didn't Vine get caught by the Iraqis a few years ago?"

"I've heard that," Grafton said, and waved dismissively. "Vine or anyone else—doesn't matter. They're human. Just use your head, take commonsense precautions." Apparently he thought that advice was all I needed. I hoped to Christ he was right.

He rose, said, "Good night!" and passed through the door. I heard him climbing the stairs to bed.

The nightmares began whenever Mikhail Goncharov dropped off to sleep. The scenes of horror and anxiety that ran through his mind were becoming more severe. Blood, bullets, betrayal, the smiling faces of venal men . . . He couldn't sleep for more than a few minutes before he began thrashing and awoke sweating and trembling. He climbed from the bed and sat in the stuffed chair that faced the window.

The walk on the beach hadn't helped. He was sure it wasn't this beach that he saw in his memory, the beach he and the woman had walked . . . so many times. The woman, he had loved her. But who was she?

"Who am I?" He asked the question aloud. Callie Grafton had told him his name, but it meant nothing. "Who am I?"

I was getting jumpy. After the week I'd had, perhaps it was inevitable. As I made coffee I listened to the television news on the small set the Graftons had on the kitchen counter. According to "sources," the president was going to choose a woman to run as VP for his second term. That wasn't exactly a scoop. The pundits had been speculating that he might for six months; the announcer was tossing around names when Jake Grafton came downstairs.

He mumbled something polite, then got a coffee cup from the cupboard and poured a dash of milk in it while he waited for the coffee to drip through.

"Have you figured out where you want to go from here?" he asked me.

"Yeah. Any country in the world that doesn't have an extradition treaty with the U.S. I'm thinking of leaving this afternoon, maybe go through Europe so I can have the once-in-a-lifetime thrill of watching Dorsey O'Shea and her boyfriend yacht by the French Riviera. Maybe she'll wave at me."

"I doubt it."

"So do I."

When we were both sipping coffee he said, "Why don't you drive up to New York today and check out the New York Hilton? Make sure you'll have what you need and enough help and backup."

"Okay."

We tried out our new cell phones—called each other—and that

was about it. I kept waiting for Grafton to give me some insight, but if he had some he wasn't sharing.

When I had showered and shaved and gotten myself togged out in clean clothes, I came back downstairs for a last cup of coffee. Callie and Goncharov were seated at the kitchen table nattering in Russian. I exchanged remarks with Callie—boy, what a nice lady she is—nodded at Goncharov, who actually noticed me and nodded back, then marched for the door.

I'd like to have a woman sorta like Mrs. Grafton in my life. Cool lady, classy, smart, understanding, loyal, tough, kind, considerate . . .

A woman like Anna Modin. As I drove toward Lewes and the ferry that would take me to Cape May, I thought about Anna, wondered where she was, what she was doing. I met her last year when she came to the United States to deliver a message for a Russian spymaster. The message consisted of computer disks that showed how terrorism was being financed through Cairo and who was putting up the money, but that's beside the point. Grafton put me to work as Anna's bodyguard. Best job I ever had.

Wish I still had it.

After I parked on the ferry, I abandoned the car and went upstairs to the top deck. From a vantage point near the men's room, I watched the people coming up the stairs. I was looking for a familiar face—I'd seen a few of these killer dudes—or a figure that tripped the alarms. A man, perhaps, who was looking for someone. That someone would be me.

I waited until the ferry got under way and the folks all seemed to be on the upper deck, then I went down the stairs and walked along the car deck looking to see who might be waiting in their car. Didn't see any men the right age with the hunter's look about them.

Of course, the most dangerous men were the ones you didn't see, even after they shot you.

I can't let myself get paranoid, I thought. Can't do my job if I'm frightened of everyone I see.

Nervous and unable to sit in the car, I climbed back to the observation deck. Gulls followed the ferry all the way across the mouth of the Delaware Bay to New Jersey. I watched people throw crumbs to the birds while thinking about Anna Modin.

Maybe I *should* jump a banana boat and permanently disappear. I had joked about it with Grafton that morning, but truthfully, it wasn't a bad idea. If only I knew how to get in touch with Anna, by God, you could color me gone.

Rolling up the Garden State Parkway, I called Sarah Houston. "Hey, kiddo. This is your favorite fellow."

That remark drew a long silence—well, two or three seconds, anyway.

"You know," she said wearily, "that crack is so off the wall I can't even think of a proper reply."

"I have that effect on women. It's a burden I've carried all my life. As it happens, I need your help with a project next week."

"Like what?"

"Are those bad vibes I feel coming my way?"

"Every time I hear your voice my skin starts to crawl. What do you want this time?"

"Much better. Professional, brisk, matter-of-fact. I like that. I need some help with a little project at the Hilton in the Bad Apple." I explained what I wanted.

She grumped some, but I could tell she was dying to help. You gotta know Sarah Houston pretty well to appreciate that fine, twisted mind. Unfortunately I knew her too well. I once made the mistake of suggesting that she leave her brain to medical science so they could study it after she's gone.

This morning I managed to exercise a bit more tact, so we were still on speaking terms when I broke the connection.

The humidity made New York a steam bath. My shirt was glued to me by the time I got the car parked in a commercial garage a half mile from the Hilton. I left the Colt 1911 under the seat. I was just going to have to outrun anyone who wanted to take a shot at me. However, should you think I was just another yokel tourist, in my pocket I did have my traveling assortment of lock picks in an expensive leather wallet, just in case. I hung my sports coat over my arm and set forth upon the mean streets toward the Hilton.

The avenues and cross-streets were full of taxis, cars, and trucks, the sidewalks crammed with people; vendors hawked hot dogs, pretzels, and coffee on every corner—all in all, New York was a happening place. I heard snatches of four languages in one block.

I paused on the corner across the Avenue of the Americas from the Hilton and looked it over. Taxis pulled up in front, uniformed valets opened doors and assisted with luggage . . . and there wasn't a uniformed policeman in sight. Nor did I see anyone who might be a federal officer.

What I did see were surveillance cameras mounted high on the corners of the buildings, focused downward. There were enough cameras to give complete coverage of the sidewalks all around the building, which took up an entire block on this avenue, and probably extended a hundred yards or so toward the avenue to the west. To the west of the hotel was the associated parking garage, a high-rise structure.

The building was at least forty stories tall, hermetically sealed with a glass and smooth metal exterior and windows that couldn't be opened. It wasn't much larger than those that surrounded it, so a listening post across one of the streets equipped with a laser or microwave to read window vibrations was technically possible.

I walked along the south side of the building until I came to the service entrance. It was equipped with an overhead door that was now open. Inside I could see three trucks at a loading dock. Beside the service entrance was the garage entrance, a ramp that led downward. No doubt there were four or five floors of parking under the hotel.

I continued westward along the south side of the building, found I would have to walk to the next avenue to circumnavigate the thing, and did so. On the north side was the employees' entrance. A uniformed security guard was visible through the door at a guard kiosk. I watched for thirty seconds and saw two people enter. He checked their IDs, then let them pass.

Also on the north side of the building was a secondary entrance to the lobby. I climbed the steps and passed through the circular door.

The ground floor of the hotel reeked of slightly overdone moneyed elegance, which was about as I remembered it. There was the usual piano bar and café off the main floor, a kiosk that sold theater tickets, the main reception desk, a bell stand, a newsstand selling papers and toothpaste, and the pièce de résistance, a jewelry store gaudily displaying large diamonds and other baubles for the dirty rich. I lingered and gazed enviously into the display windows, which were wired to guard against a smash and grab. A surveillance camera inside the store was aimed right at me. By studying the reflections in the windows, I could see other surveillance cameras mounted high up in the corners of the lobby.

The denizens of this zoo were about what you would expect: Arab sheikhs, corporate captains, African dictators, embezzlers from Iowa, rich dowagers, and shapely young women with artificially enhanced chests. Here and there a normal person. And, of course, an occasional lowlife like me.

After an inquiry at the bell desk, I made my way to the employment office. There I met a young Hollywood starlet waiting to be discovered. I thought it unlikely she would be discovered here, passing out employment applications in the bowels of this huge pile of steel and glass, but if I found her others might also.

"I've waited for you all my life," I told her, and gave her my most dazzling smile.

She lifted her head enough to see through her bangs as she handed me the employment application. She asked for my driver's license. I surrendered it, and she copied it on the machine behind her, giving me an excellent view of her back half.

"We've waited for you, too, Mr. Winston," she said, handing it back. "Unfortunately our corporate offices are all full just now, although in this frenzied age one never knows when there will be an opening. If you'll take a seat and complete our application, we'll call you when we need a new vice president."

I flashed the grin again and took the indicated seat.

CHAPTER TWENTY-THREE

M y name is Mikhail Goncharov," the Russian said slowly. He was sitting on the screened-in porch of the Graftons' beach house with Callie. Sections of the morning newspaper were strewn around. She had been translating news stories for the archivist, trying to get him interested in something . . . anything.

His declaration silenced her. She folded the section of newspaper she had been reading and placed it on her lap, then sat watching him, waiting for more. After a long pause he said, "I am retired from the SVR."

"Are you married?" she prompted.

He had to think about it. His bland, relaxed expression slowly disintegrated. "Bronislava. She is dead! They killed her."

He looked at his hands, looked around the porch as if seeing it for the first time. "She always wanted children but they never came. Now she's gone . . . Life leaks away grain by grain, like sand running through your fingers. Then one day there is no more left."

"I'm sorry," she said.

"Yes. Sorry." He stopped looking around and seemed to focus his gaze inward. His shoulders sagged and his chin dropped toward his chest.

Jake Grafton went with me to pick up the van. It was indeed ready, with a spiffy new paint job and professional lettering on both sides. The New York commercial plates looked nice, too. "How much trouble am I going to have with those plates?" I asked the fat man.

He took his cigar butt from his mouth and spat on the concrete. "Depends on how long you plan on driving that thing," he said. "Truck they're off of was in a wreck. It's in a Brooklyn shop for repairs and paint. Going to be there about ten more days. When it comes out, I figure somebody will start squawking."

"Good enough," I said, nodding.

I had visited the bank where Willie and I had our business account earlier that afternoon and had withdrawn some cash. Then Grafton and I went over to Willie Varner's, left him five hundred, and dropped off a six-pack.

I introduced him to Grafton, just gave Willie his name. "Most of the stitches came out this morning," Willie said. "Damn things were itching like crazy."

"That's good," I told him. "Now all you need are some tattoos to cover up the scars."

"I've had enough needles to last me, Tommy. Any more and they're gonna have to hold me down."

"Think you could help me out some next week? In New York. I'm going to need someone who has it together."

"Doin' what?" he asked, eyeing Grafton. In his jeans and T-shirt, the admiral didn't look like a cop, but Willie was a careful man.

"Monitoring some bugs in a hotel. I've got a guy to help, but I don't know if I can trust him."

"Don't ever do nothin' with people you don't trust. Nothin' at all. Don't even be around them. How many times I told you that?"

"That's why I'm asking. Think you can do it?"

"Long as it don't involve heavy liftin' or hard lovin', I can probably help a little. I'm stiff and sore as a diseased dick but the brain is working. I'll tell you now, though—you, too, Grafton—I don't want to go back to the joint. Shit goes down, I never heard of your sorry ass. They'll have to burn down Washington and sift the ashes to find me."

"I can live with that."

"Don't wanta shoot nobody neither."

"I'll drop by this weekend and see how you're doing. We'll talk about it then."

"No offense, fella," Willie said to Grafton, then focused on me. "You come back, be alone."

"Sure. Hang tough."

At the garage I inspected the paint job and climbed in the van to inventory the contents. The fat man stood outside with Jake Grafton, who didn't have anything to say. I could see them in the rearview mirrors, just standing there, the fat man chewing his cigar and Grafton looking like a man waiting for a bus.

I checked carefully. Even if the guy running the chop shop hadn't stolen anything, the men working for him might not be as honest. Everything appeared to be as I had left it. Then I hit the jackpot—found another dozen bugs in a small box under the computer. I checked them over. Yeah, I could use them.

Grafton was hard to figure. Sure, I had worked for him several times in the past when he was an admiral on active duty in the Navy. While he was tan and lean enough for a man his age, he didn't look like anyone special. He was, though. The people who knew him best, folks like Toad Tarkington and Rita Moravia, swore by him.

He'd been on the phone more or less continuously since he found me camping out in his beach house. I didn't think he was talking to his stockbroker. Of course I was curious. Be nice if he shared some info with me.

When I got out of the vehicle I pulled the roll from my pocket and counted out twenty hundreds, which was all of it, into the fat man's hand.

"A pleasure doing business with you," he said as he pocketed the money. He dropped the key to the van in my hand. "How's Willie?"

"Stitches came out this morning. He says they were itching like hell."

The fat man chuckled. "Tell him I say hi," he said, and went into his office. I got in the van and backed it out of the garage. Grafton followed me back to Delaware in his car.

Maybe I ought to ask the admiral for the lowdown—the straight skinny. That thought was immediately followed by another: I had assumed that he knew more than I did. Was that true? Surely he knew that I didn't help murder those people at the Greenbrier safe house. Or did he?

Why was he helping me, anyway?

Jake Grafton was following along a hundred yards behind Carmellini, just keeping him in sight, when his new cell phone rang. "Hi."

"Hi, yourself." Sarah Houston. "I am up against the wall here at work. I am supposed to be working with the cryptographers, yet I am spending scads of time on my computer." Jake well knew what she was doing on that computer—spying on Dell Royston and trying to learn what he was telling interested government agencies about the hunt for the Russian defector and the corpses that kept cropping up. "I've run out of wriggle room."

"Tommy will pick you up at your apartment on Saturday morning. Pack for a couple of days. Bring your laptop."

"Oh, Lord. You know I can't stand him."

"I can't imagine why. He's reasonably smart, well within the bell-shaped curve on looks, showers daily. Seems like every other girl in town hits on him."

"That's why."

"We need your help. He'll be there day after tomorrow."

As he drove along, Jake smiled. So Sarah liked Carmellini. Who would have suspected that?

When we got back to the beach house there was little light left in the sky. A thick overcast lay just over our heads, one churned by a stiff wind. I wasn't hungry, but when Callie offered me a beer I thanked her and took it to the porch. Goncharov was already upstairs, in bed I suspected, though I doubted he was sleeping. The man was fighting too many demons.

The Sunday papers were still there piled up, and since I hadn't read them, I pulled out the latest and turned on the reading light. After I went through the baseball standings and read about the latest tour event, I glanced through the political news.

Normally I don't read political stuff. Just not interested. Maybe that's the sign of a poor education, but I've only got one piddly little vote and one stomach lining, so I sleep better not knowing what the elected ones are doing on a daily basis. If you avoid television, as I do, they are remarkably easy to ignore.

The storyline du jour was the possibility of a female vice-presidential candidate. The five women the pundits thought most eligible for a political mating were three senators and two governors, who were given a lot of column inches.

A page over I stopped to read Jack Yocke's column. I had met him at Grafton's house a year or so ago, and he seemed like a decent sort. He had a different slant on the woman veep issue, however. According to Yocke's unnamed sources—journalese for rumor—the president was considering the possibility of nominating his wife, Zooey Sonnenberg, for the vice-presidential spot.

Wow! If it happened, that would really be news. Not the biggest story since the resurrection, but close. Sonnenberg, who didn't use her husband's name, was a politician in her own right, and a controversial one. When she was young she had used her position as the female scion of a prominent wealthy family to make a big splash in the antiwar movement during the height of the Vietnam protests. She had advocated leftist causes in the years since, although she had been moderating her stances since her husband got elected to drive the bus. According to Yocke.

He went on to analyze the political chemistry. The president's strongest support was from the conservative wing of his party. Zooey would strengthen him with the liberals, the theory went. She would even steal votes from women of the other party, which was a politician's nirvana. Jack Yocke said that Zooey Sonnenberg on the ticket would be just what the doctor ordered to reelect the president.

I tossed the paper down and turned off the light, wondering where Yocke had gotten that tidbit.

The country was overdue for a woman vice president, but Zooey Sonnenberg? The first lady? The president's wife?

After a while Grafton joined me in the darkness. "Callie says Goncharov has his memory back."

"Thank God," I whispered fervently. "What did he say?" I said, speaking louder.

"She didn't question him about the files. Didn't think this was the time."

I took a sip of beer to hide my disappointment.

I saw the flash of his teeth in the darkness as he grinned at me. "This is going to work out, Tommy. We'll get these people."

"How?"

"You'll see. Just bug that hotel. Pick up Sarah Houston at her apartment on your way to New York and take her along. She can't be of much help if she stays in her office."

"I have to go back to Washington tomorrow," I told the admiral, "to make some preparations. Probably spend the night with Willie Varner, leave for New York the following morning. Do you think I should ask Joe Billy Dunn to help?"

"You're worried he's talking to people at Langley?"

"Yeah."

"How do you decide if a person can be trusted?"

I took a deep breath as I thought about the answer to that one. I'd made my share of mistakes through the years. Kelly Erlanger sprang immediately to mind. "Gut feeling, I suppose."

"How much help do you need?"

"One or two other people. Willie can work the van. I can teach him enough in half an hour to stand in for me."

"Who would you use if you decide not to use Dunn?"

"There's a couple of folks who helped me on a couple of things in the past. Man and woman who run a little electrical business, Scout and Arlene."

"Are they honest?"

"Arlene used to be a crackhead. Was a street-corner hooker to pay for her habit. She beat it, though, which puts her pretty damned high in my book. Scout's a thief. Willie sent me to them a couple years ago, says they're good people. I can understand a guy like Scout, maybe because he's so much like me. I know when he might be tempted and when he wouldn't. And he thinks I'll kill him if he crosses me."

"Dunn doesn't believe that, does he?"

"Well, he might," I said, thinking of his reaction to the pistol I shoved in his face. "On the other hand, he might think he can kill me first. The thing is, I don't know who he's been talking to, what he really thinks, if he can be bought."

"Can you be bought?" Grafton asked.

"Hell, yes. Take a lot of dough, though. Whatever I am, I'm not cheap."

The admiral chuckled. After a bit he went on. "Dunn's been talking to your department head. He's a good man. I think it's safe to take him along, but if I were you I'd keep this conversation under my hat."

"Okay."

Grafton finished his beer in silence. I thought about asking him to level with me, to tell me all of it, but I chickened out.

" 'Night, Tommy," he said, and rose from his chair and went inside. In a little bit I heard him and Callie go upstairs.

Maybe I just didn't want to know. Maybe I wanted to think that someone smarter than I was knew where the aces and kings were. Maybe I should just write a letter to Dear Abby. She would probably tell me to get my head examined.

I kicked off my shoes and stretched out on the porch swing. Pulled an afghan over me because the evening was cool. The wind was buffeting the building, and I figured it was going to rain soon. Going to be a good night to sleep. I thought about Kelly Erlanger for a while, wondered if she was still alive. Thinking about her was a waste, so I thought about Anna Modin until I dropped off.

CHAPTER TWENTY-FOUR

Something snapped me wide awake in the middle of the night. I lay frozen, listening. Wind was driving rain against the building, and some of it was blowing in through the screen on me. I was damp, felt the mist of exploded raindrops on my face. But that wasn't what woke me.

The luminous hands of my watch read a few minutes after two. I turned my head until I could see the street through the porch screen. Rain was driving through the halo of the street-lights, but I couldn't see anyone. The parked vehicles appeared to be as I remembered them before I went to sleep.

What had awakened me?

Then I heard it above the low moan of the wind, the sound of something dragging along, scraping against . . .

The 1911 automatic was under my pillow. I wrapped my fingers around it, automatically checked that the hammer was back and the thumb safety on.

Slowly, ever so slowly, I eased the afghan away from my legs.

There was that noise again! Something rubbing against the house, it sounded like.

And someone moaning.

I eased myself off the couch and, staying low, slipped past the chairs so I could see the walkway up to the house.

I froze, listening with every fiber of my being.

Scraping again, and a low moan. Right under me.

It was a man lying on the ground, pressed up against the house. At least, it looked a little like a man. Ah, he was wearing a ghillie suit. This was one of Grafton's snake-eaters who was guarding the house.

With the pistol in hand, I slipped inside and threw the bolt to Grafton's front door. Pulled it open as slowly as I could, staying very low. I took a deep breath, then eased through, still low.

In seconds I was over the moaning man. He had lost the headpiece of his outfit somewhere. He was white, with stubble for hair. No excess fat, lots of muscle. His eyes were closed, but he was still breathing. The rags and tatters of the ghillie garment were wet from the rain. Yet there was a large dark area on his right rear side, near his kidney.

I bent down, trying to see in the dim light. Blood. The stains appeared to be blood. I reached for him, trying to see where he was wounded. He moaned as I touched him, tried ineffectually to fend off my hands.

I tore the ghillie suit with both hands, trying to see.

He had been shot. At least twice. Probably while he was in his hide.

His assailant was probably still out there . . . right now!

My cell phone was in my pocket. The light was too bad to see the numbers. I grabbed the man, hoisted him up over my back and took him into the house, laid him on the couch, ran up the stairs to Grafton's room.

Jake and Callie came awake as I burst in. "The guy guarding the house tonight has been shot. He's downstairs on the couch."

With that I went charging out. I took the stairs three at a time, half expecting to meet the would-be killer in the front room. There was certainly nothing to stop him from coming through the open front door.

No. The living room, kitchen, and porch were empty.

I closed the door, threw the dead bolt, then hurriedly checked the rest of the house.

I paused in the living room, trying to think. Hunkering down in the house and calling 911 wasn't an option. Not unless we wanted to end up like the folks at the Greenbrier safe house. There had been only one man on guard duty tonight—and the attacker didn't know that.

The back door was in the kitchen and led to an outside shower beside the house, a shower screened by an eight-foot board fence.

A man with a knife could merely cut the screen on the porch and come in that way. Or he could be waiting for us to come out. That the killer was still out there was a high probability. His target had to be Mikhail Goncharov, yet he didn't know how many guards were out there. That was my edge.

I let myself out the back door, half expecting to stop a bullet at any second.

The rain beat at me. The wind was worse than I thought. My hands were shaking and I was breathing a mile a minute.

I didn't even know where the wounded man's hide was. Nor that the hunter was there. Or perhaps he was, waiting for someone to come looking.

I crawled on the wet sand around the house and stopped under the porch, where I could see the street.

You need to think about this logically, Tommy. The hunter discovered the snake-eater and shot him, but he didn't know how many guards there were. Even if he did, he didn't know where the others were. He couldn't come toward the house until he found and eliminated them. So he was in a position where he could watch and wait until someone revealed himself.

I scanned the houses I could see on the opposite side of the street—the north side—inspected the cars, tried to remember what the houses had looked like on this side of the street, the south side. Most were built on piles and had some kind of skirting between the house and the ground to keep out critters. The hunter could be under any one of them if he found or made a hole in the skirting.

Except for the house on the south side of the street nearest the beach. It had been built too far out, on the dune, and the retreating beach had washed the dune from under it. It stood derelict now on its pilings, the ground floor at least ten feet above the sand. A few more winters or a hurricane would finish it off, cause it to collapse.

There, I thought. In that house or under it. From there he could see Grafton's front yard and walkway and everything on the street. He could have watched the wounded man crawl toward Grafton's. If I were him, I would wait there.

The wind was driving the rain in waves. By this time I was soaked and covered with sand . . . and still barefoot. I had forgotten to put on my shoes.

I watched the rain in the streetlights for a moment longer, scanned everything I could see. Okay, I was delaying the inevitable, trying to screw up my courage. The man inside needed medical attention, and the only way to get it to him was to call an ambulance or take him to the hospital. With a killer out there, neither option looked good.

I took a deep breath, then scurried forward and rounded the end of the fence, and ran into the next yard to the east. When I was completely hidden from that house at the end of the street, I slowed, made my way to the next fence, prepared to do it again.

If he was in or under the derelict home, he must have seen me dart around Grafton's fence. This time he might be ready.

I went. Fast.

Made it, with a pounding heart. As I rounded the back of this house I decided the third time would be the charm—he'd pop me then. I was only about eighty yards from the place I thought he might be.

Shielded between two houses, I scaled the fence and dropped onto the other side. Got a ton of splinters in my hands and ripped my trousers. Sneaked around the corner of the house and did the fence trick again. Now only one house lay between me and the derelict.

I heard a dog barking in the house beside me. Terrific. Sounded like a small dog, a yapper. If I could hear it, the hunter could, too.

Oh, boy.

I just hoped the householder didn't call the law and report a prowler. A patrol car in the street was the last thing I wanted.

I used both hands to chin myself on the fence, take a squint over the top. Heard something zing by my head. I knew damn well what it was and let go of the fence as if it were electrified with a thousand volts. A bullet. He had shot at me with some kind of silenced weapon.

I didn't wait. I rounded the fence and sprinted by the front of the adjoining house in my best imitation of a juking halfback as two more bullets went by like angry bees. I didn't stop. Kept going, across the sand toward the dark hulking presence of the derelict house as the driving rain pounded on my face.

He fired one more time, and I saw the muzzle flash. It wasn't much, no more light than a firefly would make, but it was enough. He was in the derelict house, on the second story.

I dove under it and rolled to a stop. Blew on the pistol to clean the sand out of the hammer channel.

Getting into that house was a mistake. He was trapped in there. Unless he killed me.

Trapped unless he had a pal out here. That thought tightened every muscle in me.

In the darkness, amid the rain and wind, I could see nothing that moved. The beach seemed to reflect what little light there was, and it was empty.

I inspected the house above me. How had he gotten in there? The underside of the first floor was ten or eleven feet above the sand. It seemed to consist of joists and wires and plumbing—in the darkness it was hard to tell. There were three entrances to the house that I could see: one off the deck, a back door, and a front door. The problem was that the steps to these entrances were suspended at least six feet in the air. He must have jumped up to one of these sets of stairs, scrambled up, and gone in. Easy enough for me to do, too, except for one thing. He would probably shoot me as I came through the door.

I certainly didn't want to take that chance.

Nor did I need to. With me under the house, he was trapped. If and when he came out, I would see him before he saw me. That would be my edge.

All I needed to do was sit.

I hunkered down behind one of the pillars, which gave me a bit of shelter from the wind and rain.

Minutes passed slowly, and I shivered. My shirt and trousers were wet and plastered to me, and I was wearing more sand than a *Sports Illustrated* swimsuit model. Not much insulation value in sand, I found.

I dialed Jake Grafton on my cell phone. After three wrong numbers I got him. I told him where the killer and I were.

"I can't get anyone here until morning," he said. "Can you keep him corked until then?"

"Yeah."

"Callie is going to take this trooper to the hospital," Grafton continued. He was the coolest man under pressure I had ever met. He sounded as if he were ordering breakfast at an IHOP. "We'll put him in the car and she'll drive away. I'll come back in the house and stay with Goncharov."

"Will he stay in the house, you think?"

"By God, he'd better," Grafton exclaimed, then the connection broke. I stowed the phone in my pocket.

Five minutes later I saw them come out of their house half carrying the injured man. They got him into the back seat of Grafton's car, then Grafton went back into the house and Callie drove away. I was glad to see that. Anyone entering that house would come face to face with one tough man armed with an MP-5.

The night passed slowly, agonizingly so. I shivered and slapped myself and listened to the wind . . . and waited.

Waiting is damned hard. You can't relax; you must remain ready. Any second you may find yourself in a fight for your life. Yet it's difficult to maintain the intensity over time. As the minutes pass you can feel the readiness leaking away.

A half hour passed, then another. Never had time seemed so heavy. Several times I thought I heard a noise from the house over my head, but perhaps not. With the wind and pounding of the rain it was hard to tell.

The night dragged as I sat shivering. The pounding of the rain being blown horizontally began to hurt after a while, but I was already doing everything I could to escape it.

I thought about everything as I fought to stay awake and alert— women, past misadventures, things I had done that I wished I hadn't, things I hadn't done that I wish I had. Every man should have a list of things to do before he dies, and I had mine. Things like kill the son of a bitch who sent killers to cut people up to make them talk, to kill them to keep them silent.

The preachers say you shouldn't think evil thoughts—they rot the soul, corrode it. All I can tell you is that I got no heat from mine.

Just when I thought I was nearing my limit of endurance, the storm eased, the wind velocity dropped. Even the rain let up. I fought the drowsiness that overcame me when I ceased shivering.

I knew he knew I was still here. Don't ask me how I knew, but I did, to a certainty. He was upstairs waiting and I was waiting down here.

Waiting . . . for his nerve to break? For him to try something. Anything.

The sky was beginning to lighten up just enough for me to see the ocean and base of the clouds when something fell from the west side of the house into the sand. I heard the sound of it hitting, just a muffled plop. That jolted me to maximum alert. I spun and threw myself prone on the sand with the pistol out in front, ready to shoot. I couldn't see what it was because of the piles that held up the house. There were perhaps two dozen.

It wasn't a man that fell—I sensed that. Not loud enough. But what was it?

I wasn't dumb enough to crawl closer to see. Maybe I wasn't that curious. I knew if I waited I would get my shot.

The seconds ticked by. I turned my head back and forth, watching, but nothing moved.

A minute passed. Two. Three. The sky seemed to be turning lighter.

Something burned across my back like a hot iron. The shock of it drew a grunt from me. There was a soft *plut* of a noise, but perhaps I imagined it more than heard it. Instinctively I knew that I had been shot.

I rolled over, pistol held in both hands. I thumbed the safety off as I scanned the ground.

Another sound, louder this time, and an angry bee whizzed by my ear.

I saw him then, on the stairs down from the deck on the beach side of the house. The only reason I was still alive was that he was lying on the deck and shooting at me upside down. All I could see was the dark place where his head and shoulders blotted out the lighter gray of the sky.

I rushed my first shot, which didn't seem as loud as I thought it should be. I settled down, began squeezing them off as quickly as I could line up the sights in that terrible light.

He might have shot at me again and I didn't hear it—I don't know—but after my fourth or fifth shot he lost the rifle. It fell from his hands.

I managed to rise. I walked toward him, the pistol pointed, ready to shoot again.

He didn't move.

Maybe I shouldn't have, but I shot him again in the neck from a distance of about eight feet.

The rifle was a compact one with a silencer on the barrel. I picked it up, tossed it up on the deck, then hoisted myself up on the bottom rung of the deck stairs, which ended in midair. My back was on fire. Somehow I knew the bullet wasn't in me; it must have grooved my back without hitting the bone.

Only when I was climbing the steps did I realize that there might have been two of those dudes in that house. My pistol was in my pocket, where it would do me no good.

One thing for certain—the shooter was really dead. Dead as hell. Blood all over the step where he had fallen. I grabbed his feet and tried to pull him back into the house out of sight of passersby on the beach. He weighed a ton, at least. With my back hurting like hell and heavy as he was, it was all I could do to get him through the door to the living room.

The house was gutted. Now I got the pistol out, stood listening. Heard wind coming through the broken windows in that ramshackle derelict, which couldn't have been over ten years old. They must have just got it completed when the storms washed the beach out from under it.

I went through the house carefully. Someone had left a lot of trash in an upstairs bedroom—camped up there, it looked like— but I was the only living person in the house.

Downstairs I paused to look at the dead man. In novels after the hero kills somebody he is supposed to pause for some soul-searching and introspection, think a deep thought. No deep thought occurred to me. I wanted to kick the bastard, but he was dead and I didn't feel like wasting the calories.

I was sitting on the steps outside when Jake Grafton came out from under the house. "How many were there?"

"One." I jerked my thumb over my shoulder.

"Help me up," he said, and extended a hand.

I helped Grafton roll him over so we could look at his face. "Is this that CIA killer Royston was supposed to have hired?"

"Stu Vine?" Grafton studied the slack face with the staring eyes. "I don't know. It's possible, I suppose. Whoever he was, he rushed it. Shouldn't have gone after the sniper in the hide. That was a silly mistake."

"Maybe the challenge of it intrigued him."

Grafton turned and studied my face. "Perhaps," he admitted. He picked up the sniper rifle with the silencer. It was a Ruger with a 3×9 variable scope. "One of these new .17 calibers," Jake Grafton said, then laid it on the floor. "Fires a seventeen-grain bullet, tiny little thing. He must have been planning for head shots."

"Quiet, too. Played hell with my back."

He inspected the wound. "Just a gouge. Bleeding some."

"He got me facing one way, then tried to pop me in the back. Would have done better if he had been right side up."

We were outside on the deck looking at the ocean when a police vehicle, a Jeep Cherokee, drove up. The officer rolled down his window. "You people aren't supposed to be in that house. Didn't you see the sign?"

Truly, I hadn't. Would have ignored it if I had, but I didn't tell him that.

"Come on," the officer said. "That building is condemned. Get down out of there before it collapses with you in it."

I jumped down facing him so he wouldn't see the blood on my shirt or the pistol tucked into the small of my back. Grafton climbed down. When we were both on the sand the officer said, "Don't let me catch you in there again."

"Yes, sir," Jake Grafton said.

Satisfied we were properly chastised, the officer drove on along the beach.

We walked back to the Graftons', where the admiral worked on my back with iodine and Band-Aids. He used at least a dozen. When he had me fixed up, he went to call some friends about the corpse. After he hung up, he told me they would come get the dead man tonight after dark.

On that happy note we sat down on his porch to drink a beer even though it was only six in the morning. A bit later Callie called Grafton from three blocks away. He told her the coast was clear. The trooper had been shot twice, but he was on IVs and stable, Callie said. She told the people at the hospital she didn't know him, didn't know who shot him or where. A policeman came by the hospital and got her name, said he would call her later.

"We aren't doing so good in this war," I remarked to the admiral.

He didn't deny it. He was always like that—upbeat, optimistic, bucking up the troops.

CHAPTER TWENTY-FIVE

We rolled into New York through the Lincoln Tunnel. With Sarah Houston, Willie Varner, and Joe Billy Dunn in the van, it had been a hell of a trip. Willie sat in the back telling Tommy Carmellini stories while he sipped beer. Houston was in the passenger seat beside me. She didn't have much to say while Willie ran his mouth, but from time to time she gave me an appraising glance.

Most of Willie's tales were lies—for reasons too obvious to mention, I had long ago learned that the less said to people about my business the better. Didn't matter to Willie. He told what he knew, what he suspected, and downright bald-faced lies, all with the same air of omniscient authority. To hear him tell it I was the worst desperado since Willie Sutton. There wasn't a safe made that I couldn't crack, a wall I couldn't climb, a man alive I couldn't con.

Joe Billy egged him on, all the way across Delaware and New Jersey. Approaching New York I turned on the radio, found a jazz station, and cranked the volume up. Even then I could hear Willie talking loudly to Dunn, telling him whatever lies popped into his crooked head.

The tunnel was a relief. I snapped the radio off and told the guys in back to shut up. Amazingly, they did. Wanted to see New York, I guess.

The streets and avenues were packed, as usual. What all these millions of people do to make a living is one of the unsolved mysteries of the modern age, but make a living they do. There they were, scurrying along the sidewalks and crosswalks like a horde of ants or a biblical plague of locusts while trucks, taxis, and limos jammed the streets, honking, creeping, oozing along like thick mud flowing down a storm drain.

We circled the New York Hilton once, looking for Secret Service agents and vehicles. True, the president wasn't supposed to stay at this hotel, and the convention was being held at the Javits Center, but they just might be in there today anyway, which would complicate our lives. Didn't see anything or anyone out of the ordinary, though.

We dropped Sarah at the corner near the front of the joint. She could do her thing anyplace that had a telephone line, but the Hilton had a high-speed cable Internet connection, so why not?

She marched away in her high heels and New York business suit, her laptop case dangling from a strap over her shoulder, pulling her overnight bag on its little wheels. With her head erect and hair stirring in the breeze, I had to admit, she was a fine-looking hunk of woman. Little twisted upstairs, but I didn't regard that as a disqualifying disability, not in this day and age. And who was I to talk?

What I found fascinating was the way her hips swayed with—

The guy behind me beeped; the light had changed. Joe Billy—now in the passenger seat—gave him the finger, and we circled the block again. In that traffic, each circuit took about twelve minutes.

We were halfway into the next one when my cell phone rang. "I'm in," she said. That meant she had checked into her room and been shown upstairs. She was now on-line and had hacked into the Hilton's central computer. That wasn't as big a feat as you might imagine, since she had explored the security firewalls at her leisure at her office at the NSA facility at Fort Meade. Indeed, yesterday she had twice crashed the hotel's video security system for ten seconds at a time. "And it's down." Down again, she meant, and couldn't be resurrected until she fixed it.

"Okay." I hung up, put the phone in my shirt pocket.

Actually, circling the hotel was sort of dumb. I headed up the avenue toward Central Park. We were rolling through the park when the telephone rang again.

"They've called a service company. I've just called the company back and canceled the call. Give them about a half hour before you arrive."

"Okay."

I returned the telephone to my pocket and told the guys, "We're a go."

Exactly thirty-two minutes later we rolled into the hotel's service entrance and parked beside two trucks off-loading supplies—one food, one liquor. At the control console in back, Willie began the final check on our bugs. Joe Billy and I grabbed our tools and got out, locking the van behind us.

"Security service company," I told the guard. "We got an urgent call a little while ago and zipped on over."

"Wow! That was fast. They just had me put you guys on the list fifteen minutes ago."

"We were on a job just down the street. This shouldn't take long. Service is our business." That motto was embroidered on our shirts, just below the company name. I had gotten the shirts done yesterday at a custom shirt shop in suburban Washington.

"I've heard that shit before," the guard said wearily as he passed us the clipboard to sign our names on. I signed as Andy Jackson Jr., and Joe Billy signed as Henry Clay. The guard glanced at the board, handed us visitors' passes to clip to our shirt pockets, and gave us directions to the security center.

It was in a windowless room deep within the bowels of the hotel. The two uniformed guards on duty were pleased to see us, especially the woman, who looked Joe Billy over with interest. She was short and dumpy and talked with a Brooklyn accent as she explained how the video feeds had crapped out all at once. Computer still seemed to be working properly, though.

He nodded sagely and began checking the cables leading to the machines and the connections. I scrutinized the bank of monitors, checked all the connections, made sure everything was getting power. This was all for show, of course. It helped that Joe Billy had actually taken a course in video security systems—completed it just a week ago, as a matter of fact. He tossed off enough phrases to convince the guards that we were indeed knowledgeable, if they had any doubts.

He played with the computer while the guards and I watched. Shut it down, rebooted it, the whole drill. The female guard got as close to him as she dared. Finally he said, "It's gotta be a problem in the camera circuit. Will you check, Junior?" I was Junior. The embroidered name on my shirt said so.

On my way out of the room I whispered to the girl, "He's single." I went back to the truck for a bag full of bugs.

"They're ready to go," Willie said. "How's ever'thing going?"

"Piece of cake." Indeed, the job was routine. I bugged four hotels in Europe earlier that spring using just this method, although with different personnel.

"By the way," I added, "I didn't appreciate you making me the topic of conversation all the way up from Washington."

"Sarah likes you. She sopped up ever' word."

"Don't blow smoke. You were talking to Dunn. The other day I stuck a pistol in his face and threatened to shoot it off. All those lies you told will make him think I'm some kinda criminal."

"You worry too much about what other people think. The people who know you like I do are damn glad to have you around."

"Do me a favor, Willy. Don't talk about me to anybody."

"Even Sarah?"

"She doesn't like me either."

"Like hell! She was all ears. Sometimes, boy, I think you're dumber than a box of rocks."

I made a rude noise, hoisted the bag of bugs, and locked the vehicle door behind me. Yeah, right. Sarah Houston—the woman who once told me I was a farm animal.

Keeping your mouth shut is a lost art. I used to think Willy knew how to do it. His injuries had affected his brain. Wouldn't surprise me if he announced he was marrying his hospital nurse.

I started at the security office and began checking security cameras. They were all fine, of course, but I set up a stepladder, climbed it, and gave the installation the once-over, checking the voltage in, the coaxial cable, and so forth. Two minutes sufficed for each camera. All these cameras sent their video by coaxial cable to the security center. The new units being installed in many commercial buildings broadcast the video, which made the problem of tapping them ridiculously simple. One merely moved a receiver within range and tuned in. To tap a hardwired video feed, one merely placed a collar with a transmitting device around the coaxial cable, and it broadcast the signal. As long as our receiver—which was in our borrowed FBI van—remained within range, we could see what each camera saw. I didn't place these collars on every camera, just the ones in the public areas of the hotel.

After I had gotten the cameras I wanted in the lobby and halls of the meeting areas, I was ready to ride up to the penthouse level, where Dell Royston had a suite reserved. I called Joe Billy on his cell phone and asked him to send a guard to key the elevator for me. Of course he sent the girl. She helped me get the stepladder onto the service elevator and used her passkey to enable it, then dashed back to the office. Apparently Joe Billy knew enough to flirt with her to keep her away from me, because I didn't want an audience. I've worked with audiences before, but you have to devise a reason to go where you aren't supposed to, and getting the bugs in place takes longer.

I collared the two video cameras in the corridor of the penthouse floor. I had a magnetic card in my pocket that would open any room door in the hotel. We had an encoder in our lock shop, and I had brought it along and Sarah had supplied the codes—but I didn't have to use it because the maid was cleaning the suite I wanted. The door was standing open. I marched in, set up my stepladder, and began placing the bugs.

The maid was Puerto Rican, and I happen to be fluent in Spanish—which I learned for one of my very first CIA assignments—so we chattered away while I worked. I had my audience after all.

She was a genuinely nice young woman, in her early twenties, and had been in New York for only six months. Her name was Isabel. She told me her life story, about the boy waiting in San Juan, about her hopes and dreams for the future, while I put bugs in light fixtures and on top of furniture and behind pictures.

These bugs were battery operated and contained transmitters. To conserve battery power and prevent them from being detected by conventional sweep gear, they could be turned on and off via radio. Some of them were so tiny they were mounted on the head of a straight pin. I had them threaded through the cloth of my shirt pocket and pinned them in the top of the window drapes, near a hook that held the drape to the curtain rod.

At one point Isabel asked what I was doing. I told her that I was placing the new high-tech insect repellers. I showed her a bug, one enclosed in a four-inch-square sheet of clear plastic. I placed it on top of a dresser and pressed it down so that it wouldn't move, and it became almost invisible in ordinary light. I pressed another into place behind the headboard of the bed while Isabelle told me all about the cockroaches of San Juan, of which she, like all natives, was justly proud.

After I had placed at least six bugs in each of the rooms of the suite, including two in each bath, I asked her to open the door to the adjoining suites on either side so I could also do them. No problem.

She stuck right with me, chattering away in Spanish. I asked about the upcoming convention. The hotel would be full, she told me, completely full.

"What do you think of a woman as vice president?" I asked, pretending I was Jack Yocke getting some deep background.

"I have met her, you know," Isabel solemnly informed me. "Zooey. She shook my hand." She held up her right hand so I could see it. Just looking, you wouldn't know that it had touched the anointed one. "It was in this hotel, just three months ago. I think she will be vice-president, and then the next president."

"Would you vote for her?"

"Oh, yes. She is very brave. She lights up the room. She will make life better for women everywhere." Isabel chattered on as I placed the bugs.

When I finished ten minutes later she was still talking politics. She pressed me for a promise to vote for Zooey. I refused, which made her adamant. Smiling, wishing I hadn't brought up the subject, I thanked her, wished her luck, and made my escape.

As I waited for the service elevator I called Sarah on my cell phone. "All done," I reported.

"Joe Billy has a pass for the truck."

"Any trouble?"

"No. The management is worried about another failure next week. He told them we couldn't come back next week if we were needed without a parking garage pass, so they gave him one."

"Terrific." Getting a place to park the van during the convention had been one of our highest priorities. I was worried that we would have to steal a pass or counterfeit one, since the City Hall office where street parking passes were issued was reputed to be hopelessly inundated with requests this late in the game.

"Guess who has a reservation at this hotel starting tomorrow?" Sarah said.

"Your ex."

"I don't have an ex, Carmellini. I'm still a virgin. How about Dorsey O'Shea?"

The virgin fastball went zipping by and I never saw it. Dorsey? My Dorsey? Did the yacht sink? "You sure?" I asked, because I couldn't think of anything else to say.

"She must have heard you were going to be in town and couldn't stay away."

"Turn on the system," I said mechanically and slapped the phone shut.

Dorsey O'Shea. Really!

What in the world is going on, anyway?

Willie Varner, Joe Billy Dunn, and I made our escape from the Hilton in the borrowed FBI van. We left Sarah Houston there to wallow in the lap of luxury for a whole night on her own dime. She had said that she was going to get a facial and massage in the spa. Whatever.

Joe Billy was driving. I had him drop me at the New York Public Library on Fifth. He and Willie wanted to find a cold beer, but I had too much on my mind.

I climbed the steps between the lions and stopped at the information desk. An hour later I was seated in a cubicle on the second
floor with a stack of books in front of me. "Are you a student?"
asked the lady who delivered the books.

"Oh, yes," I lied. "I'm working on my master's."

"I thought so," she said with the authority of one who knows
everything, and wheeled her cart away.

The books were all on the California antiwar movement in the
late sixties, early seventies. That seemed a good place to start.

I cut to the chase. I flipped to the back of each book and
scanned the indexes for familiar names. Since you're smarter than
I am, you probably know the names I was looking for.

I found Zooey Sonnenberg in the first book I tried, a serious,
poorly written tome published by an academic press somewhere. I
flipped to the pages where her name appeared and read them
carefully. She had made a splash in the antiwar movement, that
was certain. Passionate and articulate, the daughter of a rich in-
dustrialist, she was a natural leader. She did outrageous things, got
arrested once, twice, three times . . . no, five times, according to
this author, picked targets for demonstrations, convinced everyone
to follow her lead. She even demonstrated against her father's
company, accused them of war crimes. That got a lot of press.

The fifth book in the pile went further into detail, had extensive quotes from manifestos she had written. She was in all the
other books I looked at, from a few paragraphs to a chapter or
two. I merely scanned the information.

All in all, looking at it from the vantage point of thirty-plus
years, it didn't seem very earth-shattering. She had believed in a
cause and fought for it. So? Isn't that what America is all about?

Then I found another name I was looking for, one Michael
O'Shea. Yep, he was there, helping write those manifestos. I even
found him in one of the photos standing beside Zooey, who was

skinnier and had more hair then than she did now. She wore it long and frizzy in those days and sported a set of granny glasses.

O'Shea was tall, skinny, and intense. Gawky. Had a scraggly mustache and hair down to his shoulders. He looked like your average hippie . . . until you looked at the eyes. That was a very smart guy. I wondered what he would have done with his life if he had lived. Sometimes life isn't fair.

Just for the heck of it I tore the photo from the book, folded it, and put it in my shirt pocket.

O'Shea's wife, the bootlegger's granddaughter, wasn't mentioned. Not in the index of any book I examined. Maybe she was there, but she wasn't famous and didn't write manifestos or big checks or do outrageous things, and she died soon afterward.

None of the books mentioned O'Shea's fatal car wreck.

I wondered if I should check on that. All I knew about it was what Dorsey had told me.

With the help of the desk clerk, I got into the microfiche files for the *San Francisco Examiner.* Found it finally, two paragraphs about O'Shea and his wife, a fatal car wreck in 1972 on the Pacific Coast Highway south of Big Sur.

So what was the link that brought Dorsey to New York for the convention where Zooey Sonnenberg was going to be nominated for the office of vice president of the United States? Correction— *might* be nominated. I had never heard Dorsey mention Zooey. That might or might not mean anything, although Dorsey had a habit of dropping names left and right.

I stopped in the periodical room and scanned that morning's papers. Jack Yocke had stirred up a hornet's nest. Today there was more speculation by a variety of pundits, who claimed the White House was leaking Zooey's name, running it up the flagpole to see what happened. A number of politicos would welcome the nomination, they said. On the other hand, a lot of politicians of both parties thunderously denounced the possibility of Zooey's candidacy, accusing the president of wanting to start a political dynasty and attempting to evade the constitutional limit on two terms by setting his wife up to run for president at the end of his second term. One of the Internet companies had done an unscientific poll; seventy-seven percent of the respondents thought Zooey would make a good candidate.

It was raining when I came out of the library. I bought an umbrella from a street-corner vendor and walked ten blocks to a poolroom on the West Side, where I found Joe Billy and Willie Varner bent over a table. I took ten bucks off each of them before we hung up the sticks and went to find some dinner.

CHAPTER TWENTY-SIX

I was the chief archivist for the SVR, the successor to the First Chief Directorate of the KGB. With the help of the British, I defected and brought seven suitcases full of notes with me to the West. I was to be debriefed by British intelligence and the CIA when the killers came." The Russian paused and took a ragged breath. "They killed my wife, Bronislava. I saw her dead."

After Callie Grafton had translated for her husband, she waited for Goncharov to say more, but he did not.

Jake asked, "When did you first approach the British about defecting?"

"The second week of April. I had taken a train to Vilnius for a holiday. I walked into the British Embassy and asked to speak to an intelligence officer."

"Wasn't that a serious risk?"

"Yes."

"And you had no trouble leaving Russia?"

"You know the bureaucratic mind. They do not watch those

who are retired. Before my retirement from the SVR, traveling to the Baltic Republics would have been impossible."

"How did the British bring you out?"

"It was very simple, really. My wife and I took another holiday to Vilnius, brought all the files with us. The afternoon of our arrival the British flew us to London."

"Did you come straight to America from London?"

"No. We spent almost a week in Britain—just where I do not know—in intense discussions with intelligence officers. Then we came to America for a thorough, extensive debriefing."

"Were there any Americans in England during your debriefing there?"

"Yes. At least two. One named Stephen and one named Bob."

"Did the British copy your notes?"

"No. They wished to do so, but I refused to allow it. I thought that if I didn't explain the notes, the files, innocent people might be injured by what was in them."

"You didn't think the files spoke for themselves?"

"Many did, yes. Many did not. You must understand the conditions under which I made my notes, snatching a few minutes here, a few there, scanning the actual files, trying to summarize what I had learned hours or days later when I had a few moments. The luxury of verbatim copying was not possible except in a few, rare instances when the fates gave me a quiet afternoon."

"I notice that some of the files are typewritten."

"After my retirement I finally had the time to attempt to organize my notes, to fill in details that in my original haste had been omitted—details that I still recalled—and to cross-reference them. But after so many years, with so much material, I feared the task would be unfinished at my death. And if my files remained in Russia, they would be destroyed soon after I died, as soon as the authorities learned of them."

"Who, besides yourself, ever studied the actual files in the archives?"

"No one!" he said bluntly. "No one had the access I enjoyed. An intelligence agency is highly compartmentalized. True, the director of the agency could send for any file he chose, but directors came and went, and they had agendas. They had no time to sit and read. Only I did. The realization came upon me one day a few years after I was appointed archivist that only I was in a position to know the complete story, the awful, blood-soaked story of how the Communists ruled. Lenin, Stalin, Beria, Andropov, all of them. Only I could read every word, every jot and comma, of their crimes.

"That is why my notes are so precious. No person has ever studied the archives as I have. No one else knows as much as I do about the activities of the Soviet intelligence services."

Goncharov searched the faces of his listeners. "Don't you understand? The intelligence services kept the Communists in power. They were the right arm of the Communist state. They arrested, framed, betrayed, silenced, murdered, and discredited the state's enemies, who were everyone who voiced the slightest doubt that the Communists were always right. They fought their enemies worldwide. My notes are the evidence against them. They must be studied and understood in the West. And they must be publicized, be made available to the Russian people, who must learn the truth."

"Only one box of files remains," Jake gently remarked.

"True, much has been lost. But the files that remain are the most precious. They detail the KGB's operations against internal enemies."

"And you. You remain. You can write of what you know."

The pain in Goncharov's face was difficult to look upon. "Without the files to refer to . . ." he whispered, his doubt palpable.

Jake Grafton moved on. "Did any British intelligence officers accompany you to the American safe house?"

"To the best of my knowledge, no. An Englishman named Nigel came to the United States with me, but I didn't see him after the first day. I was told that specialists were coming from London to study the files and question me, yet they had not arrived."

When she had finished translating, Callie said to her husband, "You don't really think the Russians attacked the safe house?"

"No," he replied softly. "It happened too soon, and the people who did it were Americans. The safe house strike was an American operation all the way." He studied his toes. "Goncharov's defection was a huge intelligence coup. No doubt his extraction from Russia received minute-by-minute attention from the very top. The British must have been ecstatic. A peek into the inner workings of their archrival, a chance to purge the traitors in their midst, uncover sleepers, plug leaks, ahh . . . ! This twist of fate was so wonderful they decided to share the good fortune with their allies, the Americans, who must have been equally ecstatic.

"And yet, somewhere on this side of the Atlantic, the news must have been the last thing on earth someone wanted to hear. The archivist for the KGB was coming with seven suitcases full of meticulously copied notes, the labor of his life, his monument to the venal criminality of the Communist system. Someone heard that news with morbid dread."

"But wouldn't Goncharov's defection be a closely held secret?"

"Oh, yes. Extremely closely held. A half dozen people in the CIA perhaps, the director of the FBI, the president, the national security adviser, the president's chief of staff, perhaps the chairman of the Joint Chiefs, three or four other highly placed, key people—you can make your own list. Yet someone in that circle felt mortal terror when he heard it."

"Which one?"

"That is the question," he said, and rose from his seat. "You need to question him, carefully, thoroughly," he said to Callie, "find out everything he can remember on American agents, American moles, anything American. Take your time, make notes. Talk as long as you can, take breaks, resume where you left off."

Grafton paused. "Until we find that guilty secret, Goncharov's life isn't safe. Someone has risked everything—spent money, compromised himself, put himself in mortal peril—to destroy the files and kill the archivist. And he isn't going to stop now."

As he walked from the room he placed a hand in passing on Goncharov's shoulder. The Russian glanced at his retreating back, and a shadow of a smile crossed his face.

Jake walked out to the screened-in porch and absentmindedly flipped though the stack of newspapers. Dell Royston had been the chief of staff until six months ago, when he became head of the president's reelection efforts. He wouldn't have been in that select circle that heard the glad tidings of Goncharov's defection, would he?

Ah, here it was. A Sunday supplement piece on Dell Royston in the *Post*. He had recalled seeing it a month or so ago. Fortunately he and Callie had been at the beach that weekend.

He dropped into a stuffed chair to read the article again. It was about what he expected, a puff piece by a political admirer. Dell Royston was the son of two American expatriates who were living in Spain when they were killed in a highway accident. He had two kids, one in college and one just graduated from law school. Royston had attended Harvard Law after the war, married, worked for a few years at a firm in Washington where he had been bitten by the political bug, then left for the hinterland and allied himself with a rising political star who later became president.

Jake tossed the paper back on the pile and stretched. The sun was out and the wind smelled of the sea. Over the muted sounds of traffic on the highway he could hear snatches of Russian coming from the kitchen.

He went inside, turned on the television in the living room, and flipped to the Weather Channel. He glanced at his watch—had he missed the weekly planner again? Ads, more ads, the Weather Channel seemed to have more advertisements than weather these days.

There was a box on the coffee table. He opened it, pawed through the aviation sectional charts it contained, glanced at a couple, then tossed them back in the box.

Back on the porch, he removed his new cell phone from his pocket and made a call. Callie and Goncharov were still in the kitchen talking an hour later when the telephone buzzed. "Grafton."

"He insisted his files should not be copied, but of course they were. The Brits worked every night frantically duplicating everything while he and his wife slept."

"You know what I want."

"We'll do our best."

"As soon as possible."

"Jake, it will take years to assess what's in those files, which as you probably can guess are incomplete. The notes are cryptic, made hurriedly."

"Do the best you can. Please. And please call me the moment you know anything."

"So is it the president?"

"I don't know. I think—well, it's too early to say. I wish there were some way to read all those files."

"There isn't."

"I suppose not."

A sigh came over the phone. "The man Tommy shot was named Joliffe. He was a retired cop, just went through a nasty divorce and a bankruptcy."

"Any possibility he was Stu Vine?"

"No. He was on the Washington police force when Stu Vine

was reputed to be cleaning up the Middle East. Someone wired ten thousand dollars to his checking account day before yesterday from a bank in the Caymans."

"An amateur."

"Lucky for you."

"We need some more guys around this place."

"I've got people on the way. You had enough of retirement yet?"

"No. Callie and I are going flying. The summer weather pattern is setting in, and there is a lot of this country we haven't seen."

"Going to be aerial gypsies, eh?"

"Yes, sir. For a while, anyway."

Grafton snapped the telephone shut. He was reading a newspaper when Callie came into the living room. "Let's go shopping. We'll take Mikhail along."

An expedition should be safe enough, Jake decided. "Okay."

The first place they stopped was the supermarket nearest the beach house. As they walked through the entrance, Jake heard Goncharov's sharp intake of breath. He muttered something in Russian to Callie, who nodded. Jake pulled a shopping cart from the stack and followed along behind them.

A minute later Jake became aware that Callie wasn't really shopping. She was wandering along, pointing out this and that to the Russian, who was handling everything. He picked up vegetables and sniffed them, squeezed fruit, inspected meat, opened the doors of coolers and poked his head inside, strolled up and down the aisles examining the pictures on the cans and the contents of various shoppers' carts. He seemed intrigued by the selections the shoppers made.

Every few minutes he stopped to take a deep breath. "The food stores in Russia stink of rotting food," he told Callie. "The vegetables were never fresh unless you bought them on the black market. We had to wash them very carefully. Some of the vegetables were grown on radioactive soil."

A few minutes later, Goncharov asked, "Do all Americans buy their food in places like this?"

"There are supermarkets in every city and town in the nation," she replied.

"Are the items expensive?"

"In relative terms, no. Food is not a huge expense for most people."

"My wife used to shop for hours every day. When she found something we needed she bought all she could carry. Cakes in boxes, baked goods in bags . . . there was nothing like that."

He said no more, merely watched as Callie filled the cart with the items she wanted and they joined a line at a checkout counter.

"The mall," Callie murmured to Jake as he piloted the car from the parking lot.

"We need to get this food in the refrigerator," he objected.

"We won't stay long," she replied.

He thought he knew why she wanted to go there. They entered through one of the anchor tenants, a Sears store.

Goncharov was visibly shaken as Callie led him through the usual crowd of shoppers of all ages. He looked at the clothes, the appliances, the tools—he was fascinated by the tools, picking them up, fingering them, then parting with them reluctantly. The display of televisions filling one wall, all showing the same channel, mesmerized the Russian. Callie led him on, out into the mall past shop after shop filled with toys, clothes, electronic gadgets, more clothes, posters, stuffed animals, sporting goods, jewelry, watches, and still more clothes.

Goncharov came to a stop, finally, at the top of an escalator where one could see the crowds and stores on both levels of the building.

"If the Russian people had seen this in 1991, they would have murdered all the Communists," he said to Callie. "Everything they said about the West was a lie. Everything!"

On the way back to the car the archivist said, "I lived in the prison that they ruled, watched them all my life, and one day I realized that they were in it only for themselves."

"Isn't that true of most rulers?" she asked gently.

"Perhaps," he admitted grudgingly. "I copied the files because I wanted the world to know what the Communists did. I wanted their victims to know, so they could never do it again. And it cost my wife her life. Was I a fool?"

American political conventions today are built around television prime time, probably for historical reasons since the modern primary system has eliminated the drama of who will win the presidential nomination. Still, the politicians arrange the convention so that speeches by bigwigs take place in the prime viewing hours of the evening, when presumably the political faithful are home glued to the boob tube, waiting to cheer every carefully honed syllable. The political groupies come to the convention to bond, cheer, and get interviewed, sure that somehow, in some way, it all matters. And maybe it does, although I doubt it.

Watching partisan political speeches ranks on my list with watching paint dry and grass grow. The conventioneers who crammed every bar and restaurant in Manhattan that weekend seemed to share my opinion. They ignored the governors, congresspeople, and senators dropping ten-second sound bites on the televisions mounted high in the corners and lubricated their throats while indulging in loud conversation, handshaking, and backslapping.

A weeklong party was under way, and the folks from the hinterlands were there to enjoy it. Renewed my faith in America, so it did. That Saturday night Willie Varner, Joe Billy Dunn, and I circulated through three Irish bars—we were seriously into Guinness—mixing and mingling. We met car dealers, doctors, lawyers, farmers, implement dealers, two guys who owned dry cleaners, and a bunch of teachers and state officeholders, all here to party and make their voices heard in the national arena. We also met a couple of hookers, one of them a high school teacher who normally worked Vegas in the summer but thought that this year she would try New York, and a working girl from Chicago who looked like she would be a lot of fun. Both of them knew how to party. They soon had a crowd of admirers buying them drinks, so we circulated on. The whole scene reminded me of a plumbers' convention I stumbled on in Vegas a few years back, although the plumbers were more high-toned.

We spent Saturday night at a motel in Jersey and drove back Sunday to check out the scene. Our New York Hilton parking garage pass worked like a charm. Sarah checked out of the hotel at eleven that morning after a spa treatment; Joe Billy met her at the desk and took her luggage to the van, then Sarah went shopping. While Dunn went back to the van to monitor the bugs I had planted, Willie Varner and I purchased a tube steak from a sidewalk vendor. I got kraut and mustard on mine.

I was still munching when my cell phone vibrated. Trying to get the phone out of my pocket and juggle the dog, I managed to smear mustard on my shirt. Joe Billy was on the phone.

"The only spot I could find in the garage was three floors below the hotel. I can't activate the bugs from there or receive their signals."

"How about aboveground in the garage?"

"Not in a commercial van. I even offered the valet a twenty."

"Okay."

"We've got to get this buggy out on the street."

"Where are you now?"

"Out of the garage, cruising Fifth Avenue. Even the cell phone won't work down there."

"Okay. Let me see what I can do. Call you back in a little while."

I explained the problem to Willie as we walked. "We need a street parking pass," I remarked superfluously.

"Doesn't seem like a difficult problem," he replied. He finished his dog and tossed the napkin in a corner trash barrel. We hailed a taxi and rode over to the Javits Convention Center.

The street around the center was lined with television and radio service trucks, corner to corner, one after another. People were everywhere, coming and going, carrying equipment and boxes, rolling loaded dollies. One outfit was using a small forklift. There were cops around, but only a few, strolling and observing.

"Even if we get a pass, we have to find a space near the hotel to park," Willie said.

"The space is tomorrow's problem," I told him. "The pass is today's."

The passes were taped to the passenger's window of the trucks.

We intended to walk around the entire building, looking for a likely truck, but we were only halfway when our moment came. A crew was unloading the back of a truck using dollies. The passenger door was standing open; the cab was empty. Without a word Willie climbed into the cab and closed the door.

I stood on the sidewalk with my back to the cab, watching the men loading boxes on a dolly at the back end of the truck.

Two minutes later Willie joined me. "Got it," he said. "Cut it off with my pocketknife."

We walked away. When Joe Billy motored by the corner we were on ten minutes later, we gave the pass to him. All he had to do was tape it in the window. And find a parking place near the hotel.

Willie and I rode the subway out to Yankee Stadium to improve our minds. We bought tickets from a scalper on the sidewalk for a mere ten-buck premium and settled into seats way up high behind first base.

Joe Billy called in the second inning. He had found a spot near the hotel. The bugs worked. He was now on his way back to Jersey. The game was a dilly, the Yanks versus Boston. Low clouds hung over the city all afternoon, but it didn't rain.

That evening Willie and I were outside the Hilton watching the limos roll up when it began drizzling. By then the police had the sidewalk in front of the joint cordoned off to keep riffraff like us at a safe distance. Willie and I were huddled under the umbrella when I saw Dorsey O'Shea get out of a long black limousine.

She had apparently been shopping in Paris; the outfit she was wearing was definitely not off a rack. She strolled across the red carpet looking neither right nor left and disappeared into the maw of the hotel while the limo driver and bellman wrestled with her luggage, four hard brown suitcases and a smaller vanity case. I would have bet my last dollar those suitcases were leather.

So that's the way my life was shaking out. I was standing on the sidewalk in the rain under a too-small umbrella that I was sharing with an ex-con when the multizillionaire hot woman that I wasn't good enough for marched into the Hilton on her way to a penthouse suite. They weren't going to put her in one of the suites I had bugged, according to Sarah Houston. Oh, too bad! It would have been fun to hear what in the world she was up to.

And yet, it wouldn't. The last thing I needed was to listen to Dorsey and some schmuck getting it on in a fifteen-hundred-dollar-a-night hotel suite overlooking Manhattan. And she would probably pick a schmuck, like that outside artist I ran off. After the episode with the porno movie dude, I knew Dorsey's taste in men was undiscriminating, to say the least. Hell, she had even rolled in the hay with me. I rest my case.

"Wanta go get a toddy?" Willie asked.

"Like what?"

"Like an Irish coffee."

"How about Scotch on the rocks?"

"Man, if you're buying I'll drink any damn thing except soda pop."

So away we went, two really cool unattached dudes with money in our jeans, out on the town in the Bad Apple on a Sunday night.

CHAPTER TWENTY-SEVEN

Monday morning the sun illuminated a hazy, gauzy summer sky. The humidity was already high and going higher at seven in the morning when we set out from New Jersey for Manhattan. Joe Billy Dunn, Willie Varner, and I were in the van, and Sarah Houston was still sacked out in her motel room, which she announced last night was a far cry from her digs at the Hilton. Her observation almost broke my heart. Slumming can be so hard on a girl.

"I have to go back to Washington this evening," Joe Billy said. "I thought I'd hop a train this afternoon."

"Can't you tell them you're still sick?" He had called in sick before we left the motel.

"No. And I haven't earned enough vacation to get days off. It's back to work or go looking for another job." Fortunately Sarah had taken a week's vacation, so I knew I could count on her. That is, if and when she woke up and got sufficiently caffeinated to be of some use.

"Maybe we could take Joe Billy on at the lock shop," Willie said to me. "He could sweep out and work the counter while we teach him how to duplicate keys and stuff."

"Maybe you could sorta cut class like I'm doing and hope everything shakes out okay," I said, and turned the rearview mirror so I could see Dunn's face. "After we've saved the free world from the forces of evil, all will be forgiven."

Joe Billy made a rude noise. "With your luck, Carmellini, you're going to be still rotting in prison when they find a cure for the common cold."

"Hey, man, don't be so negative," Willie chided. "Too early for bad vibes."

"Take a train," I told Joe Billy. "The Musketeers will soldier on without you."

"Mail me a little medal when you get your big ones, okay?"

"Negativity sucks, you know?" Willie said, continuing his soliloquy. "You gotta think positive as you travel the road of life. Tommy gets prosecuted, they'll probably let him plead to desecration of a body or obstructin' justice, something like that. Hell, he'll only be in eight, ten years max."

"Desecration of a body?"

"Yeah. You know, fuckin' a corpse, something along those lines. Tommy will make out all right. Have faith."

Easy enough for Willie to say, but mine was shaken an hour later, after we parked on a narrow east-west street just north of the Hilton. Willie was listening on the bugs, I was working the computer making a digital recording, and Joe Billy was munching a banana, three spies in the house of love, when Willie asked, "Who in hell are these people, anyway?"

"Whaddaya mean?"

"You listen a while. You tell me what we're listenin' to." He handed me the earphones.

A guy and a gal, talking about getting it on with another couple they knew from Tampa. The guy sounded lukewarm, the woman enthusiastic, trying to persuade him.

"What suite are they in?"

"Royston's."

"Naw."

"Yep."

"These aren't the right people. That couldn't be Royston. His wife is in Washington."

"For Christ's sake, I know that, Tommy. These are two god-damn swingers from California. They were talking about car dealerships in L.A. a minute ago. Who are they?"

I called Sarah Houston, woke her up, sounded like. "We've got a problem. Get on your computer and find out who the hotel put in these suites we bugged."

"Please."

"Get on your computer, please."

"Okay."

She called back twelve minutes later. "They're registered as a Mr. and Mrs. Bronson Whitworth from Beverly Hills, California."

Joe Billy and Willie were both wearing earphones now. "It's the woman she's got the hots for," Joe Billy said gleefully. "This one's a switch-hitter."

"What suite did the hotel put Royston in?"

I slapped one phone on my left ear in time to hear the woman say, "Bronnie, you can watch. You know how much you enjoy that."

He didn't think the convention was the place.

"Royston's party is in Penthouse Ten, Twelve, and Fourteen," Sarah said.

"We bugged Fifteen, Seventeen, and Nineteen."

"A delegation from California got all three of those suites. Someone shuffled the parties around. There is a notation in Roys-ton's reservation about a good view. Royston must have demanded a view room."

"What suite is Dorsey O'Shea in?"

In the silence that developed while she checked, I heard the woman in the suite cooing softly in my left ear.

"They're gettin' it on," Willie announced gleefully. "She's goin' to screw him around to her way of thinkin'."

"God almighty," Joe Billy said with a smile on his face. "Wish we had put a little video camera in there."

"What is going on?" Sarah asked. Apparently she could hear the comments of my colleagues.

"Gimme Dorsey's room number, huh? I don't want to run into her when I'm in the hotel trotting around."

"You're going in again?"

"Someone has to move the bugs. I planted everything we brought."

"Twelve twenty-one," she said crisply. Then she added with a trace of envy in her voice, "She paid several hundred extra for the room. It must be a small suite."

"Next time around inherit some money, please," I snarled, and snapped the cell phone shut. Damn women, anyway.

Years ago I learned that prior planning prevents piss-poor results. I call it my P^{5}R rule. Sarah could check to ensure the master code I had put in my plastic door pass the other day was still in use. Or I could put in the new code. Getting into the rooms was not the problem.

However, getting in without arousing the suspicions of the people monitoring the hallway surveillance cameras was a problem. Unfortunately my suit, white shirt, and tie were in the motel room in New Jersey, and I didn't want to drive two hours to retrieve them. Should have brought them along, just in case.

I left Willie and Joe Billy to be audio voyeurs and got out on the sidewalk to walk and think about the problem.

I didn't have enough cash left to pay for a suit, and my Zack Winston credit card was bogus. I had high hopes that I would eventually be able to convince the powers that be that I had been merely defending myself and others since that Tuesday at the Greenbrier River safe house, but I didn't want to try to explain credit card fraud. Some people get downright pissy about money.

If I used my own personal credit card, would it light up alarms in Dell Royston's universe?

Maybe I should go back to Jersey and get the damned suit. We couldn't move the van without losing the parking place, and I didn't want to waste cash on a taxi.

What the heck, I had plenty of time. I couldn't go into those rooms until the people were out of them. The dinner hour would be the most likely time.

Over on the East Side on Lexington I found a large men's shop that opened at ten. Looking in the window, I thought I saw some sports coats on manikins that might fit. The problem is my shoulders and arms, which are so big that an off-the-rack coat that I can get around my shoulders doesn't hang right around my small waist.

I strolled along soaking in the sights, sounds, and smells of New York, had a bagel and cup of coffee at a small breakfast place, then wandered back up Lexington to arrive at the men's shop a few minutes after ten.

The owner was a former prizefighter, I surmised. Scars on his eyebrows, one permanently mashed ear, and huge shoulders and arms.

"You have a pair of trousers and a sports coat that might fit me without alteration?"

"You some kind of athlete, ain't you?"

"Rock climbing."

"Yeah. I got the stuff to fit guys who work out, take care of theirselves. Lot of pro athletes come here for their duds. Not the high dollar guys, but the guys who watch their wallets."

"That sticker in the window says you take credit cards."

"MasterCard and Visa."

He did have a sports coat that didn't make me look like an ape, and the price was reasonable. I decided the risk of using my own credit card was small, so I surrendered my Visa card with TOMMY CARMELLINI embossed on the bottom. He ran it through the machine, I signed the invoice, and he bagged my purchases, which included a tapered shirt and subdued tie.

Walking crosstown, I called Sarah. "Where are you?"

"Eating breakfast," she said.

I told her what I needed. "I don't want the entire surveillance camera system to crash, just temporarily go on the fritz floor by floor as I move around. I'll call you on your cell."

"The motel doesn't have a high-speed Internet connection. I dropped off the Net twice this morning and had to log back on and go back into the system. Takes about four minutes to get through."

"I don't have the money to pick up another night at the Hilton, Sarah, if that's what you're asking."

"I don't have the bucks either. No, I was merely warning you that there may be problems."

"Okay. Warning received."

"You're going into Dorsey's room, aren't you?"

"I haven't decided," I answered, a trifle evasively I suppose.

"You will. I know it."

"What's it to you?"

"I think you have a thing for her, that's all. Very unprofessional, I must say."

"Are you jealous?"

She made a noise and hung up.

I knew she wasn't jealous—heck, I knew what she thought of me. Still, the fact that she guessed right on Dorsey bothered me a little. Maybe I was getting too predictable. If Sarah Houston could guess my next move, so could someone with lethal intentions. It was a thing to think on.

Joe Billy Dunn shook hands with me and Willie and left about two in the afternoon. Just when I needed someone that Dorsey didn't recognize to act as a lookout, there he went.

After he closed the van door, Willie and I sat in the back of the thing—which was about the size of my closet at home—looking at each other. "Well, nothing ever goes perfectly," the Wire remarked.

I was in no mood for philosophy. I grunted unpleasantly.

"How do you get yourself into these messes, anyway?" he asked.

"Do you want to go play pool or get a beer or something?" I said. "There's nothing to do until I get ready to move the bugs."

"You want me to go inside and act as lookout?"

"No. I want you to sit right here in the van and watch the floor surveillance camera on that monitor"—I pointed to the one mounted high in the corner—"and communicate with me on the cell phone. The cameras will still work even when Sarah diddles with the computer downstairs."

"I could do that, I reckon," Willie Varner admitted as he picked at a scab on his arm. "I just don't want to put myself in harm's way. Can't handle it, the shape I'm in. I'm already runnin' on two gallons of other people's blood. Been gettin' these urges to read romance novels, drink white wine, and listen to white music—I figure the blood was from some white women. Republicans, probably. I'm all crippled up from that cuttin', still wearin' bandages, and here I am workin' anyway. You know I oughta be on that Social Security disability, gettin' a little check in the mail, takin' life easy till I'm feelin' myself again."

"Take a hike, goddamn it."

He went, leaving me in splendid solitude in the back of a stolen FBI van parked beside a fancy hotel in New York that I couldn't afford to stay in. Ah, the glamour of the clandestine life. And to think I could be heisting jewels on the French Riveria!

I felt like a fool strolling in the side entrance of the hotel in my new duds. Dorsey O'Shea was in there somewhere, and I certainly didn't want to run into her.

I had waited until six in the evening—the cocktail hour in civilized climes. Willie was out in the van; he'd come back an hour ago well hydrated with beer. He didn't have a set of Hilton clothes, and he would have drawn security men like flies if he had walked in there in his jeans and ratty T-shirt. Not that I could have used him as a lookout even if he had the right clothes— Dorsey might recognize him. She might recognize me, too, but putting more people she knew in the building made no sense. Willie had the penthouse corridor surveillance camera on the monitor when I left the van.

The three penthouse suites where we had our bugs were empty just now; I had listened carefully before leaving the van and locking Willie in. Knowing Dorsey, she would be someplace swilling white wine with the beautiful people while nattering about outside artists and spiritual advisers.

I dialed Sarah on my cell phone. "I'm going up to the penthouse now."

"Give me one minute, then call me back."

I paused just inside the entrance and surveyed the lobby. The cocktail bar was in a slightly raised area on the right, and it was packed. Every seat was taken, and people were standing around and talking loudly. I didn't see Dorsey. Nor did I see Dell Royston. I had certainly seen enough photos of him through the years to be able to recognize him in the flesh, I thought. For a brief second I wondered if the California car dealer and his AC/DC wife were in this crowd. Might be.

I glanced at my watch, then dialed Sarah again.

"Coast is clear," she whispered conspiratorially.

"Terrific."

I walked on through the lobby, past the desk to the elevators. The penthouse had its own elevator. A group was coming out. I held my breath, half expecting to find myself face-to-face with Dorsey, but my luck held. The person who did step out was Dell Royston, surrounded by four guys in expensive suits. They didn't even glance at me.

A plastic door key was required to activate the elevator. My master key worked like a charm. The door closed and I ascended.

I met one matron on the penthouse level. She was dolled up, apparently heading for dinner. This being New York, she avoided eye contact with me. After all, we hadn't been introduced.

I knocked on the car dealer's room door. Rapped several times, then used the master key.

The place was empty. I scrambled around collecting bugs, which I tossed in an attaché case I had brought along for that purpose, and was finished in ninety-five seconds flat. Standing in front of the door, I called Willie. Who knew who would be standing out there when I opened this door? Years ago Willie had met the guest as he opened the door of a room he had just robbed— that twist of fate sent him up the river. He was supposed to call me if anyone showed up in the hallway, but I wasn't willing to run on faith, not with him half potted.

"Anyone out there?" I asked when he answered.

"Hey, dude, I'll call you."

"Right."

I took a squint through the security glass anyway, saw no one, and opened the door. Corridor was empty. Walked to the adjoining suite and repeated the procedure.

When I had all the bugs, I used the phone by the wet bar in the third suite to dial Royston's suite. No answer. I dialed each of the other two in turn. The telephone rang in each suite until the hotel's automatic message system picked up.

Without further ado I marched down the hall and proceeded to scatter the bugs through the three suites in places the maid and guests were unlikely to discover them. About the only rule was to avoid placing them by a television or radio speaker or near a water faucet or toilet. It didn't really matter where in a particular room the tiny microphones and transmitters were—the computer would synchronize the audio if two or more bugs picked up the same conversation. The operator could filter out extraneous noise picked up by the bugs or be selective in which bugs he wanted to monitor. Unless we left them on continuously, the batteries in each unit would last about ten days, more than enough for our purposes. Our ability to turn the units on and off remotely made them impossible to sweep with conventional gear unless they were transmitting.

Standing in front of the elevator twelve and a half minutes after I arrived on the floor, I called Sarah.

"I'm on the red level. The bugs are in place. I have to ride the elevator back to the level above the lobby to catch a regular one. Give me one minute, then turn on the cameras on this level. Then call Dorsey's room. See if she's there."

"What will I say if she answers?"

"Ask her to confirm her dinner reservation. I'll call you from downstairs."

The elevator arrived and I stepped aboard for the trip down. Unfortunately Willie couldn't monitor the surveillance camera on that floor, since I hadn't put a tap on the coaxial cable. No time to do it now, even if I had another cable tap, and I didn't.

I bailed out on the so-called balcony level, which had its own lobby with meeting rooms leading off in various directions. My choice of floors was not a good one. This lobby was jammed with people, too, although they appeared somewhat more sober and subdued than the crowd around the bar on the floor below. Apparently many of the convention committees were meeting here, wrestling with things like credentials, the platform, and so forth.

I stood by some sort of artificial potted plant that some of the conventioneers had watered with beer and called Sarah one more time.

"She doesn't answer her phone. Perhaps she's in the shower."

"Did you do the cameras on twelve?"

"No. I've lost my Internet connection. Do you want to wait?"

"No."

Without a lookout on the floor, I was playing Russian roulette darting in and out of Dorsey's suite. The sooner I was out of this building, the better.

I took a regular elevator to twelve and marched along the hall to Dorsey's room. Rapped three times loudly. No answer.

"Room service," I called in what I judged to be the proper volume.

When I received no answer I took a deep breath and used the master key.

The door opened, and I surveyed the room before I entered. Indeed, Dorsey had popped for a small suite, with a sitting room with wet bar, a bedroom with a king-sized bed, and a bath off the small hallway leading between them.

I stepped in, pulled the door shut, and stood poised, ready for anything. When nothing happened, I did the tour. The place was empty.

Wasting no time, I put a bug behind the head of Dorsey's bed and one under the counter of the wet bar. I had to short Royston two bugs to have these for Dorsey. He would have felt slighted if he knew, but I hoped he never would.

I had just placed the bug under the bar when someone knocked on the door. "Maid!"

Before I could get to it the door clicked, then opened.

Thank heavens it wasn't Isabel from Puerto Rico. "Oh," she said. "So sorry. Turndown service."

"I'm just leaving, thank you," I said, and left carrying the attaché case.

In the hallway I stole a chocolate chip cookie from her cart and pocketed it for later. We thieves have no morals.

A couple was waiting by the elevator. I joined them, then followed them into the elevator for the trip down.

"Where are you from?" the lady asked. She was in her sixties, a dried-up wizened thing wearing a choker of plastic pearls.

"California, originally." See, I can tell the truth on occasion.

"We're from Arkansas. My husband is a Southern Baptist minister."

He beamed at me. I smiled at him.

"What religion are you, young man?" she asked seriously.

The tone of her voice must have irritated me a little. As the door opened at the main lobby, I said, "I'm a nudist," and made my escape.

"A Buddhist!" she exclaimed. Behind me I heard her ask her husband, the Southern Baptist, "Did he say he was a Buddhist?"

Scanning for Dorsey, walking confidently, assuredly, I headed for the side entrance where I had entered the building. I was five feet from the door and a clean getaway when who should come through it but Dorsey O'Shea! Through a side door, no less! What was the world coming to?

"Tommy Carmellini! Of all people! My God, what are you doing here?"

CHAPTER TWENTY-EIGHT

A man followed Dorsey through the door. He was maybe mid-thirties, with collar-length blow-dried hair and wearing an expensive silk suit cut in the Italian style.

I ignored her question and exclaimed, "I thought you were yachting in the Med!"

"It didn't work out, so I came home."

"I see." I turned toward the man. "And you are?"

"Just a friend," Dorsey stated firmly. She turned to him. "Carlo, I'm so sorry, but I need to talk to Tommy. Perhaps later. Would that be okay?"

Carlo was no fool. When you hang with rich girls you must get used to being brushed off when a better deal arrives unexpectedly. "Of course, darling. Call me." He squeezed her hand and was out the door before I could blink twice.

"One would think he did exits professionally," I observed as Dorsey led me across the lobby to an empty couch far removed from the bar and piano player.

290 — Stephen Coonts

She sat down as close to me as she could get—thigh to thigh—took my hand, and looked me straight in the eyes. "What are you doing here, Tommy?"

I looked straight back into her deep brown orbs and said, "They're having a political convention in New York in the age of terror to make a statement to the world. The feds have pulled in security people from all over." Notice that I didn't say that I was one of the security people, I merely implied it. For a spur-of-the-moment falsehood, I thought this was one of my better efforts.

"But what about—?"

"Over. Finished. Highly classified and buried."

"Oh." She examined my hand as if seeing it for the first time, then a knee, then the carpet. "Oh, my."

"These things happen."

"Then I'll never be questioned about that man?"

"I doubt it, but really, I wouldn't know. If you are, I suspect that you'll have to sign a secrecy agreement."

"I see. Very convenient for me."

"Yes. Isn't it?"

"Of course, it was strictly self-defense. You and that other woman were witnesses, and he was armed. After all, he had just broken into the house to do God knows what. I didn't do anything illegal. And I would be delighted to tell anyone about it."

"As I said, the whole thing is classified. I suggest you not mention it to anyone or, indeed, you *will* be visited by the FBI."

"I certainly don't need to tell anyone anything. That was one of those episodes best forgotten."

"You got that right."

"Difficult to forget, though."

This was my cue. She was still holding my hand, so I covered hers with my free hand and squeezed gently. "Have you had dinner?"

"Why, no. Have you?"

"I was just on my way. This place is packed. There's no way we will get into one of these hotel restaurants without reservations."

"I have a reservation." She glanced at her watch. "I'm sure they held it. It's at Gallagher's on West Fifty-second." I had heard of it. Gallagher's was a classy beanery where the political honchos liked to hang out. Getting a table at this hour was probably impossible unless you knew the maître d' or were willing to slip him two or three photos of Jackson. "Would you like to eat there?" she continued. "Or perhaps someplace more intimate?"

Uh-oh. That was an invitation if ever I heard one.

She made the decision for us, as I knew she would. "I know a little neighborhood place in the Eighties that shouldn't be crowded," she said. "Not too many people know of it, but the food is delicious and we can visit and talk. Let's go there."

Looked as if I was going to be the main course for Dorsey this evening. Too bad for Carlo.

"So," I said as we walked out the front entrance of the hotel, "why are *you* in New York?"

"Haven't you heard? The convention is going to nominate a woman for the vice presidency."

"I didn't know you cared about politics."

"Tommy, I like to be where the action is, and this week that's New York. Can't you feel the electricity in the air? Nothing will ever be the same. No woman who could afford to be here would dare miss this."

That evening Callie Grafton joined her husband on the porch of their beach house after dinner. Jake put down the sectional aeronautical charts he had been annotating and slipped his pencil into his pocket. Their guest, Mikhail Goncharov, had gone upstairs to lie down. He and Callie had been talking all afternoon.

"He is a very brave man," Callie said forcefully.

"I suspect so," Jake murmured.

"He was a Communist and got into the KGB through his uncle, who was a bigwig there. A major general, I think he said. He'd worked in the Fifth Directorate for eight years when he was picked for the archivist job. He didn't get along with his boss, who campaigned hard to get rid of him. I think by that time he was disillusioned with the KGB and the Communists, but if he resigned from the organization he would have been unable to get other work."

"And he would have been a security risk."

"Yes. He was stuck and knew it. So he made the best of the archivist assignment. It was actually a very low-pressure, low-visibility job. He said that in effect he was merely the head clerk, overseeing the typists who transcribed handwritten notes, overseeing the clerks who logged the files in and out, preparing the department's budget, supervising the guards who were on duty twenty-four hours a day, and so forth. The amazing thing is that the files for all the directorates were kept in his archives—all of them—for security purposes. Regulations forbid anyone, even the top people, from keeping files in their private safes."

"Why did he begin making notes?"

"Disillusionment, he says. He doesn't want to talk of that decision, but it is the key to his personality. He saw the reports and reviewed the files for completeness for every single activity the KGB engaged in—everything—from internal security to bugging foreign embassies in Moscow and overseas, running spy rings and counterintelligence operations, the campaigns against the dissidents, the show trials, covering up scandals among the party elite, all of it. And he had time to review the old files in the archives, the files from Lenin's and Stalin's time. Those files were sometimes incomplete, he says. In the past highly sensitive material was removed from the files. The example he gave me was of the arrest record of Stalin when he was a young man. The file was there because it was numbered and had to be accounted for, but the folder was empty."

"You like Goncharov, don't you?"

"I admire him, yes. The pressure he put himself under by betraying the state! Living with that day in and day out for all those years, living with the constant fear of being found out. He doesn't say so, but I think they would have executed him if they had learned what he was doing."

"I have no doubt they would have," Jake agreed.

"His wife is now dead because of what he did."

"She must have known what he was doing. At some point all that paper accumulating in their small apartment had to be explained."

"Oh, she knew, all right. And shared his conviction that he was doing the right thing. Still, the guilt is hard to bear." Callie fell silent, thinking about the afternoon's conversations.

Finally she passed her hand over her face, then said, "I asked him the questions you suggested. He can't remember anything on any of those people."

Jake studied his toes. "Can't or won't?" he prompted.

"I believe he can't. He has nothing to hide. He risked his life and his wife's life for all those years to make notes on the files and threw their fate to the wind to bring the information to the West."

Jake Grafton nodded.

"But Jake, if he can't remember, perhaps those files don't exist. Perhaps they never existed."

"The copies are being reviewed. Quickly read, not analyzed. We'll know more in a day or two. Perhaps three."

"Who knew the files had been copied?"

"MI-5, of course, and probably a few senior people in the CIA. But no one else. British intelligence had secretly copied the files without permission, and the people who knew it didn't want that fact leaking back to Goncharov. They wanted his cooperation."

"So whoever went after him thought the files had not been copied?"

"Apparently."

"But I don't understand. If he can't remember, perhaps the files they thought were there never existed at all."

"Perhaps."

"Then why would any of those people want him dead and non-existent files destroyed?"

"That's the nub of it."

They talked on, and even went on to other subjects, but after a while Callie came back to this one. "If it had been your decision and Goncharov refused to allow the files to be copied, would you have betrayed his trust and copied them against his wishes?"

"In a heartbeat," Jake said. "When Kelly Erlanger said he had been in Britain a week and a few days in America and there was only one copy of the files, his, I knew that couldn't be true. No competent, responsible intelligence officer would take the chance that the most precious intelligence treasure of modern times might be lost in a plane crash or house fire. Not one. Those files were duplicated the instant they were out of his sight."

"So who ordered the files destroyed and Goncharov murdered?"

"Someone who isn't an intelligence officer."

Dorsey O'Shea was as forthcoming about her reasons for being in New York as I had been. Baldly, she was evasive, but unlike me, she didn't have the classified information laws to hide behind, not that she needed them. Over white wine at the restaurant on the Upper West Side, she told me that she and the yacht dude hadn't hit it off, so she decided to come home.

"I felt like a fugitive," she said earnestly, leaning forward to give me a good view of her ample cleavage. "I wanted to come home so if anyone wanted to question me, they could see that I had nothing to hide." The irony of that remark was not lost on me.

"Been home yet?"

"To Maryland? Not yet. I thought I'd spend a few days in New York and do some shopping, see some friends. The political theater is just a bonus. Tommy, I need something to take my mind off that—." She made a gesture.

Well, that certainly was plausible. Shopping and socializing was all Dorsey had ever done since she left college—without a degree, I might add. The educators had gotten stuffy about the difference between required courses and electives, according to her, so she packed her checkbook and told them good-bye. After all, people who know things can usually be hired by the hour. I suspected there was a young male involved in Dorsey's college adventure, but I had never pressed her on it.

Inevitably our conversation returned to the convention. "What do you think of the chances of having a woman vice-presidental candidate?"

"The country is ready," she said matter-of-factly. "I think it will happen this week. I hope it does. I meant it when I said the moment is historic. If it happens, life will be different for every woman in America."

I wasn't about to argue that. "Think Zooey has a chance to be picked?"

"God, that would be awesome! She's presidential timber. But whether the president has the guts to make the choice, I don't know."

"You've given a lot of money to the president's campaign," I remarked, "so why don't you tell Dell Royston what you think? He has to listen to big contributors." Actually I didn't know that she'd ever given a politician a dime, but I felt that this shot in the dark was likely to hit something.

And it did. For a second she looked startled, but she said, "Perhaps I should talk to him." She laughed to cover up letting her face slip. "And maybe I should write the president a letter. If enough people want her, he will have to choose her. Right?"

Our dinner arrived, and she picked at it. Skinny rich women never eat much. "Have you ever personally met Zooey?" I asked casually.

She took her time before she answered. "Several times, as I recall. Parties and receptions."

"Did you ever go to the White House?" I asked warmly, as if that were a big deal.

Again the hesitation. Her answer could be checked, and she knew it. "One of the receptions was at the White House. I've forgotten the date and occasion, though."

"Must be cool, getting invited to the big house."

"It was, believe me. I bought a special dress for the occasion from a well-known designer"—she named him—"and believe me, I don't do that very often."

That didn't cut much ice with me. I had seen her closet, which was about the size of my apartment. I kept my mouth busy with my pork chop.

We went on to other subjects, split a dessert—she had exactly one bite—and lingered over a coffee and liqueur. She palmed the tab expertly, and I let her. My guess was that the dinner and tip had run to at least $250. She was used to it. No doubt Carlo would have stuck her with the bill, too.

When we left she put her arm around my waist. "Where are you staying in New York?"

"With friends. That way I can pocket the per diem."

"Would they miss you if you didn't go there tonight?"

"Might telephone in a missing persons report. I'm willing to take a chance, though, if that was an invitation."

"It was."

Oh, boy. Willie was going to get an earful.

When we got back to the hotel there were two uniformed cops and two plainclothes dicks standing in front of the penthouse elevators checking credentials. It looked to me as if I got the bugs shifted just in time. They also gave the story I told Dorsey more credibility.

Sex with Dorsey was always a workout. She was one of the new moderns who believes that a woman's sexual satisfaction is her own responsibility, so she went after hers with a will. Of course it was fun for me, too, since she was trim and tuned up and filled out in all the right places.

After the first round of bedroom gymnastics, she played with my chest hair and took another shot at my reason for being in New York.

"Hey, babe, a terrorist incident this week is a risk no one in government is willing to tolerate. The town is packed with feds and fuzz and badge-toters from all over."

"But you're not FBI."

"I go where I'm told. Have to to keep getting paid."

She left it there, and we got after it again.

I sneaked out of Dorsey's room at six in the morning while she was still asleep. Waking up alone would be hard for her ego, but I'd had enough of her company. I got a cup of coffee and a bagel from a street-corner vendor and went around the block to the van, which was locked up and empty. I went inside and locked myself in. Willie must have got a cab or train back to New Jersey last night.

They were awake and playing politics in Royston's suites by nine. He got telephone call after telephone call, and I listened to his side of the conversation. He had a deep, gravelly voice, so I quickly learned to pick it out no matter how many conversations were going on in the room.

Tuesday was the first day of the convention. The platform committee had a large faction, I quickly learned, with an agenda that didn't match the president's. Royston spent the morning on that issue when he wasn't meeting the heads of state delegations who came to call. I suspected Royston was going to be talking to delegations all week.

Each and every one asked Royston who the president wanted on the ticket with him. Royston was coy. If he knew, he wasn't saying. After I heard him dance around the issue for the fifth time, I decided that he probably didn't know. He did, however, ask each delegation what they thought of Zooey.

That was more for show, I figured, than anything else. The presidential nominee was going to get whoever he wanted to join him on the ticket. True, years ago a Missouri senator was announced as the presidential nominee's selection, then dumped by the nominee, George McGovern, when it became plain that the senator's mental health history worried the delegates. McGovern apparently dumped him on the theory that if the delegates were worried the voters would be, too. Of course, the voters turned out to be extremely worried about McGovern, so the veep choice didn't really matter. Yet it might have.

This president hadn't announced his choice, and no doubt he would not until the very last minute. Royston was merely taking temperatures and weighing support.

Yet when he had mentioned her name to eight delegations by eleven o'clock, I would have bet my pension, if I live to collect one, that Zooey Sonnenberg was going on the ticket with her husband. Dorsey was going to be thrilled.

I wondered why. I'd spent a lot of time with her during our torrid affair a couple years ago, and she had never once mentioned a single political issue. I didn't know her party affiliation or if she was even registered to vote. If I had been forced to guess, I would have labeled her a nonpolitical independent who voted her conscience. She certainly didn't need to vote her wallet.

The idea that she supported Zooey because she had met her was ludicrous. With her money Dorsey got invited everywhere in Washington. She had met everybody worth meeting at one time or another. Rubbing shoulders with the smart and powerful hadn't changed her much, from what I could see.

I was listening to Dell Royston and wondering how much of anything we were going to get out of all this political wind when my cell phone rang. I checked the number before I answered it. Sarah Houston.

"Yo."

"I heard you spent a hot night with Dorsey O'Shea."

Ol' Willie. Can he keep his mouth shut or what? "We need to know what she knows," I said.

"So you were pumping her. Jerk!" The connection broke.

What was she hot about? It's not like she and I had something going.

Willie Varner arrived around noon. He greeted me with a giggle and "Hoo boy, what a night you had!"

"Being a gentleman on a mission, of course you listened all evening to Royston's suite."

"When Dorsey wasn't moanin' and tellin' you what a stud you are, yeah, I channel surfed to Royston's station. Big political stuff goin' on there, lots of drinkin', no women."

"Great. And you called Sarah to give her the hot news about where I was spending the night."

"Actually she called me. Said you had turned off your phone. Wanted to know where you were. She's got the hots for you, too, you lucky devil. How in the world do you manage to walk down the street carryin' your cojones?"

"Gimme a break, goddamnit!"

"Royston and his bootlickers came poppin' into those suites about ten minutes after you left. You cut it mighty fine."

"Yeah, that's the way I do things."

"At least ol' Dorsey says what you got is mighty fine."

"Hey, it was in the line of duty, man! As your friend, I ask you to say no more about it."

"Tough shit, Carmellini. I'm goin' to talk about it ever' chance I get for the next fifty years. She says you're a real stud, big guy, and I think you oughta go with that endorsement. Take it to the bank. She's a prime piece of ass and you did a good job fuckin' it. Be proud. Be happy."

I let him have the last word. It was the only way to shut him up.

CHAPTER TWENTY-NINE

O n Wednesday amid much pomp and circumstance the convention nominated the president to run as their party's candidate in the election that fall. Actually they nominated three men, the president and two favorite sons, then dragged the speeches out for most of the afternoon and didn't get around to the voting until prime time, when the proceedings were televised. Surprise, the president received most of the votes to be the standard-bearer, then someone moved that the convention make the nomination unanimous, which was done by yeas and nays.

Throughout the afternoon Royston hung out in his suite and received a steady stream of visitors—governors, senators, congresspersons, cabinet secretaries, big party donors, and people who wanted to be governors, senators, congresspersons, and foreign ambassadors. It was quite a parade and boring as hell to listen to. And difficult. The rooms where Royston was not receiving visitors were full of people; to select individual conversations from that hubbub, you had to use the computer and zero in on a voice print. Willie did it a few times with my coaching, but it hardly seemed worth the effort. All the talk was about a woman VP candidate. The fact that the president's selection would be female was a foregone conclusion with that crowd, most of whom assumed that the soccer moms and working mothers of America would flock to the banner of the party with a woman on the ticket; the only question was which woman. Zooey Sonnenberg seemed to have the most supporters.

The president called Royston once, and he called the big guy twice to report on the visitors and what they said about the chances of the party carrying their states. I could only hear Royston's side of the conversation, and it wasn't anything earth-shattering. I became convinced these two knew the local politics of every county and hamlet in America.

Royston made no big promises, and neither did the president. Apparently they didn't think this was the time or place for promises—they didn't need them. Not yet, anyway.

There was some opposition to Zooey for the vice-presidential spot on the ticket, an undercurrent, but how significant it was I didn't know. To the best of my knowledge neither did Royston, because I didn't hear anyone give him actual polls of state delegations.

I was listening to this pablum while contemplating my navel when the telephone rang. Thinking it was probably Sarah or Jake Grafton, I clicked it on.

"Tommy, this is Dorsey."

I almost dropped the telephone. "Just a second while I turn off the television."

I frantically turned the volume knobs as far down as they would go. Silence filled the van, and Willie stared at me while I took several deep breaths.

"Hey, Dorsey, how you doing?"

"Fine. Where are you, Tommy?"

"Working. By the way, how did you get this telephone number?"

"Oh, I turned on your phone and got it while you were asleep Monday night. You don't mind, do you? I realized that I didn't know how to get in touch with you, and that seemed like an easy way."

Sleeping around can get you in trouble—I learned that in high school. "Enjoying New York?" I asked brightly.

"Oh, yes. I was wondering if you would like to go to dinner?"

"This evening?" I kicked the brain into gear. Did she just want a repeat of Monday night? Was she going to try to wheedle information from me? Or was something else on her mind?

"I'm pretty busy right now, Dorsey. If this is social I probably should work."

"It's important to us."

"Us?"

"You and me."

Willie couldn't hear what Dorsey was saying, but he heard enough of my side to get the drift. He winked and leered lasciviously. I shut my eyes so I could concentrate.

"Could we discuss it over a hamburger?"

"That's not the venue I would choose, but if you only have a little time . . ."

"If it's important, let's wait until after the convention. I'll have several days free then."

"It can't wait."

"Okay. Ten o'clock in the hotel café. They do salads, too, I suspect." Dorsey O'Shea might munch a burger on her way to hell, but not otherwise.

"Ten o'clock," she said. "I'll see you there."

" 'Bye."

"Good-bye, Tommy," and she hung up.

As I folded up the phone, Willie chortled. "She can't get enough."

"You think?"

"What else could it be?"

Indeed. If only I knew how Dorsey was mixed up in this, maybe I could guess. What I did know for certain was that she wouldn't tell me. No way.

"Was she in her suite when she called?"

"No. I checked while you were talking. No audio from the bugs there."

I opened the phone and checked the number of the last call received, then wrote it down. I called Sarah and asked her to find out where the phone was. Almost an hour passed before she called back. The delay she blamed on a lack of a high-speed Internet connection. As if I cared.

"So where is it?"

"It's a cell phone belonging to one Dorsey O'Shea."

"Thanks." Well, no help there.

"So how is everything with you two?"

"Really, Sarah, I'm not in the mood."

"Never mind. I'll ask Willie."

Jake Grafton wandered aimlessly through the beach house looking at everything and seeing nothing. He was engaged in the most noxious task known to modern man—waiting on a telephone call. From time to time he flipped through his sectional charts, read his airport directory again, measured distances and calculated flying times. Occasionally he looked up from his task and watched a few minutes of convention coverage. Then he went back to wandering.

Callie and Mikhail Goncharov chatted from time to time, ate, and napped. Callie managed to read a few chapters in her current novel. Goncharov had nothing in Russian to read, so he, too, paced, but he did his pacing upstairs.

"He's a kind, gentle human being," Callie told her husband at one point.

"Who is?" he asked distractedly.

"Mikhail."

"Uh-huh."

"I'm trying to imagine how I would have managed to get from day to day if I had been in his place, trapped in a bureaucracy I loathed, one engaged in subversion, murder, framing innocent people for crimes they didn't commit, all to prop up a criminal regime. I think I would have just quit. Would have gotten a manual labor job to eat."

Her husband gave her a long look, yet said nothing.

"On the other hand," she mused, "quitting would have been a cop-out. If you don't fight evil, you become evil."

"That's a platitude," her husband murmured.

"Every deep human truth is a platitude," his wife shot back. She was no shrinking violet, which Jake Grafton well knew.

"You would have done what he did," Jake said. "If fate had put you in that place, you, too, would have written down the secrets, hoping that someday you could find a way to make the truth known. That choice took courage and commitment. Goncharov may be a kind, gentle man, but he's got guts. So do you. That's one reason I married you."

He squeezed her hand and wandered out into the yard to look at the grass.

Ten o'clock came all too quickly. I left the van fifteen minutes early and walked completely around the hotel so that I would approach the main entrance from the side opposite the van. I had on my sports coat and tie.

Dorsey was fashionably late, arriving in the café at six after the hour. She saw me at a table in the corner and joined me.

She bussed me on the cheek and squeezed my hand before she sat down. "Thank you for coming."

"You look ravishing this evening, Ms. O'Shea."

Actually she looked like she was under a lot of stress. I had seen her in that condition before—chasing the porno tapes, and after she shot the intruder in her house—and knew the signs.

The waitress came, and Dorsey ordered a salad, as I had predicted. I ordered a sandwich and a glass of wine. Dorsey also thought a glass of wine would be good.

"Do you think I look old?" she asked.

Of course I denied it. She was in her early thirties and looked maybe twenty-five.

"I feel as if life is passing me by," she continued as if she hadn't heard me. "I am wasting my life."

This was a new Dorsey, introspective. I've always believed that the idle rich should avoid introspection. "What do you want out of life?" I asked politely, trying to guess where this gambit was going.

"I want to be happy," she said flatly. "I want a man who loves me, and I want kids."

This was the first I'd heard about kids. That comment jarred me. Dorsey wasn't my idea of the maternal type.

"What is happiness?" I offered, just to keep her talking.

"I'm not sure," she mused. She began playing with that idea and was still chattering when our drinks came. The wine was cool and delicious. As I sipped it and listened to Dorsey the thought occurred to me that maybe I should have ordered something stronger. I was beginning to suspect that Dorsey was on her way to a destination I wasn't going to like.

And by God, damn if she didn't go there!

"Tommy, you're the only man I ever met who didn't want something from me."

"I don't do platonic relationships," I muttered.

"I'm not talking about sex. I'm talking about money. Every single man and half the married men who meet me have dollar signs in their eyes. I've heard every investment opportunity and charitable scheme you can imagine. I hear a new one almost every day."

"You need to find a better class of people to hang with."

"I need a man who wants me, not my checkbook."

"They're out there. You'll meet one."

"Why not the two of us, Tommy? You and me. Is that so crazy?"

So there it was. I was being proposed to. And I had no idea how to handle it.

The waitress arrived with our food, which gave me a few seconds to think. When she disappeared I sat watching Dorsey toy with a little tomato with her fork. Finally she put the fork down.

"Dorsey, I don't think you're in love with me."

"I don't know. Perhaps I am. But I think we could love each other. I like you so much . . . Oh, Tommy, can't you see us together? We could travel all we wanted, see the world, enjoy the people and places and find a perfect spot for us. And we could have children. Two, I think, a boy and a girl. You and I living life together could be so perfect."

Wandering aimlessly through life on an eternal vacation was not my idea of how I wanted to spend my days. "I'm not going through life with a woman paying the bills," I said as gently as I could.

"We could do a prenuptial agreement," she said earnestly. "I'll give you half of everything I have when we're married. Then you can pay the bills."

I took a healthy gulp of wine. I was right—I should have ordered whiskey.

"If we were married we couldn't have any secrets from each other," I stated, trying to turn this ship to a different heading.

"That's true." She was watching me like a hawk, her salad and wine untouched.

I took a bite of my sandwich, chewed it and washed it down with wine while I waited in vain for her to take another step on the subject of secrets. She wasn't going to, I concluded.

"Dorsey, I'm flattered. I have never been proposed to before. I've never had a woman care that much for me. I don't know what to say. I care very much for you and don't want to hurt your feelings. Yet I doubt that we would work as a couple. We tried dating regularly once, and that didn't work so well. You are you and I'm me, and that's sort of an unchangeable fact. Maybe we should accept that. Make love when it suits us, go to dinner when we can fit it in, now and then a play or party, and each of us go on with our lives."

Her eyes were glued on me. I had never seen her so intense. "Tommy, I'm offering you me and half of everything I own. I want you as a husband. And a friend who trusts me. I am trying to do the right thing for both of us. Do you trust me?"

Oh, boy! "I believe you are trying to do what you think best. But I am not convinced it would work."

"If we want it badly enough, we can make it work."

The divorce courts were full of people who once thought that. I did not make this comment to Dorsey O'Shea. What I said was this: "I need time to think. I confess, I haven't been thinking of marriage. I need some time to get a handle on where I'm at."

She reached for my hand. "Spend the night with me. Let's go up to my room. I need you now, this evening."

A roll in the hay with hot, wanton Dorsey pulling out all the stops while Willie Varner listened to the action was the last thing on earth I needed that night. I told her I had to go back to work. I signaled for the check, stood, and dropped money on the table.

"I'll put the tab on my room," she said distractedly.

Truthfully, she was a very beautiful woman. And she wasn't the woman for me.

"No, Dorsey. You won't." I bent, kissed her on the lips, and headed for the door.

It was raining when I came out of the hotel. I was in no mood for Willie Varner, so I went walking. Bought another umbrella and I didn't even have an expense account. There was a little bar on Ninth Avenue at about Fifty-seventh, and I dropped in. Quiet. Two drunks at a little table in the back of the room. Tending bar was a defrocked priest or a disbarred lawyer—I didn't ask which. The place reeked of old wood and wasted lives. High at one end of the bar was a television with a Yankees game going, with no sound. They were playing someplace with sunshine. I wished I were there.

I ordered a double Scotch, the oldest stuff they had, and sat at the end of the bar by the window and watched the rain and the traffic and the people hurrying by.

Dorsey wasn't a bad person. Oh, she was a poor little rich girl, and I believed her when she said every man in her life wanted money. Still, I wasn't the guy to rescue her. I didn't want her money. I didn't want the frantic indolence, the eternal vacation, the doomed-to-failure effort to stay young and trendy and with it. I wanted to look my age, to keep busy with things worth doing, and to find a woman who loved me.

Dorsey didn't.

At least, I didn't think she did.

So why in hell did she ask me to marry her?

Didn't she know that wasn't done in middle-class circles? Any woman worth her salt could maneuver the object of her affections into getting on his knee and popping the question. Or maybe, being a hip young modern, Dorsey didn't give a damn.

Wonder if I was the first man Dorsey ever asked to wed.

Can a husband testify against a wife in New York? Maryland? Why did I have this suspicion eating on me that she was somehow involved in this mess with Royston? She knew everyone in Washington; she admitted she'd been to the White House. Why not Royston? Or the president?

Naw—she was no Monica.

I sipped the Scotch as slowly as I could, but it went down way too fast, so I ordered another.

I pulled my cell phone from my pocket and laid it on the bar beside my drink. After a while I picked it up and dialed a number I had memorized.

He got it on the second ring. "Grafton."

"Tommy. Been a hell of an evening. Dorsey proposed."

"Proposed what?"

"What the hell you think? Marriage, goddamn it!"

"How much is she worth, anyway?"

"My guess is about four hundred million. Give or take."

"Why didn't you get the number?"

"She was proposing marriage, not a merger." That wasn't strictly true, but I was in no mood to get into the messy details with Jake Grafton. I had all the respect in the world for him, but there is a limit.

"Girls that rich don't come along every day," he observed tactlessly. "My old man always told me that I should marry the first time for love, the second time for money."

"If you and Callie ever split the blanket, I'll give you Dorsey's telephone number."

"He also said it's as easy to love a rich girl as a poor one, although I don't think he had any experience to back that up. It was a naked assumption on his part."

"Terrific."

"So did you say yes?"

"I called because I think it's time for you to tell me what is going on. Everything you know."

"Don't know much," the admiral muttered, "and that's a fact."

"Everything you suspect."

"All of it?"

"All of it. Who, what, where, when, why."

"It'll take a little bit."

"Believe me, I've got nothing but time."

So he told it. Dumped the whole load on me. When I hung up thirty minutes later I tossed the phone on the bar and sat watching the rain through the window. When the barman came around I asked if he had coffee. He said he could make a pot. And he did.

CHAPTER THIRTY

It was after midnight when I got back to the van. As I put my umbrella on the floor to drain, Willie sniffed and said, "Been drinkin', huh?"

"If you were a better cook you'd make some lucky man a good mother."

"So what'd she say?"

"She wants to marry me," I said flippantly.

He snorted in derision. "That'll be the day," he said, turning back to the computer. "Royston got a call a while ago I think you should listen to. I got his end of it."

"Who was he talking to?"

"You tell me." He handed me the headphones, then went back to punching the keyboard. Rain drummed on the top of the van, making a pleasant sound.

I donned the headphones and got comfortable. A proposal from Dorsey. That'll be the day! And yet, this *was* the day. Four hundred million genuine American dollars, half to me, and I told her I'd think about it.

If half of that pile wasn't enough, Carmellini, just what was your price?

If Willie only knew the truth, my reputation as a corruptible bastard would be in jeopardy. Yet knowing Willie, he'd probably just tell everybody that Carmellini wanted to steal it, not marry it.

My ruminations were interrupted by Dell Royston's gravelly voice in my ears.

"Hello."

After mumbles and grunts and some long pauses, Royston said, "You're going to have to announce your decision soon. Like tomorrow. Heston's set to make the nominating speech, but he has to have a name to plug in." Heston would be Senator Frank "Piggy" Heston, the senior senator from one of the smaller states—he got his nickname from his addiction to pork projects for his constituents. By reputation, he had never seen an appropriations bill he didn't like.

Another long pause followed that comment, then, "I see . . ."

Finally, "I can hold the train in the station for a few hours, but by tomorrow afternoon it's got to pull out . . . Sure. See you tomorrow evening." Tomorrow evening, I knew, the president planned on making his acceptance speech to the convention, to be broadcast nationwide on all the networks.

Willie raised a finger and pushed a button.

I took off the headset.

"Well?"

"The president hasn't made up his mind," I said.

"His own wife! You'd think the bastard could say yes or no."

Which left me speculating about the relationship between the president and first lady. Theirs was a political marriage, sure. But they had four years to figure this out!

Willie leaned back in his chair and scratched a scab. "Well, you ready to go back to Jersey and snatch a few winks? Or will you be sleeping over somewhere?"

WAGES OF SIN — 315

"Maybe the president isn't sure he could be reelected with Zooey on the ticket. Reelection is the first priority."

"Bullshit!" Willie pointed to a stack of newspapers on a ledge. "The pundits say he's a shoo-in. The economy is humming, he's hell on terrorists, working on the Mideast thing . . . There's a landslide shaping up."

" 'Dewey Defeats Truman!' "

"Maybe he just doesn't like the bitch." The bitch he was referring to was Zooey.

"You think likes and dislikes matter in politics?" I mused.

"Oh, I know, these politicos would bend over and spread 'em for the devil if he would deliver the sinner vote. But unless someone catches him in bed with a live boy or a dead woman, this president doesn't *need* help. That's my point."

"Beats me," I replied.

"Well, Jersey or what?"

"You go. Take a cab. I'm going to stay here a while."

"At this time of night?"

"Get one in front of the hotel." I dug in my wallet and gave him sixty bucks from my dwindling cash supply.

His parting shot was, "Try to stay out of trouble. I know it's tough for you, but tonight, for my sake, give it your best shot."

"Yeah."

He took my umbrella and locked the door behind him.

But what, I wondered, if it came out that the president did a deal with the Russians, way back when? In that event, my guess was that he would need every vote he could beg, borrow, or steal. Say hello to the devil, folks!

I wondered what the Big Dog was thinking tonight as he sat in the White House.

The rain kept pounding on the roof.

An hour later I was having trouble staying awake. I sat watching the comings and goings on the penthouse floor of the Hilton on the monitors and listening desultorily to the conversations in the suites. And this convention was going to run on for two more days. Friday was the last day; the delegates couldn't stay longer even if God asked them to. The television networks had other programming scheduled for the weekend and next week. The prez had to decide his choice for VP, get him or her nominated, and the delegates would vote on Friday. The cleanup people would work all weekend swabbing out the Javits Center, then next Monday a home products industry convention was opening there. Come hell or high water.

The crowd in Royston's suite emptied out. A bunch of drunks were finishing a bottle of Scotch in one of the adjoining suites, and in the other some aide was getting laid by one of the true believers from Iowa, some woman who had something to do with the school system. No one in Dorsey's suite on twelve.

Ah, me.

Just where was I going to be next week? Lodged in a jail someplace with a platoon of FBI agents shouting questions at me, or puking my guts out on a banana boat, sailing south under a false name? Wish I knew more about extradition treaties.

Of course, I could be making wedding plans with Dorsey, renting a tux and visiting lawyers' offices and making big plans to spend a huge heaping pile of cabbage. On which the taxes had already been paid, thank you very much. Assuming the FBI didn't latch on to me in the meantime.

What kind of yacht should I buy? What ocean should I put it in? Should I pop for gold faucets in the head? How big should the bed in the master suite be?

Say what you will about poor, rich Dorsey, the woman was flat-out dynamite in bed. Sure, she had been spreading it around—so had I—but with marriage and all, I could negotiate some sort of exclusivity deal.

Choices. Eenie, meenie, minie, moe, catch a tiger by the toe . . .

I checked Dorsey's pad one more time and managed to hear a woman say, "Thank you, gentlemen. Please wait for me downstairs."

The sound of a closing door. Water running in the bathroom. The faint sigh of a chair taking weight.

Who was that? Wasn't Dorsey. I was sure that wasn't her voice. Had she checked out?

I punched the button to record this.

As I looked up from the control panel, I got a glimpse on the monitor of Dell Royston coming out of his suite. Still wearing that suit and tie, of course. He walked to the elevator and pressed the down button. The camera beside the elevator gave me a good look at the thinning hair on the back of his head.

The elevator door opened and he entered.

Hmm . . .

Five minutes later someone rapped on the door of Dorsey's suite.

"Oh, Dell. Come in, come in."

Was this his wife? A secretary? The California car dealer's AC/DC wife? Or a working girl who sucked toes for fun and profit? I guess I'm naive: Prior to this week I had no idea how much screwing went on at these conventions.

The door closed, and I heard the sound of the privacy latches being thrown. I doubted that Isabel from San Juan was bustling about at that hour, but a man in Royston's position couldn't be too careful.

A short silence followed, then the sound of the bed taking weight. Oh, boy.

After a bit I began to hear moans and so on. There was serious fucking going on, or I miss my guess.

It was over pretty quick. Four minutes by my watch. One thing about Dell Royston, it didn't take him long to breed.

"Oh, baby, that was so good," Royston said, panting.

"I needed that, darling. It's been too long."

"I talked to him a few hours ago. He still hasn't made up his mind."

"The bastard! He's stringing this out to make me sweat."

My eyebrows shot up into my hairline. Holy cow! The "gentlemen" who accompanied her to the door must have been Secret Service. Royston was fucking Zooey Sonnenberg, the first lady!

"Whoever he picks is going to be the next president of the United States," Zooey declared. "With the vote of the party faithful and a huge chunk of the female vote from the other party, she'll be unstoppable four years from now."

"Maybe he isn't thrilled about being first husband in four years."

"Pffft."

"Maybe he doesn't want to spend the next four years in bed with the heir apparent."

"Dell, he doesn't—"

"You know what I mean."

"I don't know what he thinks. The troll sits in the Oval Office all day talking to his cronies, making deals, parading before the press, trotting off for photo ops and speeches in front of every civic group that will have him from Maine to San Diego—I am about at the end of my rope. He has my life—my future—in his hands and he plays with it. Sometimes I wish he would just drop dead."

"Let's hope you're the vice president if he does."

"He's healthy as a hog." She sighed. "No, my chance is selection as his running mate. Give me four years to line up support and be seen by the public and I could beat Jesus Christ in the next election."

"Maybe he's worried you'll steal the limelight now, during this election and during the next four years. The man has a titanic ego. He's spent his whole life fighting to be in the center of the stage."

"Perhaps." She paused, then launched into an assessment of the strengths and weaknesses of the other female politicians who had been prominently mentioned as possible candidates. As Zooey saw it, she was the logical choice.

"Sometimes logic doesn't carry the day," Dell said gently.

Amen! I added.

"So what should I do?" Zooey asked poignantly.

"There's nothing you can do except wait. It will happen or it won't."

"By God, I hate that son of a bitch!"

"Hang tough! You're almost there."

"Almost but not quite."

I heard the bed creak. "Let's get dressed. I have to go up to my suite and get some sleep. Thanks for coming. I needed you badly."

"Why didn't we meet in your suite? He wouldn't find out, and he wouldn't care if he did."

"It's bugged."

Goddamn, I muttered. *How in hell did he learn that?*

"Oh." That was her only comment. Not "Who?" or "Why?" Just "Oh."

They dressed in record time, kissed some more—I think—and whispered good-byes at the door. Royston left first. Three minutes later I watched on the monitor as he popped out of the elevator on the penthouse level and marched briskly to his room.

After some serious bathroom noises, Zooey left Dorsey's room ten minutes after that, pulled the door closed until it latched and rattled it to be sure.

I stopped recording and sat staring at nothing.

Well, well, well.

After a few minutes of thought I pulled my cell phone from my pocket and dialed Jake Grafton.

When he finished his conversation with Tommy Carmellini, Jake Grafton got out of bed. He held on to his cell phone. "Who was that?" Callie asked.

"Carmellini."

"Are you getting up?"

"For a while. Go back to sleep."

Grafton checked on his houseguest, made sure he was in bed asleep, then descended the stairs, trying to avoid the creaky one.

He looked out every window, then opened the door to the porch and settled on the couch, pulling an afghan over him. Royston and Sonnenberg. That was one piece of the puzzle, certainly, but he still didn't have enough.

It was maddening that Goncharov could not remember. Lord knows, Callie had tried. The silver lining in all this mess was that her command of Russian was increasing dramatically.

The admiral leaned back and closed his eyes, but he couldn't get his mind off the problem. It was almost an hour before he drifted off.

There weren't many people in the lobby of the Hilton at a quarter to four in the morning. The serious people were in bed—theirs or someone else's—and the drunks were sleeping it off, trying to get sober for the big doings of the coming day. I was still togged out in my sports coat and tie and trousers, though the crease was starting to go in the trousers and the shoes desperately needed polishing.

I walked to the elevator, rode up to twelve. The master key still opened Dorsey's door, so they didn't change the code daily.

Once inside, with the door closed behind me, I stood looking over the scene of the action. The bed was a wreck. The bathroom was not too bad, but Isabel was going to think Dorsey had a male visitor during the night. Of course, Zooey didn't care a whit what the maids thought. Probably never even gave it two seconds of thought.

The hotel provided a few sheets of embossed stationery for the guests who wanted to impress the folks at home. There were also a couple of envelopes. I helped myself to one.

Then I went through the sheets very carefully, looking for hair. Picked up a strand or two here and there . . . nothing out of the ordinary.

Dorsey had a brush in the bathroom. A few strands of hair were wedged between the bristles, and I carefully added them to the envelope. Got down on my hands and knees and examined the floor. Found a few more short strands for my collection.

I didn't linger at my task. Having Dorsey march in just now would be a major embarassment . . . and probably get me arrested, unless I read this situation all wrong. At this stage of the game, I doubted that I would ever live to leave any jail cell the police put me in.

After a glance through the security peephole in the door, I was out of there.

Along the empty hallway without seeing anyone, then waited for the elevator. Rode it down, did the gut check as the door opened, saw the coast was clear, and marched across the lobby and out.

At least the rain had stopped.

CHAPTER THIRTY-ONE

I was waiting for Willie Varner to arrive at the van late Thursday morning when my cell phone rang. I checked the number before I answered. Uh-oh.

"Good morning, Dorsey."

"Are you working?"

"Just getting off, actually."

"I was wondering if we might have breakfast."

"Sounds fine to me. Where and when?"

"My room at the Hilton, in about an hour."

I hadn't showered or shaved since the previous morning, and my clothes were beginning to smell, but I had to see her. "Okay. See you there."

I flipped to the bugs in her room and listened. A steady buzz on both bugs, though stronger on one than the other. It sounded as if the maid was vacuuming.

More activity in Royston's suite. People talking business and investments. The political situation in California in one of the adjoining suites. In the other they were worrying the bone: Was or wasn't it Zooey? Would having her on the ticket help or hurt the president?

I flipped back to Royston's suite in time to catch him on the telephone. "When will you arrive?" he asked. Then, "Are you staying with the first lady?" Some more grunts, then, after a long pause, "We could work up some spontaneous demonstrations if I could at least hint as to how it will go, have the signs and banners ready to unfurl. It would look terrific on television, get the ball rolling . . .

"I see," he said after another long pause, then he hung up the telephone. Someone came in and said the maid wanted to clean the room.

I was examining the sad state of my shoes when Willie unlocked the side door and climbed into the van.

His very first words were, "You look like something the cat coughed up."

"That bad, huh?"

"Don't you get valet services out here?" He plopped into the other chair. "What's happening?"

"Nothing much."

"The cabbie had a radio talk show on. They said the president hasn't announced his VP choice yet."

"That's about the size of it, I think."

"Have you had any sleep?"

"I napped for an hour or two in this chair."

"So are you going back to Jersey?"

"After a while. First I have a date."

His head jerked up. "Dorsey?"

"Yeah."

"In her room?"

"Yeah."

"Well, why not? I could use some red-hot sex to get the juices flowin', speed the healin', but I guess listenin' is the next best thing. 'Course, watchin' would be better."

"As your friend, I'm asking you not to listen."

"Ask away. The answer is no. Just remember every moan and grunt and compliment on your equipment is being recorded for posterity. When the FBI catches up with you, this stuff is going to be played at the Hoover Building, before the grand jury, in court, maybe even on TV. I'll bet I could even sell it to some of those talk show shock dudes. Maybe Jerry Springer—he's kinky enough. Imus would like the political angle."

"This is how you repay me for saving your miserable life?"

"Hey, man, sellin' recordings of your sexual exploits sounds like a career to me. Man's gotta do what a man's gotta do to keep body and soul together. Next week nobody will give a shit about this political crap, but sex always sells. Gonna buy a Lincoln Town Car and move to the suburbs."

Willie thought about that prospect for a moment, about the car and the lawn and the barking dogs next door, then shifted gears. "There's two sisters livin' in Andover who I might be able to hook you up with. They're a pair of fine lusty ladies with big tits. These gals are sorta Hershey's chocolate, but with you that'd probably be no nevermind. I've noticed that big tits seem to bring out your best performances. We get back and—"

I climbed from the van. When Willie the Wire got rolling, leaving was the only way to shut him up.

There was a copy store a block crosstown. I went in, waited for a moment until the clerk was available, and filled out a fax form. I handed her the document; she pushed buttons on the machine. The paper fed through the thing, and she handed it back.

"Have a nice day," she said. Her tits were medium-sized.

"Yeah."

Right beside the copy story was a drugstore. I bought tooth-paste and a brush and put them in my pocket. Found the remnants of that chocolate chip cookie I stole the other day in that pocket. Had forgotten I had it. It was a mess now. I threw it in the trash on the way back to the hotel. Bought a cup of coffee off a bagel vendor and drank it, although it was acidic enough to take the enamel off my teeth.

In the hotel men's room I answered nature's call, brushed my teeth, and washed my face. Yes, I could smell myself. If Dorsey wanted me in this condition, she was really serious about marriage. Or randy as hell.

For some reason as I stared in the mirror at my unshaven mug, the image of the burning house in the forest near the Greenbrier River flashed through my mind. The feel of guns bucking in my hands, falling people, smiling killers, broken bodies . . . Would I see those images at odd moments all my life, or would they fade into static amid the zillions of electrical impulses that stored memories inside my brain?

Blood and murder, sex and politics. One fine stew, you must admit.

And Dorsey, with her millions and her marriage proposal. I could almost hear her saying, "Let me take you away from all this."

The unshaven mug in the mirror stared back at me.

Dorsey obviously had lots on her mind when she opened the door. Yet she took one look at me and her nose wrinkled. "Did you sleep in those clothes?"

"I've been working all night."

"Strip. I'll send everything to the laundry on an emergency cleaning order. They'll have them back in an hour or two. Then get in the shower."

It was an offer too good to pass up. I went into the bathroom and stripped to the skin, piled wallet, cell phone, keys, .38 revolver, and ankle holster on the counter, and dumped my clothes in the hallway. I could hear her on the phone to room service.

The shower was running and the bathroom steamy when I heard the door open. I peeked around the curtain. She was examining my pile of hardware on the counter. "Uh-uh. Leave that stuff alone."

"Do you always wear a pistol?"

"Only on duty." I had forgotten to leave it in the van, where I stored it prior to my last tryst with Dorsey.

She took her clothes off. It always amazed me how fast she could strip for action. Then she asked, "Do you have room for one more?"

It was a big shower. After all, this was a big hotel, with big prices.

She tried to get me excited, but I guess I was too tired. I nearly yawned in her face. The downside was that I could tell she was working at it. We turned the shower off and toweled dry, and I grabbed my stuff. Put the watch on the bedside table and the rest under the pillow on the bed and crawled in. She got in beside me, I think, but I was asleep before she got settled.

Knocking on the door awakened me. I heard Dorsey's voice at the door, then silence. I checked my watch. A little after two in the afternoon, and I felt a lot better.

She came into the bedroom with my clothes on hangers and my underwear and socks in a brown paper bag. "See," she said brightly, "the system works."

She was wearing a frilly thing with a matching robe. Her hair was piled up on top of her head.

Dorsey O'Shea, sexy half-billionaire, sat on the bed and kissed me gently on the lips, then licked my lips with her tongue. I caught the scent of something expensive.

The thought occurred to me that I was in the same bed where Dell Royston got laid in four minutes a mere twelve hours ago, which took some of the luster off the moment.

"I love you," she whispered.

No doubt ol' Willie Varner was all ears out in the van. It takes talent for a man to get himself in fixes like this, and by God, I have it.

A man with more character might have handled this situation differently, but I figured I would probably never pass this way again. Although she was in this mess to her eyes, I really didn't believe she meant me any harm. I wrapped my arms around her and pulled her across me into bed.

A half hour later as she nibbled on my ear, she murmured, "So have you been thinking?"

"It would never work, you and me."

She stopped the nibbling, put her face inches from mine, stared into my eyes. "I want to go away. Now. Today. As quickly as we can pack. Anywhere on earth you want to go. I want to go with you, Tommy."

"You don't need to be rescued," I muttered.

"How would you know what I need?" The muscles were drawn taut in her face. She wasn't pretty now. "Do I have to beg?"

"Don't. It wouldn't become you."

"What's wrong with me?" She sat up. "Aren't I good enough for you?"

"Please, don't do this. You're a wonderful person—don't do this to yourself or me."

She leaped from the bed, went to the dresser, and jerked open the drawer. Took out a bra and put it on. Then panties. She was in a hurry, and she was angry. Not furious or spiteful, but deeply angry. At least I thought so at the time.

I got up and began dressing, too.

She grabbed clothes from the closet and stormed into the bathroom.

I took the time to examine her pillow. I found a couple of long dark hairs, which I put in my wallet.

She was crying when she came from the bathroom wearing a cocktail dress.

"Hey," I said.

"Oh, Tommy, when I really need you, you say no."

"It takes more than need to make a marriage. It takes love."

"We could love each other. My God, when I think of you, I— we could—"

"Did Royston ask you to do this?"

That stopped her tears. She looked at me hard, then said, "Go. Please."

I pulled on my sports coat, debated if I should try to kiss her, and decided against it. I put my hands on her shoulders, and she tried to pull away. I held her still.

"There are bodies scattered all over," I said, watching her eyes. "Dell Royston is in this up to his neck. I don't know how or why, but I'm going to find out. If you have any role at all in whatever has happened or is going to happen, you better make like a rabbit. Go as far away as you can as fast as you can and change your name. Or trust me and tell me what you know."

I couldn't read the muscle movements I saw in her face, around her eyes.

"Please go, Tommy," she said, so I did.

I wondered if I would ever see her again.

Jake Grafton's cell phone rang while he was fixing a late lunch for himself and Mikhail Goncharov. Callie had gone to the library. Standing in the kitchen amid the sandwich makings, he opened the phone.

"Grafton."

"It's the way we figured," the man's voice said. "The Brits say they can't find anything along the lines we talked about. Everyone in the files has a code name, the dates are coded, some of the files are nearly incomprehensible. They really need the archivist to explain what they're seeing."

"I see."

"Jake, the bottom line is they can't find it. If it's there to be found."

"Okay."

"So what are you going to do?"

"I don't know. How long do I have?"

"The FBI is chomping at the bit. They have bodies scattered from hell to breakfast, and they've been stonewalling Justice. I can't hold these people off much longer."

"I understand. I'll call you back."

He watched Goncharov eat his ham and Swiss on rye. Watched his face, his hands, his mannerisms. Wondered what he was thinking.

Callie returned as he rinsed the dishes. She came in, said hello to Goncharov in Russian, and handed Jake an envelope. He ripped it open, examined the faxed photograph. The quality wasn't perfect, but the faces were recognizable.

"Ask Goncharov if he has ever seen this man or knows who he is."

Callie handed the Russian the page and translated the question. Jake saw the recognition in his eyes.

Yes!

Words were gushing from the archivist when the telephone rang again. Jake glanced at the number, then opened it.

"Yes, Tommy."

It was nearly five o'clock when I got back to the van. Willie gave me a long look but said nothing. That I found hard to take.

"What's eating you?" I asked. He had the convention on the

monitor, video without sound. Some politician I didn't recognize was pounding the podium.

"You."

"Right."

"I thought I knew what was goin' down, but then you have that little conversation with Dorsey this afternoon and the thought crosses my dishonest mind that I don't know shit."

"Who does? They say anything on TV about the president's choice?"

"All this time I think you just gettin' some nookie on the sly, and turns out you're up to your ass in shit with that rich bitch. What's this about going away?"

"You had anything to eat today?"

"Don't brush me off, goddamnit! The feds are going to swarm us both and send us so far up the river we won't get out for a hundred years. And I'm takin' the ride not even knowin' what the fuck went down. Shows you how fuckin' smart I am! You keep tellin' me I'm your friend and you don't tell me shit."

"What do you want me to say? There are two dozen bodies spread all over the East Coast, and we're trying to figure out who and why. You think I know?"

"You know more than me, and that's a fact. Goddamn, Carmellini, it was *me* those assholes carved up. I'm gonna carry the scars all my miserable life. Don't all that blood buy me some truth?"

I took a deep breath and exhaled slowly before I answered. "The truth is I don't know what's going down. I just pray to God that Jake Grafton does. If he doesn't, we'll share a cell someplace."

"I ain't sharin' nothin' with you ever again," Willie declared. "You in the same prison with me, you're a dead man, Carmellini."

He meant it, too—I could see that. "Maybe you should go home," I suggested.

He didn't say anything to that for at least a minute. I could see he was thinking it over. After a while he muttered, "I go home, they'll arrest me before the goddamn sun sets. I'll stay."

I turned up the sound on the monitor. This guy thumping the podium was a fire-breather.

"And I don't want to hear any more shit 'bout you savin' my life," Willie said, "like I owe you somethin' and ain't payin'. You're the one sicced those assholes on me. You owe me, man, not the other way 'round."

CHAPTER THIRTY-TWO

The president will speak in about twenty minutes," Callie told her husband, who was looking out the window. She was adding the final items to an overnight bag. "Do you want to stay to hear what he has to say?"

"No. Doesn't matter."

"Is going to New York really a good idea?"

"Maybe not, but it's the best one we have—the only one we have—so we're going to run with it."

He glanced at the television. On this channel a panel of "experts" was debating why the president would or wouldn't choose to run with his wife, Zooey Sonnenberg. In an upper corner of the picture was a smaller picture in which the governor of some Midwestern state was addressing the convention delegates, who weren't paying any more attention to him than the panel of experts were.

A wry grin crossed Jake Grafton's face; this was, he reflected, the Americans' freedom of speech in full flower. Card-carrying members of the chattering class were talking, exercising their constitutional right to say whatever they wished, and no one was listening.

He carried the overnight bag down the stairs and set it by the door.

He was about to ascend the stairs again to check on Goncharov when someone rapped on the front door.

He opened it and found a soldier in full camo wearing grease paint and carrying a short submachine gun on a strap over his shoulder. "Just thought I'd drop by, Admiral, and tell you we're leaving now."

"You are? Now?"

"Just got the orders, sir. They said you were leaving shortly so we were to pull out ASAP."

"Thank you, major. We are indeed leaving shortly."

"Any time, Admiral. It's been good training. Sorry about that villain last week."

"Right." Jake stood in the doorway and watched the major go. His men sifted out of empty houses and hides and joined him as he walked under the streetlight toward the highway.

The sound of loud rock music drowned out the sounds of traffic and surf tonight. It seemed to be coming from a house three doors closer to the beach, on the south side of the street. Cars filled every parking place.

Jake closed the door as Callie and Goncharov came down the stairs. "I think something is about to happen here," Jake said as he reached for the MP-5 Carmellini had stashed in a corner. "Come with me, now."

They followed him out the door.

"What's wrong?"

"Maybe nothing," Jake said. "The helo is supposed to pick us up at midnight and take us to New York. The general didn't mention that he was going to pull the security people away, but they all left. Called off, the major said."

"Why don't you call the general?"

"I will. In the meantime I think we should get out of the house."

Moving quickly, they walked under the light past the party into the darkness beyond. Jake told Callie to hide with the archivist under the derelict building near the beach, the one in which Carmellini had killed the rifleman. They disappeared over the boardwalk. Jake lay down in the sand beside a fence on the yard of the last house on the north side of the street, which was empty just now.

Yesterday a pack of college-age youngsters had loaded the garbage cans in front of the party house, packed their cars, and departed. Another bunch had arrived today. Tonight they were settling in.

There was a shrub of some kind at the end of the fence. Jake shoved the nose of the silenced submachine gun between the shrub and the fence and pointed it at the junction of this dead-end street and the highway, then lay down to wait. Fortunately this yard was slightly elevated, so he could see over the hoods of the cars parked on the street.

There was not enough light to see the keys of his cell phone. Still, he managed to get the general on his second dialing attempt.

I watched the president's acceptance speech on the monitor in mission control, surrounded by computers, radio and television receivers, and the remnants of sandwiches, potato salad, and pickles from a deli down the street. Willie had stopped his grousing and watched without comment.

The president wore a dark suit and burgundy power tie. He was carefully made up and used the TelePrompTer with obvious skill. He recited the accomplishments of his first term and laid out the goals for his second, the themes he wanted to run on. He denounced the dogs in the other party who had impeded his legislative program and stymied some of his judicial nominations.

It was a tub-thumping political speech, just what the pundits and everyone else expected him to say. Made you wonder if there were any good movies on the cable channels. Near the end of the speech, he got around to the subject that had consumed the delegates all week, the identity of his vice-presidential running mate.

"This party needs a woman on the ticket," the president declared, "a competent, capable, highly intelligent woman. This nation wants a woman on the ticket who understands the goals and aspirations of the American people and is ready to assume the burdens of the presidency in an emergency."

Apparently the prospect of his demise was merely "an emergency." That wasn't the word I would have chosen. Which is why he's a politician and I'm a thief.

"This party and this nation," he continued, "are ready to put behind us the tired, obsolete, bigoted ways of the past and step into the future, a future where all Americans, regardless of race, religion, national origin, or gender"—here he paused to thunderous applause—"have an equal opportunity. The time has come. *We* must carry the torch forward into the future, lighting the way for all the people of the earth. *Our* time has come . . ."

"Get on with it," Willie muttered impatiently.

"Senator Heston will make a formal nomination tomorrow, yet tonight I wish to ask the delegates to this convention to put the most competent, capable, trusted woman politician and statesman in the country on the ticket with me." Growing, swelling applause. "Tonight I ask you to nominate my wife, Zooey Sonnenberg, to run with me for—"

The rest of the sentence was drowned out by cheering and applause. For a moment the president looked as if he were waiting until the applause died so he could finish his peroration, but then he gave up. He turned, stepped over to Zooey, who was beaming broadly, took her hand, and led her to the podium. As a million camera flashes strobed continuously, the president and first lady stood before the nation and the world with hands clasped together over their heads while they waved to the crowd with their free hands.

I studied Zooey's face when the television cameras zoomed in for a close-up. She was one happy human, beaming at the audience, her husband, and the cameras as the world watched. It occurred to me that she and the president had both labored for most of their adult lives for this moment.

Power—the ultimate aphrodisiac.

They wanted it badly.

Then I remembered Dell Royston. I flipped switches to hear what was going on in his suite. Cheering and applause, an audio overload. Individual voices were indistinguishable. I tried the adjoining suites, right and left. More of the same, although in one they had the television audio cranked way up and I could hear the commentator's voice-over.

I tried Dorsey's room. Got her on the telephone, apparently, because I could only hear one side of the conversation.

". . . Never seen her so happy . . . That's right . . . Um-huh . . . Uh-huh, yes . . . Yes, I see that. She deserves it, but deserving or not, sometimes life doesn't work out."

Then Dorsey hung up, and I was stuck with the television commentator. I cranked the volume way down and called Sarah Houston, who, God willing, was still monitoring the hotel's computer system.

"Hey," I said when she answered. "You still on the job?"

"No, fool, I'm at Radio City getting in my seat to watch the Rockettes."

That stunned me for a second, until I realized that was supposed to be a joke. Sarah has a rather sick sense of humor, which she trots out at the oddest times.

"Dorsey was just on the telephone. What can you tell me about that call?"

"Very little."

"Did it originate within the hotel?"

"Yep."

"Who made the call, damn it?"

"It came from Royston's suite. As you know, I don't have the capability to listen in. If a certain burglar had done a better job last week, we'd be able to monitor both sides of every telephone conversation made through the hotel's switchboard."

"It's hard to get competent help."

"Impossible, sometimes."

"Thanks," I said, and hung up. I used my cell phone to call Jake Grafton.

He listened to everything I had to say, then said, "We'll be up there later tonight. I'll bring Callie along to translate."

You could have knocked me over with a feather. I mumbled something, I can't remember what, and he said, "Someone set us up down here. The guards were called off, and the general who sent them here knows nothing about it. He's checking now."

"You'd better clear the house," I said.

Jake Grafton swatted my advice right back at me. "You have been a stationary target in that van for five days now," he said. "I'd hate to come up there and find you dead."

"Ahh . . . You don't think—?"

"You know far too much, Tommy. So do I. So do Goncharov and Callie and Willie Varner."

"Where should I meet you?"

"The hotel lobby at two or two-thirty."

I looked at my watch. Three hours from now.

"Okay," I said, and hung up.

"Let's go," I said to Willie.

"Go where?"

"Go get a drink. Take a leak. Go. Now. Come on."

"But who is going to listen to—?"

"No one." I pushed him out of the seat and started him toward the door.

There was just enough moonlight for Callie to spot the two figures moving swiftly south along the beach, near the dune. They were apparently fit men in dark clothes that covered their arms and legs completely, trotting along carrying something in their hands.

She whispered to Goncharov, who moved even deeper into the shadow under the pilings that held up the abandoned house. Callie joined him there. Showing him by example, she lowered her face into her hands so her eyes wouldn't reflect light. She also did not want the eyes of the hunters spotting the lightness of her face amid the darkness.

Head in her hands upon her knees, sitting in the darkness beside Goncharov, she waited.

Callie Grafton and the archivist were saved by the simple fact that the two men did not expect to find them here, so they weren't looking. Their quarry, they thought, was still in the Graftons' beach house, and the guards were gone. As a matter of fact, they had sat in a van parked along the highway to the south and watched the guards leave in a government bus.

Jake had just turned off his telephone so it wouldn't ring when he saw the two black-clad figures come over the boardwalk. One took a position behind the porch of the rambling old house opposite Jake; the other dropped behind a car just in front of him. The man nearer Jake looked around quickly, scanned the houses and porches, then spoke into a small radio or cell phone.

It was a radio, Jake decided, because he heard the answering transmission end. Didn't hear the words.

The man was no more than ten feet away from the admiral.

It was a small miracle the man hadn't seen him. Perhaps he had seen Jake and, since he was not expecting to find a man there, had ignored the shape.

Whichever, if he turned his head ninety degrees to his right and took any look at all, he would see the admiral. This Jake knew. Needless to say, the MP-5 wasn't pointed in the proper direction. If he tried to extract it from the bush and point it at the man near him, the man would probably be alerted by the movement. Alerted too soon.

Jake felt sweat begin to accumulate on his forehead.

Soon a young man came out onto the porch of the party house. Music and laughter poured out the screen door. Standing on the porch, he lit a cigarette. He was joined by a young woman in a snuggling mood. The young man tossed his butt toward the street. The couple leaned against the railing and wrapped their arms around each other.

The party made the man in front of Jake uneasy. He eyed the young lovers repeatedly, glanced at his watch, shifted his grip on his weapon. Apparently he had not anticipated witnesses at this hour.

Welcome to the beach, buddy, Jake said silently to himself.

A minute passed, then another. A second couple joined the first on the covered porch and settled into a recliner.

The man in front of Jake said something into his two-way radio. Even as he did a van rounded the corner onto the street and drove the thirty yards to Grafton's house. It passed it, double-parked in front of the next one. Two men climbed out, the driver and one from the passenger door. The passenger went around the house while the driver walked up to Jake Grafton's door and knocked.

Another vehicle, a convertible, careened around the corner from the highway and came barreling down the street. Slid to a stop beside the van. The passenger leaned out, shouted at the man in front of Grafton's door. "Hey, buddy, you can't leave that thing parked there in the street."

Jake heard the reply. "I'll move it."

The convertible spun its tires getting under way, then braked hard and threaded its way between two parked cars onto the lawn of the party house. Four people climbed out. "Hey, Vinnie! We're here. Where's the beer?"

The man standing on Grafton's porch must have been frustrated. The party was unexpected. The witnesses might be a fatal problem. And he still wasn't in Grafton's house.

He turned back to the door, worked on the lock.

Jake tried to remember if he had used the key to lock the dead bolt or merely pulled the door shut until it latched.

No dead bolt, apparently. Thirty seconds after he attacked the lock, the man on the stoop opened the door. And disappeared inside.

There were at least eight people on the porch of the house across the street, drinking beer, laughing, talking loudly over the music. There was an elderly lady who lived on this side of the street who routinely called the police when parties got loud. Jake wondered if she was there tonight. If she was, this situation could get interesting.

The man in front of Jake picked that moment to move to a position where he could get a better view of the party. When his back was completely turned, Jake extracted the muzzle of the submachine gun from the bush and leveled it.

"Freeze," he said in a low, conversational tone, "or I am going to splatter you all over that car."

CHAPTER THIRTY-THREE

We locked up the van and strolled across the street to a bar on the corner. Inside were small tables along the window where we could watch sidewalk traffic and people coming and going from the Hilton. If I craned my head I could see the side of our parked van. There was a television truck of some kind in front of it, so the side was all I could see. Willie Varner ordered a beer and I ordered coffee.

When the waiter left, Willie said, "Okay, man, what's going down?"

"Grafton says he's got it."

"Got what?"

"*It,* goddamnit."

Willie nodded vigorously. "Fuckin' *it,* man. He's got *it* and I've been lookin' for *it* all my life. That what you're sayin'?"

"Yeah."

"So why'd we bail out of the van?"

"Shit happens."

"You mean there's a good chance another bunch of assholes are lookin' for us?"

"Maybe. Maybe not. Why take a chance when we can sit here drinking beer and good coffee?"

"Well, I'm here to tell you, I really hope Grafton does have *it!* I'm tired of that crappy little motel room in New Jersey and tired of New York and tired of that van and tired of you."

"Okay." I was watching people on the street, looking for folks I might recognize. Didn't see a one. Amazing, isn't it, how with all the millions of people in New York, everyone is a stranger.

The drinks arrived, and Willie drank deeply of his beer. When he put the mug down he sighed. "I want to go back to the neighborhood, man, where I can sit at my window and watch the kids sell crack. Watch the *po*-lice hassle the niggers 'cause they're poor and black. Watch the winos get drunk and vomit and sleep it off on the sidewalk. Watch the buildings crumble down." He took another long swallow of beer.

"Home sweet home," I said.

"Manhattan ain't America. Too busy, y'know? Ever'body goin' somewhere to do somethin', ever'body in a hurry, all day, all night, ever' day. Never stops. Wears you out just watchin'."

He finished the beer and signaled the waiter for another. I called Sarah Houston.

"Hey."

"Hey yourself."

"We're in a bar across the street from the van. Keep an eye on the penthouse video, will you?"

"How long have you been there?"

"Oh, ten minutes or so."

"Then you missed the show. Zooey Sonnenberg went into Royston's suite five minutes ago. You would have thought she was Britney Spears or the queen of Xanadu from the way those fools were acting."

"I have a weak stomach. Glad I missed it."

"So why are you in a bar?"

"Grafton thought it would be a good idea. He'll be here in a couple of hours. I've got my cell."

"Stay sober," she remarked, and hung up.

Willie wiped the beer foam off his lips and asked, "What's the it that Grafton's got?"

"I don't know."

"Or you ain't tellin'."

"One or the other."

For Jake Grafton time seemed to stop. The gunman ten feet in front of him against the car was frozen like a statue, across the street was another gunman who didn't know what was happening on this side, and two killers were double-parked near his house while they searched it, looking for him and Callie and the Russian archivist. Both sides of the street were lined with cars. Over this tableau floated the sound of rock music, loud voices, and laughter. At least ten people were crowded onto the porch of the party house, having a fine old time.

"Are you Grafton?" the man in front of his gun muzzle said, barely loudly enough to be heard.

"Yes."

"It's Goncharov we want, not you and your wife."

When Jake didn't reply, the man shifted his weight slightly. "You're one trigger squeeze away from the Pearly Gates, Jack," the admiral said softly, which stopped all movement.

"Tell us where Goncharov is and we'll let you go."

"You're not a very good liar."

"These are very heavy people. Regardless of what happens here in the next few minutes, if they want you, you're dead."

"They want Goncharov and he's still breathing."

"Not for long."

Seconds ticked past. One of the women on the porch began taking off her blouse as her audience clapped and urged her on.

"How long are we going to do this Mexican standoff?" the man asked.

"Until I let you move."

Jake could see him breathing deeply, thinking.

"Maybe you should drop the weapon before you get tempted."

The man released his gun, and it fell with an audible clatter on the gravel. In the darkness it was hard to see what it was, but it appeared to be a submachine gun of some sort.

"You know," the man said, his tone matter-of-fact, "I'm thinking of walking across that boardwalk and up the beach."

"Your funeral."

"Those guys come out of your house, they're going to come looking for me and the guy across the street."

"I've got enough bullets for them, too."

The girl on the porch threw her bra onto the lawn as her audience cheered appreciatively.

"When they come out of that house," the gunman said just loudly enough for Jake to hear, "I'm going to leave my weapon where it is, get up, and walk toward the boardwalk to the beach."

"I wouldn't."

"You won't shoot me in the back."

"This isn't a cowboy movie. Why don't you just lie down right where you are and put your hands behind your head? Tomorrow you'll still be alive."

Perhaps the man would have obeyed the admiral if he had had time to think about it. But time was up. A bus braked to a halt on the highway, blocking the entrance to the street, and a dozen soldiers carrying weapons piled out of the door and came running down the street.

The man in front of Jake simply started to his left, toward the boardwalk and the darkness beyond it. He walked normally, his hands at his sides.

Jake Grafton pointed the MP-5 at the center of his back and pulled the trigger. The silenced weapon bucked and coughed; five bullets hammered the gunman to the ground before Jake released the trigger.

"There's two of them in the house," Grafton roared at the top of his lungs.

The man across the street fired a burst toward Jake. The weapon wasn't silenced—the thunder filled the street. The man tossed a burst toward the oncoming soldiers, then turned and dashed for the boardwalk.

As he ran he sprayed bullets in Jake's direction. He managed four running steps before Jake's bullets scythed him down. The dying man held the trigger of his weapon down as he fell, emptying the remainder of the magazine into the ground and a nearby car in one long drumroll.

Curses and screams came from the party porch. Half the people there tried desperately to crowd through the door into the house; the others threw themselves flat.

Five minutes passed before the gunmen in Grafton's house surrendered. The soldiers had them lying facedown on Jake's small front lawn when the first police officer came running from the highway with his pistol in his hand.

Willie was on his third beer when the van blew up. I was scoping out a hot chick two tables over who was giving me the eye over her boyfriend's shoulder when I heard the detonation and felt the concussion, which rattled the window and caused glasses behind the bar to fall off the shelf and break. I looked toward the van in time to see the expanding fireball and pieces flying into the air.

"Damnation!" Willie exclaimed. "Somebody blew the son of a bitch up! Did you see that?"

Pieces began raining down on the sidewalk and street outside the bar. The bigger ones fell first and bounced, then the little bits fluttered down. Metal snow.

"Shit like this don't happen in Washington," Willie remarked, which was of course a lie without a hair on it. His collection of scars proved that.

"Stay here!" I ordered, and charged for the door.

I couldn't believe my eyes. The van wasn't crumpled or burned out—it was *gone!* Whoever had decided to take it out had not stinted on the explosives. Anything worth doing is worth doing right, I suppose. The asphalt where the van had been parked was on fire, giving off stinking black smoke. The carcasses of two of the tires were on fire—where the other two and the spare had gone I had no idea. There was a misshapen lump of metal in the middle of the asphalt fire that might have been the remains of the transmission and drive train. The vehicles parked in front and behind the van were severely damaged, smashed in as if they had taken hits from Thor's hammer. I looked around for the bodies of pedestrians or winos—didn't see any, which was a miracle.

The bomb was detonated by either a timer or radio device. I assumed that whoever had blown up the van probably didn't know Willie and I weren't in it. They didn't care about the van; they wanted us dead.

The windows of the ground floor of the hotel were missing, blown to bits and fired as shrapnel into the hotel by the blast. Across the street a jewelry store and drugstore had lost their windows, and indeed, smoke was coming out of them. Burning debris must have been thrown in there by the blast.

As I watched, security people began running out of the hotel, milling around with drawn weapons. A police cruiser roared up and screeched to a stop—in the distance I could hear a wailing siren. And onlookers were beginning to gather. Gawkers arrived in twos and threes, wandered up and stood staring at the smoking, stinking fire and rubble, a scene made all the more ghoulish by the flashing lights of the police cruiser's beacon.

There *was* a body, ripped up by flying debris. The onlookers pointed it out to the police.

Then someone found the remnants of a second person.

The hell of it was that I had a pretty good idea who had planted the bomb. I wondered if he was the button pusher or if he left that chore to someone else. Or did he just use a clock? If he were real smart he would be two states away when the thing blew. Then again, people who plant bombs often have this sick desire to be around when the thing goes off so they can watch the fire and the firemen, see the blood and gore, smell it, count the bodies . . .

I thought he might want to be close by.

But where was he?

About that time the gas tank in the truck that had been parked in front of the van ignited. Perhaps the burning asphalt got to it.

The first fire truck roared up, then another; police vehicles came from all directions. Extinguishing the fires in the street was the firefighters' first priority, so that they would have room to attack the blazes taking hold in nearby buildings.

How much explosives had that guy used?

The sidewalks were filling up with onlookers as the firefighters fought the fires in the drug and jewelry stores, police investigators and paramedics examined the corpses, and investigators poked and prodded at the remains of our van. The police quickly rigged yellow crime scene tape. A uniformed female cop pushed me and a bunch of other folks back as the tape went up in front of us. She was a slip of a thing, her hat cocked at an angle. She looked like a sausage in her bulletproof vest, complete with belt, holster, gun, spare ammo, mace, and radio. I don't know how she walked.

I knew it was time to leave when the first television crew turned on their lights and got their reporter on the air.

That's when something jabbed me in the back and a familiar voice said softly, "I didn't think you'd be in that van when it popped. Told them that, but they said to blow it anyway. I think the bugs you planted pissed him off."

The lady cop immediately in front of me had her back to me and was oblivious to my situation.

If I tried to elbow the pistol out of my back as I turned, more than likely he would put one in my kidney.

He grabbed my upper left arm and jabbed the pistol barrel deeper into my back, then whispered in my ear. "I owe you for sticking that gun in my face, Carmellini. Just wanted you to see it coming. Adios, motherfucker."

I had run out of time and options. I spun left, trying with my left elbow to sweep the gun aside, while I gathered up the female cop with my right arm.

A tremendous force hit me in the lower back, nearly dropping me. The sound of the shot came simultaneously with the impact—and for that reason didn't really register.

Somehow I stayed on my feet and kept turning.

Joe Billy Dunn's second shot hit the cop in the lower abdomen—I heard her grunt as the bulletproof vest absorbed the bullet's energy.

I pushed her forward into Dunn. His muffled third shot went off point-blank against the vest. Squeezing the trigger had been a reaction, probably, not intentional.

She collapsed at his feet. As he turned to run, trying to create space between us, the crowd impeded his progress. I leaped over the cop at him . . . too late. I sprawled on the sidewalk.

He ran as the crowd parted.

The cop sprawled and groaning, the noise, flashing lights and stench, screaming, running people . . . that was the way hell was going to be when I got there, probably in the very near future.

The only bright spots in this mess were that the right side of my lower back was numb, and I could still make my legs work, so the bullet hadn't hit my spine.

I scrambled up and ran after Joe Billy.

CHAPTER THIRTY-FOUR

J oe Billy Dunn ran, so I chased him. It never occurred to me to wonder why he was running away. He had tried to kill me, had even put a bullet in my back—although I didn't know if he knew that—and if he hadn't run I'd have taken his pistol away from him and killed him with my bare hands. Maybe it's my overdeveloped male ego, too much testosterone shrinking the brain, but I thought getting away from me was the natural thing for him to do.

Of course, the other possibility was that he didn't want to stand around shooting me until twenty cops in bulletproof vests got their pistols out and used him for their monthly target qualification. If his first point-blank shot had killed me, he could have turned and walked away and no one would have noticed his face. That was probably his plan; it didn't work out because he got to talking when he should have been shooting. I had absolutely no intention of making that mistake myself. Shoot first and talk later—I learned that from Jake Grafton.

Whatever his reason, Joe Billy ran like a deer.

I wasn't running like a deer, believe me. Not with a bullet in my back. I put my hand back there and pulled it away wet. A glance was enough. I was leaking blood at a fair rate. And I was beginning to hurt. Really hurt. I thought maybe the bullet had nicked a rib or something, because I got a stab of pain with every breath, and it got worse with every passing second. I ran like an old woman in tight shoes.

I didn't think he'd run far. When he got away from the crowd and the cops around the obliterated van, I figured he'd turn around and wait for me. To finish the job of killing me. I didn't figure he'd be doing much talking this time.

I had him in sight ahead of me when he dived down a subway entrance.

That was where it would happen.

I stopped at a fire hydrant, put my right foot up on it, and pulled the Smith & Wesson snub-nose .38 from the ankle holster. Just lifting my foot made my back scream.

I crossed the street and went down the entrance there. Went down very carefully.

These subway entrances join up at the bottom of the first flight of stairs . . . if I picked the right entrance to descend.

I had. Joe Billy wasn't in sight.

I kept going down, easing around corners. Got to the turnstiles and looked for my man Dunn. He wasn't in sight. No one was.

Of course, being an ex–Boy Scout who is always prepared, I didn't have a MetroCard. I had to heist myself over a turnstile, which cost me some pain. There was a surveillance camera pointed at the turnstiles; I gave the unseen watcher the finger.

I went slowly down another flight of stairs and got my first look at the platform. Not a soul in sight, not even a mugger or gangbanger. Everyone in town must have gone to bed after the president's stirring speech.

Dunn would be to my right or left, waiting to plug me again

when I came out of this stairway. I stopped at the bottom of the stairs and leaned against the left wall.

"Joe Billy!" I shouted. "Have you figured out why Willie and I weren't in the van?"

No answer.

"Because we knew you had sold out to Royston. And we told Grafton. Even if you kill me, you're going to prison for the rest of your life, maybe even the chair. How many people have you killed, anyway?"

"If I'm doomed, I might as well take you with me, Carmellini." The voice came from the platform behind me.

I crossed over to the right side of the entryway, leveled the pistol with two hands. It's impossible to hit anything beyond ten feet with a pistol with a two-inch barrel unless you use two hands and aim carefully.

I waited. I could feel a warm wetness soaking the back of my shirt and trousers. How much blood I had lost I didn't know—I wasn't feeling very chipper. Just holding the pistol at arm's length with both hands took about all I had.

I saw him a second before he fired. He had climbed off the platform down onto the tracks and sneaked along until he was almost abeam the entrance. Then he popped up, leveled his pistol with both hands, and fired. In that masonry tunnel, his pistol sounded like a cannon.

I was going forward by then, and the bullet gouged the tile on the wall behind me.

I went all the way down onto my stomach and leveled the snubbie.

Of course, he wasn't in sight. He had dropped down below the level of the platform the instant he fired.

The next time he popped up, he was going to be to my right or left, and he was going to nail me. I was going to die right here, lying on this subway platform.

As panic flooded over me, I sprang up and dashed for the stairs I had come down. Another cannon shot boomed and the bullet whacked the stairs just to my right—I saw the chips of concrete fly out. I went up those stairs like my tail was on fire.

I was scared, truly scared. I was an amateur facing a consummate professional in a fight to the death, and I didn't like my chances.

The reason he ran from me on the sidewalk outside the Hilton was that he knew I was stupid enough to follow him. I thought I was the hunter and he was the prey. Ha! It was a miracle Joe Billy had missed me with his first two shots. He wouldn't keep missing—oh, no! You could bet my life on that.

I was so scared I didn't even feel my back. I went up the stairs three at a time, running for my life.

At the turnstile level I looked around wildly for some cover. Got behind a pillar with a trash can in front of me, got down on my knees and stuck the toy pistol out so I could shoot quickly the instant I had a target.

That was when I realized I was gasping for air. Getting to here had cost me all my strength.

I listened for his footsteps.

Nothing.

My pulse and breathing rate were slowing when I heard a subway train roar up to the platform below and stop. Thirty seconds later it got under way again.

So where was this asshole?

Someone coming up the stairs. I heard the footsteps.

I leveled the pistol. A black kid in a T-shirt and pants that were held up only by the dictates of fashion popped out of the staircase and headed for the exit. He didn't even look at me.

He went through the turnstile and on up the stairs.

Oh, Christ, my back was killing me! Maybe I needed to go find an emergency room right now, before I passed out and bled to death waiting for a good Samaritan. I doubted if there were many Samaritans good or bad in the New York metropolitan area.

Where was he?

Fuck!

And where were the goddamn transit cops?

My back was on fire. I was on one knee and couldn't stay there. I sank to a sitting position.

Tried to keep the pistol up and couldn't.

Where was the bas—-

I glimpsed him on the other side of the turnstiles. He was leveling his pistol.

I rolled and fired all at the same time. Missed, of course.

His bullet clipped me on the scalp, just a glancing blow, like a friendly tap from a baseball bat.

I concentrated on the sight picture. The good news was that I was now flat on the floor, lying on my left shoulder, steady as a rock. I squeezed off one, reaimed the piece and sent another on the way.

His pistol was firing, and I tried to ignore it.

I fired again . . . and knew I had only one more left. He was a small target by then, down on his knees. I cocked the hammer, aimed as carefully as I could, and touched her off.

Joe Billy Dunn sprawled on the concrete.

It was all I could do to get to my feet. Went over and looked at him. He had at least two bullets in his chest and one in his throat. The throat wound was bleeding badly. I kicked his gun out of his hand, then bent down and picked it up. If I left it there the first kid who happened along would snatch it.

"You knew, huh?" he whispered.

"Royston said his suite was bugged. He said it in O'Shea's suite, which I bugged after you left. It had to be you who told him." Blood was leaking down over my ear from my scalp wound. I wiped at it. "How much did he pay you?"

"Not enough." He breathed in and out, fighting to stay conscious. "I've had a good run," he whispered.

"Your luck ran out."

"How'd you know I was behind you?"

"Heard something. Maybe your foot scraping. Maybe I just sensed it. For sure you weren't coming up those stairs."

He coughed blood. When the coughing subsided he whispered, "Just ran out of luck. That's all. Yeah."

I left him there. Didn't want to watch him die.

I felt better when I got up to the street. The night was misting rain again, and it felt good on my face. I was weak and tired and suffering from adrenaline aftershock, but I could still put one foot in front of the other. My back didn't cause me agony—I was just sore as hell.

I put the empty snubbie in one trouser pocket and Joe Billy's shooter in the other. Swabbed at the blood on the side of my face, wiped my hand on tree trunks, those baseball-bat-sized saplings growing up through holes in the concrete.

I wondered if Joe Billy Dunn was Stu Vine. Probably should have asked him that, but I didn't think of it. Don't guess it really mattered.

A wino staggered over. "Hey man, can you spare a dollar?"

"No."

"How about some change, a quarter or two? Ain't much. I need it bad."

"No."

"You're bleedin', dude. What happened?"

"Fell down."

"Better get that looked at." He turned and retreated to the store entrance that he was homesteading.

A young couple in expensive, fashionable clothes came along

the street from the direction of the Hilton. They studiously avoided looking at me and passed on by.

I was leaning against a building, taking stock, when my cell phone went off. Took me a while to dig it out of my pocket. It was still buzzing.

"Yeah."

"Where are you, Tommy?" It was Jake Grafton. I'd know that voice anywhere.

"Holding up a building. Had a little run-in with Joe Billy Dunn. He blew up the van and got a bullet in me."

"Where are you precisely?"

I looked around, saw a street sign and read it off.

"The driver says we're two minutes away. Stay right there."

If I was going to get a ride, there was no reason to continue to stand. I staggered over and seated myself on the curb.

Sure enough, a couple minutes later a stretch limo pulled to the curb and Jake Grafton got out. He looked at my head and back, helped me into the car.

Callie was sitting beside Goncharov, and there were two men in suits who I didn't recognize.

"What happened?" Jake asked as he inspected the hole in my back.

I told it as plainly as I could, about leaving the van and sitting in the bar, hearing the explosion, and rushing outside. I told him about the cop and her bulletproof vest, and I told him about Joe Billy.

Grafton felt my pockets, got the pistols out with my help, and passed them to one of the men in the car, who inspected them and slipped them into his jacket pockets. "The police officer is going to be okay. They took her to the hospital. She's shaken up and badly bruised."

"I didn't mean to hurt her, but there was no other way. He'd have killed me where I stood."

Callie went to work on my head with a hand towel that the limo driver passed back. "We should take him to a hospital," she said.

Jake Grafton looked at me with those cold gray eyes. "We can take you to an emergency room now or after we visit Dell Royston in his penthouse suite. Which do you prefer?"

"You got it, huh?"

Grafton grinned. He had a wicked grin when he was fighting mad, and he was that way now—I could see it in him.

"What about Willie?" I asked.

"Some of my friends picked him up and took him back to Jersey."

"I want to be there."

Callie made a last swipe at my forehead. "You may be bleeding internally, Tommy. Delay could be really bad. It could even kill you."

"You only die once. Let's go see the man." Okay, I was being an idiot, but that son of a bitch owed me. I intended to collect.

Jake Grafton nodded at the driver and the limo got under way.

CHAPTER THIRTY-FIVE

The limo wheeled up to the main entrance of the Hilton and stopped with the rear passenger door precisely centered on the red carpet. The suits got out first, and when I followed them two more suits showed up to assist me, one on each arm.

"Who are you guys?" I muttered to the one on my left.

"FBI," he replied in an almost inaudible whisper, as if it were a big secret.

That's when the importance of the moment hit me between the eyes. If Grafton didn't have Royston in the bag, the next ten to twenty years of my life were going to be spent in a very small place communing with rodents. Of course, I wasn't really guilty of any crime except stupidity—and prosecutions for that are thankfully rare—but it wouldn't go down that way. Too many bodies. Someone would have to take the fall. There wasn't a shadow of doubt in my crooked mind that I was the prime candidate.

At two in the morning there were only a few stragglers loafing in the lobby. Pretending to be someone they should know, I ignored them. As our little parade marched through the ornate, cavernous lobby, I was surprised to see it was growing rapidly. Over a dozen of us gathered at the elevators.

One of the FBI guys beside me flashed credentials at the two cops on duty. The plainclothes guy wanted to know about the rest of us, but the federal agent announced, "They're with me," in a don't-screw-with-me tone that moved the cops out of the way. It was heartening to see such deference paid to a federal wage slave.

I looked at the plainclothes cop and said, "I'm with the government, too."

If he was impressed he hid it well. He must have thought that with a burly escort latched on to each arm as I dripped blood on the carpet, I was under arrest. I sorta thought he might be right.

Admiral and Mrs. Grafton, Goncharov, and the suits from the limo got on the first elevator. My escorts and I got on the second along with the flotsam we had picked up in our voyage through the lobby. "Who are those guys with the Graftons?" I asked.

"Myron Emerick, director of the FBI, and Special Agent in Charge Harry Estep."

"What's Estep in charge of?"

"New York."

In the tight quarters of the elevator I could smell myself. At least I assumed it was me, reeking of stale sweat and old fear. Yeah, I was really scared back there in that subway station. That was perhaps as close as I've yet come to being launched into eternity. We all must make that journey sooner or later, but like most folks, I'm not anxious to be on my way.

When we got to the penthouse level of the Hilton, my two agents marched me out of the elevator and down the hall. I could see that three of the agents had two guys who must have been Secret Service backed against the wall. The Secret Service types were examining credentials and talking into their lapels. I expected that; bad news travels fast. The only question in my mind was how many minutes would pass before the president and his

Secret Service entourage showed up. He was spending the night someplace in town—where, I didn't know.

My escorts stopped twenty feet from Royston's suite. A minute slowly passed. I could hear someone rapping on a door.

I was close enough to hear voices. "They aren't here." Darn if that didn't sound like Dorsey.

It must have been, because a moment later Dorsey O'Shea walked past me. She didn't even notice me. Her eyes were focused on infinity as she walked past the crowd and led the way toward the elevator.

Grafton paused in front of me. "They're apparently down in Dorsey's suite on twelve."

I figured as much. I handed him my plastic-card skeleton key. "This will open the door if Dorsey doesn't have a key. Unless the hotel management has changed the code."

We trooped back to the elevator, waited for it to reappear, then climbed aboard. Dorsey went aboard the first one with the admiral and the big FBI bananas.

My back was hurting like hell, I was getting light-headed, and my scalp was still leaking. One of the FBI guys passed me a hankie, which I pressed against the scalp wound. As long as I was upright, I wasn't going to complain. The next few minutes would have a huge impact on the rest of my life. I wanted to be there.

To tell the truth, I was also hoping against hope that I would get a chance to lay some hurt on Royston, who I figured was behind everything. Maybe one of the FBI guys would loan me his pistol. Strangling the bastard would have been fun, but I doubted if I was capable of it in my delicate condition. Weak as I was, I'd be lucky if I could bite him on the ankle.

I don't know if Grafton or Emerick, the FBI honcho, pounded on the door, or if Grafton just used the master key I gave him, but everyone was piling into the suite when my escorts and I got there, so we followed the crowd.

It was a crowd. Dorsey's sitting room was smaller than Royston's upstairs. I guess Dorsey went back to the bedroom. In a moment she came back. "They're getting dressed," she said, not too chipper. She perched on the arm of a soft chair.

Then she saw me—my face actually registered on her consciousness. Her eyes widened, then she averted them.

Callie Grafton went behind the wet bar and found a towel. She motioned me to sit on a bar stool. She wet the towel and went to work cleaning my scalp. I noticed idly that I had left a trail of tiny blood drops behind me on the carpet as I came into the room.

The room swirled around. I grasped the bar to steady myself. That was when I saw the bottle of cognac and two glasses, neither completely empty. I pointed at the bottle, and Callie shook her head no.

"Medicine," I said with all the command I could muster. "Gimme."

She rolled her eyes, then shoved the bottle and one of the glasses my way. I drained it and poured myself some more. Ahh . . .

Dell Royston came out in shirt, trousers, and shoes. Zooey Sonnenberg was right behind him, wrapped in a bathrobe with the Hilton New York logo on the left chest area.

"What in hell is going on?" Royston demanded hotly. He looked from face to face. The only one he recognized besides Dorsey was probably Emerick, because he addressed his next question to him. "What are you doing here?"

"Dell, Ms. Sonnenberg, I'd like you to meet Rear Admiral Jake Grafton." Just polite as could be. "He has some things he wants to say."

They looked at Grafton, but I looked at them. Zooey's hair was messy, she wasn't wearing makeup, and she looked ten years older than her photos. Royston also had a case of bed head and needed a shave. I wished I had a camera in my pocket—a photo of them now would be worth a year's pay.

"On Tuesday, two weeks and two days ago," Jake said conversationally, "a gang of assassins attacked a CIA safe house in the Allegheny Mountains. They killed everyone there except for two people, Mikhail Goncharov"— he gestured toward the Russian —"and a young woman, a CIA translator named Kelly Erlanger. Ms. Erlanger is now deceased; her floating body was recovered from the Chesapeake the day before yesterday and has been tentatively identified. The killers would have probably made a clean sweep of the safe house if Tommy Carmellini, an officer in the CIA, hadn't shown up to do a week of guard duty. He killed several of the assassins and rescued Ms. Erlanger and a suitcase full of notes that Mr. Goncharov, the retired archivist for the KGB, had spent twenty years painstakingly assembling. Mr. Goncharov escaped the burning house after the assassins were driven off. He isn't sure how he did that, but he doesn't remember seeing Carmellini or Erlanger. They might have already escaped, or he might have exited in another direction—it doesn't matter."

All eyes in the room were on him except mine. I was watching Royston, who was standing with his back to the bedroom door, and Sonnenberg, who was immediately behind him, yet slightly to one side. She had her hands jammed into the pockets of her robe. I wondered if she had a pistol in there. She and Royston looked very pale.

From the inside pocket of his sports coat, Jake Grafton removed a folder with a red cover. He had had it folded double in his pocket. Now he unfolded it and bent it the other way to minimize the damage the folding had caused.

"This is the file the assassins wanted," Grafton said simply, unfolding it and smoothing it. "Mr. Goncharov and his files were extracted from Russia by MI-5 after he visited a British consulate in

Lithuania and asked to defect. After a cursory debriefing, he came to the U.S. to be extensively debriefed by both British and CIA personnel. Unfortunately, the assassins showed up before that could be accomplished."

"This is ridiculous," Royston declared, and made a show of looking at his watch. Apparently he had decided to go on the attack. "Why are we discussing this in a New York hotel room in the middle of the night?"

"That will become apparent in just a few moments," Grafton said smoothly. He opened the red folder and passed around the five or six sheets of handwritten notes it contained. I had seen hundred of pages like that, with the tiny, cramped, Cyrillic handwriting. "This is a file on an American turncoat with the code name of 'Rollo.' Don't ask me why this code name was assigned—I don't know.

"In any event, Rollo was an American who was recruited by the KGB while he was in college. He was politically progressive, very much so—so much so that he willingly went to work for the KGB to attempt to derail American military efforts in Vietnam. He joined antiwar movements, made speeches, wrote pamphlets, donated money to the antiwar movement—oh, yes, he had money. None of his own, you understand, because he came from a modest, lower-middle-class background, but that of his wife. He married an heiress to a large automobile dealership fortune while he was in college, an only child who received a very healthy allowance from her parents."

"Cut to the chase," Royston said impatiently. "I am embarrassed and humiliated that you people burst in here tonight, and I want an explanation damned quick. And by God, it had better be good."

"It will be," Jake said. "Let me meander on." He collected the papers and returned them to the folder, then put the folder under his left armpit and crossed his arms over his chest. "Rollo's duties for the KGB took him to California, the hotbed of the antiwar movement. There he continued to do everything within his power to further the KGB's goal of helping the various groups who were against the war influence American foreign policy. While he was in California, he met a woman, a brilliant, dynamic, ambitious young woman who was passionately against the war. One thing led to another, and they became lovers."

"I don't think you can prove a solitary word of this," Royston snarled.

Grafton smiled gently. "Oh, but I can. Then the woman became pregnant with Rollo's child. The couple calmly assessed the situation. He had no money of his own, yet she did, and she loved him. They were both extremely ambitious. They realized that their experience at the cutting edge of the antiwar movement could provide them—or one of them—with a start in politics, an entry to a political career that could take them in the fullness of time to a very high place. If only she weren't pregnant—remember, this was the early 1970s. And if only he hadn't agreed to work for the KGB.

"Ah, yes, they had finally grasped the enormity of that foolish mistake, the truth of which he had shared with her. The KGB had a marvelous blackmail tool to force him to obey their orders all the days of his life. If he refused, they could ruin him at any time by revealing the Soviet connection.

"So Rollo and his lover concocted a plan. The woman dropped out of sight before her pregnancy began to show. A few days after she delivered, Rollo and his wife adopted the infant. The adoption was highly irregular, but since everyone involved had plenty of money, certain regulations were bent or ignored in the interest of the unfortunate lady's good name.

"In any event, a month or so after the adoption, the new parents were in a fatal automobile accident on the Pacific Coast Highway. The car went off a cliff into the ocean and was swept away. The wife's parents were called and informed their daughter and her husband were dead. They rushed to California and took the baby home to Maryland."

During Grafton's explanation I had been keeping an eye on Dorsey while I worked on the cognac, which was damned good. She was having difficulty looking at anything except the red folder under the admiral's arm. She was pale, licking her lips and swallowing repeatedly. I thought she might be on the verge of throwing up.

"Of course, Rollo wasn't really dead. His wife was—he killed her."

A gasp came from Dorsey. She got off the arm of her chair, walked over to Royston, and confronted him from a distance of six inches. "Say it isn't so."

"I have no idea why he's telling us this tale," Dell Royston said, and put a hand on his daughter's shoulder. "Nor if there is a word of truth in it."

She pushed his hand off, glanced back at Grafton. "Go on," she ordered.

"Rollo had made preparations. He had already equipped himself with a false name and legend, complete with a birth certificate, driver's license, and all the other sheets of paper that memorialize our past. He cut off the fashionable mop of hair, shaved, went back east and ditched the hippie clothes, gained a fast thirty pounds, and entered law school.

"The risk was that someone would recognize him as Michael O'Shea. It was not a very large risk—he had switched coasts, lifestyles, and social circles, and significantly altered his appearance. If anyone noticed the resemblance, they were probably aware that Michael O'Shea was dead and dismissed the fading resemblance as a coincidence. And so the years rolled by, everyone aged, and Michael O'Shea slipped further and further into the past in a world that rapidly changed. The risk of someone realizing he was O'Shea dropped toward zero. Only the KGB was interested in O'Shea, and it had lost him.

"In fact, O'Shea and his girlfriend had done such a good job of faking his death in the car wreck, the Soviets thought he was dead. The file on Rollo at KGB headquarters on Dzerzhinsky Square in Moscow was closed." Jake gestured with the red file, then patted it against his leg.

"Michael O'Shea and his girlfriend believed they had pulled it off. Their ambition brought them together again. They resumed their journey toward that high, windswept place they had glimpsed when they were young. And they had the presidency in sight when Mikhail Goncharov defected with his treasure-trove of notes from the KGB archives. The worm of suspicion began to gnaw relentlessly on them. What if the KGB *knew*? What if evidence of treason and murder was contained in those files?" The file was in the admiral's right hand; every eye in the room went to it.

"O'Shea and his lover decided they couldn't live with the risk," he said softly. "The notes must be destroyed. Anyone who had read them must die."

Royston made a rude noise. "I have never heard such a vile slander in all of American politics!" he said belligerently. "You haven't a shred of proof of any of these accusations."

You've got to give him credit—he was trying. His face glistened with perspiration.

"Not a shred of proof," he continued hoarsely. "Even if it's true, it has nothing to do with us. Now get the hell out of here, and if I hear a whisper about you being here tonight—from any of you people—the world is going to cave in on you."

Dorsey continued to study Royston's face. Sonnenberg put a hand on her arm to draw her away, and she brushed it off.

"I do have proof," Jake Grafton said simply. "In the last few days we have done DNA testing. Michael O'Shea has living relatives. One of them is Jimmy O'Shea, a brother who lives in Brooklyn. With the help of his barber, we obtained samples of his hair. There is no doubt, Mr. Royston. You are Jimmy O'Shea's brother and Dorsey O'Shea's father. You, Ms. Sonnenberg, are Dorsey's mother."

Dorsey approached Zooey. "You never told me Dell was my father."

Zooey couldn't avoid those eyes.

"Your whole life has been a lie, Mom," Dorsey continued, her voice cracking like old glass. "You helped him murder that woman! Everything you said, everything you did was a lie designed to get you elected to the presidency."

"Dorsey, I—"

"Don't touch me!" She backed up slowly, a step at a time. "All these years I thought my father was dead. You told me he was dead. But you never told me he murdered his wife and you helped him do it!"

She wheeled and slapped Dell Royston with a sound that cracked like a pistol shot.

"Royston," said Myron Emerick, "you're under arrest."

"What's the charge?"

"First degree murder of Kelly Erlanger. One of the admiral's friends was listening to her cell phone conversations. That will do for starters, but I think by arraignment time we'll have a couple dozen murders to charge you with. We picked up your executive assistant earlier this evening—he hasn't stopped talking. Then two men broke into the admiral's house tonight. They are now under arrest and are also telling everything they know."

You could have knocked me over with a feather when Royston said, "Do you have a warrant?" I didn't think he had any juice left at that point, but apparently he was tougher than I thought.

"As a matter of fact, I do." Emerick removed a document from a coat pocket and passed it to Royston. He glanced at Sonnenberg. "I have one for you, too, Ms. Sonnenberg, charging you as an accessory."

Zooey turned on Royston. "You could take care of it, you said. The presidency of the United States was——." She held out both hands and closed them into fists. "*You!*" I had never in my life heard such venom in just one word.

She turned and stalked into the bedroom, slamming the door behind her.

I was hanging on to the bar by this time. My trousers were sodden with blood, the room was spinning, the faces were going in and out of focus. I knew it was loss of blood, not the cognac—which was mighty tasty—so I had another gulp.

On the bar beside me was a phone. I saw one of the two lines illuminate. I waited a decent interval—like maybe thirty seconds while Dorsey sobbed and one of the agents installed a set of handcuffs on Royston—then I picked up the phone and punched that line.

Zooey was talking. ". . . Emerick arrested Dell and—who is listening on this line?"

Of course they could hear the commotion going on around me. "Uh, Tommy Carmellini, Ms. Sonnenberg. Eavesdropping's a bad habit, I know. Hope you don't mind."

Apparently the president didn't care who else was listening. Before she could tell me to hang up and go to hell, he said, "Zooey, the attorney general is here along with the chief of staff. They tell me that if you are alive when Emerick is ready to leave that suite you're in, he intends to arrest you as an accessory to murder. He has a warrant in his pocket. Tomorrow morning I am announcing a new choice for vice president. You decide how you want the headlines to read."

"Those are my only choices?"

"Those two."

"You bastard! All these years holding your hand and smiling while you tomcatted around and made me a laughingstock! This is what I get for all those years of humiliation! Well, I'm not going silently in a box so you can weep at the funeral and march bravely on. Oh, no! I'm going to tell the press everything—*everything!*" Her voice rose to a shriek. "When I get through you won't be able to win an election for constable in any county in the country."

"Good-bye, Zooey," he said tightly, and broke the connection.

I cradled the telephone and drained the last of the cognac.

Emerick jerked his head at one of his agents. "Get him out of here," he said, pointing at Royston.

They cuffed Royston's hands in front of him. "Listen, Emerick—" he began.

"Can it," the director shot back. "They'll read you your rights down in the car."

"For God's sake—my wife! My kids!"

"You'll get your telephone call after they book you." Emerick again jerked his head at the agents, and they hustled Royston out of the room.

Dorsey shrank into a fetal position in one corner. I wondered if I ought to try to say something comforting, but the truth was I was in no condition to even walk over to her. Time passed—I don't know how much—while everyone in the room stood around waiting . . . waiting for Zooey to slit her wrists in the tub or come strutting out of the bedroom dressed for a press conference, I guess.

How long they stood there looking at each other I don't know. I remember thinking I should have said something to the president—I had missed my only chance to talk to a head of state. Somewhere in there the evening ended for me. I passed out about that time and did a header off the stool. Never did have much of a head for liquor.

CHAPTER THIRTY-SIX

The ambulance crew was still in the suite loading Carmellini on a stretcher when Mikhail Goncharov whispered to Callie, "May I leave now?"

"Certainly." Callie didn't know what the CIA or FBI honchos would think of Goncharov's departure, but she didn't intended to ask them. They were huddled in the corner with Jake Grafton.

After catching her husband's eye, Callie followed Goncharov out into the corridor and through the crowd in the hallway to the elevator. Secret Service, police, FBI agents, paramedics, and hotel executives—the crowd was beginning to thin now that the first lady and Royston had been taken away in handcuffs. Callie and Goncharov boarded the elevator, watched the door close. No one made any move to stop them.

They made their way through the lobby. People were whispering, watching the paramedics and police hustling about, speculating on what had happened.

Outside the main entrance on the Avenue of the Americas, under the awning, Goncharov told Callie, "I don't want to go back to the CIA or British intelligence."

"I don't think they really need you," she said. "The British copied your files."

Goncharov snorted. "I suppose I knew they would." He laughed without humor. "I was very naive."

Callie ignored that comment. "Where do you want to go?" she asked.

Goncharov took a deep breath as he considered it. He looked right, then left, looked up at the buildings, then back at Callie. "I don't know. Somewhere. I don't speak a word of the language, I have no money, but this is what I want. This—." He gestured grandly with his hand.

Callie opened her purse, took out all her cash, and held it out to him. "Here."

"No."

"Yes." She said the word in English. "Yes." Then in Russian, "This isn't much, but it will feed you for a while. Tens of millions of people have come to America and started over—thousands do it every day—and you can, too. A little money will help."

"Yes," he said, trying the English word.

"Yes." She echoed him, still holding the money in her hand, offering it.

"Yes." He reached for the cash, inspected the bills, then put them in his pocket.

Callie Grafton smiled and held out her hand.

He shook it. "Good-bye," she said in English.

"Gude-by." The archivist, Mikhail Goncharov, turned and walked away into the night, into the great city of New York, into the heart of America.

The second day after my operation, the hospital moved me from intensive care to a private room. I thumbed the television on and flipped channels until I found a baseball game. I was just drifting off to sleep when Jake Grafton came into the room and shut the door.

"Hey," he said. "We almost waited too long to get you to a hospital. The doctors had some real nasty things to say to me."

"It was worth it," I said. "After all the shit I went through, I really wanted to see Reactor and Zooey take the fall."

"Reactor?"

"Royston was a fast breeder."

Jake Grafton nodded and lowered himself into a chair.

"That scene in Dorsey's suite—I was really surprised when you trotted out the DNA results. I thought those tests were going to take a week."

"That's right. We still don't have the results. Should have them tomorrow."

It took a long ten seconds for me to get it, what with my delicate condition, generally honest nature, and low mental ability. "You mean you lied to them?"

"Yeah."

"And that red folder. Was that really it?"

"Oh, no. That was just one we had at home. What the hell— none of those people could read Russian."

" 'Rollo'?"

He shrugged. "Goncharov couldn't remember O'Shea's code name, and I doubted if O'Shea ever knew it. I made that one up."

I had to smile. Jake Grafton gave me a grin in return.

"How come I haven't had every reporter in the free world in here today offering me millions for my story?"

"The story the FBI gave the press was that Zooey and Royston were lovers. I don't think the press understands who was in the suite or what was said. Perhaps that could have been explained better, but the FBI didn't bother. Zooey has held three jailhouse press conferences, and the media is having a field day. The country is eating it up. Royston's lawyer refuses to let his client say a word and refuses to say a word for him. The bail hearing isn't until next week, and the prosecutors will oppose it, they say. Some opposition senators and representatives are promising an investigation. The president refuses to discuss the matter."

"He's a cold-hearted bastard," I remarked, remembering his short conversation with Zooey. But perhaps that wasn't fair—he knew her a lot better than I did.

"This election is going to become a circus," Grafton predicted. "It's going to make the California governor's recall look like a tea party. Politics has become an afternoon soap opera. In an era when the country is deeply divided over complex issues without easy answers, perhaps that is inevitable."

I took a deep breath and moved on to the most important question. "Am I going to be arrested?"

Grafton chuckled. "Apparently not. I am informed that you are still a valuable employee of the CIA."

"Long as I'm getting paid."

We talked for a while about this and that, about Mikhail Goncharov and Kelly Erlanger and Dorsey O'Shea and my former boss, Sal Pulzelli.

"Was Joe Billy really Stu Vine?" I asked.

"I think so," Jake said. "The CIA holds little tidbits like that very tightly indeed."

"How come he was assigned to my shop?"

"I think the decision was made somewhere to bring him in-house. They just needed a place to stash him for a while. What the agency didn't know was that he had agreed to do a job for Royston. Do you remember? Pulzelli was told to send Dunn to be a guard at the safehouse. Since Dunn was scheduled to go to a training session, Pulzelli changed the assignment without telling anyone."

"That was Sal . . . the born administrator. He lived his life by the schedule and thought we should, too."

We were still chatting when a nurse came in and told the admiral he would have to leave. "See you, Tommy," he said.

"Thanks, Admiral, for everything."

"Any time."

"You and Callie going flying?"

"All over the country. We'll call you when we get back."

Then he was gone. Just like that.

Maybe it was really over. God, I hoped so. If some wild man with murder in his eye came charging in here, I didn't even have a pocketknife to defend myself with . . . if I could stay awake, which I couldn't.

I drifted off while the nurse was working on my IVs.

The next day two guys from the agency and one from the FBI showed up with a cassette recorder. After reading me all the warnings, they wanted the whole story in my own words. I ran them out after half an hour. The next day they were back and we did two hours. Three hours the day after that, then for the next two days they asked questions, hundreds of them. I did the best I could, but when I got tired I told them to return tomorrow. They didn't come the last day I was in the hospital. In midafternoon, after giving me a cursory exam and a new set of bandages, the hospital released me.

I was ready to go. I had channel surfed when the law wasn't there and had had more than my fill of the made-for-TV political circus. I took a cab to Pennsylvania Station and then a train to Washington.

My apartment was a wreck. Someone had ransacked the place during my big adventure, maybe one of Royston's thugs or perhaps Joe Billy Dunn.

It took courage to open the refrigerator. There was something green in there, and I didn't think it was lettuce. I threw everything in a garbage bag and spent twenty minutes wrestling it down to the cans in the basement. I was weak as a cat. I wasn't ready to tackle that mess the goons had made. I even thought about moving in with Willie . . . for ten whole seconds.

The agency guys had said my old Mercedes was parked in the lot, so I went looking for it. Found it finally, decorated with bird droppings, parked under a tree. It even started on the third attempt.

I called Jake Grafton on his cell.

"Hey, I'm out of the hospital. Where are you guys?"

"Wisconsin. Getting gas. We'll be in Minnesota tonight. How are you doing, Tommy?"

"The agency gave me a couple weeks off, but I may never go back. I'm still thinking about taking a banana boat south."

"It's like that, huh? Why don't you go over to my beach house, loaf there until you feel better?"

Now that was an idea! The beach.

"You wouldn't mind?"

"Oh, heck no. Just make sure you buy your own beer."

"Where did you hide the key?"

Grafton made a rude noise and hung up on me.

Well, why not? I put the Mercedes in gear and let 'er rip. Stopped at a Wal-Mart on the Eastern Shore for the bare essentials—underwear, beer, swimsuit, and toothbrush.

At Grafton's place I quickly settled into a routine. Every morning I walked all the way to the corner to buy a paper from the vending machine, read it as I poached a couple eggs and made toast, finished it over coffee, then walked to the beach and lay around on the towel frying in the sun.

Willie Varner had all his stitches out, he said, was getting laid again by his semiregular girlfriend, and was working in the lock shop. He gave me some grief over the phone, but not too much. Like me, he was very happy life was getting back to normal.

The papers were full of the political news. I thought Zooey was in danger of overplaying her hand, but she was fulfilling her promise to her husband. She accused him of a dozen infidelities, cheating on his income tax for eight years, and screwing a couple million out of two former business partners. I thought the president would have a huge political problem with all this, but no. Apparently in the post-Clinton age the public was becoming inured to personal scandal. The party's honchos picked a new vice-presidential candidate, a woman the president recommended, and the president refused to discuss any of his wife's jailhouse revelations, declaring that the issues were more important than the personal life of any candidate.

The president played it like a harp and actually gained in the polls. It turned out he had the ability to work a little quaver into his voice when the reporters hounded him about his wife and Royston. People actually felt sorry for the S.O.B.

The world is full of wackos—what can I say? I figured that in a few weeks the president would probably file for a divorce and in a year people would be asking, Zooey who? One of the pundits suggested that he get a dog to help him through this difficult time.

The guy who owned the house three doors closer to the beach on Grafton's side of the street stopped me on the second day I was there. He wanted to chat.

"I see you're staying in that retired admiral's house."

"Yeah."

"You know him?"

"Enough to get permission to use the place. Why'd you ask?"

"Oh, man! About ten days ago we had the goddamnest shootout you ever heard of right here on this street. That admiral killed two guys"—he pointed—"right there and there. A busload of military guys surrounded his house and dragged two more men out of it."

"Wow! Sounds like a movie or something. But it was real, huh?"

"I was having a party. Had a house full of guests. Normally this house is rented out to whoever, but that was the first night of my summer vacation—take a month every year. Had lots of people here from the office. Goddamnest thing you've ever seen. Submachine guns blasting, bodies all over, blood, soldiers with weapons, enough cops to arrest the Capone mob, all right here on this street about midnight."

I shook my head. "Sorry I missed it."

"You know anything about it?"

I shrugged. "This is the first I've heard."

He scrutinized my face. "Who is that admiral, anyway?"

"Some retired ship driver. Name's Grafton."

"Well, here is the amazing part. I've got a couple dozen people here partying, and we all see and hear this shootout and watch the police and ambulance people clean up, and they wouldn't tell us a goddamn thing."

"They wouldn't?"

"Nothing. The next morning we check the television and newspapers to see what in hell the shootout was all about, and you know what? There wasn't a word in the paper or on television. I even called the local paper and talked to the editor."

" 'Zat right?"

"He listened to what I had to say, said his reporters would look into it . . . and he printed zilch. *Nada!* Not a single word on the air or in print. Like it never happened. All the television and papers are full of the political mess—there isn't room for anything else. But I'll tell you, if I read or hear another word about Zooey Sonnenberg I think I'm going to puke."

"I know what you mean."

"Thought you might know something about the shootout."

"Naw. Not a thing. By the way, you gonna have any more parties?"

"Next Saturday. Wanta come?"

So Jake had some explaining to do with his neighbors. I made a mental note to tell him so when I talked to him again.

Try as I might to think of something else, the events of the last few weeks occupied most of my thoughts. Joe Billy Dunn, Royston, Zooey Sonnenberg . . . the guy who had tried to kill me from the abandoned house with the little Ruger rifle—I carefully inspected that house every time I passed it.

Of course I wondered about the president and Zooey. I thought about that conversation I had overheard. Did he know that Zooey was cheating on him with Dell? Did he care? Did he ever care for her, or was theirs a political union, a marriage in name only?

Someday some idiot publisher would pay the president millions for his memoir, and the public would read what he chose to say— just that and nothing more. I decided there are some rocks no one will ever see under.

One morning I climbed in the car and headed for the Bethesda Naval Hospital to get checked for infections and have the last of the stitches removed. Dorsey O'Shea was on my mind. The way I figured it, she wanted to marry me and take me away in order to save my life. She knew or suspected Royston was going to have me hit. She may have thought that if I were her husband, he'd lay off.

Perhaps Dorsey had fallen in love with me . . . a little teeny tiny bit. Loved someone besides her mother, Zooey Sonnenberg. Maybe she cared.

That's what love is, isn't it? Caring.

I cared for a woman who was somewhere out there in the big wide world and might never return.

Was I capable of loving another person, one who was physically here?

The thing about Dorsey . . .

What if she called? She had my cell phone number. What would I say to her?

I thought about that, about the murders and Zooey and all that stuff. As I drove over the Bay Bridge, I threw the phone out the window into the Chesapeake.

On Saturday morning I was basting in the sun, reading a novel and enjoying a stiff breeze, when a shadow fell across my book. I looked up.

Sarah Houston. In a huge, floppy sun hat and a skimpy two-piece suit that didn't hide anything. I don't know why they even bother to wear those things. She spread a huge beach towel beside mine and handed me a tube of suntan lotion while the wind whipped at the brim of her hat. "Do me, will you?"

"Did you just happen by?"

"I hike the beach from Maine to Florida every summer. Saw you lying there and decided I could use a break."

"Going to be here long?"

"As a matter of fact, Admiral Grafton called me. He said you were staying at his beach house and asked if I would like to use it, too. Said he had a couple of bedrooms and plenty of toilet paper."

I turned on my side and looked her over while she settled herself on her towel and told me this tale. I wondered if Grafton really called her or she called him. I sat up and went to work with the lotion.

"So," she continued as I slathered her, "I thought, I'm due for some vacation, and why not?"

"Indeed! Why not?"

"Give me a chance to get the real inside scoop on Zooey and Royston. Grafton said you were in the suite when they were arrested."

"I'm sorry, I can't discuss it. I'm saving it for my autobiography."

"Darn. I'll just have to wheedle it out of you. A project like that will help fill the long evenings."

"Heck, yeah. As a matter of fact, I have a party invite for tonight. Want to go?"

"If we can leave the party early. There's a certain man I'm looking forward to making love to."

You could have knocked me over with a feather. Sarah Houston! Who would have ever suspected?

ACKNOWLEDGMENTS

The very real defection of Vasili Mitrokhin, the retired archivist for the KGB, to Great Britain in 1992 was the inspiration for this tale. He left Russia with six suitcases full of notes that he had taken from classified KGB files over a period of twelve years. (See *The Sword and The Shield: The Mitrokhin Archive and the Secret History of the KGB* by Christopher Andrew and Vasili Mitrokhin, Basic Books, 1999.) I have wanted to write this tale since I read that book. My editor, Charles Spicer, and his colleagues at St. Martin's Press offered me the opportunity, for which I am extremely grateful.

My wife, Deborah Coonts, had a large creative input to the plot of the novel as it developed. Engineer and physicist Gilbert "Gil" Pascal read the manuscript and offered technical suggestions, as he has been kind enough to do many times in the past. A heartfelt Thank You to both of them.

This story is a work of fiction. As usual, the author is solely responsible for the plot, characters, incidents, and dialogue contained herein.